HOT SPOTS

HOT
SPOTS

All-Inclusive Vacations

JASON G. VOGEL

E. P. DUTTON
NEW YORK

Published in the United States by E. P. Dutton,
a division of Penguin Books USA Inc.,
2 Park Avenue, New York, N.Y. 10016.

Published simultaneously in Canada by Fitzhenry and Whiteside, Limited, Toronto.

Library of Congress Cataloging-in-Publication Data

Vogel, Jason, G. 1959–
    Hot spots : all-inclusive vacations / Jason G. Vogel. —1st ed.
       p.   cm.
    ISBN 0-525-48507-4
       1. Resorts—Guide-books.   2. Ocean travel—Guide-books.
    I. Title.
    TX907.V64   1989
    647.94—dc20   89-33839
                                              CIP

Designed by Stanley S. Drate/Folio Graphics Co. Inc.

10 9 8 7 6 5 4 3 2 1

FIRST EDITION

EDITED BY Sandra W. Soule

RESEARCHER COORDINATOR: Adina Hamik

CONTRIBUTING EDITORS: Matthew Joyce, Maureen Mattingly

EDITORIAL ASSISTANT: Annie Tin

CONTRIBUTORS: Alan Forst, J.D., Valerie Gardner, Elliott Mincberg, J.D., Alan Paley, Gail Ross, J.D., Jeffrey Schaider, M.D., Irene B. Vogel, Ph.D., Kenneth Vogel, J.D., Jeffrey Wolf

Cover photographs courtesy of Sandals Resorts, Inc.

To my grandparents,
whose houses
forever seem like
all-inclusive resorts

CONTENTS

HAWAII

CLUB MED

CRUISES

YACHT CHARTERING SERVICES

LAND TOUR

ACKNOWLEDGMENTS

Hot Spots was made possible by the work of many people. I had no shortage of volunteers to take vacations, but few realized in advance how much effort each review would take. They all performed admirably in helping me get the story. Adina Hamik, in particular, researched the trips, took great photographs, and acted as my personal travel agent.

Sandy Soule helped me form an amorphous collection of ideas into a readable format. I'm constantly amazed at her knowledge of geography and the travel industry, and I thank her for her friendship. Victor Block acted as my mentor, adviser, and friend. He helped me in intangible ways that took concrete form in this book.

Hot Spots was made economically viable by the generosity of airlines, resorts, public relations firms, and tour companies. Other resorts and people too numerous to mention have helped. I hope they will forgive their exclusion from this thank-you; please know that I am grateful. The following people and companies have been especially helpful:

The staff of the El San Juan and Condado Plaza hotels and their public relations firm A.C.&R., including Lisa Brainin and Ann Campbell; Air Jamaica; American Airlines, especially Donna Schlotzhauer and Joe Humphrey; American Canadian Caribbean Line, including Yvette; Sharon Roonie at American Hawaiian Cruises; the Bahamas Department of Tourism; Rick Pereira at Banana Bay; Bermuda Starlight Cruises, including Steven Hirshan; Bitter End Yacht Club; Blackbeard's Cruises; Limetree Beach and Tennis Club; Mary Jane Enterkin at Bonaventure Spa; all the staff at the SuperClubs of Jamaica, especially Andrea Hutchenson; Bill Smith at Brazilian Scuba and Land Tours for having faith in this project early in the game; Varig Airlines; CSY; RockResorts; Caribbean Adventures; Caribbean Information Office; Carnival Cruises; Sigmund Kaufmann at the Cloister; Savoy Resorts; a special thanks to Steve Perillo at Club Perillo; Linda Darling-Mann at Coco Palms; Commodore Cruise Lines' Kristy McElroy; Maggie Gibbs at Costa Cruises; John Ribbler at Creative Resources, Inc.; Yolanda for extraordinary efforts for Dolphin Cruise Lines; Judy Baer Associates and the Elegant Resorts of Jamaica; Sheryl Stein at El Al Israeli Airlines; Fontainebleau Hilton Spa; Harbour Island Spa; Jekyll Island Club Hotel; Kona Village Resort; Chuck Edelstein at Lido Spa; M. Silver & Associates, Martha Gates and Pam Bloom at Palm-Aire

Spa; Piedmont Airlines; Premier Cruise Lines; Cindy Weir at Princess Casino Vacations; Princess Cruise Lines' Julie Benson, Nancy Lowenherz, and Carolyn Speidel; Pritikin Longevity Centers; Pyramid Island Resort; Rum Cay Club; Sandals; Saturnia Spa; Heidi Patty at Stevens Yachts; the generosity of Kevin Tolkin at Travel Impressions; the staff of Trelawny; and Angie Chantrielle and Debbie Kelly at Windjammer Cruises.

INTRODUCTION

WHY ALL-INCLUSIVE VACATIONS?

In a perfect resort, everything is effortless. The staff picks you up at the airport, transfers your luggage, then shows you a great time. You don't have to worry about tips. You leave your wallet in the safe and simply enjoy the sports, food, water, and relaxation without even having to sign your name. You can spend your time simply enjoying yourself, without a care in the world. These vacations resemble Erica Jong's fantasy of "zipless" sex.

The mood at an all-inclusive resort comes closest to this fantasy, differing from conventional vacations because everything is paid in advance. You don't have to worry about the cost of another drink, ordering dessert, or going waterskiing because of the cost. In fact, the all-inclusive nature encourages you to experience everything. Think of it as a vaction buffet.

Moderately priced all-inclusives also break down the barriers of class and income, creating an egalitarian atmosphere. Loosen your tie, take off your hard hat. It doesn't matter if you are a lawyer or a bricklayer. Everyone pays the same amount and goes for the same reason: to have a good time. Go ahead, order drinks for the house.

The proliferation of all-inclusives poses the question of which one is the best. The answer depends on who you are, what you like and how much you want to spend. Some resorts cater to couples only, others to families, a number to singles. Your choice should depend on the atmosphere and features that you want. *Hot Spots* reviews a variety of world-class resorts that offer excellent accommodations, food, sports, and locations.

Every resort looks great in the brochures. They seem to echo one another in amenities, services, and entertainment. In reality, each has its own personality that is not readily apparent from the handouts. Some brochures are accurate down to the color of the bedspreads; others take more artistic license.

Not every place that we visited made it into this book. Some claimed to be all-inclusives but did not even come close. Others were so poorly maintained that we could not recommend them. In a few cases, the quality of an all-inclusive did not warrant a review, but its market share and aggressive advertising gave it so much public recognition that we had to mention it. In more than one case, we found a place so appealing that we stretched the rules to include it, even though it would not meet a strict definition of an all-inclusive.

No one person could have stayed at all the places reviewed within the limited time available. We relied on a staff of researchers who

1

were given very strict criteria. As often as possible, we consulted multiple sources for opinions.

In reviewing resorts, we asked the question Who, if anyone, would like this vacation, and why? These questions, ultimately, gave us the basis for making judgments.

HOW TO CHOOSE AN ALL-INCLUSIVE RESORT

What's the best place? Where should I go? Depends on who you are and what you want to do. We selected the best all-inclusives and tried to figure out who would most enjoy them. You, the travel consumer, must use the reverse logic: Where do I want to go? What do I want to do? How much do I want to spend? These will lead you to a resort. Remember that location alone rarely indicates the best path to a resort.

1. Who am I? (single, couple, children, age)
2. Who am I looking to meet, if anyone?
3. What do I like to do? (sports, tours, activities, sight-seeing, shopping)
4. What level of activity do I want?
5. Length of stay? (The shorter your vacation, the more the travel time plays a factor.)
6. Location?
7. Cultural experience?
8. Food?
9. Travel irregularities? (sea/motion sickness, physical limitations)
10. Price range?

HOW TO READ THIS BOOK

All resorts are reviewed in the same general format. They can receive from zero to five symbols in each category, going from worst (zero) to best (five). The ratings may seem a bit inflated because the least desirable places were left out of the book.

Judgments were based on category. You cannot expect the same quality of food on a small chartered yacht that you would in a gourmet restaurant. Each place has its own virtues, judged in context.

"Vital Features" that are "Not rated" means that the reviewer did not have a chance to evaluate that item or service fairly. A "0" rating means that a vacation is wholly unsuitable in a specific category. For example, a couples-only place would get a zero for "Child appeal" and "Singles meeting ground."

Costs are given per person, double occupancy (ppdo) for a seven-day, seven-night vacation, unless otherwise noted. Our calculation includes the base price plus a realistic, but somewhat modest, number of drinks and tours, making it easy to compare vacation costs. We did not, of course, figure in heavy gambling losses or substantial shopping expenses.

In "The Real Story" section we have tried to give you a *feel* for the resort in the way a friend would describe it. Salient features include the general environment, what makes it special, and how it differs from other offerings in its class.

The "Included" section lists all the items that are covered by the all-inclusive price. "Activities, Sports, & Excursions," on the other hand, lists everything available, with "extras" noted as such.

"Aesthetics & Environment" judges the resort's natural beauty and the maintenance of its physical plant. Some people find this section to be very important, others less so. If you really don't care if the paint has yellowed, or if the gardener has taken a two-month siesta, do not let us spoil your bliss.

The "Rooms" section, by its very nature, demands a subjective evaluation. "Luxury Level," on the other hand, lists features in a straightforward manner. Some people consider it a luxury *not* to have modern electronics like TVs, telephones, and clocks.

Our food ratings display a heavy bias toward local cuisine. If a place offers only standard American fare, it lessens the incentive to travel there. We realize that people prefer a variety of cuisines, and that kids can be picky, so we gave the highest ratings to the resorts that offered the widest range of fresh, well-prepared food. Many people go on a vacation just to relax. The "Privacy & Relaxation" section tells you how busy a place is, if you will feel rushed, and if there are secluded places for escaping from the crowd.

Some people best remember their vacation because of the exotic piece of art they bought, or how they saved $20 on their Japanese camera by buying it in the Caribbean. If shopping's your bag, our observations should give you some idea of how to fill it.

The "Honeymooners" section closely relates to privacy and aesthetics. It additionally mentions any special wedding or honeymoon packages. In "Singles," we judge the likelihood of finding company of the opposite sex. This is based on conduciveness of the environment and the likely number of prospects. The "Child Appeal" section tries to see a vacation from a kid's perspective, with both activities and playmates of key importance. For the parent to have a vacation, baby-sitting and supervision are essential.

The attitude and competence of the staff often determine the quality of a vacation. "Staffing & Service" evaluates the on-site staff and rates the equally important home office. The latter should produce clear, comprehensive brochures and should also handle the reservations, transfers, and all the little details that make a big difference.

TRAVEL AGENTS

Travel agents can be your best allies when you try to put together a trip. They offer one of the few remaining free services and can even save you money. A good travel agent can get you the best combination on an air/land package or can help you find a special deal on a cruise. Often, when a resort or airline says that it is fully booked, your travel agent will know which wholesaler has blocks of tickets.

Unfortunately, many people ask too much of a travel agent and subsequently have a disappointing trip. A travel agent, like anyone else, sometimes recommends a vacation based on limited information. The resort operator may be one of the four or five with whom the agent deals on a regular basis, or the agent may make the recommendation based on personal experience or the feedback of a few clients. The problem here is that another person's vacation experience may not be relevant to you. Someone may have had the greatest vacation of his life lying in the sun, but you could go to the same place and be bored out of your mind. A California travel agent might know all about Hawaii and Mexico, but far less about diving in the Caribbean. If you go to Club Med, for example, you need to know which clubs are more couple-oriented, which are geared for singles, and which are best for families.

Hot Spots was written to help you select the vacation that best suits your needs. The couple of weeks a year that you get to take off are precious; the money that you spend is hard earned. It is worth spending a couple of hours doing a little research—and it's fun too.

When you know where you want to go, ask a travel agent to find you the best price. If the agent recommends a different place, listen, then do some research on that destination. Your travel agent and *Hot Spots* should complement each other.

SOME GENERAL TIPS

BUT IT'S FREE! You can have a great time and leave only a few pounds heavier. People tend to go wild the first couple of days. Relax. You have all week. Go easy on the buffets, and do your exercises before you get too sloshed. Pace yourself. Have a good time. Don't try to set a consumption record—the human body can only absorb so much.

FIRST IMPRESSIONS: Sometimes your first impression fails to live up to your expectations. Don't despair. Many times the reviewers of this book faced similar situations. Often we have found that if you can let go of your expectations, you will also let go of your disappointments. Many great vacations have emerged from less than ideal surroundings. Hang in there—and enjoy yourself.

THE BIG LUG: Official airline policy usually limits passengers to two pieces of checked luggage and one carry-on bag. Bags are measured by the sum of total inches, meaning length plus width plus depth. One bag should be under 62 inches, the other should not exceed 55 inches. The carry-on bag may not exceed 45 inches. No bag may weigh over 70 pounds.

Airline enforcement of luggage restrictions varies widely among carriers. They tend to be stricter on the longer flights. Unless you bring scuba gear, none of the trips reviewed should require more than one checked bag per person. Some people choose to bring an extra suitcase in which to lug back souvenirs.

HIDDEN COSTS: Hidden costs pose pitfalls for travelers. For example, how much could the local room and departure tax add up to? Much more than you would ever believe. Many travelers on cheap package trips have discovered that governments often base room taxes on the full retail price of the room—not the deeply discounted package price. This adds a significant chunk of money to the price of the trip. Use our convenient worksheet to calculate the true cost of your vacation. You avoid rip-offs by getting all the information up front.

PRESSURE: Pack your scuba gauges in your carry-on bag so the nonpressurized cargo area does not ruin their calibration.

SCUBA INTRODUCTION

As much sight-seeing as sport, scuba diving and snorkeling open up the two thirds of the planet covered by water. Under the sea, you can explore a world much different from any foreign country. Colorful coral forests, exotic fish, and warm, friendly waters offer as much variety as the land. You can also play in the near-weightless environment, do in-water flips, or catch a lobster dinner while hanging upside down on a reef. It's a little like being in outer space.

On a hot tropical day, nothing feels better than a half hour of cool (below body temperature) water against the skin. With a little study, you soon appreciate the differences among reefs, which range from hard black rock to spongy orange tubes.

Scuba provides the greatest getaway. Underwater, you can leave the outside world behind. You have complete relaxation. There is nothing to think about but your immediate environment. All worries dissipate—you are a guest in a different society. You communicate with your buddies in sign language. Enjoy it before they invent underwater cellular phones.

Scuba divers need a cool head and more than raw strength. Age is hardly a factor in diving. Many people in their sixties take up diving, although they tend to set more moderate limits. Good health and swimming ability are required, of course, but you need not be a triathlon star. Mental control will help you think your way out of potential problems.

What about the danger from sharks and barracuda? Those fish are down there, but they almost never attack humans. In fact, the IRS takes a bigger bite, and the Feds are far more predatory.

Many of the resorts discussed in this book offer both snorkeling and scuba diving. Scuba (self-contained underwater breathing apparatus) allows you to explore the undersea world closer, longer, and deeper. Most American resorts and boats require scuba participants to be certified by one of the national or international associations. These include PADI (Professional Association of Diving Instructors). NAUI (National Association of Underwater Instructors), and the YMCA. Offshore, many tour operators offer a "resort course" that allows you to take a diving day trip. This does *not* give you the certification necessary to dive in the United States, or at most other resorts, for that matter. And tour operators will not let you dive if you have trained in someone else's noncertification course.

If you don't want to commit to learning scuba, you can still snorkel on top of shallow reefs. Snorkeling offers some of the attractions of scuba, but of course you only scratch the surface. Here, the biggest danger is burning your back and the back sides of your legs. A T-shirt and waterproof suntan lotion with sun blocker are strongly recommended. Also, cotton work gloves will keep you from scraping your hands. Please do not touch the coral. It can sting you, and you will almost surely destroy the delicate plant life. Tropical fish aren't stupid: they prefer the same warm, clear water that makes for the most pleasant diving vacations. So prepare for many enjoyable hours in the water.

The scuba locations and resorts featured in *Hot Spots* offer some of the best diving in the world. They also offer exciting and different vacations.

BEATING JET LAG

Warm-weather vacations have traditionally involved a north-south trip. North Americans tended to stick close to their coast: Easterners going to the Caribbean, and Westerners traveling to Hawaii or the Mexican Riviera. It's true that cost, time, flight availability, and habit placed a damper on east-west travel, but the jet lag caused by crossing time zones has also dissuaded many travelers.

Beating jet lag can make a trip more enjoyable, productive, and time efficient. It can also open up areas of the world that would otherwise be difficult to visit for a short period of time because of the stress travel would have placed on the body.

Jet lag occurs when the body's sense of time becomes disoriented by a profound change in time zones, that is, when your body tells you that it's time to sleep but the local clocks show midday. Luckily, jet lag can be mitigated using simple changes in eating and sleeping patterns.

In their book, *Overcoming Jet Lag* (New York: Berkley Books, 1986), Dr. Charles Ehret and Lynne Waller Scanlon outline a three-step process that helps air travelers prevent or quickly recover from the negative effects caused by crossing time zones. They recommend the following procedure when traversing three to eight time zones:

The preflight step requires changing eating habits three days before the trip. In general, this means adhering to a diet of high-protein breakfasts and lunches, and high-carbohydrate dinners. On the day of the flight, you should change to an eating schedule based on the time zone of your destination.

The second step involves acclimating yourself to the daytime cycles of your destination. People react naturally to light and darkness. From the moment you enter the airplane you should tinker with natural and artificial light to place yourself on the day schedule of your destination. Use the airline shades, eyeshades, sunglasses, and reading lights to trick your body into thinking that it is on the new schedule. Also, resist the urge to sleep or stay awake on the old time schedule. Avoid the impulse to take a nap, because this will disturb your pattern of sleep.

Caffeine also dramatically affects the body's sense of timing. It can be used to reset the body's internal clock in much the same way that you would reset a real clock. It is important to avoid caffeine on the few days preceding the flight (except between 3:00 and 4:30 P.M.). If you are traveling westward, drink two to three cups of *black* coffee the morning of the flight, then avoid coffee the first day of arrival. If traveling eastward, drink two to three cups of coffee after 6:00 P.M. (old time) on the day of the flight. Do not add real dairy products or sugar to your coffee.

Other recommendations are:

Avoid alcoholic beverages. They alter the body's chemistry and have a much greater impact in flight.

The air in airplanes is usually extremely dry. Drink plenty of water to compensate for this.

Avoid taking drugs, especially sedatives or those drugs containing caffeine. This can negate the effects of the program.

Try to avoid missing sleep.

Try to arrive during the day or early evening, local time. In this way you will go through the disembarking hassle during what would be the normal "active time" for the destination.

Become physically active and socially engaged during the new local time.

These tips outline the simple but specific plans found in *Overcoming Jet Lag*. The book gives more detailed schedules; we strongly recommend consulting it and following its advice.

Many of the land tours described in this guide allow time for overcoming jet lag. Following the three-step program can return this day to your travel itinerary and make the rest of the trip more enjoyable. Avoiding jet lag can also allow you to extend your trip closer to the day when you have to return to work.

SAFE SUNTANNING

If sunbathing is high on your list of vacation priorities, alert yourself to the hazards of the intense tropical sun before it puts a red alert on you. Even with that faded base from summertime sunning, the tropical sun demands respect because of its low altitude.

To protect sun worshipers from merciless ultraviolet rays, the U.S. Food and Drug Administration has classified six skin types, each with a specific sun protection factor (SPF) that should be used in the form of sunscreen or lotion. A product with an SPF of 6, for instance, enables sunbathers to stay in the sun six times longer than they could unprotected.

As a general rule, the safest times of day to tan are during the hours before 10:00 A.M. and after 3:00 P.M., when the sun is less intense. Only when you have a good base tan should you lower your SPF or spend long periods in the sun during midday.

Don't increase exposure time or lower the SPF of your lotion for the first week of sunning, as it takes five to seven days for most people's skin to change pigmentation. After a week, increase exposure gradually. Keep in mind that ultraviolet rays are transmitted below the water, so you should include swimming in your exposure time and choose a waterproof sunscreen.

The list below will help determine your personal skin type. Follow the safe tanning guidelines, and you can bask in the island sun fully protected from its intense rays.

1. Type 1s, often redheads, have light skin that freckles, burns easily, and never tans. They should never sunbathe without sunscreen, or for longer than 20 minutes the first week. SPF: 15, or SPF 23, which blocks out nearly all of the sun's ultraviolet rays.
2. Skin type 2s have fair skin with light eyes. They burn easily but can get tan after careful exposure—15 minutes when still, 30 minutes if moving around. SPF: 8 on body, 15 on face.
3. Type 3 individuals burn minimally and tan gradually if they limit unprotected exposure to 20 minutes or so. SPF: 6 on body, 10 on face.
4. Type 4s, often olive-complected, rarely burn and turn a deep bronze if they build a base slowly—no longer than half an hour if unprotected. SPF: 6.
5. Type 5, usually of Middle Eastern or Hispanic background, tan profusely to a chocolate brown and never burn. They can spend about an hour in the sun unprotected. SPF: 4.
6. Type 6s, usually black, need minimal sun protection. SPF: 2.

THE
BAHAMAS

INTRODUCTION

A chain of nearly 700 islands, the Bahamas extend in a southeasterly curve from the east coast of Florida to the Windward Passage between Cuba and Haiti. The Bahamas were the first stop in the ocean blue that Columbus sailed in 1492. Today, the water is still blue, and Columbus is memorialized as the first tourist. A myriad of pirates and privateers used the natural ports of the Bahamas before the British colonized the islands. English ships brought Africans as slaves, and the mixture of peoples created a rich culture. Now tourists are attracted to the warm water, soft beaches, shopping, casinos, and fine restaurants.

Most of the tourism is clustered on Providence Island, home to Cable Beach and the capital, Nassau. Paradise Island lies just across a bridge. A lot of cruise ships and smaller vessels ply the waters, stopping off at the port of Nassau. Freeport, on Grand Bahama Island, also attracts a considerable crowd.

Bimini is called the Gateway to the Bahamas.

Smaller craft often stop at Bimini or stay for a weekend. The island, which lies just across the Straits of Florida from Miami, found fame for the Compleat Angler bar, once the digs of Hemingway and the downfall of Gary Hart.

When the British granted independence to the Bahamas in 1973, they left their system of law, a parliamentary democracy, and English customs. These have blended with the African and other traditions of the Bahamians to form a local culture complete with its own music, festivals, and charm. The government has many of the failings common to the Third World, but it recognizes the importance of tourism. The people go out of their way to accommodate visitors; 60 percent of the population depends on tourism for its livelihood.

The all-inclusive resorts reviewed here are located in the Nassau–Paradise Island area. All the major resorts were renovated in 1987, in a successful attempt to upgrade the area's image. Transportation among Cable Beach, Nassau, and Paradise Island can easily be accomplished by bus, taxi, or on foot.

The Bahamas have become a haven for people interested in sport-fishing, cruising, diving, and all types of water sports. Other people just come to relax on the beaches. Both groups will find good food in the wide variety of restaurants and nightlife in the clubs. Many honeymooners and families find that the large resorts offer the variety, service, and privacy that they desire.

11

If your ideal vacation involves shopping, the straw market in Nassau attracts those who like to bargain for trinkets. Although no one is offering a clean deed to the island of Manhattan, good deals can be had on native handiwork, which many artisans create in their marketplace studios.

Other "bargains" can be made for duty-free liquor, if you don't mind carting it home. Camera and radio deals probably do not equal those found at a U.S. discount store.

NUTS & BOLTS

CONTACT INFORMATION

Bahamas Tourist Offices

10 Columbus Circle,
Suite 1660
New York, NY 10019
212-758-2777

Chicago: 312-787-8203
Dallas: 214-742-1886
Los Angeles: 213-385-0033
Miami: 305-442-4860

85 Richmond Street West
Toronto, Ont. M5H 2C9
416-968-2999

CURRENCY: The independent Bahamian Republic issues its own currency, the Bahamian dollar, which is freely exchangeable for the U.S. dollar.

CUSTOMS/DUTY: The Bahamas are a key stop-off point for drug smuggling into the United States. Head government officials of the islands have been accused of complicity in moving the contraband. This has caused strain between the two countries and unsettled the internal political situation of the Bahamas.

If you look like a possible customer, street drug dealers will approach you for a deal. Some of these supposed dealers are police informers who collect money for tipping off the local gendarmes. An arrest looks good for the Bahamas government. If this happens, you'll wish that you were in a U.S. jail.

The United States has a policy of zero tolerance. The boat *Monkey Business*, infamous because of Gary Hart, was later seized because one of the crew members allegedly possessed a small quantity of marijuana. Drug smuggling is not only illegal, it's foolish as well. Don't even try. It ain't worth doing time for.

ELECTRICITY: 110 volts 60 cycles; no adapter required.

FESTIVALS/HOLIDAYS: From June to August you can share in the local Goombay festival. This is a time of colorful street parades,

Bahamian music, and big smiles. The natives tend to be extremely friendly and have a touch of British charm. While you're getting into the Goombay beat, be sure to try the Goombay Smash, a grafting of a whisky sour with a Piña Colada.

LANGUAGES: English.

PACKING: You might expect the sunny Bahamas to be as informal as the Caribbean islands. Wrong. The former British colonials dress more like the inhabitants of their rainy motherland. Proper women, unlike the daughters of France, do not bare their breasts on the beach, nor do men show up at a nice restaurant without a jacket.

TIME: The Bahamas are on Eastern Standard Time. They switch to Daylight Savings Time when the United States does.

TRAVEL TIME BY AIR

Chicago: **4 hours**
Los Angeles: **5 hours**
New York: **3 hours 30 minutes**
Toronto: **4 hours**

ARRIVAL AIRPORT: Nassau.

VACCINATION REQUIREMENTS: None.

VISA/PASSPORT REQUIREMENTS: United States and Canadian citizens need only proof of citizenship in the form of a passport, birth certificate, or certified copy of birth certificate with photo ID.

WEATHER

	WINTER	SPRING	SUMMER	AUTUMN
Air:	70	75	80	75

Rainfall: **50 inches per year**
Wind speed: **5–25 knots**
Daily duration of sunshine: **8 hours on average**

CLUB PERILLO

Type of vacation: **Resort**
Target market: **Everyone, all ages**
Location: **Paradise Island, Nassau, Bahamas**
All-inclusive cost per week: **$1,399 including airfare**

RATINGS

Value: $ $ $ $ $

Fun quotient: 🌴 🌴 🌴 🌴

Honeymoon suitability: ❤ ❤ ❤ ❤

Singles meeting ground: 👫 👫

Child appeal: 🍦 🍦

Management professionalism: ☎ ☎ ☎ ☎ ☎

Service: 💡 💡 💡 💡

Food: 🦞 🦞 🦞 🦞

THE REAL STORY

Do you find that even the best foods and most gorgeous places get old after a few days? If so, you may appreciate Club Perillo's all-inclusive stay in the Bahamas. Its version of a complete vacation serves up theme dinners, many restaurants of varied cuisines, gambling, island tours, nightclubs, and a beautiful sunny environment.

Club Perillo in the Bahamas feels like a combination between a resort vacation and an all-inclusive club. It places more emphasis on restaurant choices and tours than on water sports. You may spend your days soaking up the sun, shopping in the straw market, touring the island, playing tennis, or engaging in any of the activities that the hotel has to offer. The evenings are much more structured. Perillo

14

alternates between theme dinners with shows and dine-around nights, when you can choose among seven restaurants. After the show, you can shake it on the dance floor or roll some dice in the casino. The emphasis here is clearly more on tourist activities than on sports and participatory games. The resort does offer full water sports for a fee, but your all-inclusive dollars pay for other things, including a luxurious room.

If you like to gamble, the hotel lets you take your shot at winning the big one. Other close-by casinos stand ready to sell you chips as well.

Club Perillo adds a warm touch to a large resort beach vacation. Although a part of the Paradise Island Resort and Casino complex, Perillo pampers its guests with gourmet meals, native shows, and a concierge who makes everyone feel at home. A recreation register gives you a way to communicate with other members of the "inner circle." This way you can easily find a tennis partner, a fourth for bridge, or just a pal. The private club suite gives you a place to meet, by design or serendipity. Activities that are open only to Club Perillo guests have the same effect. Most important, the club hostess (or host) gets to know the guests in a short period of time. She (or he) floats as a combination troubleshooter, socialite, matchmaker, camp counselor, and friend.

Everything is effortless, from the baggage handling prearrival check-in through the week to the return flight. Perillo guests fly regularly scheduled Pan Am jets, which supply service that generally exceeds that of charters and gives scheduling flexibility if a special situation arises.

 Jason's Tips:

Why would you go to the Club Perillo rather than check into the Paradise Island Resort itself? First, the concierge takes care of all your needs, making the vacation hassle free. Second, you'll know the cost up front: the total air/land/food/activities package probably costs less than you could arrange yourself. Next, Perillo guests form their own friendly clique, which isn't a bad thing for a one-week vacation. Of course, you can cruise the hotel and island if you want to explore and meet people on your own. Finally, you could not organize this trip on your own. Club Perillo sponsors its own parties, events, and other activities.

Considering the time, care, and dollars, Club Perillo guests can have a much better experience than tourists who just check into the hotel on their own or buy an air/hotel package.

INCLUDED

Accommodations
Activities
Airfare
Child care
Entertainment & dancing
Food

Taxes
Tips
Tours
Transfer to and from airport
Wine with dinner

ALSO INCLUDED

2 cocktail receptions with
    open bar
Bahamian night theme party
Le Cabaret Theatre
Club Perillo dinner party
Sight-seeing tour of Paradise
    Island

3-hour catamaran cruise with
    calypso band
Free admission to Tradewinds
    Disco and Club Pastiche
Fashion show

VALUE

Club Perillo costs about the same as other quality all-inclusive resort packages. It caters to a sight-seeing and luxury-seeking clientele. It takes care of its guests very well. Most guests feel that the Perillo experience exceeds their expectations and that the money is very well spent.

Most water sports are available, but they cost extra. If you plan on occasional use, this should not throw your budget off. If you are a sport fanatic, you should probably choose a different trip. Come to Perillo in the Bahamas to luxuriate, eat well, gamble, and see the island.

ACTIVITIES & SPORTS

ACTIVITIES

Arts & crafts
Board games
Culture/music/language
    classes
Dancing

Entertainment/shows
Movies
Nude sunbathing
Sunbathing
Underwater vision boat

SPORTS

Basketball
Jogging trail

Swimming (pool and ocean)
Tennis (12 lighted courts)

AT EXTRA COST

Canoes	Scuba
Golf	Scuba resort course
Horseback riding	Snorkeling
Jet skiing	Swimming (not for laps)
Parasailing	Waterskiing
Pedal boats	Weightlifting
Sailing (sunfish)	Windsurfing

ITINERARY & DAILY SCHEDULE

Trips go from Saturday to Saturday or Sunday to Sunday. With either schedule, you get the full range of activities and meals.

NIGHTLIFE & ENTERTAINMENT

You'll only be bored at night if you don't like to eat gourmet meals, see shows, gamble, dance and socialize, and watch movies. In other words, there's lots to do.

Club Perillo guests spend several evenings together, enjoying the dinner dance, Bahamian Night party and dinner show, and the band/dinner show. Other nights you can choose your own restaurants and nightclub entertainment.

Perillo guests gain free entry to the two nightclubs on the property. The Tradewinds Disco has a deejay who spins records and gets the crowd moving. Club Pastiche has a native show, a live band, and a great dance floor.

AESTHETICS & ENVIRONMENT

Paradise Towers at Paradise Island Resort and Casino is a first-class resort.

FACILITIES

Bars	Entertainment coordinators
Beaches	Gift shop
Beauty salon	Medical station
Casino	Piano bar
Concierge	Safety-deposit box (in room)
Disco	Swimming pools (2)

ROOMS

Perillo sells only deluxe land view and deluxe ocean view rooms. Each has two double beds and a private balcony. The hotel was recently renovated.

LUXURY LEVEL

Air-conditioning	Porter service
Clock	Radio
Laundry service (extra)	Refrigerator in room
Maid service	Room service (extra)
Phone in room	Television in room

FOOD & DRINK

All meals are included in the Club Perillo plan. Guests choose from among seven restaurants for dinner. You won't get to try them all in a week, because some nights are taken up with the Bahamian Night party, the nightclub dinner/show, and the dinner/dance.

The following briefly describes the restaurant choices for the free "dine-a-round" nights.

Grill Room: Steak and seafood. Dressy. Jacket for men, dresses for women.
Villa d'Este: Italian. Dressy.
Coyaba: Polynesian. Casual to dressy.
Spices: Continental. Sandwich to lobster. Casual.
Paradise Pavilion: Continental. Casual.
Sea Grapes: Casual.
Terrace Garden: Continental. Dressy.

At orientation they will give you a membership card, which allows people to use their dine-a-round privileges. Dinners include a carafe of wine.

PRIVACY & RELAXATION

In between tours, you should find lots of time to relax. The large hotel atmosphere does not offer lots of secluded places, but its large grounds give you space.

SHOPPING

The Nassau straw market features all sorts of handiwork, art T-shirts, and of course, straw products. Go on a day when there are few cruise ships in town to get the most attention and the best prices. Street vendors also sell fruits, which make great snacks.

STAFFING & SERVICE

Perillo Tours is a worldwide, family-run organization. In 42 years, it has expanded its operation to include tours to Italy, the Bahamas, and Hawaii. By any definition, it is a major player in the travel market.

More important, it adds pride and a caring attitude to its business. Mario Perillo started the company, operating tours to Italy. The company grew, but his personal touch is still found throughout.

Mario's son, Steve, not only works with the company but stays active in guest relations. The Perillo charm and service pervade the whole organization.

HONEYMOONERS

Club Perillo attracts lots of honeymooners. It doesn't have any special packages, but does host a champagne party for newlyweds.

SINGLES

Spring break, Christmas, Easter, and summer draw some singles. In general, however, this resort's not geared to this crowd. It will pair same-sex singles in rooms on request, if available.

CHILD APPEAL

Children are welcome, although the club is not geared for them. There is no special day-care or activities program, although the concierge will find a baby-sitter if you desire.

NUTS & BOLTS

BOOKING & CONTACT INFORMATION: Book the trip through your travel agent. Most people do. Or you can contact Perillo Tours directly by calling 800-431-1515 or 201-307-1234.

The number for Paradise Island Resort and Hotel is 809-326-3000.

DEPOSITS/REFUNDS: Various cancellation penalties apply. Perillo strongly recommends cancellation insurance. Purchase it when you buy the package from your travel agent.

HANDICAP ACCESSIBILITY: The resort is fully ramped and almost 100 percent accessible. However, none of the bathrooms is handicapped equipped. They will pull the bathroom doors down to allow for wheelchair entrance.

RELIGIOUS SERVICES: You can probably find a service that you'd be comfortable with in town within a 15-minute taxi ride.

RESERVATION SCHEDULE: For holidays you probably will need to book at least three months in advance. At other times, you should be able to get a room within several weeks.

TRAVEL TIME FROM AIRPORT: 20 minutes (Nassau Airport).

SPENDING MONEY: $200 should cover drinks and gambling losses for two. Drinks cost what they would in a U.S. hotel bar, about $2.50 to $3.

Cost Worksheet

	High Season[1]	Off-Season[2]
Accommodations		
(8 days, 7 nights)	$1,339[3]	$1,099
Food	incl.	incl.
Drinks		
Departure tax	5	5
Sports	extra	extra
Airfare[4]	incl.	incl.
Sight-seeing		
Tips		
Additional, sports[5]		
Souvenirs		

[1] High season dates: Christmas week, Presidents' week
[2] Off-season dates: After Easter up to Christmas week. Regular season dates: New Year's through Easter, except high season week
[3] Premium for single person: $200
[4] Airfare from New York City on Pan Am is included in the price. Additional charges for airfare from other cities range from $60 for major Eastern Seaboard cities to $285 for Los Angeles and San Francisco.
[5] Offered for extra charge: All sports

THE PALM CLUB
(Nassau Beach Hotel)

VITAL FEATURES

Type of vacation: **Beach resort**
Target market: **Couples, families, singles, most guests in their thirties and up**
Location: **Nassau, Bahamas**
All-inclusive cost per week: **$1,199 plus airfare**

RATINGS

Value: 💲💲💲💲💲

Fun quotient: ⛱⛱⛱⛱

Honeymoon suitability: ❤❤❤❤❤

Singles meeting ground: 🚹

Child appeal: 🍦🍦

Management professionalism: ☎☎☎

Service: 💡💡💡

Food: 🦞🦞🦞

THE REAL STORY

Housed in a wing of the Nassau Beach Hotel, the Palm Club offers the privacy and luxury of a large resort and the simplicity of a prepaid vacation. Set on Cable Beach, a short bus ride from Nassau, this resort gives travelers a chance to stay on the grounds or to visit the nearby casinos and attractions of Nassau.

The 50-room Palm Club grants its guests free run of the hotel and provides special services. Palm Club members enjoy a private lounge with an open bar, a full-time club director, and concierge service. The Palm Club package includes a full American meal plan with dining at six restaurants, excursions to nearby islands, greens fees at the Cable Beach Golf Club, day and night tennis, water sports, native shows, cocktail parties, and more drink coupons than you can possibly use.

Palm Club vacation packages come in varying lengths. Eight-day/seven-night, five-day/four-night, and four-day/three-night trips are available. Piedmont Airlines flies guests free from certain East Coast cities.

The Palm Club is located in an older section of the Nassau Beach Hotel. The rooms aren't quite as nice as those in the rest of the hotel. In spite of this, you're sure to have a good time at the Palm Club. You'll enjoy yourself from the moment the limo picks you up at the airport and the driver begins pouring the champagne, until the end of your stay when they drag you, kicking and screaming, back to civilization.

INCLUDED

Accommodations	Sports
Activities	Taxes
Airfare (on Piedmont Airlines)	Tips
Champagne on arrival	Tours
Drinks	Transfer to and from airport
Entertainment & dancing	Wine with dinner
Food	

VALUE

Overall, the Palm Club offers an excellent value. You get a lot for your money, and you'll use almost everything in the package.

ACTIVITIES, SPORTS, & EXCURSIONS

ACTIVITIES: Dancing, entertainment/shows, sunbathing.

SPORTS: Guests have free access to the resort's beach, swimming pool, and health club. The spa has an exercise room, sauna, and massage facilties. Palm Club members enjoy complimentary greens fees at the Cable Beach Golf Club and unlimited tennis on the resort's two courts. The tennis club features a pro shop and two teaching professionals. All nonmotorized water sports also are free to Palm Club members. Equipment includes snorkeling gear, pedal boats, sailboats, catamarans, and Windsurfers. For an additional charge, guests can go scuba diving, parasailing, waterskiing, and deep-sea fishing. Each winter the Nassau Beach Hotel hosts the Bahamas International Windsurfing Regatta, the richest pro-am board-sailing event in the North Atlantic.

Aerobics/exercise class   Swimming
Golf   Tennis
Sailing   Volleyball
Snorkeling   Windsurfing

EXCURSIONS: Palm Club guests choose one of the two free tours. The first option involves an all-day boat tour to Rose Island with a live band, lunch, and unlimited wine. The second choice takes you on a tour of Coral World, an underwater observatory that allows you to see marine life without getting wet. Guests also receive free admission to Nassau's longest running native show. The hotel provides free scheduled transportation to downtown Nassau.

ITINERARY & DAILY SCHEDULE

You create your own schedule at the Palm. Club. After breakfast, some people leave the resort to go shopping or sight-seeing. Many guests head to the beach for a day of suntanning and water sports. Once or twice a day, the activities director may organize a group activity like volleyball. How you spend your time depends on your energy and imagination.

NIGHTLIFE & ENTERTAINMENT

Evening entertainment at the resort centers on the nightclub, where local bands play music until the early morning. Depending on the band, you may dance to Caribbean music, rock and roll, or disco. Local Bahamians come to the club to mix with the tourists. Hotel guests get in without a cover charge. If drinking and dancing aren't your style, the casino next door provides other forms of entertainment.

Thursday evening is Junkanoo Night at Pineapple Place, where Palm Club guests enjoy a lavish Bahamian buffet and Nassau's longest running native show. Acts include fire dancing, the limbo, and calypso singers. First-time viewers have a great time, veterans will still find it enjoyable.

AESTHETICS & ENVIRONMENT

The uniformed guard at the hotel entrance dresses like a British colonial soldier. He personifies the atmosphere of the Nassau Beach Hotel. Tropical gardens, fountains, and scenic walkways highlight the hotel's grounds. Inside, wide window expanses, louvered doors, and partitions create a feeling of restful elegance. The large lobby feels spacious and open, yet little clusters of sofas and chairs give you private places to sit and talk. A 3,000-foot beach fronts the resort, giving the Nassau Beach Hotel and Palm Club the largest beach in Nassau.

FACILITIES

Bank
Bars
Beaches
Beauty salon
Casino
Concierge
Disco
Entertainment coordinator

Gift shop
Medical station
Piano bar
Safety-deposit box
Snack bar, grill
Swimming pool
Water sports center

ROOMS

The Nassau Beach Hotel has two sections; the Palm Club rooms occupy the older wing. Guest rooms have wall-to-wall carpeting, tropical furnishings, spacious closets, and mirrored areas. Each room opens onto a private balcony or terrace with a ocean view or garden view. All rooms have color cable TV, a radio, a telephone, and individually controlled air-conditioning. Palm Club guests trade off a new room for good, old-fashioned fun and games. Most guests feel that they get the better part of that deal.

LUXURY LEVEL

Air-conditioning
Bar in room (on request)
Clock
Hair dryer
Laundry service (extra)
Maid service
Phone in room

Porter service (extra)
Radio
Refrigerator in room (on
  request)
Room service
Television in room

FOOD & DRINK

Palm Club guests may choose among six restaurants serving a variety of menus from Bahamian to burgers to Continental. The American Café serves breakfast, lunch, and dinner from 7:00 A.M. to midnight. The menu and quality of food resemble that of a Denny's restaurant, except the American Café serves Bahamian specialties as well; the service is extremely slow. The Pineapple Place serves a buffet breakfast. If you can get out of your room before noon, you will probably eat lunch at the Beachcomber Grill and Pizzeria. At dinner, guests can return to the American Café or choose from two more-formal restaurants. The Lobster Pot offers a well-stocked soup-and-salad bar, as well as fresh seafood from local Bahamian fishermen. The Beef Cellar serves beef and seafood, charcoal grilled tableside. Both these restaurants provide quality food.

The Palm Club also offers several other dining experiences. Once during your stay, you dine at the Frilsham House, a French gourmet restaurant with four dining rooms and a veranda overlooking the ocean. This is a swanky place with great-tasting food. You'll want to dress for the occasion.

 Jason's Tips:

> On another night, you may get a pass for dinner and a show in town. If you go, eat at the hotel first. One look at what other people at the show are eating will convince you that you made the right decision to satisfy your appetite earlier.

After each meal you will receive a bill, just like the paying customers. All you do is sign the tab and write down your room number. You can add in the tip if you like, or leave something extra at the restaurant. Use your drink coupons to pay for your wine and liquor.

STAFFING & SERVICE

Service moves at the slow Bahamian pace. The staff at the Nassau Beach Hotel seem friendly and eager to help, although they are sometimes uninformed. The Trusthouse Forte reservations staff comes across in a similar way. The stateside office staff can be less than helpful. Don't judge the resort by the stateside staff's phone manner—it's actually a nice resort, in spite of the way they deal with you over the phone. The hotel is owned by Trusthouse Forte Hotels, a London-based chain with over 800 hotels on five continents.

PRIVACY & RELAXATION

The laid-back Bahamas pace pervades the Palm Club atmosphere. No street noises disturb you. No boom boxes blare tunes on the beach. You relax, revive, regroup, and go home feeling refreshed and rejuvenated.

SHOPPING

Nassau has some excellent shopping opportunities. Good prices can be found on T-shirts and Bahamian arts and crafts. The hotel has 11 boutiques, including a beauty salon, jewelry shop, gift shop, newsstand, liquor store, and drugstore; prices are a bit higher than in town.

HONEYMOONERS

The beach and subtropical climate create a very romantic setting. The Palm Club contains all the ingredients necessary for a great honeymoon, including lively activities, private retreats, and room service. The Nassau Beach Hotel offers an almost all-inclusive honeymoon package, but the Palm Club provides no special honeymoon perks.

SINGLES

We met no single guests while reviewing the Palm Club. The resort does not organize singles mixers, although you may meet another single at a cocktail party. The dance club attracts singles from town.

CHILD APPEAL

The resort provides no special kids' activities. Kids may get bored, and you could spend a lot of time running after them on the beach. The hotel requires that children stay in the same room as their parents.

NUTS & BOLTS

BOOKING & CONTACT INFORMATION

Palm Club, Nassau Beach
    Hotel
P.O. Box N7756
Nassau, Bahamas
800-225-5843 or 809-327-7711

Trusthouse Forte
Hotel Plaza Athenée
37 East 64th Street
New York, NY 10021
212-734-9100

Trusthouse Forte Westberry
Madison Avenue and 69th
    Street
New York, NY 10021
212-535-2000

DEPOSITS/REFUNDS: Palm Club requires a 25 percent deposit to be paid no later than 14 days after the time of booking. Reservations made fewer than 14 days before arrival require an American Express Card or a Trusthouse Gold Card. The balance is paid at the end of your stay. Full refunds will be returned if you notify the hotel or reservation office at least 21 days prior to arrival. If you cancel with fewer than 21 days' notice, you will forfeit the deposit.

ELECTRICITY: 110 volts 60 cycles; United States standard.

HANDICAP ACCESSIBILITY: No special handicap facilities are available.

LANGUAGES: Staff members at the Palm Club speak English, French, Italian, and German.

PACKING: Bahamians tend to be more formal than their Caribbean cousins. Typical cotton clothes are fine during the day, but you'll want to bring nicer clothes for going out in the evening. Some men wear jackets and ties to the better restaurants. Women need comparable attire. If you plan on going off the grounds at night, bring a flashlight because the streets are dark.

RELIGIOUS SERVICES: The Palm Club does not provide or arrange transportation to religious services.

RESERVATION SCHEDULE: A month's notice is usually sufficient for reservations.

NUMBER OF ROOMS: 50 Palm Club rooms; 411 rooms in Nassau Beach Hotel.

NUMBER OF EMPLOYEES: 450.

TRAVEL TIME FROM AIRPORT: 10 minutes (Nassau airport). Guests are transferred in a chauffeur-driven limousine.

SPENDING MONEY: You'll probably want to bring money for souvenirs, gambling, cab fare, and side trips that are not included in the base price. A few hundred dollars will easily cover costs.

Cost Worksheet

	High Season[1]	Off-Season
Accommodations (7 days)[2]	$1,199	$1,099
Food	incl.	incl.
Drinks	incl.	incl.
Departure tax	$5	$5
State tax	incl.	incl.
Hotel tax	incl.	incl.
Sports	incl.	incl.
Airfare[3]	_____	_____
Sight-seeing		
Tips	incl.	incl.
Additional sports		
Souvenirs	_____	_____

[1] High season dates: December 15 through April 26
[2] Premium for single person: $500
[3] Airfare on Piedmont Airlines can be built into some packages if you are traveling from certain eastern U.S. cities.

CARIBBEAN

Aruba

INTRODUCTION

Aruba, a mere speck of an island, offers much more than most tourists see. The landscape and people are very atypical for the Caribbean. If you get to know the real Aruba, you may find that it redefines your idea of an island retreat.

Located off the coast of Venezuela, Aruba is only 20 miles long and 6 miles wide. The population is racially mixed—of Dutch, South American, and African ancestry. Unlike many of the other islands, it has practically no racial tension, crime, beggars or cheats. What it does have is a dry climate that hovers around the low 80s year-round, a friendly local population that could not be more accommodating, and consistent trade winds that make this island a major windsurfing draw.

Most people come to Aruba for the gambling, and there is plenty of that. Every one of the large hotels has a casino, and there are a few independents as well. If you gamble a lot, ask the pit bosses to give you complimentary meals. They are stingier here than in Las Vegas, but they will usually accommodate you if you ask.

A large percentage of guests never get off the hotel strip. They miss the nicest parts of the island, which has natural desert beauty. Driving around the perimeter of the island gives you a view of its real geography. You'll want to visit Lover's Cave and take the guided tour by flashlight. The owner is a young entrepreneur with a U.S. computer science degree. Although the cave is not spectacular, you can learn a lot about the island from the guide. Good snorkeling and secluded, uncrowded sands can be found at Baby's Beach. Bring your own drinks, food, and gear, because no concessionaires have made it there. At the extreme west end of the island, the California Lighthouse stands next to a hilltop restaurant and bar. There is no better place to watch the sunset.

Because much of the terrain does not have paved roads, you'll need a Jeep or motor scooter to access the most beautiful parts of the island. Avoid driving through the tar pits, because the dust will leave a residue on your skin and hair.

Fewer than ten years ago, Aruba had one of the largest oil refineries in the world. The old Exxon compound is on the east side of the island, standing like a ghost town, just past San Nicolas. If the guard will let you in, it's worth touring. You can see the smokestack from Baby's Beach.

Along the beach, water-sports companies rent jet skis, sailboats, sailboards, and most other water sports equipment. There are also several companies that run scuba diving trips for both certified and noncertified divers. During the off-season you can even take a true certification course if instructors are available. During high season, forget it. Snorkeling can be a group activity or a solo enterprise. If you're down at Baby's Beach you may even get equipment free. The waiter at Charlie's bar will give you an unadvertised special—free loaner mask, fins, and snorkel. They don't ask for a deposit, and claim that no one has walked off with their equipment. Please keep up this tradition.

Most of the beach action happens outside the Holiday Inn. The hotel has a volleyball net and it's easy to get up a game. Tourists seem equally divided between gringos and South Americans. The native Arubans often come to the beach to join in the fun. The island's temptations come at a pretty stiff price if you stay along the row of high-rise hotel-casinos.

Most nightlife takes place in the casinos of the big hotels. They offer a plethora of gambling games, which can raise the price of your trip substantially. The Alhambra Casino and Aladdin Theatre form the centerpiece of a ten-shop complex with restaurants and nightclubs. The complex can be found near the Divi Divi hotel. A couple of nightclubs in town attract nongamblers who prefer a fair exchange for their money. Visage, in Oranjestad, draws the largest crowd with its giant fish tanks and disco music. Every day from 6:00 to 7:30 P.M., one of the hotels or restaurants sponsors a manager's hour when drinks, and sometimes snacks, are free. Some sort of live entertainment usually accompanies the party. Your hotel concierge should be able to supply you with a list of locations. If not, ask around.

If you haven't blown all your money in the casinos, your dollars can buy lots of things to take home. All the big boutiques are here, and they sell goods at almost duty-free prices. Check prices carefully, though, because true bargains require informed shopping. You'll do best on Scandinavian porcelain, pottery, pewter, and silver. Some local crafts can be found at the Bon Bini (Welcome) Festival that takes place every Tuesday from May to December from 6:30 to 8:30 P.M. There, you'll find handicrafts and local dishes well worth the small admission price. Most of the shopping on Aruba is clustered on Oranjestad's main street, Nassaustraat.

As in Aruba's parent country, Holland, prostitution is legal. The working girls supposedly frequent the major hotels in the late afternoon and early evening, but the practice is so discrete that you probably won't recognize it. Later at night they haunt sleazy dives in the town of San Nicolas, where the practice is very open.

The quality of food on Aruba ranges from good to excellent. The island has a wide variety of cuisines that originated with the home countries of the immigrants. These include Dutch, Indonesian, Chinese, French, Continental, and Caribbean. Everything is imported, so prices are high. Ask the concierges and taxi drivers for restaurant recommendations. The Brisas del Mar in San Nicolas serves fresh seafood and island dishes with a local flair. Try this on the day that you rent a car. Other good restaurants include Gianni's (great seafood, skip the veal), Talk of the Town (Continental-French), the Dutch Mill, and the Buccaneer. Many of the hotels have cookouts and buffets that include music and a show for about $20 per person, plus drinks. These usually are good deals.

 Jason's Tips.

Travel Impressions, a package tour company, offers its customers a meal plan that includes seven breakfasts at your hotel and five dinner coupons that may be used at different restaurants or hotel buffets. In light of island food prices, this can be a good deal.

The temperature and weather remain spectacular year-round. Aruba is located outside the hurricane belt, so storms and rain are rare. The high season corresponds to the northern cold, and lasts from December 15 to April 15.

The following list gives Aruba's temperature during our winter. Conditions remain fairly constant throughout the year.

Air temperature: 82–85°F
Water temperature: 72–75°F
Humidity: 76 percent
Rainfall: 17" (mostly during the winter months)

Wind: steady 16 mph
Daily sunshine: 8 hours on average

SEASONS: The most interesting time to visit is during Carnival. The activities begin around the first of the year, but the atmosphere gets increasingly exhilarating as the climax approaches in late winter.

BUSHIRI BEACH RESORT

VITAL FEATURES

Type of vacation: **Beach resort**
Target market: **Singles, couples, families of all ages**
Location: **Aruba, off the coast of Venezuela**
All-inclusive cost per week: **$875–$1,085, plus airfare**

RATINGS

Value: 💲💲💲💲

Fun quotient: 🏖️🏖️🏖️

Honeymoon suitability: ❤️❤️❤️❤️

Singles meeting ground: 👥👥👥

Child appeal: 🍦🍦🍦

Management professionalism: Not rated

Service: Not rated

Food: Not rated

THE REAL STORY

Travel Impressions and the Bushiri Beach Resort combine forces to offer a very affordable vacation on Aruba, an island that otherwise could be prohibitively expensive. Bushiri Beach offers what you would expect from an all-inclusive: food, tennis, water sports, a great beach, theme parties, and the like. It recently completed a large expansion of the property. The reason to choose Bushiri over another all-inclusive is the island of Aruba.

Life at Bushiri revolves around the large pool courtyard. Beyond the man-made structure lies the real beauty, a white stretch of sand leading to a warm turquoise sea.

34

INCLUDED

Accommodations	Sports instruction
Activities	Taxes
Drinks	Tips
Entertainment & dancing	Tours
Food	Transfer to and from airport
Sports	Wine with dinner

VALUE

Travel Impressions' packages make Aruba affordable. The Bushiri Beach, in particular, offers a good alternative to E.P. hotel prices.

ACTIVITIES, SPORTS, & EXCURSIONS

ACTIVITIES

Arts & crafts	Entertainment/shows
Board games	Movies
Culture/music/language	Sunbathing
classes	Underwater vision boat
Dancing	

SPORTS: The sailboats and Windsurfers at Bushiri are often grounded because of the high winds. People who really want to learn or improve their skills will find the conditions ideal, but the week-end boardsailer may find the conditions too difficult.

Aerobics/exercise class	Scuba resort course
Basketball (for kids)	Snorkeling
Horseback riding (extra)	Swimming
Jet skiing (extra)	Tennis
Parasailing (extra)	Volleyball
Pedal boats	Waterskiing (extra)
Sailing (extra)	Weightlifting
Scuba (extra)	Windsurfing

EXCURSIONS: Bushiri offers sight-seeing tours of the island by bus, shopping trips, and a nightly ride to a nearby casino and disco. All are free and bring you back to the resort, except the night trip to the casino and disco. Night owls will have to find their own way home. The tour desk also arranges extracurricular tours and sports.

AESTHETICS & ENVIRONMENT

The Bushiri is a low-rise hotel that is located close to the town of Oranjestad. Although not plush, the Bushiri is modern, tastefully decorated, well kept, and clean.

FACILITIES

Bars
Beaches
Entertainment coordinators
Gift shop
Jacuzzi

Piano bar
Safe in room
Snack bar, grill
Swimming pool
Water sports center

ROOMS

The rooms are well maintained and tastefully decorated.

LUXURY LEVEL

Air-conditioning
Laundry service (extra)
Maid service
Phone in room
Porter service

Radio
Refrigerator in room (deluxe
   rooms)
Television in room

FOOD & DRINK

Three meals a day and snacks are included in the room price at
Bushiri. A manager's cocktail party should get your buzz going for
the week.

PRIVACY & RELAXATION

Many people use the Bushiri as a relaxing retreat after a busy
night of getting their clocks cleaned at the casinos. The wide stretch
of beach and the quiet nature of the pool will let you decompress
from your regular life and the spinning roulette wheel.

HONEYMOONERS

The honeymoon package includes T-shirts, a commemorative
photo, champagne on arrival, flowers in the room, a three-minute
phone call home, a sunset cruise, and limo transportation to and
from the airport instead of the normal bus transportation.

SINGLES

The mix varies from week to week. In general, Aruba tends to
attract an older crowd and couples. Most young singles frequent the
discos in town and the beach outside the Holiday Inn.

CHILD APPEAL

Supervised activities for children span the day and evening so
parents can enjoy time to themselves. Activities include kite flying,
basketball, felt darts, movies, exercises, pool games, and beach contests such as sand castle contests and a water balloon toss.

NUTS & BOLTS

BOOKING INFORMATION: Ask about the Travel Impressions air/land packages.

CONTACT INFORMATION

Bushiri Beach Resort
141½ Main Street
Norwalk, CT 06851
800-622-7836
203-846-4140
Fax: 203-849-1892

Bushiri Beach Resort
Lloyd G. Smith Boulevard #35
Oranjestad, Aruba
011-297-825-216

CURRENCY: You get 1.77 Aruba florin to the dollar. Currencies are freely exchangeable and the exchange rate is steady.

CUSTOMS/DUTY: Standard U.S. and Canadian customs apply.

DEPOSITS/REFUNDS: In the winter you must pay a three-night deposit to confirm space. Cancellations must be made 21 days in advance for a full refund. During the summer season the resort requires a one-night deposit for a confirmed reservation. For a full refund, you must cancel at least 14 days prior to arrival. No refunds are returned if deadlines are not met.

ELECTRICITY: 110 volts 60 cycles, same as in the United States.

HANDICAP ACCESSIBILITY: The hotel features wheelchair-accessible concrete paths, ramps, and elevators. Public rest rooms come equipped with handicap facilities. The rooms are large enough for wheelchair access, and the baths have bars mounted in the tube.

LANGUAGES: All of you who took Papiamento language courses will get a chance to practice here. Dutch is the other official language. Almost everyone also speaks English and Spanish.

PACKING: Aruba is more formal than many other tropical islands. Tourists often walk around town in shorts, although Arubans rarely do. Bushiri Beach tends to be pretty casual, with beachwear OK except for dinner. At night, the casinos and nicer restaurants require nice sports clothes. Men often wear jackets, but not ties.

RELIGIOUS SERVICES: The resort holds no religious services. Aruba is predominantly Catholic, but other Christian faiths are also represented and there is a Jewish synagogue.

RESERVATION SCHEDULE: Reservations should be made at least two months in advance. For vacations during the Christmas holidays, you should book six months ahead of time.

NUMBER OF ROOMS: 150 rooms, 4 suites.

TRAVEL TIME BY AIR

Chicago: **5 hours 40 minutes**
Los Angeles: **7 hours 30 minutes**
New York: **4 hours 30 minutes**
Toronto: **6 hours**
Arrival airport: **Beatrix International Airport**

TRAVEL TIME FROM AIRPORT: 10 minutes (guests are met at the airport).

VACCINATION REQUIREMENTS: None.

Cost Worksheet		
	High Season[1]	*Off-Season*[2]
Accommodations		
(7 days)[3]	$875–$1,085	$560–$770
Food	incl.	incl.
Drinks	incl.	incl.
Departure tax	8	8
State tax	none	none
Hotel tax	incl.	incl.
Sports	incl.	incl.
Airfare	depends on package	
Sight-seeing	incl.	incl.
Tips	incl.	incl.
Additional sports		
Souvenirs		

[1] High season dates: December 23 to April 2
[2] Off-season dates: April 3 to December 21
[3] Premium for single person: high $1,295–$1,505, low $840–$1,050

VISA/PASSPORT REQUIREMENTS: U.S. and Canadian citizens need only proof of citizenship and a return/continuing ticket. You are also required to give notice of where you'll be staying when you enter the country. If you don't have advance reservations, you can make them at Aruba's airport. Its staff will call guesthouses and smaller hotels to get you a bargain, if you wish.

SPENDING MONEY: You'll want to bring extra money for shopping items and gambling expenses. Unless you're a big spender a few hundred dollars should cover additional expenses.

All rates per person, based on double occupancy for a seven-night stay.

Always ask if any special packages, promotions, or airfare discounts are in effect before booking.

All vacations described in this guide can be booked through any competent travel agent; we advise you to do so.

See the general introduction and area introductions for more details.

Belize

PYRAMID ISLAND RESORT

VITAL FEATURES

Type of vacation: **Beach resort on private island**
Target marget: **Divers, sailors, adventurous beachgoers of all ages**
Location: **Caye Chapel, Belize, Central America**
All-inclusive cost per week: **$1,000 plus airfare**

RATINGS

Value: 💲💲💲💲

Fun quotient: ☂ ☂ ☂

Honeymoon suitability: ♥♥♥♥

Singles meeting ground: 🧍🧍

Child appeal: 🍦🍦🍦

Management professionalism: ☎ ☎ ☎ ☎

Service: 💡💡💡

Food: 🦞🦞🦞

THE REAL STORY

If you dream of being marooned on a deserted island, without giving up the comforts of home, then Pyramid Island could give form to your fantasy. The moment you land on Caye Chapel's private runway, you enter a tropical haven with no cars or crowds. Palm trees rustle in the constant breeze, and a pale sand beach begins at your bedroom door. The island has no roads and only 32 guest rooms. The world's second largest barrier reef stretches past the island, attracting scuba divers and snorkelers.

Pyramid Island Resort is located on an island a mile long by a quarter mile wide. The hotel has two tennis courts, sailing dinghies, Windsurfers, and snorkeling equipment. Diving and fishing boats dock in the marina or at the pier. A large, comfortable room serves as lobby, lounge, and recreation center, and two wings of guest rooms extend from this central area. Each guest room opens directly onto the beach—it's only 20 steps to the clear, blue, very clean water. The patio bar and restaurant survey the great barrier reef, while a thatched roofed lounge provides a place to sip cocktails.

Where is this seeming paradise? Belize. Located on the Caribbean coast of the Yucatán Peninsula, Belize is an unknown, unspoiled, and underdeveloped nation. It remains largely undiscovered by tourists. From the air, the countryside appears to be a mosaic of inland mountains, dense jungle lowlands, coastal mangrove swamps, and untouched offshore keys. (Pilots who flew choppers in Vietnam may be subject to flashbacks.) On the ground, the climate feels warm and humid. Few resorts and fewer cities await travelers. The vast majority of visitors to Belize vacation on the chain of islands just off the coast.

Belizeans come from a mixed stock. The original inhabitants were Mayan Indians. Next came British settlers and black slaves from the Caribbean. Later, Mestizos, Asian immigrants, and refugees from other Central American countries added to the population. Today, Belize is a true melting pot that is refreshingly free of the prejudices that cause separations in many societies. Although the country has a low per capita income and simple living conditions, Belizeans are truly proud. The people are warm, friendly, and interesting. Pyramid Island's staff can tell you stories about the days of English rule, when the country was called British Honduras, as well as about the heady times that followed their country's independence on September 21, 1981.

INCLUDED

Accommodations	Taxes
Activities	Transfer to and from airport
Airfare from Belize City	Unlimited beach dives, free
Food	tanks and weight belts
Sports	

VALUE

Pyramid Island provides solid value for those looking for a remote getaway vacation, but the tab adds up quickly if you take extra-cost trips to other islands.

ACTIVITIES & SPORTS

Pyramid Island offers PADI diving certifications. The resort manager instructs neophyte divers from the first classroom hours through the momentous first open water dive. The fee of $300 (in U.S. currency) covers certification, books, classroom hours, scuba gear, and boat excursions for the first four dives. Dive trips visit remote and interesting locations, including the Blue Hole, a famous dive spot. Full-day dives provide lunch on the boat, or you can stop to picnic on one of the numerous low coral islands. Overnight dive trips can be purchased for extra cost.

If a diving package is not for you, you can arrange one-day outings. For an additional cost, boat tours visit Mayan pyramids, and small planes fly to nearby islands. Deep-sea and bonefishing charters can be arranged for full-day and half-day trips. The glass boat does two-hour tours with stops for snorkeling and swimming along the way. Each trip costs $12 per person.

Back on Caye Chapel, volleyball games can start on the beach at any time. Guests play tennis, Ping-Pong, pool, and basketball. Sailors use Windsurfers and Sunfish whenever they wish. For an extra cost, you can rent motor scooters and roam around the island. Those who prefer to walk can explore the mangroves or the bird sanctuary with its freshwater pond.

ACTIVITIES

Board games	Sunbathing
Glass-bottomed boat	Underwater vision boat (extra)
Nude sunbathing	

SPORTS

Basketball	Shuffleboard
Fishing	Snorkeling
Jogging trail	Swimming (ocean)
Motor scooters (extra)	Tennis
Sailing	Volleyball
Scuba	Windsurfing
Scuba resort course (extra)	

ITINERARY & DAILY SCHEDULE

The scheduling at Pyramid Island is casual and loose, as is the constant mood of this vacation. You can literally stumble out your door, land on the beach, and stay there all day. If you feel more active, the water sports equipment awaits at any time. The glass-bottomed boat goes out for one guest or a full load of passengers. One of the managers makes arrangements for off-island excursions. Diving and fishing trips can be arranged at your request.

NIGHTLIFE & ENTERTAINMENT

Most guests congregate in the bar in the evening. A boom box plays reggae music or any other tapes guests may happen to bring. The atmosphere feels like that of a family get-together. On any given night, you might find yourself playing cards, shooting pool, or partaking in a lively discussion. On such a small island, everyone feels part of the group. Guests trade stories of the day's lives like old friends at a class reunion. Belizean beer flows easily and tastes good.

AESTHETICS & ENVIRONMENT

Pyramid Island Resort completely occupies this privately owned island. Guests enjoy free run of the cay, from the beaches to the mangrove swamps. The facilities at Pyramid Island do not compare with those found in multimillion-dollar vacation complexes that allow guests to "escape" in American-style luxury. Instead, the resort offers a warm and relaxing environment far removed from the stresses and hustle of modern society. The hotel shows signs of wear and age, but it stays clean and functional. The toilet seats don't quite fit the commodes, and sometimes you have to let the water run a while before it gets hot. Still, these minor inconveniences become insignificant when you consider the remote natural setting. Tropical fish abound in the warm, clear waters, providing a bounty for fishermen and divers alike. Calm seas and consistent winds create excellent sailing conditions. Empty beaches let you soak up the rays without disturbance.

FACILITIES: Bars (2), beaches, library/TV room, snacks at the bar.

ROOMS

All 32 spacious rooms open directly onto the beach. The decor and furniture are rather plain. Standard features include air-conditioning, louvered windows, a desk and dresser like you had in your college dorm, and twin or double beds. The tiled floors show signs of age. All rooms come with private bath and freshwater showers. Room service is available, but since there are no phones, you have to get up to go ask for it, or request it the night before. The housekeeping staff does a nice job keeping the rooms clean.

LUXURY LEVEL

Air-conditioning
Laundry service (extra)
Maid service

Porter service
Room service

FOOD & DRINK

The kitchen staff at Pyramid Island take great care and pride in the meals they serve. The food is fresh and tasty, but it's closer to home cooked than gourmet. The kitchen will make conch chowder and special seafood dishes with fish you catch. The waitresses move a bit slowly, but the generous helpings fill you up. The resort is small enough that the staff know who is on the American plan and who is just visiting for the day.

The resort starts the day with a hearty breakfast of eggs, meats, flapjacks, and French toast, as well as juevos rancheros and fruit; the coffee could stand improvement. For lunch and dinner, the resort offers a standard menu as well as daily specials. The fresh fish brought in daily comes barbecued, grilled, baked, or fried. At least one dish always follows a Spanish/Mexican theme. Deserts are made fresh every day. Between meals you can eat potato chips at the bar. Pringles seem to be a Belizean favorite. You can sample the entire product line from lightly salted to barbecued.

The bar serves standard drinks, as well as such tropical favorites as banana coladas. Belikin Beer is the local brew. It's also the cheapest drink at the bar. Prices are comparable to what you would pay at any stateside hotel.

STAFFING & SERVICE

Life in Belize tends to move at a slow pace; so does the staff. Staff members relate to you as a person instead of as servant to guest. They often pull out a chair and chat in the middle of a chore. It may take a little longer to get things done, but you won't complain about the quality of the job or the friendly service.

PRIVACY & RELAXATION

Pyramid Island is the perfect place for relaxing in the sun. An almost unpopulated beach begins literally at your doorstep. A deck near the bar keeps refreshments close at hand. The constant breeze will lull you to sleep in the warm sun. (Be careful!)

SHOPPING

Caye Chapel has no stores. The few items you will find for sale in Belize City and on other cays will probably be made in Guatemala or Honduras.

HONEYMOONERS

If you and your fiancé are looking for a deserted island getaway, this is as close as you can get while still enjoying modern conveniences and services. No special honeymoon packages are offered.

SINGLES

Once a month Pyramid Island throws a weekend-long party with barbecues, bands, and beach activities. Fun seekers come from other islands to join the festivities. Belizeans, resident foreigners, and tourists all attend. People camp on the beach or stay on their boats. The party starts Saturday morning and continues into Sunday. During the rest of the month, the pickings are fairly slim. You may meet single divers or soldiers, who visit the island on their days off.

CHILD APPEAL

If your kids are easy to please and travel well, this could be a great place for the family. Pyramid Island provides plenty of activities, and safety is not a concern.

NUTS & BOLTS

BOOKING & CONTACT INFORMATION

Pyramid Island Resort
P.O. Box 193
Caye Chapel, Belize
Central America
011-501-44190
800-325-3401

CURRENCY: Belize dollars exchange two for one against the U.S. dollar. American money is widely accepted, but change comes back in Belize dollars.

CUSTOMS/DUTY: On the way into Belize you pass the customs officer at his desk in the one-room airport. On the way out you pay a $10 (U.S. currency) departure tax. Since there is little to buy, you probably won't have much to declare. Standard U.S. customs apply upon returning to the States.

DEPOSITS/REFUNDS: Confirmed reservations require a first night's deposit to be paid within two weeks of booking. The balance is due at the end of your stay. Credit cards and traveler's checks are the preferred method of payment. Cancellations receive credit toward another stay within one year.

ELECTRICITY: 110 volts, 60 cycles, same as in the United States.

HANDICAP ACCESSIBILITY: The small planes that take guests to the island cannot accommodate wheelchairs. Once on the island, however, no steps inhibit handicapped guests. Although the rooms are not modified, they are spacious enough for wheelchair maneuverability. With help, handicapped guests can use the bathrooms. Concrete walkways connect the rooms and main facilities. Wheelchairs will have a tough time negotiating the soft sand.

LANGUAGES: English is the official language of Belize, but you'll hear it with a variety of accents ranging from British to Spanish to Caribbean.

PACKING: You won't need dresses, collared shirts, slacks, or a jacket on this trip. Light cotton clothing will be most comfortable. Pack T-shirts, shorts, jeans, walking shoes, and sandals. A light jacket or sweatshirt feels nice on cool evenings. You'll also want to bring all your own lotions and toiletries, because none are available on the island. If you run out of something, the managers may pick it up for you on their weekly boat trip to the mainland.

RELIGIOUS SERVICES: None.

RESERVATION SCHEDULE: Reservations for the Christmas holidays should be made at least six months in advance. Winter months fill up rapidly, particularly the last weeks of each month. Book at least two or three months in advance to ensure that you get the room and date you want.

SIZE: 1-mile-long by 1/4-mile-wide island.

NUMBER OF ROOMS: 32 guest rooms.

TRAVEL TIME BY AIR

Chicago: **5 hours**
Los Angeles: **7 hours 35 minutes**
New York: **5 hours**
Toronto: **5 hours**

ARRIVAL AIRPORT: Cave Chapel via Belize City.

TRAVEL TIME FROM AIRPORT: When you land, you're at the resort.

VACCINATION REQUIREMENTS: None.

Visa/passport requirements: U.S. and Canadian citizens need a valid passport. No visas are required.

Spending money: All items at Pyramid Island can be charged to your bill. The few sundries available cost several times what you would pay for them in more developed areas. You will want to bring money for tips, drinks, and trips and tours off the island.

 Jason's Tips

The management normally adds gratuities to the bill. You might want to ask that they be left off the bill so you may distribute the tips directly and according to the quality of service.

Cost Worksheet

	High Season[1]	Off-Season[2]
Accommodations (7 days)[3]	$820 diver	$795 diver
	$545 nondiver	$520 nondiver
Food	incl.	incl.
Drinks		
Departure tax	10	10
State tax	incl.	incl.
Hotel tax	incl.	incl.
Sports	incl.	incl.
Airfare		
Sight-seeing		
Tips	at your discretion	
Additional, sports[4]		
Souvenirs		

[1] High season dates: December through April
[2] Off-season dates: May through November
[3] Premium for single person: $200
[4] Offered for extra charge: Pyramid Island offers rental equipment and night dives for extra cost. PADI open water–I certification costs $300. All excursions, except the 12 local boat dives, must be purchased at additional cost.

Honduras

INTRODUCTION

Vacation in Honduras? This question is likely to generate a look of dismay and a wisecrack such as "Yeah, right! Good luck getting a tan through a bulletproof vest." The news media has created the impression that Honduras is a troubled country caught between the war zones of Nicaragua and El Salvador. Needless to say, this image doesn't help the country attract pleasure-seeking vacationers. But there is more to the story. What the media don't tell you is that the restless winds of the mainland calm as they head out to sea. By the time the winds reach the Bay Islands, forty miles off the Honduran coast, they become gentle and serene. The Bay Islands may be adjacent to Central America, but the tranquillity there is so profound that you'll find yourself laughing at the paranoia you entertained before your trip.

Adventurous visitors to the Bay Islands will find unpopulated beaches for tanning and swimming, unspoiled reefs for scuba diving and snorkeling, and prime waters for sailing and deep-sea fishing. You won't see casinos, shopping strips, or high-rise hotels. Instead, you stay in small familylike inns and resorts, often in bungalows built on stilts above the placid azure waters. In short, visitors enjoy exotic locales that resemble the Caribbean of years ago.

Located 300 miles south of Mexico's Yucatán Peninsula, the Bay Islands are composed of three large islands and a scattering of smaller cays. The larger islands appear rugged and mountainous with a profusion of tropical vegetation. Secluded beaches and protected bays punctuate their serrated shores. Some of the smaller cays contain only a few coco palms and clearings big enough for a picnic.

Beneath the waves, these tropical islands display a diversity of life and colors. Staggering walls, deep canyons, and spirelike pinnacles form the backdrop for a myriad of Day-Glo fish that dart among the coral, sea fans, and giant sponges. Many people consider the Bay

Islands to be one of the top ten scuba diving destinations in the world.

For years divers have quietly whispered their Honduran secret to others. Now tourism is beginning to increase, making regular visitors nervous that "their" unspoiled islands will fall victim to hordes of tourists. Fortunately, change comes slowly on the Bay Islands, so new visitors still have a chance to savor this special place. The gradual growth of tourism also allows the islanders to prepare their businesses and personnel for the demands of being a thriving tourist destination. For now, Bay Islands residents remain friendly and welcome visitors to their islands as warmly as you would welcome someone into your living room.

Although Spanish is the official language of Honduras, most Bay Islanders speak English as well. Many trace their ancestry back to the British and Dutch buccaneers who plundered rich Spanish galleons loaded with silver and gold. Today's population also consists of descendants of the Spaniards, escaped black slaves, and Carib Indians, as well as mainland Hondurans and a growing number of North Americans. This heterogeneous mix is pleasantly void of prejudice and excessive differences between opulence and poverty.

Now that you know about the Bay Islands, let's tackle your other fears: the water, the food, and the distance. Not only is the water safe to drink, it tastes like mineral water compared to some tap water in North America. The food on the Bay Islands comes predominantly from the surrounding area. Seafood makes up a significant portion of the weekly menu. Lobster, shrimp, conch, and grouper are all common dishes. The variety of tropical fruits makes the produce section in your local supermarket look dull in comparison.

The Bay Islands are only a three-and-a-half-hour flight from Miami, Houston, and New Orleans. They are served on a regular basis by Tan Sahsa, a Honduran airline. Presently, the flights stop on the Honduran mainland, but soon you may be able to fly nonstop to the islands. With the completion of a control tower and other safety features, Roatan will be able to receive planes directly from the United States, making the only dangerous part of your trip the layover in Miami.

In spite of the natural tropical setting and friendly population, the Bay Islands are not for the ordinary Caribbean vacationer. You've got to have a sense of adventure to enjoy the remote setting. Even Roatan, the largest and most developed of the islands, lacks broad boulevards of hotels, restaurants, and fashionable shops. The roads are only now being paved, and a few dozen stores comprise the "business district." Because there are no phone lines, islanders communicate by CB radio. Guanaja, the second largest island, remains even less developed than Roatan. It has a crushed-coral-and-dirt airstrip, and no roads at all. The other islands are even less de-

veloped and populated. They can be reached only by boat or sea-
plane.

If you're willing to exchange amenities for vistas of stilt houses in
quiet bays, glimpses of wild parrots among the palms, and views of
neon-colored fish in clear, warm waters, you'll love the Bay Islands.

NUTS & BOLTS

CURRENCY: All the resorts and many other Bay Islands businesses
accept U.S. currency in payment. They prefer cash or traveler's
checks. Many places will not accept credit cards. Almost all of the
resort guests pay in U.S. currency.

The official exchange rate is one U.S. dollar for two Honduran
lempíras. At press time, the black market rate was approximately
three lempiras to the dollar, but don't expect to get that rate at the
resorts. Their prices are set in U.S. dollars.

CUSTOMS/DUTY: Entering Honduras, customs tend to be lax. Upon
exiting, airport security checks carefully for dangerous weapons.
Standard U.S. and Canadian customs apply upon returning north.

LANGUAGES: Both English and Spanish are spoken on the Bay
Islands. The resort staffs speak English.

PACKING: When traveling to third-world countries, you are advised
to make your carry-on items count. Bring the essentials you'll need
in case your bags get delayed. Pack your toiletries, bug spray, sunscreen, sunglasses, sensible shoes, bathing suit, mask, and regulator.
If your bags get delayed, you should be able to borrow or make do
without anything else.

TRAVEL TIME BY AIR: The Bay Islands are served by Tan Sahsa, a
Honduran airline. Its planes fly direct from Miami, New Orleans,
and Houston to La Ceiba, on the mainland of Honduras. From La
Ceiba you may continue on, or change planes and take a DC-3. It
takes approximately three and a half hours, including stops, to get to
Roatan, and four hours to get to Guanaja. Be sure to check in with
Tan Sahsa at least two hours before the flight.

VACCINATION REQUIREMENTS: None.

VISA/PASSPORT REQUIREMENTS: All visitors to Honduras need a
valid passport. The Honduran embassies give inconsistent information on customs regulations. We were told that U.S. citizens needed
an advance visa, but upon arrival all that was necessary was a
passport and a tourist information card (obtained on the airplane).
Canadians supposedly need an advance visa as well. Visitors to
Honduras should check with the Honduran embassy for regulations.

ANTHONY'S KEY RESORT

VITAL FEATURES

Type of vacation: **Resort and dive club**
Target market: **Divers and people of all ages who like water sports**
Location: **The Bay Islands, Honduras**
All-inclusive cost per week: **$650**

RATINGS

Value: 💲💲💲💲💲

Fun quotient: ⛱⛱⛱⛱

Honeymoon suitability: ❤❤❤

Singles meeting ground: 🧍

Child appeal: 🍦

Management professionalism: ☎☎☎☎☎

Service: 💡💡💡💡💡

Food: 🦞🦞🦞

THE REAL STORY

You don't just "wake up" at Anthony's Key Resort; you gently glide into consciousness. The macaws begin cawing about 5:00 A.M., just as the sun filters through the wood blinds, filling your bungalow with a warm glow. The early morning breeze blows through the hut and gently nudges you out of bed. Upon opening your eyes, you first see the water sparkling against a very blue sky. You wonder why you ever settled for a cup-of-coffee wake-up.

Most people venture to the Bay Islands for the underwater aesthetics. Anthony's Key Resort is definitely one of the best places in the world to dive. It has immense walls, lavish amounts of coral, honeycombed reefs, and profuse underwater growth.

51

On land, the resort has the same untouched feeling. Mother Nature decorated it with lush vegetation. On the main island, wood bungalows are suspended on stilts over the sea. A small motorboat delivers guests to the key, where more bungalows are scattered among palm trees and dense floral growth. You'll find plenty of privacy here; sitting on your sun deck you feel as though you own the island.

Once at the resort, you slip into "calm mode." Guests move in slow, languid movements, as if they were underwater. The hostess greets you with a tropical rum drink. You can spend the rest of your vacation without worries, drifting from diving, snorkeling, windsurfing, and horseback riding to the dining room, bar, and the beach.

INCLUDED

Accommodations	Sports
Activities	Sports instruction
Diving	Taxes
Entertainment & dancing	Transfer to and from airport
Food	

VALUE

Anthony's Key Resort is a tremendous value for divers, even for couples where only one person dives. Most of the resorts on the Bay Islands concentrate on diving. Other resorts on Roatan may offer you a better price, but fewer water sports.

ACTIVITIES, SPORTS, & EXCURSIONS

If your idea of a good vacation is to have a thousand activities at your fingertips, then you should look elsewhere for a vacation spot. Serious divers stay occupied the entire day and are usually too tired to care about activities in the evening. Nondivers can ride on the dive boats and snorkel. Windsurfers, Sunfish, kayaks, and a pedal boat also keep them amused. The bar attracts more activity than the common room, which has several games and a VCR.

ACTIVITIES: Board games, movies, sunbathing.

SPORTS: Seven experienced dive masters attend to the guests. Anthony's Key Resort is a good place to become certified. The dive masters slowly lead you through a comprehensive set of lessons, allowing even the most nervous students to feel at ease. You may become spoiled if Roatan is your first diving experience. The seven dive boats are maintained carefully and are never crowded.

Horseback riding	Kayaks/canoes
Jogging trail	Pedal boats

Sailing	Swimming
Scuba	Volleyball
Scuba resort course	Windsurfing
Snorkeling	

EXCURSIONS: Once a week the resort staff pack the dive boats with guests, employees, and supplies and head down the beach for an all-day picnic. Nondivers frolic on Tabiyana Beach while divers do the first dive of the day. The long stretch of white beach and palm trees provides an idyllic setting for the picnic. A sunset cruise on the resort's 52-foot sailing vessel ends the glorious day.

ITINERARY & DAILY SCHEDULE

In the morning you have two choices: you can eat a hearty breakfast, get your gear ready for the first dive, and stay active all day, or you can walk out to your sun deck, slip into a hammock, and watch the sun change positions.

Divers do one to three single-tank dives. The boats leave at staggered times to prevent lines. In the evening, many people dive to see the fluorescent fish and the nocturnal feeders. You may also choose to participate in the channel dives, which cost extra.

NIGHTLIFE & ENTERTAINMENT

It's easy to lose track of time at Anthony's Key Resort. Many people get so engrossed in the atmosphere and the sports that they never leave the property. The town doesn't offer much in the way of nightlife, and taxis are difficult to find after dark. Most of the nightlife occurs at the resort's open-air bar. People wander off to their bungalows early in the evening so they can get an early start in the morning. Every few months the resort hosts a party for all the island folk.

AESTHETICS & ENVIRONMENT

Anthony's Key Resort keeps its grounds impeccably groomed and in sync with nature. Groundskeepers sweep the sand, pick up debris, and groom the flowers.

FACILITIES

Bars	Disco
Beaches	Gift shop
Casino	Safety-deposit box
Concierge	

ROOMS

The 50 airy bungalows at Anthony's Key Resort are made of a light wood. Many have decks attached. Some rest on stilts over the sea.

Several of the bungalows are clustered together and share a deck. If you come with a partying group, these will serve you well. All huts have running hot water and ceiling fans.

LUXURY LEVEL: maid service, porter service.

FOOD & DRINK

The food is good and plentiful, but very basic. You'll rave about the tuna you saw swimming in the water more than the one lying on your plate. The hearty breakfast has a buffet table laden with fresh fruit. Lunches often come picnic style. At night you can choose between a fish or meat entrée. A dinner buffet makes a weekly appearance. But you might not notice the food too much as you sit in the open-air restaurant and watch the sun set over the sea.

STAFFING & SERVICE

The staff at Anthony's Key Resort make you feel like a close friend rather than a guest at a hotel. They are interesting and articulate people.

The resort maintains a no-tipping policy. Guests are asked to contribute to the Children's Fund at the end of their stay. This program was developed by the owner to help educate the children on the island.

PRIVACY & RELAXATION

Couples gather on the key at six o'clock every evening. They lean against palm trees and watch the sun sink into a blazing spectrum of pink. Even if you are standing right next to someone, you feel as if you're the only one on the island. You will find this is true of the entire resort. There are never any lines or chaos. You can easily slip into one of the hammocks scattered throughout the grounds.

SHOPPING

Photo Roatan, next to the gift shop, provides daily film-processing instruction. It also rents still and video cameras. Prices for trinkets range from reasonable to very expensive.

HONEYMOONERS

The romantic, secluded setting is perfect for diving honeymooners.

SINGLES

This is not a good place to come to alone, unless all you want to do is dive.

CHILD APPEAL

Children over the age of 12 may become certified and participate in diving. There are not any planned activities for children, although the paddle boat, canoes, and horses should keep them busy during the day.

NUTS & BOLTS

BOOKING INFORMATION

Anthony's Key Resort
1385 Coral Way
Suite 401
Miami, Florida 33145
800-227-3483
305-858-3483

CONTACT INFORMATION

Anthony's Key Resort
Bay Islands
Roatan, Honduras
011-504-45-1003 (Rarely works)
Fax: 011-504-45-1140

DEPOSITS/REFUNDS: A $100 deposit is due 10 days after booking. The balance is due 45 days prior to your vacation. If you cancel less than 45 days after booking, you will be charged $25. After 45 days, the deposit will be kept by the resort, although it may be applied to another vacation date within six months of the cancellation.

You are charged a 50 percent penalty if you cancel less than 30 days before departure date. If you tell them more than 30 days in advance, you will be charged a $100 penalty.

ELECTRICITY: 110 volts 60 cycles, same as in the United States.

HANDICAP ACCESSIBILITY: None.

PACKING: If you own diving and snorkeling equipment, bring it. The resort keeps its equipment maintained, although a well-fitting mask may be hard to find.

You will need to wear only what feels comfortable. There is no need to pack eveningwear.

RELIGIOUS SERVICES: There are no services offered on the property.

RESERVATION SCHEDULE: You should book six months in advance for the winter season and up to a year in advance during holidays.

NUMBER OF CABINS: 50.

NUMBER OF EMPLOYEES: 78.

FUTURE PLANS: Anthony's Key Resort may expand and build another resort at Tabiyana Beach. The extension would concentrate on water sports such as windsurfing, sailing, parasailing, and jet skiing.

A building next to the resort will soon house a school of dolphins. Guests will be able to observe and swim with the dolphins.

ARRIVAL AIRPORT: Roatan International Airport.

Cost Worksheet		
	High Season[1]	*Off-Season*[2]
Accommodations		
(7 days)	$650	$550
Food	incl.	incl.
Drinks		
Departure tax	12	12
Sports	incl.	incl.
Airfare		
Extra[3]	_____	_____

[1] High season dates: December to mid-April
[2] Off-season dates: Mid-April to December
[3] Offered for extra charge: scuba certification—resort course, $75; PADI, $300.

BAYMAN BAY CLUB

VITAL FEATURES

Type of vacation: **Scuba diving resort**
Target market: **Scuba divers, singles, couples, groups**
Location: **Guanaja, Bay Islands, Honduras**
All-inclusive cost per week: **$650 (divers) or $550 (nondivers) plus airfare**

RATINGS

Value: 💲💲💲💲💲

Fun quotient: 🏖️🏖️🏖️🏖️

Honeymoon suitability: ♥♥♥

Singles meeting ground: 👫

Child appeal: 🍦🍦

Management professionalism: ☎☎☎☎☎

Service: 💡💡💡💡

Food: 🦞🦞🦞🦞

THE REAL STORY

You know you're headed for a week of adventure when the DC-3 lands on a dirt runway between two tropical hillsides. A smiling group of islanders greets you beside a simple one-room building that serves as the control tower, terminal, and baggage claim area. Someone says, "Bienvenidos a Guanaja." Welcome to Guanaja.

Bayman Bay guests board a small boat that serves as taxi on this island without roads. The ten-minute ride begins as the driver negotiates a mangrove-and-palm-tree-lined canal. The boat's wake disappears in the mass of roots along the channel's edge. Soon the canal empties into a bay, and the boat skims across placid, blue seas.

Rounding a rocky promontory, you see a steep hillside covered

57

with dense jungle growth. At its base rests a sandy beach and a dock. As the boat draws closer, you spot a small bungalow hidden in the trees. Soon you notice another and another. When you reach the dock, you see a three-story building that looks like a fantasy treehouse. You have arrived at the Bayman Bay Club.

The claim tickets on your bags say "Guanaja—The World's Best Scuba Diving." Many experienced divers would agree with that claim. The marine life beneath the waves parallels the profusion of tropical life on the island. Countless neon fish and virtually every type of Caribbean coral abound off the island's shore. Giant canyons, sheer cliffs, dark caves, and narrow crevices await exploration.

Scuba divers discovered Bayman Bay soon after it opened in the mid-1970s. The word has spread since then, but veteran visitors are selective about whom they tell. After all, if too many people hear the secret, such a great deal might be harder to come by. Bayman Bay offers week-long, all-inclusive diving packages that include accommodations, food, two boat dives a day, and unlimited air for shore diving. Special nondiver rates include a scuba resort course.

Bayman Bay calls itself "a civilized resort in a tropical jungle." The bare wood, exposed beams, and open-air construction of the buildings create a rustic atmosphere that fits perfectly with the lush surrounding foliage. Parrots fly overhead; iguanas sun themselves on the rocks; spotted eagle rays patrol the beach and dock after dark.

The pace and mood at Bayman Bay are relaxed and casual. Guests come to escape their busy lives. T-shirts and shorts dominate the scene. Meals are served buffet style and are eaten at large dining room tables, where the talk naturally turns to diving stories. After a week-long trip to Bayman Bay, you should go home with lots of great stories of your own.

INCLUDED

Accommodations
Activities
Dancing
Food

Scuba resort course for
    nondivers
Sports
Transfer to and from airport
Welcome cocktail

VALUE

Bayman Bay offers exceptional value. The tropical setting and palm-studded beach alone merit a trip. The value gets even better when you dive beneath the surface. If you are prepared for the rustic setting, you're virtually guaranteed to have a good time.

ACTIVITIES, SPORTS, & EXCURSIONS

ACTIVITIES: Diving is the only organized activity at Bayman Bay. Other activities depend upon your motivation. Many guests simply relax between dives. They lie in the sun, or read a book while swinging in a hammock. The upper floor of the clubhouse has a well-stocked library, a pool table, and board games to pass the time.

SPORTS: Bayman Bay offers a wide variety of diving experiences. Every dive offers something special. The steep hillsides of Guanaja continue beneath the sea and create a wonderland of coral fingers, caves, and mazelike canyons. Sheer cliffs plunge 100 feet or more, inviting divers to swim deeper and deeper as they discover giant sponges and interesting coral formations. In some places, the canyon walls are so close together that the coral has grown over the top, creating tunnels and caves. At times, visibility extends to 200 feet, making the waters off Guanaja some of the clearest in the Caribbean.

With more than 20 dive sites within 20 minutes of the Bayman dock, you'll spend little time on the boat and much time in the water. The resort schedules two boat dives each day. No other resorts regularly dive the reefs, so the dive sites remain uncrowded and unspoiled. Free air and unlimited beach dives guarantee that even the most avid divers will get their fill of diving each day. Weights and weight belts come free with your stay.

The dive masters at Bayman Bay are just that, masters. Both are native to Guanaja and each knows the island's surrounding reefs like you know your backyard. Prior to each dive, they orient you on the layout of the reef, mention things to look for, and describe what to avoid. They also recommend a dive plan. Dive buddies can follow the plan or agree on their own. The dive masters take the time to familiarize new arrivals with their equipment and surroundings to ensure that everyone remembers their diving skills and safe diving practices. The dive masters are present and available when you want them, but they don't intrude.

Nondivers receive a free scuba resort course that gets them in the water and introduces them to the equipment. For an additional charge of $265, Bayman Bay will arrange for an intensive, four-day NAUI Openwater I certification course. The dive instructor gives no breaks, but she patiently works with students until they have mastered their scuba skills. Her students graduate as safe and knowledgeable divers.

Besides scuba diving, Bayman Bay's water sports include snorkeling, swimming, and fishing. Land-based activities depend upon your energy level. You can hike or jog on the trails above the resort, or play volleyball and soccer on the beach. Bayman Bay's resident nurse leads aerobics/aquacise classes on the beach once a day.

Aerobics/aquacise class	Scuba resort course
Dories	Snorkeling
Fishing	Soccer
Jogging trail	Swimming
Scuba	Volleyball

Excursions: Bayman Bay plans several free excursions. On Saturday night one of the dive boats takes guests to the local disco in Bonnaca, Guanaja's major settlement. The boat leaves for town about 9:00 P.M. and returns around midnight. During that time, Bayman guests have a chance to drink, dance, and mix with some of the locals. It's a worthwhile trip, but the morning gong sounds rather early the next day. On Wednesdays guests enjoy a sunset cruise that stops at a nearby bar for drinks and dancing to jukebox music. The trip starts around 5:00 P.M. and returns at 8:00 P.M., in time for dinner.

The hiking at Bayman Bay begins with a steep trail that winds its way up through banana and pineapple groves. The vista from the ridge rewards early morning hikers with views of parrots flying above mist-cloaked valleys. The same spot at dusk shows off tropical sunsets over distant islands. Several trails lead inland and down to the beaches. One path wanders through a large banana plantation and down to Columbus Beach, where the explorer supposedly came ashore for water and supplies. Another trail leads to Michael's Rock and a secluded white sand beach perfect for swimming and nude sunbathing.

Beyond Michael's Rock is a trail to a 30-foot-high waterfall. The hike is moderate to strenuous, but a boat ride from the resort to the trailhead saves several miles of walking. The path goes through dense tropical foliage as it parallels and crosses a clear-running stream. At times the going is so rough you need to climb with your hands to safely traverse slick rocks. The journey rewards hikers with a chilling shower beneath the falls. The waterfall hike makes a nice variation in the daily dive schedule.

For extra cost, the dive masters will take a small group of divers to nearby Barbarette Island for diving on pristine reefs. Because no dive resorts visit Barbarette on a regular basis, most reefs remain unexplored and unnamed. The reefs radiate a healthy glow. No finger marks or broken coralheads detract from the scenery. Colors appear more vibrant and intense. Tropical fish travel in bountiful schools and swim up to divers instead of going the other way. The trip begins at 7:30 A.M. and lasts all day. The boat charter costs $200 and can be split by up to six people. The price includes three tanks, lunch, snacks, and beer and soda for the duration of the trip. The boat ride takes approximately an hour and a half each way. Considered among the most spectacular diving excursions in the Bay Islands, the trip is well worth the $40 or $50 per person.

Would-be archaeologists can take a guided tour to a nearby site where they can dig for 400-year-old Indian artifacts called *yabadingdings*. These figurines and pottery shards date to the pre-Columbian inhabitants of the Bay Islands. Bayman Bay has some on display if you'd like to see them. The trip costs $25 and lasts a half day. The money could be a good investment, since buried pirate treasure was recently discovered near the site.

ITINERARY & DAILY SCHEDULE

A gong announces meal time, and a bell tells you that the dive boat leaves in 15 minutes. Most people make two dives a day and relax the rest of the time. Almost everyone wakes up with the sun and goes to bed by 10:00 P.M.

On Saturday night, guests go to town for an evening at the local disco. Tuesday night is the night dive. The sunset cruise sails on Wednesday. The waterfall hike usually happens on Thursday afternoon. All these outings depend on the weather, and may be rescheduled if necessary.

NIGHTLIFE & ENTERTAINMENT

Bayman Bay does not have a swinging nightlife. After two dives and a day in the sun, most folks feel rather low on energy. Guests sit at the dinner tables and talk until nine or ten. The bar serves drinks, but people seem to drink more coffee than alcohol. Guests can bring tapes to play on the clubhouse stereo or make selections from the house tapes. Upstairs you can shoot pool or play board games. The dock is a great place to look at the stars. If you want to party, that's OK too.

AESTHETICS & ENVIRONMENT

The Bayman Bay Club resembles Hollywood's Swiss Family Robinson's treehouse. A three-story wooden structure, it clings to a steep tropical hillside. Banana and other trees shade the 68-step climb from the dock. The resort has no glass windows. Instead, the main structure stands open to the tropical breeze. Wooden shutters cover the windows during bad weather.

Bayman Bay is not for people who feel squeamish at the sight of lizards or insects. With the open-air dining rooms, you may really end up with a fly in your soup. Sand fleas inhabit the dock and beach. Although these little pests normally live off the crabs and other native wildlife, they view humans as a special delicacy. While we were there, some people complained of being eaten alive, others were hardly touched. To avoid the fleas altogether, be sure to bring bug spray.

The air and water temperatures hover around 80 degrees. A laid-back Caribbean feeling pervades the resort, and the limited number of guests guarantees that you will have a quiet and uncrowded stay.

The entire resort appears well maintained and constantly cleaned. Construction projects update existing facilities and add new ones.

FACILITIES

Bar   Medical station
Beaches   Safe
Gift shop

ROOMS

Bayman Bay features 13 bungalows and 3 suites. All the rooms are spaced about the hillside and hidden by the dense tropical foliage. Each cottage stands separate from the others, giving guests privacy and space. All the bungalows feature hot and cold water, flush toilets, and fans to circulate the air. Some rooms have hammocks, as well as queen-size or king-size beds. Like the clubhouse, they are decorated in natural wood. The bungalows don't offer anything fancy, but they have a decidedly rustic charm. Unlike the open-air clubhouse, all the rooms have louvered windows with fine mesh screens to keep out the bugs. Each bungalow has a private balcony. Most view the ocean.

LUXURY LEVEL: Ceiling fans, laundry service (extra), maid service, porter service.

FOOD & DRINK

Bayman Bay serves meals buffet style and they are eaten family style at large dining room tables. The menus feature fresh foods from the local area and goods brought from the mainland. The resort raises its own pigs and grows numerous types of fruits and vegetables, including pineapples, mangos, yaca, bananas, plantains, breadfruit, papaya, bell peppers, hot peppers, and patastia squash.

The dinner entrees almost always incorporate fresh seafood. In one week you may sample lobster, shrimp, conch, grouper, and more. The seafoods come with rice or noodles, fresh steamed vegetables, soup, and salad. On other nights you may get chicken or spaghetti. Nightly desserts range from fresh key lime pie to breadfruit pudding. Breakfast usually consists of eggs, refried beans, spiced and diced meats, toast, and orange juice and great Honduran coffee. To add variety, the kitchen serves French toast or pancakes once or twice a week. Lunch can be anything from hamburgers and chicken to a salad or burritos made with fresh tortillas. Watch out for the salsa satanica. A few drops go a long way.

Dietary restrictions can usually be accommodated, but don't wait until the food is on the table to speak up. Mention your special needs at the beginning of your stay—or, better yet, in the questionnaire that you receive when you book your stay. The more advance notice you give, the better your chances are.

The Bayman Bay bar is well stocked with brand and off-brand liquors, Coca-Cola, and two types of Honduran beer. Both beers taste great. Bar prices range from $1 for a Coke and $1.50 for a beer to several dollars for blender and brand-name drinks. All drinks are added to your final bill.

 Jason's Tips:

Bayman Bay management allows you to bring your own liquor, but it asks that you don't drink it in the common areas. It's OK to bring your own wine to dinner.

STAFFING & SERVICE

The staff at Bayman Bay are helpful and extremely friendly. The entire resort runs smoothly and efficiently. The managers learn guests' names in no time. The dive masters plan and execute safe and interesting dives. They share their knowledge of the reefs and the aquatic life, and tell you about local island lore. You'll easily make friends with the entire staff.

PRIVACY & RELAXATION

Privacy and relaxation come easily at Bayman Bay. The bungalows offer a pleasant retreat, but there are so many other great places to relax you probably won't want to spend many daylight hours in them. Most of the day you can have the whole beach to yourself. A sun deck above the dive shed and the end of the dock offer other hideaways. A hammock on the top floor of the clubhouse provides the ultimate hangout. From there you can view the ocean below and listen to the calm breeze rustle the leaves. The casual atmosphere and slow island pace are almost sure to send you home 100 percent more relaxed than when you arrived.

SHOPPING

Bayman Bay features a small gift shop with T-shirts, earrings, and other small mementos to remind you of your trip. It also features a small selection of Guatemalan and other handmade goods. Prices are on the high side of reasonable, but you can just sign for your purchases and pay when you settle your bill at the end of your stay.

Bannaca, Guanaja's main town, is more of a fishing village than a tourist center. The shops import most of their goods from the Honduran mainland or the United States, and they charge premium prices. Don't expect many bargains on handmade goods either. The best deal on Guanaja is vanilla, which sells for $3 a pint.

HONEYMOONERS

If you and your spouse are avid divers and adventurous souls, Bayman Bay Club would make a terrific honeymoon spot. You won't get breakfast in bed, but the resort creates such a rustic, romantic atmosphere you probably won't care. Lovers can walk on the beach as the sun sets. You may fall asleep to the sound of a light rain dripping off the tropical leaves and running down the roof of your bungalow. You will wake up to the cries of wild parrots and the crash of ocean waves.

You can get married at the resort too. Civil services are available, or you can pay to have a minister flown out from the mainland. Since both options are expensive, you'll probably be better off getting married at home and going there for the honeymoon.

SINGLES

The singles-meeting opportunities vary with the week. Your best chances are when a large dive club comes to visit. At other times most guests come as couples. Local singles hang out in town, but the fare for the water taxi is expensive. Your best bet is to bring your significant other, or pray to meet a mermaid (mer-man?).

CHILD APPEAL

Bayman Bay places no age restrictions on children, but it discourages kids under the age of 12. The steep hillsides, rocky areas, and high decks create potentially dangerous places for youngsters. Fifteen-year-olds are usually the youngest ones allowed to go diving.

NUTS & BOLTS

BOOKING INFORMATION: Most guests book directly through Bayman Bay's stateside office. Travel agencies and scuba dive tour companies can also handle reservations. Bayman Bay recommends that you consult with them to get the inside scoop on Tan Sahsa's best flights and itineraries.

CONTACT INFORMATION

Bayman Bay Club, U.S. Office
801 S.E. 16th Court, #2
Fort Lauderdale, FL 33316
800-524-1823
305-525-8413

DEPOSITS/REFUNDS: Confirmed reservations require a $100 deposit, with the balance due 45 days before arrival. If cancellations are made between 45 and 31 days prior to arrival, the balance will be refunded and the deposit will be held in escrow for one year to be applied toward a re-booking. If cancellations are made between 30 and 15 days before travel, only half the deposit will be returned, and the rest is held in escrow. At 14 days before arrival the entire amount is held and applied toward re-booking.

ELECTRICITY: 110 volts 60 cycles, same as in the United States, 24 hours a day.

HANDICAP ACCESSIBILITY: None.

PACKING: Bring your C-card, dive log, and dive gear, if you have it. You can also rent equipment at Bayman Bay. Casual dress consists of T-shirts, shorts, sandals, and similar attire. A sweatshirt or light jacket will keep you warm if temperatures dip down. Supplies are limited in the Bay Islands, so bring any specialty items you may need or want, including herbal tea, diet sodas, munchies, sunscreen, and bug spray to ward off the sand fleas. To fight the insects, people at Bayman Bay recommend a diluted mix of Avon Skin-So-Soft and bug spray. Ask the stateside office for details.

RELIGIOUS SERVICES: The resort holds no religious services, but the town has Baptist, Seventh-Day Adventist, and Church of God services. Many are in English. You'll have to be fairly devout though, because the water taxi costs $40 per boat round-trip.

RESERVATION SCHEDULE: Bayman Bay vacations begin to fill up a year in advance. February, March, and April are the busiest times of the year, and October and November are the slowest. Guaranteed airline reservations should be made at least two months in advance.

SIZE: 30 acres.

NUMBER OF ROOMS: 13 bungalows, 3 suites.

NUMBER OF EMPLOYEES: 25.

TRAVEL TIME FROM AIRPORT: Guests are met at the airport by a Bayman Bay employee and taken to the resort by water taxi. The ride takes eight to ten minutes.

Sometimes Bayman Bay Club offers discounts from September 30 to early December, when Honduras has its rainy and hurricane season. This can be a good deal if the weather stays nice. The lower rates reflect the fact that there are no guarantees and no refunds if the seas become too rough for diving.

SPENDING MONEY: If you have your own dive gear, you can get by with just enough money for tips and the entrance and departure taxes. You'll probably want to bring some extra cash for drinks and excursions. Around $200 per person should cover everything.

Bayman Bay accepts credit card payments at the stateside office but not in Honduras. On Guanaja, cash or traveler's checks are preferred. Almost all of Bayman Bay's guests pay in U.S. currency.

Cost Worksheet

	High Season[1]	Off-Season[2]
Accommodations (7 days)[3]	$650	$600
	(Nondiver, $550 year-round)	
Food	incl.	incl.
Drinks		
Entrance tax	2	2
Departure tax	10.50	10.50
Hotel tax	incl.	incl.
Sports	incl.	incl.
Airfare	_____	_____
Sight-seeing		
Tips[4]		
Additional sports[5]		
Souvenirs	_____	_____

[1] High season dates: December 15 to April 14
[2] Off-season dates: April 15 to December 14
[3] Premium for single person: Single rooms cost $10 extra per day and are available only as space permits. If you are willing to share a room, you can pay the PPDO rate. Group rates: If five divers pay the full rate, the sixth gets a 50 percent discount. With nine divers, the tenth diver stays free.
[4] $20–$40 per person for the house, plus comparable tips for the dive masters
[5] Offered for extra charge: Dive equipment is available for rent at the following daily rates: buoyancy compensator—$10; regulator—$10; mask, fins, and snorkel—$5 for the set; dive skins—$7; dive light—$4. A complete rental for one week receives a 10 percent discount. Tanks and weight belts are free. See "Excursions" section for prices on optional trips. Essential extras: All visitors to Honduras must pay a $2 (U.S. currency) entrance tax. Upon leaving they will have to pay a 50-cent departure tax on Guanaja and a $10 departure tax (both in U.S. dollars) when leaving the country.

COCO VIEW RESORT

VITAL FEATURES

Type of vacation: **Scuba diving resort**
Target market: **Scuba divers, singles, couples, groups**
Location: **Roatan, Bay Islands, Honduras**
All-inclusive cost per week: **$600 plus airfare**

RATINGS

Value: 💲💲💲💲

Fun quotient: 🏝️🏝️🏝️🏝️

Honeymoon suitability: ❤️❤️❤️

Singles meeting ground: 🚹🚺🚹

Child appeal: Not applicable

Management professionalism: ☎️☎️☎️

Service: 💡💡💡

Food: 🦞🦞🦞

THE REAL STORY

A little is good. More is better. And too much still isn't enough. This statement describes the scuba diving at Coco View. Divers come to Coco View for some of the best wall diving in the Caribbean. Just 100 yards off the beach, a set of 110-foot walls plunges into the sapphire-blue depths. The wreck of the *Prince Albert*, a 140-foot tanker, adds wreck diving to the already diverse scuba opportunities.

Located on a secluded bay on the south side of Roatan, Coco View offers week-long scuba diving packages that include accommodations, food, two boat dives per day, unlimited air for shore diving, and more. In short, it provides all the ingredients necessary for a dive fanatic's ideal vacation.

The atmosphere at the resort is relaxed and casual. Guests wear T-shirts and shorts most of the time. They eat buffet-style meals and mingle in the main room or on the beach between dives. On any given week you may meet a doctor from Alaska, a fashion photographer from Chicago, and a farmer from Kansas. Ages range from late teens to late sixties. Friendships form quickly at Coco View, and by the end of your stay you could have pen pals from around the country.

Coco View adds another twist to the scuba business by chartering a 43-foot dive boat. The vessel carries up to six passengers, plus a crew of two. The boat comes with a full provisioning plan and an air compressor. The captain and cook will take you wherever you wish to go, including to premier dive sites off Barbarette Island, Guanaja, and Cayos Cochinos. The number of dives is limited only by your endurance and decompression limits. You can charter the boat for seven days, or split your time between surf and turf with three nights on the boat and four nights at the resort.

INCLUDED

Accommodations	Taxes
Activities	Transfer to and from the
Entertainment & dancing	airport
Food	Welcome cocktail
Sports	

VALUE

Coco View provides solid value for dive fanatics. This is the place if you want to dive to the point of exhaustion. Tanks and dive buddies are always ready for another trip into the water. For nondivers, the resort offers a nice place to relax but few activities.

ACTIVITIES, SPORTS, & EXCURSIONS

ACTIVITIES: Coco View concentrates on what it does best—diving. It offers no organized activities other than the two boat dives a day. Board games, dive videos, and bar drinks fill the time between dives.

Board games	Entertainment/shows
Dancing	Sunbathing

SPORTS: Coco View sits virtually on top of more than a dozen premier dive sites including reverse ledges, volcanic cracks, and mammoth walls.

Every morning, one of the dive masters gives a briefing that describes the reefs and he recommends a dive plan. You keep track of your own dive tables and decide on appropriate depths and bottom times. The dive masters don't hold your hand—unless you ask them to.

Both the morning and afternoon dive boats go out for one-tank dives. You may request that an extra tank be loaded on the boat so you can do a drop-off dive on the way back. Just tell the dive master where you want off, and then swim back to the beach.

Other water sports include snorkeling, swimming, and windsurfing. Motivated guests can organize a game of volleyball.

Jogging	Swimming
Scuba	Volleyball
Snorkeling	Windsurfing

EXCURSIONS: Once a week Coco View arranges for island tours of Roatan. Half-day trips head west to Coxen Hole, Roatan's major town. This trip costs approximately $10 for transportation and lunch. Guests can also tour the entire island including the east end. This full-day trip costs $25 to $30 and includes land transportation, a water taxi tour of the mangrove canals, lunch, drinks, and tours. Island tours by seaplane are also available.

Coco View arranges one-day to four-day escorted tours on the Honduran mainland. Leaving from San Pedro Sula, guests travel to Copan, one of the most impressive Mayan ruins in Central America. Stone monuments rise up from the jungle-covered mountains. Visitors leave in awe of the great mathematical, scientific, and cultural attainments of the buildings' pre-Columbian architects.

ITINERARY & DAILY SCHEDULE

Most guests arrive on Saturday evenings. On Sunday mornings, the resort holds an orientation session to answer frequently asked questions. On Wednesdays, guests have the opportunity to take tours of Roatan. Steak and lobster grill on Thursdays. Carib dancers often entertain after dinner.

NIGHTLIFE & ENTERTAINMENT

The nightlife at Coco View centers on diving. You can make night dives from shore every night. If you don't want to go back into the water, you can also watch dive videos or brush up on your species identification by looking at books of underwater photographs.

If you need a break from the dive scene, there is always someone around the bar to get to know. The guests and staff at Coco View are friendly and easy to talk to. The casual atmosphere invites you to kick off your shoes and relax. Music plays on the bar stereo, and the drinks flow until the last barfly retires for the night. Most guests go to bed by 10:00 P.M.

AESTHETICS & ENVIRONMENT

Coco View occupies the tip of a small peninsula. Although attached to the island, the resort has no road access, so guests arrive by taking a brief boat ride across a small bay. The first view of the property reveals red-roofed buildings, a white sand beach, and pale blue Caribbean waters.

Waking up at Coco View is an expereince in tranquillity. The sun comes up over the island, and a gentle breeze blows across the water. The ocean is only five steps from your door. Between dives you have time to relax on a sun deck or on the beach, if you're willing to brave the sand fleas. If you come armed with bug repellent these pests should not present a problem.

More visitors come to Roatan each year as jet access improves and roads get better. These conveniences make travel easier, but they come at a price. A tourist orientation now begins to replace the remote island feeling. Although Coco View's own construction projects are doing much to improve the surroundings, another resort under construction nearby does the opposite. Across the bay, a new resort takes away the remote secluded feeling that makes Coco View so special. Don't despair, though. The local cattle, fishing boats, and plantations still outnumber the resorts on Roatan. The waters are still warm, clear, and unpolluted. The diving remains among the best in the Caribbean, and Coco View continues to offer excellent scuba diving vacations in a beautiful tropical setting.

FACILITIES: Bar, beach, gift shop, lock boxes in rooms.

ROOMS

Rooms at Coco View vary from spacious and romantic bungalows on the water to cramped rooms where the bathroom is so small that the sink sits in the bedroom. Coco View recently constructed four bungalows with natural wood interiors, large beds, and private decks that overlook the quiet bay. The other rooms are grouped together in two two-story buildings. Most of these rooms come with a pair of double beds, or a queen and a twin. Hand-painted murals decorate the walls. A chair or two augments the simple closets and dressers. Most bathrooms appear fairly large and feature hot and cold running water. Several upstairs rooms were recently remodeled. These newer rooms have walk-in closets and balconies that look out over the beach and ocean. Coco View plans to remodel the older rooms and add new bungalows in the near future.

Guests can also rent brand-new beach houses equipped with bedrooms, bathrooms, full kitchens, and living rooms. Renters can purchase maid service and full or partial provisioning, unlimited air and weights, and a private dive boat with skipper.

LUXURY LEVEL: Ceiling fans, maid service.

FOOD & DRINK

When diving on a regular basis, many people find that their appetite doubles. Coco View understands this and provides hearty food in substantial quantities. Although the cuisine is not gourmet, the meals taste like quality home cooking. Seconds and thirds are readily available. All meals are served buffet style. In a week, dinners feature fish, chicken, and pork for one night each, shrimp twice, and steak and lobster once each. The evening meal comes with rice, noodles, or potatoes; salad; cooked vegetables; and dessert. Lunch always includes a homemade soup, fresh fruit, and salads. Breakfast ranges from eggs to pancakes and crêpes. Meat, potatoes, rolls, and fruit complete the meal. The kitchen can accommodate vegetarian diets, but not salt-free requests.

Iced tea is available free throughout the day. Coffee appears each morning and evening. The bar serves sodas, beers, and mixed drinks at average U.S. prices. All drinks can be placed on a tab and paid for at the end of your stay.

STAFFING & SERVICE

The staff at Coco View works quickly and quietly. They leave behind clean rooms and tasty meals. The owners live in residence and take an active role in running the resort. You'll probably eat with them over the course of your stay. The dive masters are top-notch. They know the reefs well and constantly choose interesting dive sites.

PRIVACY & RELAXATION

The resort harbors several quiet places to chill out. A gazebo at the end of the jetty offers benches and a hammock. A nearby swim platform invites sunbathers. The beach, sun deck, and dining room remain calm and quiet while the dive boats are away. Walls tend to be thin in the older buildings, and sounds carry amazingly well through the walls.

SHOPPING

Coco View's gift shop stocks T-shirts, hats, earrings, postcards, and other souvenirs. Vanilla and Honduran coffee are the only real bargains to be found in Coxen Hole, the main town on Roatan.

HONEYMOONERS

Coco View could be a nice honeymoon location if you are more interested in scuba diving than in spending amorous hours alone together. The cabins on the water are very romantic, but you must reserve them at least a year in advance. Usually they go to return guests. No special honeymoon packages are available.

SINGLES

A fair number of singles come to Coco View, and vacation romances do occur. The guest list remains small and intimate. This gives you a chance to know people, but it also cuts down on the number of potential candidates. Singles will do best when a dive group comes to visit.

CHILD APPEAL

No children under ten are allowed at Coco View, except during the annual family week, the last week in July. During this week, two counselors take care of kids who are old enough to participate in games and activities. Baby-sitters watch the younger children. During the rest of the year, kids aged ten and up can play on the beach and with the dogs. Board games entertain them when they want to stay inside. Most kids come to dive with their parents. Sometimes they can take an introductory diving course.

NUTS & BOLTS

BOOKING INFORMATION: All bookings, whether by travel agents, dive groups, or individuals, must go through Coco View's U.S. office.

CONTACT INFORMATION

Coco View Resort, U.S. Office
P.O. Box 877
San Antonio, FL 33576
800-282-8932
904-588-4131

DEPOSITS/REFUNDS: To confirm your reservation, you must send a deposit of $50 per person or $500 per group within 10 days of booking. The balance is due 30 days before arrival. Deposits will not be refunded less than 60 days before the start of your trip. Cancellations made less than 30 days prior to arrival will not be refunded. Instead, the amount, minus a $25 cancellation fee, will be held for a future trip to be made within one year.

ELECTRICITY: 110 volts 60 cycles, same as in the United States. Management discourages the use of hair dryers because they drain the electrical system.

HANDICAP ACCESSIBILITY: Accessibility is limited. Sandy areas make wheelchair navigation difficult. The resort has no hills and few steps, so semimobile people might be able to get around.

PACKING: Be sure to bring your C-card, dive log, and dive gear. Dress is very casual. A light jacket and long pants may come in

Cost Worksheet

	High Season[1]	Off-Season[2]
Accommodations		
(7 days)[3]	$600	$500
	(Nondiver rates $100 less)	
Food	incl.	incl.
Drinks		
Entrance tax	2	2
Departure tax	10	10
Hotel tax	incl.	incl.
Sports	incl.	incl.
Airfare		
Sight-seeing	$10–$30	$10–$30
Tips	$15–$20 per person	
Additional sports[4]		
Souvenirs		

[1] High season dates: December 15 to April 14

[2] Off-season dates: April 15 to December 14

[3] Premium for single person: Single rooms depend on the space available. Rates don't change for singles or doubles. Over-the-water bungalows cost an additional $40 per week. Second week rates drop to nondiver prices. Group rates: For every 11 paying guests, one diver comes free.

[4] Offered for extra charge: For $290 you can take an Openwater I scuba certification course with an American-trained Scuba Schools International instructor. The course takes several days of intensive training.

Dive equipment is available at the following daily rates: buoyancy compensator—$8.50; regulator—$12.50; buoyancy compensator and regulator—$15; individual gauges—$6 each; mask and snorkel—$3; fins—$3; dive light—$5; edge—$15. Weekly rental rates get you a 30 percent discount. Weights and tanks are free. No wet suits or dive skins are available for rent.

The live-aboard dive boat costs $3,350 in the high season and $3,300 in the off-season. The charter lasts six nights and accommodates up to six people. The Surf-n-Turf (land-and-boat accommodations) program costs $650 per person during high season and $625 per person during the off-season.

Beach house rentals are available by the week and by the month. Weekly rental rates for up to four people are as follows: 2 bedroom/1 bath—$800; 2 bedroom/2 bath—$850; 3 bedroom/3 bath—$950. Provision prices vary depending on the supplies you order. A dive boat and skipper cost $360 per week. Weights and unlimited tanks run $12 a day per guest. Round-trip airport transfers cost $40 per car.

handy. Sunglasses, sunscreen, and bug spray are essentials. Also bring your own snacks and toiletries, since none are available at the resort.

RELIGIOUS SERVICES: The resort holds no religious services. A $35 round-trip taxi ride to town can take you to Catholic, Methodist, Baptist, and Seventh-Day Adventist churches. Roatan has no synagogues.

RESERVATION SCHEDULE: Most guests book a year in advance. Specific rooms go on a first-come first-served basis. September to late November is the slowest time of year; January through April is the busiest.

SIZE: 6 acres.

NUMBER OF ROOMS: 20.

MAXIMUM NUMBER OF GUESTS: 38.

NUMBER OF EMPLOYEES: 20.

TRAVEL TIME FROM AIRPORT: Guests are met at the airport. The complimentary taxi ride takes 20 minutes.

SPENDING MONEY: Your stay is prepaid in the United States, so you'll only need money for drinks, tips, tours, and souvenirs. Around $200 per person will suffice. Bring cash or traveler's checks with you, because Coco View only accepts the credit cards of desperate guests.

All rates per person, based on double occupancy for a seven-night stay.

Always ask if any special packages, promotions, or airfare discounts are in effect before booking.

All vacations described in this guide can be booked through any competent travel agent; we advise you to do so.

See the general introduction and area introductions for more details.

Jamaica

INTRODUCTION

Jamaica's beauty is found in the lush interior farmlands, in the influential culture and music, in the beautiful resorts, in spicy native food, and in the soul of its people.

Jamaica derives its name from the old Indian word *Xaymaca* meaning "land of wood and water." Situated 600 miles southeast of Miami, the 4,244-square-mile island is the third largest in the Caribbean. Its fame and popularity stem from its blue-green mountains, lush forests, beautiful beaches, and consistently warm weather.

The island was first inhabited by Arawak Indians. Christopher Columbus landed on the island during his second voyage in 1494. The British found the island to their liking, and conquered it in 1655. They didn't leave until August 6, 1962, when they granted Jamaican independence within the Commonwealth.

ALL-INCLUSIVE RESORTS

Jamaican resorts occupy more pages of this book than those of any other destination. As they have nowhere else, all-inclusives have proliferated here—and for good reasons. The natural and cultural beauty of the island makes it a natural tourist destination. The resorts allow visitors to relax in a secure and scenic compound. The staffs organize a plethora of activities and serve mountains of food. Visits to the outside culture can be arranged at the frequency and timing desired.

THE PEOPLE

"Psst. I'm Jamaica. Touch me."

The island calls out to tourists in the same way that the street vendors extend their hands to visitors. Jamaicans reach out for sensory contact, literally. In this way, astute vendors get your attention and make you deal with them as individuals. Touching the people also makes the Jamaica experience real and personal.

The Jamaican national motto, "From many, one," describes the

75

wish, and in many ways the reality, of Jamaican society. The people are remarkably free from racial prejudice. In fact, most people tend to have a mixed background: black, white, and Asian. Jamaicans have a reputation for being proud, an attitude that is sometimes seen as arrogance. This independence enabled them to create a strong culture of reggae music, art, and national pride. Combined with intense poverty, it has also turned off some people to Jamaica because visitors sometimes feel hassled.

Jamaicans have also earned the reputation of being surly. Its blacks are heir to a legacy of escaped slaves who fought colonialism from the mountains. They passed their pride to their descendants. In the past, many Jamaicans regarded service jobs as being tantamount to slavery. They performed such jobs unwillingly. This attitude has now changed drastically. Jamaicans have retained their national pride, but they view tourism differently. The government has made efforts to get people to greet visitors. Billboards proclaim the benefits of tourism, and this education starts in the primary schools.

In most all-inclusives, you don't need to use cash. We recommend that you deposit all valuables and currency in the hotel safes. Only bring the jewelry that you will wear at all times, or better yet, none at all. The people are generally honest, but they're poor; you don't want to wave a steak under the nose of someone whose family may be hungry.

Should visitors feel guilty about living in luxury while many locals live in poverty? No! It is the height of chauvinism to compare life in the Northern Hemisphere with that of a third-world country. The economic system, climate, and culture differ greatly. If some of the abject conditions bother you (and they should), remember that you are contributing to the economy by coming to Jamaica. With the decline of bauxite, tourism is the most important industry on the island. You can further help by spending money in the straw market. Buying drugs, on the other hand, undermines Jamaican society.

The all-inclusives employ many people. Further, they provide valuable training for workers who go on to be hotel managers and better-paid staff of cruise ships. Some resorts have very enlightened management. At Sandals, for example, the employees receive no tips, but they get a bonus based on the occupancy rate of the hotel.

The staff at many resorts dine with guests. Jamaicans tend to be naturally convivial, so it is easy to strike up conversations. Very often they will invite people to their homes. Go. This is a better way to meet the locals than staying at a hotel, where vendors surround you every time you leave your room.

To let visitors know what the islanders are really like, the Jamaican Tourist Board also offers the "Meet the People" program, where you spend time with a Jamaican family that has interests similar to your own. They might, for example, invite you to a family picnic, for tea at the King's House, or for an afternoon of golf. Your children could become pen pals with Jamaican youths. The people truly want to establish friendships with you. This program complements the all-inclusive resort, making the Jamaican experience whole. Participation can be arranged through the Jamaica Tourist Boards, which are listed later in this introductory material.

POLITICS & TOURISM

All-inclusives also took hold as a reaction to some earlier negative experiences and bad press about the island. Unfortunately, the aggressive nature of Jamaican politics—democratic, but violent—makes international headlines. Fear not. The true nature of the people differs greatly from the news clips, and the all-inclusive resorts are located away from Kingston, the city that makes the news.

A friend went to Hedonism II and came back thinking that Jamaicans were the friendliest people in the world. Another fairly seasoned traveler stayed in a European plan hotel in Montego Bay and came away feeling harassed and weary. The difference, we later figured out, was that our friend spent most of his time within the confines of a controlled club environment, and the seasoned traveler was mobbed by peddlers, dope pushers, and con artists every time he left his hotel room. On his second visit, the seasoned traveler went to an all-inclusive resort and ventured into town only a few times. He came away loving Jamaica.

Think of Jamaica as a favorite wine. Take your time to sip it. Enjoy the bouquet. Admire the color. Drink it in good company. The same bottle gulped, while surrounded by a mob, does not give the same pleasure.

EXCURSIONS

Most resorts also offer various tours of the countryside, marketplaces, rivers, and plantations. Visitors can experience as much solitude, or explore as much of the island, as they want. Some jaunts outside the resort are strongly recommended. You can experience the lively marketplace, but not have to deal with the hucksters on a constant basis, as often happens during stays at European plan hotels.

In many cases, the excursions cost extra. The good short ones provide a needed chance to see the island. The all-day trips, which occasionally require a long bus ride, are best done when staying at a European plan hotel, since you'd be missing meals and activities you paid for. If time permits, tack on a few days at the end of your visit to raft down the rivers or see a different side of the island. The Sandals and SuperClubs have resorts in both Montego Bay and Negril. Often they will let guests split their trips between the two locations, an excellent way to experience the island.

Couples includes several tours in the base price. A two-masted schooner takes guests, buccaneer style, to Pigeon Island. Resort buses also take guests into Ocho Rios for shopping excursions, to Dunn's River Falls (you pay only the nominal entrance fee), to Prospect Plantation, and to White River Gorge. Each tour is worthwhile. Trips to Kingston, a rafting trip, and a ride on a catamaran are also available.

TOURIST MECCAS

NEGRIL: This fishing village originally gained fame when it attracted a counterculture element in the 1960s and 1970s. That generation "greened," and its members opened up shops and guest houses. Gradually hotels appeared, including the Negril Beach Village, now known as Hedonism II.

The major all-inclusive operators have discovered the beauty of Negril. Sandals has just constructed a new resort on this western extreme of the island. SuperClubs selected property adjoining Bloody Bay as the location for its ultraluxurious Grand Lido resort, also an all-inclusive.

Despite the recent development, Negril retains much of the charm of its humble beginnings. If you are daring, rent a moped to go into town. Rick's Café has attained the status of an institution for visitors to the Negril resorts. Built on the side of a mountain, the restaurant/bar offers views of the opposing cliffs, where amateur divers perform acrobatics as they fall into the water. Tourists often take the plunge also. Most just look on, sipping beers as they wait for the large orange sun to fall into the water. Rick's serves good food at moderately expensive prices, by Jamaican standards.

 Jason's Tips:

Bring your camera and a tripod for the best pictures. Don't forget to use a fill-flash if you want to take a picture of someone with the sun setting in the background. A polarizing filter should also help reduce the glare.

Rick's allows people in the door for free. Most resorts charge about $5 for the bus ride into town. Bring a tip for the driver. Those looking to extend their trip to different states of consciousness often ask the bus driver to stop on the way back for special tea or brownies. Many people cannot handle this, however, and get sick. This rather open practice is also illegal.

MONTEGO BAY: Most tourists land at the Montego Bay airport. MoBay, as the locals call it, also contains the greatest concentration of hotels, motels, guest houses, and tourist shops. Several all-inclusive resorts are located there as well.

The hills rise around the bay, giving some of the hotels spectacular views. Many Jamaicans have made sizable fortunes from the tourist trade, and they have built large houses in the hills. Their in-town shops tend to be well-organized and highly commercialized. The straw market too is cleaner than most and orderly, but be prepared for an onslaught of street peddlers and beggars.

Some resorts, such as Sandals, offer long-weekend trips. For these, we recommend going no further than MoBay.

Popular nightclubs attract tourists. The Cave at the Seabreeze is one of the most popular. A moderate entrance fee is charged. You have to duck under the entrance and buy beads for drinks. The young crowd mixes with Jamaicans, who do not pay for entrance.

OCHO RIOS: Ocho Rios, meaning "eight rivers," is located 1½ hours east from MoBay. The straw market, various shops, and Burger King draw visitors. Many of the all-inclusives bring visitors here so they can haggle for goods. If you look past the usual T-shirts and trinkets, you can also find fine pieces of original art.

RUNAWAY BAY: Runaway Bay is located on the north shore of Jamaica between Ocho Rios and Montego Bay. It has beautiful beaches, and local sailors swear that it gets the best winds.

FOOD & DRINK

You can drink the water and eat food in local restaurants. Avoid the slush vendors and questionable "jerk" pork stands on the side of the road, as some people have gotten sick eating there. The locals will point you to the good stands, which your stomach should withstand. When Jamaicans talk about their food being spicy, they mean flavorful, not hot. Don't expect quite the same quantity of red peppers that one finds in Mexico, although they do appear in some dishes. "Jerk" pork stands usually offer two sauces on the side, one of which is devastatingly hot.

Curried goat and a local version of British oxtail stew find their way into the all-inclusives as Jamaican specialties. Hot sauce and

 Jason's Tips:

The Jamaican food at the resorts is no substitute for absolutely authentic Jamaican "jerk" chicken or pork, which can be bought in the big cities. Try the food before adding the spicy condiments.

"Pickapepper," a spicy steak and fish sauce, give the dishes an authentic island flavor.

STAFFING & SERVICE

Throughout Jamaica service often seems slow by U.S. standards. But once you get their attention, personnel tend to be extremely attentive. That is part of the laid-back nature of this country, and most other Caribbean islands as well. You should know it before you go, expect it, and go with the flow. In general, the service is friendly and the people congenial. If slowness will bother you too much, go somewhere else. The service also won't be invisible. Jamaicans have too much personality. They love to talk to you.

SHOPPING

Jamaica is a free port, "in-bond," where you can buy internationally made goods duty free. With "in-bond" products, you pay for the goods with American or Canadian dollars and produce a North American passport. You may then take the goods with you from the store. Consumable goods, such as liquor and cigars, must be picked up at the airport. The duty-free, in-bond, shops congregate in the tourist areas.

GANJA

Ganja (marijuana) remains one of the chief reasons that some people go to Jamaica. Anyone who has been to the country has probably experienced the open selling techniques of the street peddlers. Some tourists choose Jamaica primarily because ganja is so cheap, good, and readily available.

Before you decide whether to indulge, know the facts. Ganja remains illegal and those convicted of possession face harsh penalties, which theoretically apply equally to tourists, although the law is hardly ever enforced. Use is covert but widespread at some resorts.

Ganja is not tolerated as much as it used to be. Since 1987, the U.S. government has been pressuring the Jamaican government to burn the ganja fields, thus decreasing the supply and increasing the price. Visiting U.S. military personnel should avoid it completely. All others should know that the fines for getting caught are extremely stiff.

Ganja is like a rental car: you pay a premium for the privilege of picking it up at the airport. The sellers always quote a high initial price, comparing it to the U.S. price, which they follow as if they were commodity dealers on the Chicago exchange. However straightfaced the dealer is, his price quote is only the initial offer for bargaining purposes. You can lower the price substantially, and let the dealer save face, by changing the price to Jamaican dollars.

The management of almost every all-inclusive denies that its employees sell ganja. They do, in fact, but very discreetly. If you talk to the workers, some will tell stories of ganja fields and help you score some if you wish. If you don't wish, they will not hassle you.

A favorite Jamaican con trick is to tell tourists that ganja will be mailed to the United States if it is paid for in advance. The peddlers relate stories of how they wrap and address it so it goes through the mail, and of how they have many good customers in the United States. There are good reasons not to fall for this trick. It is illegal and the penalties for importing marijuana are severe; besides, the package would probably not make it through the post office anyway. Finally, chances are extremely small that the seller would even send the package. The whole act is simply a way to rip off tourists, who fall for it time and again.

NUTS & BOLTS

CONTACT INFORMATION: The Jamaica Tourist Board strives to be extremely helpful. It can give you information about the island resorts, culture, and the Meet the People program. Its local offices can be reached by writing or calling the Jamaica Tourist Board at the following locations:

UNITED STATES
866 2nd Avenue
10th floor
New York, NY 10017
800-223-5225 or 212-688-7650
Chicago: 800-621-5232 or
    312-346-1546

Dallas: 800-654-7998 or
    214-361-8778
Los Angeles: 800-421-8206 or
    213-384-1123
Miami: 800-327-9857 or
    305-665-0557

CANADA
1 Eglinton Avenue East, Suite
    6161
Toronto, Ontario M4P 3A1
416-482-7850

1110 Sherbrooke Street West
Mezzanine Level
Montreal, Quebec H3A 189
514-849-6386/7

JAMAICA
Kingston: 809-929-9200
Montego Bay: 809-952-4425, 952-2462
Negril: 809-957-4243
Ocho Rios: 809-974-2570, 974-2582/3

CURRENCY: You must exchange foreign currency for the Jamaican dollar. One third of what you exchange can be cashed back if you keep your receipts. Traveler's checks get a slightly better exchange rate than cash. Most stores also accept American Express, Visa, and MasterCard. Most resorts will change money.

If you haven't been to Jamaica in a few years, you should note some changes. The currency floats and the government does not tolerate black market currency changers. Change money at official places only.

In general, prices are higher in Jamaica than in many countries with devalued currency, such as Mexico and Venezuela.

CUSTOMS/DUTY: You can expect to be frisked, sniffed, and searched upon returning from Jamaica. U.S. customs looks closely at all bags; some people even get strip-searched. Customs also checks the mail. The U.S. government has a policy of zero tolerance. Bring back only memories. You may bring back to the United States $400 worth of goods, not exceeding $50 value for each item. You can also bring back one bottle of hard liquor duty free.

DRIVING: Renting a car is a risky and expensive idea. Roads in Jamaica tend to be narrow and winding. People drive on the left side of the road. It takes a while to drive what seem to be fairly short distances because you must watch constantly for the maniacal driving habits of the locals and road obstacles, which include livestock, goats, chickens, carts, and slow-moving pedestrians. For a week's trip, this does not present a serious problem. For a long weekend, visitors would do well to stick to the Montego Bay area.

It's much better to hire a taxi or a minibus for the day. You get a driver who really knows the country, so he can take you to the best native restaurants. He may also show you his home, if you express a real interest. It can also be a better experience than going on a tour because you can stop when you want to take pictures or to get a drink. Make sure you set a fixed price in advance.

Mopeds can be rented for about $15 a day, after a hard session of bargaining. You often have to go through a Byzantine series of middlemen to get to the owner, but there seems to be no advantage in renting a moped directly.

ELECTRICITY: Current varies on the island but all the resorts reviewed in this book use 110 volts and 60 cycles. A hair dryer should work, but a clock might need an adaptor. Electrical shortages are endemic to Jamaica. We ran out of hot water several times during our stay.

FESTIVALS/HOLIDAYS: Jamaica's famous reggae festival, "Sunsplash," happens every August. It is often difficult to get airline tickets during the festival, but that makes it easier to get resort reservations. If you can take an extended holiday, you may want to combine festival time and resort time.

LANGUAGE: English is the official language of Jamaica, and the people speak it quite well, although with an accent that North Americans sometimes have trouble understanding. Black Jamaicans speak a dialect called Patois among themselves.

Jason's Tips:

It would be a waste of money to stay in an all-inclusive while attending Sunsplash because you will want to party all night, sleep all day, thereby missing most of your prepaid meals and activities.

MARRIAGES: Jamaica is a very popular place to get married, but the required papers make it very difficult to do so spontaneously. You need birth certificates (passports won't do), and divorce papers or a death certificate of a former spouse, if applicable. Catholics also need a letter from their priest. However, you need only a 48-hour residency. Ministers will usually counsel the couple for an hour. A Jamaican marriage is as legal as one performed anywhere else. In fact, there are very restrictive divorce laws; in Jamaica people marry for life.

MUSIC: Most people have heard of Bob Marley and reggae. House cover bands play a lot of his music, which seems to get better with time. Young Jamaicans have continually developed this music form, and they now play many different variations. Legitimate stores sell quality tapes, and bootleggers sell copies that are usually several generations stepped down in quality. Dance hall reggae, a combination of rap and reggae, is currently very popular in the nightclubs and on the streets. Be sure to listen to some before you buy a tape.

PACKING: Pack light, because you will spend 90 percent of your time in your swimsuit and flip-flops. You need 1 pair of rubber-soled shoes for the Dunn's River Falls tour. When restaurants or a dining room demand casual-formal outfits, that means a shirt with collar and long pants for men. Women need nice summer dresses. Bring a jacket and tie only if you plan to get married; even then, the tie is optional. Don't forget tennis and golf shoes if you plan to participate. An old T-shirt is recommended for diving (leave your equipment, including booties, at home; warm water gloves are optional). Wind-surfing gloves and booties help if you have them, but are not necessary. Bring jeans and boots (tennis shoes will do) for horseback riding.

Laundry service is available at most resorts, but tends to be slow and very expensive. Bring enough clothing for your stay. The sun demands that you protect your eyes. Bring two pairs of sunglasses, if possible.

The radio reception in Montego Bay is not very good, either on the room radio or on a portable. A tape player is necessary to play the tapes you want while tanning or exercising. A small one will also let you try out the tapes of the many reggae cassette dealers, many of which are bootlegged.

SEASONS: When asked about the weather the Jamaican Tourist Board says, "Don't worry, mon. It is warm all year." May and October average the most precipitation, but this varies from year to year. "Liquid sunshine" is no problem. It only rains for a short time in the afternoon. You can set your watch by it. Wind speed varies from day to day. During the day, Jamaica often gets cool trade winds that the natives call Dr. Breeze. Only in the evening does it really cool down, when the "undertaker breeze" comes to the coast from the mountains.

TELEPHONES: It's easier for someone to call Jamaica than it is to make outgoing calls. In many cases, hotel phones are not capable of direct dialing, so you must go through the hotel operator. A room phone makes the wait for an overseas line more pleasant.

TIME: Jamaica lies in a time zone that is one hour earlier than Eastern Standard time. This changes with Daylight Savings Time. You can leave New York at a reasonable hour, say 9:00 A.M., and arrive in Jamaica before noon local time. The island is closer to the equator, so the days are longer in the winter and shorter in the summer than the days farther north. The day's activities tend to be driven more by the sun than the clock.

TRAVEL: Sangster Airport in Montego Bay presents the best arrival airport for all resorts listed in this book. Departure tax is $8 (U.S. currency).

TRAVEL TIME BY AIR

Chicago: **4 hours 30 minutes**
Los Angeles: **5 hours 30 minutes**
New York: **3 hours 45 minutes**
Toronto: **4 hours 30 minutes**

ARRIVAL AIRPORT: Sir Donald Sangster International Airport.

VACCINATION REQUIREMENTS: None.

VISA/PASSPORT REQUIREMENTS: For stays up to 6 months, Americans and Canadians need only proof of citizenship (passport, birth certificate, voter's registration card) and an outgoing ticket.

EDEN II

VITAL FEATURES

Type of vacation: **Club**
Target market: **Heterosexual couples, honeymooners in their early twenties and up**
Location: **Ocho Rios, Jamaica**
All-inclusive cost per week: **$900–$1,200 plus airfare**

RATINGS

Value: $ $ $ $

Fun quotient: 🏖 🏖 🏖 🏖 🏖

Honeymoon suitability: ♥ ♥ ♥

Singles meeting ground: Not applicable

Child appeal: Not applicable

Management professionalism: ☎ ☎ ☎ ☎

Service: 💡 💡 💡 💡 💡

Food: 🦞 🦞 🦞 🦞

THE REAL STORY

Couples enter Eden II through a lush tropical entrance with a fountain and a goldfish pond in the middle. Exotic plants are everywhere. Birds are chirping. It feels as though you have entered the Garden of Eden. It wouldn't come as a surprise if a snake came slithering out of the brush to offer you an apple, but at Eden II it would more than likely be a rum drink. The welcome makes you want to peel off your winter-tainted clothing and dive right in.

Eden II, located on the northern coast of Jamaica, offers almost every activity and sport imaginable. At the beach, there is a laid-back feeling, but near the pool and volleyball net, they practically drag you out and make you participate.

85

The service is exceptional. The staff do everything they can to make the guests happy. Eden II is located near the beach where they filmed the movie *Doctor No*. but that may be the only no you hear at Eden II, because the staff say yes to just about everything. They make your body feel good by giving you unlimited oil massages, which are included. You can have several a day if you want. They have a great aerobics and stretch instructor. The class's music and view of the ocean draws a lot of people, even though it takes place early in the morning. Bubbling hot tubs overlook the ocean. They fit up to ten of your closest and most intimate friends. After midnight, couples tend not to bother with putting on a bathing suit before going into the hot tub.

There are parrots in the lobby, which adds to the tropical aura, and they are amusing at first. But they make it a little hard to concentrate on your next chess move. They look guilty of something, making you wonder whether the parrot over your left shoulder is giving away your game. After a couple of minutes of listening to them chatter at each other you'll long for that Jamaican culinary specialty, "jerk" bird.

The resort has a nude beach, but it is no longer promoted. The living fence of trees tends to bend down during heavy winds, exposing the bathers to the stares of the neighbors. Go there if you like to show what you've got. There is also a prude beach, which is cordoned off for swimming.

The drink specialty is a Jamaican Flag, which has many types of liquor in it and is set on fire. The object is to drink it—in one big gulp—before the flame goes out.

If you like activities and mixing with other talent, you'll have a great time. With so much going on, how can you not?

INCLUDED

Accommodations	Taxes
Activities	Tips
Drinks	Tours
Entertainment & dancing	Transfer to and from airport
Food	Water sports
Sports	

VALUE

Eden II offers every type of activity and includes several tours, all for reasonable prices. You won't walk away feeling as if you got the deal of the century, but you will feel that you got your money's worth.

Perhaps no other place includes as many different activities, especially water sports. The only drawback rests in the rooms, which were somewhat older and less elegant than those of the competition. Many have great views, but they need to be redecorated.

ACTIVITIES, SPORTS, & EXCURSIONS

ACTIVITIES

Beach volleyball
Beer-drinking competition
Best tan/burn/peel
    competition
Bingo
Board games
Egyptian mummy wrap
    contest
Glass-bottomed boat
Horseshoes
Massage classes
Massages
Nude sunbathing
Olympics
Patois/Jamaican history
    classes
Reggae dancing lessons
Scrabble tournament
Sunbathing

SPORTS: The sports equipment always seems to be available if you sign up, and many times even if you just show up. Also, plenty of instructors gladly give lessons and will offer to play a game with you. You not only don't have to ask twice, sometimes they will ask you. No problem, mon.

If you want to scuba dive, you must be certified or pass a vigorous swimming test. A resort course is free; PADI certification costs $260.

Rates include unlimited greens fees at Upton Golf Course, 25 minutes away. Caddies, clubs, and carts are extra.

Aerobics
Croquet
Golf
Horseback riding
Jogging trail
Kayaks (for 2)
Paddleball
Pedal boats
Ping-Pong
Pitch-and-putt golf
Sailing (Sunfish)
Scuba
Shuffleboard
Snorkeling
Swimming pool
Tennis (lighted courts)
Volleyball
Waterskiing
Weight room (Nautilus, free
    weights)
Windsurfing (Mistral School)

EXCURSIONS

Catamaran rides (extra)
Dunn's River Falls outing
Garden tour
Horseback riding near falls
    (extra)
Jet skiing (extra)
Kingston (extra)
Ocho Rios shopping tour
Parasailing (extra)
Plantation tour
Rafting (extra)

ITINERARY & DAILY SCHEDULE

It's best to arrive on the weekend, because the resort builds a spirit during the week. By the last day, you feel as if the program has reached a crescendo.

NIGHTLIFE & ENTERTAINMENT

Organized nightlife abounds, but guests tend to avoid it in favor of more intimate activities. Maybe this is because of the high percentage of honeymooners.

An after-dinner show really pleases the crowd. The resident band, Cabaret, plays every night except Tuesday from 7:30 until midnight. It accompanies a floor show, which features folk singers, fire-eaters, and limbo dancers. The fire show keeps the crowd gasping—Oooh, ahhh.

The disco pulses until 3:00 A.M. but does not attract a full crowd. After the main show is over, at 9:30 to 10:00 P.M., people tend to disappear. The resort gets kind of quiet. Many head for the beach or hot tubs to get intimate. The grounds are well lit, so you can slip off for a midnight swim and feel secure. The weekly schedule includes:

Sunday: **Fashion show and cabaret**
Monday: **Shipwreck Shenanigans**
Tuesday: **Jamaican dance contest, Oldies but Goodies costume parade and dance contest**
Wednesday: **Akanga (Jamaican Toga) Parade, Jamaican Showtime**
Thursday: **Guest and staff talent show**
Friday: **Buccaneer Night**
Saturday: **Jamaican showcase**

AESTHETICS & ENVIRONMENT

The driveway leading to the resort is surrounded by a beautiful, long stretch of green grass with vibrantly displayed flowers. It looks almost perfect.

The dining room is very attractive, with big, family-style tables. The floral, pastel decorations add to the Caribbean ambience.

The rooms could be maintained better. Their condition detracts somewhat from the overall aesthetics of the resort.

FACILITIES

Bank	Gift shop
Bars	Hot tubs
Beach	Medical station
Beauty salon	Piano bar
Concierge	Pool
Disco	Safety-deposit box
Entertainment coordinators	Water-sports center

ROOMS

Go for the ocean view in the new wing. The old wing of the building faces straight toward the ocean, but to see the ocean you have to look over the physical plant, the new building, and listen to the air conditioner running.

The balconies in the new wing are completely private: you can do whatever you want on them. You have a somewhat angled view of the ocean, but this is probably the best view and it is very quiet. The pieces of furniture don't match well and the hallways are a little dingy, but chances are that you won't spend much time inspecting the decor.

The Lanai rooms are the cheapest. They are in a two-story building, and rooms have a private patio or a walkway balcony. The motel-style rooms are small, and have an older feel. Since none of the Lanai rooms have much of a view, choose a first-floor room for convenience and the usable patio. They are fairly well decorated, with new carpeting and decent furniture.

LUXURY LEVEL

Air-conditioning
Clock
Laundry service (extra)
Maid service
Massage (included)
Phone in room
Porter service
Radio
Room service (for Continental breakfast only)
Television in room

FOOD & DRINK

They keep you well fed at Eden II. Breakfast and lunch are served on an open veranda overlooking the pool and ocean. If you don't want to leave your bed early, room service will bring you a Continental breakfast. Each week includes four nights of à la carte dining with waiter service and three nights of buffet-style dining. Monday features a buffet on the beach; and island cuisine is offered at the Wednesday and Saturday buffets. A steel band plays on Sunday while you enjoy a champagne brunch. Wine is served with lunch and dinner.

In the dining room or at the buffets, you can be seated with other people, which most people prefer, or you can request to eat with your significant other. The dining room was the only place in Jamaica where we found smoking and nonsmoking areas.

If you get hungry between meals a beachfront grill serves hamburgers, hot dogs, and barbecued chicken. Afternoon tea and a midnight buffet are also offered.

All beer and bar drinks are included, and there is waiter service at the pool and beach. They serve drinks at two outdoor bars: Cain for hard drinks; Abel for fruit drinks.

The meals and snacks are complemented with plenty of fruit and fruit drinks. Food is always fresh, well presented, and bountiful. The resort features many different varieties of cantaloupes, oranges, papayas, pineapples, and bananas.

Breakfasts and lunches are served buffet style, with juices, cold cereal, and hot entrées, including custom-made omelets. Most people prefer to take their lunches by the pool so they can stay close to the games and other action. The grill serves barbecued chicken, hamburgers, and hot dogs. The luncheon buffet features lots of seafood.

"Continental" best describes the sit-down, full-course dinners. You choose from such menu items as lobster Thermidor and beef Wellington. You can always get seconds, which many people do on lobster night.

STAFFING & SERVICE

Management is very professional. It advises you to leave your valuables in the safety-deposit box. We agree.

The staff are also responsible for the entertainment; they get people involved in the shows and games.

PRIVACY & RELAXATION

There are lots of private places that allow you to slip away from the other guests. The nude beach has plenty of room; the long stretch of white sand is perfect for private walks. Lots of palm trees allow you to duck into the shade.

SHOPPING

Ocho Rios offers a straw market for trinkets and crafts. (There are vendors on the property, so you can look and purchase without being harassed.) There is a trick to shopping in the straw market. If you go on a day when the cruise ships are in town, the vendors will be more diverted and will leave you alone. If you go on an off day, the vendors will practically drag you into their shops, but you might be able to get a better deal. They love good, name-brand sneakers. You may be able to barter a pair for a work of art.

HONEYMOONERS

All the reasons that make this a great couples resort also make it good for a honeymoon. Eden II attracts a young crowd, most of whom come on their honeymoon.

The $150 marriage package includes: the license, minister, boutonniere for groom and attendant, bouquet for bride and attendant, one 8 × 10 color photo, reception table, Eden II video and poster. A videotape costs $100 extra. The marriage ceremony takes place in a little gazebo (which might work as a *chupa* in a Jewish wedding) or by the fountain. Both spots are on the front lawn and are very appealing. The resort will provide a clergyman of your choice.

NUTS & BOLTS

BOOKING & CONTACT INFORMATION: Most travel agencies can book you. Try to find one that can give you an air/land package. Air Jamaica tends to have the least expensive flights. Or write or call:

Eden II
Ocho Rios, Jamaica, W.I.
809-972-2382
800-223-1588

DEPOSITS/REFUNDS: Payment for three nights of the total cost of the package is due at the time of booking. Full payment is due seven days prior to arrival. The deposit is fully refundable up to three days prior to arrival. If cancelled less than three days prior to the scheduled arrival, there will be an assessed penalty of three nights.

HANDICAP ACCESSIBILITY: None.

LANGUAGE: English.

PACKING: You will spend most of your time in your bathing suit since there is no need to dress for meals during the day. Bring nice, casual clothes for the evening. Bring sneakers, sport clothes, and an extra swimming suit. (Who wants to put on a wet one? Yech.)

RELIGIOUS SERVICES: There are none on the property, although a list of local services is provided.

RESERVATION SCHEDULE: Make high season reservations three to four months in advance.

NUMBER OF ROOMS: 265.

MAXIMUM NUMBER OF GUESTS: 530.

TRAVEL TIME FROM AIRPORT: 1½ hours (Sangster International Airport in Montego Bay).

Cost Worksheet

	High Season[1]	Off-Season[2]
Accommodations		
(7 days)	$ 975 (standard)	$ 880 (standard)
	1,098 (superior)	963 (superior)
	1,198 (deluxe)	1,018 (deluxe)
Food	incl.	incl.
Drinks	incl.	incl.
Departure tax	8	8
Sports	incl.	incl.
Airfare	_____	_____
Sight-seeing	incl.	incl.
Tips	incl.	incl.
Additional sports		
Souvenirs	_____	_____

[1] High season dates: December 7 to January 27, December 7 to March 31
[2] Off-season dates: April 1 to December 21

All rates per person, based on double occupancy for a seven-night stay.

Always ask if any special packages, promotions, or airfare discounts are in effect before booking.

All vacations described in this guide can be booked through any competent travel agent; we advise you to do so.

See the general introduction and area introductions for more details.

THE REAL STORY

The Elegant Resorts of Jamaica are six hotels, each of which offers a variety of environments, activities, and sports. Normally European plan hotels, they also offer all-inclusive packages called the Platinum Plan. This means that you can tee off on an 18-hole golf course or whack tennis balls to your forearm's exhaustion. Or you can just sit back and enjoy a drink on the beach and watch other guests fill the sails of their skiffs. The price for all this totals much less than you might expect to pay for so much luxury.

It makes sense that the Elegant Resorts have joined together for marketing purposes, because they resemble each other in many ways. They each cater to the "high end" of the resort market, competing with the finest hotels in the Caribbean in luxury level, cuisine, and service. Each resort differs significantly in the sports and amenities that it offers.

Author's note: A tight deadline limited us to reviewing three of the six Elegant Resorts: the Half Moon Club, Tryall, and Roundhill. The other three hotels—Trident, San Souci, and the Plantation Inn—seem to be from the same mold.

While these hotels sell rooms on a European plan, *Hot Spots* reviews only the Platinum Plan, which makes these fine resorts feel like all-inclusives.

INCLUDED

Accommodations	Sports
Activities	Sports instruction
Drinks	Taxes
Entertainment & dancing	Tips
Food	Transfer to and from airport

VALUE

The Elegant Resorts charge more than many other Jamaican hotels, but they offer a higher standard of luxury. While the prices vary widely according to your room and the number of days that you choose to stay, rates are generally the same at each of the Elegant Resorts.

All rates include airport transfers, luxury accommodations, three meals daily, all drinks, most sports, activities and entertainment, a bottle of champagne on arrival, flowers, a fruit basket, towels, beach and pool chairs, and all taxes and gratuities.

The following per-person rates apply to all six resorts and are based on double occupancy.

		Peak Season December 15–April 15	Off-Season April 16– December 14
7 nights	Superior room	$1,395	$ 995
	Deluxe room	$1,570	$1,065
	Superior suite	$1,710	$1,135
	Deluxe suite	$2,235	$1,345
	Each additional adult	$1,085	$ 805
	Each additional child	$ 560	$ 420
4 nights	Superior room	$ 818	$ 583
	Deluxe room	$ 918	$ 623
	Superior suite	$ 998	$ 663
	Deluxe suite	$1,290	$ 783
	Each additional adult	$ 310	$ 230
	Each additional child	$ 160	$ 120
Extra night	Superior room	$ 192	$ 138
	Deluxe room	$ 218	$ 148
	Superior suite	$ 238	$ 157
	Deluxe suite	$ 315	$ 187
	Each additional adult	$ 77	$ 58
	Each additional child	$ 40	$ 30

RESERVATION SCHEDULE: For December through February, make reservations at least nine months in advance. For the spring months, reserve at least three or four months in advance. For the summer months, reserve about three to four weeks in advance of your desired departure date.

PACKING: As their name implies, these resorts call for attire that is a bit more formal than elsewhere in Jamaica. Men should bring along a good sports coat, and women cocktail dresses. Plan on whites for tennis and appropriate golf gear.

NUTS & BOLTS

BOOKING INFORMATION

Elegant Resorts of Jamaica
1320 South Dixie Highway,
    Suite 1102
Coral Gables, FL 33146
800-237-3237

Interested groups can contact:
JBD Associates
P.O. Box 16086
Alexandria, VA 22303
703-370-1189

Cost Worksheet	High Season[1]	Off-Season[2]
Accommodations (7 days)[3]	$1,395	$995
Food	incl.	incl.
Drinks	incl.	incl.
Departure tax	incl.	incl.
Sports	most are included	
Airfare	_____	_____
Sight-seeing		
Tips	incl.	incl.
Additional sports		
Souvenirs	_____	_____

[1] High season dates: December 15 to April 15
[2] Off-season dates: April 16 to December 14
[3] Premium for single person: Deduct $100 per day from the double room rate.

HALF MOON CLUB

VITAL FEATURES

Type of vacation: **Resort**
Target market: **Couples, families, singles, all ages**
Location: **Montego Bay, Jamaica**
All-inclusive cost per week: **$1,400 to $2,250 plus airfare**

RATINGS

Value: 💲💲💲

Fun quotient: ⛱⛱⛱⛱

Honeymoon suitability: 🖤🖤🖤🖤

Singles meeting ground: 🧍🧍

Child appeal: 🍦🍦

Management professionalism: ☎☎☎☎

Service: 💡💡💡💡

Food: 🦞🦞🦞

THE REAL STORY

Stretching across 400 acres of Jamaica's sandy north shore, the Half Moon Club offers a tropical, sports-oriented resort. Its size offers you plentiful stomping grounds, a beautifully manicured retreat, and a plethora of activities. In fact, the Half Moon Club not only occupies the largest acreage of all the Elegant Resorts, it also offers the most sports and activities.

ACTIVITIES, SPORTS, & EXCURSIONS

ACTIVITIES: Guests can spend their days enjoying the beach or trying to find their golf balls in the sand traps of the resort's golf

96

course. They can also lounge by the pool, swim in the surf, play tennis, scuba dive, or drink tropical libations.

Dancing	Nightly entertainment (in
Entertainment/shows	winter)
Glass-bottomed boat	Sauna
Massages	Sunbathing
Movies	

SPORTS: Platinum Plan guests may golf as often as they wish; the package price even includes the cart and caddy. The depths of the Caribbean await certified divers and those willing to take the certification course. Less dedicated folk can borrow snorkeling gear and view the reefs from above. Those who favor the dog paddle can swim in the freshwater pool or along the one mile of white sand beach. A Mistral School will teach you to windsurf or help you with the advanced water start maneuver.

Aerobics/exercise classes	Sailing (Sunfish, catamaran)
Deep-sea fishing (extra)	Scuba diving
Golf	Snorkeling
Health & fitness center	Squash
Horseback riding	Swimming
Kayaks	Tennis
Nautilus	Volleyball
Night tennis	Windsurfing
Pedal boats	

NIGHTLIFE & ENTERTAINMENT

The spirit of good fun and good times at Half Moon is captivating and contagious. You can meet old friends and make new ones at an evening hospitality party, cheer on a favorite at a riotous crab race, watch calypso and limbo shows with scintillating music, and dance after dinner every night. Later, a quiet stroll along the beach provides the perfect path to bed.

AESTHETICS & ENVIRONMENT

One of the largest resorts in Jamaica, Half Moon features incredible variety. It has colorful gardens, manicured lawns, and a mile of private white sand beach.

FACILITIES

Bank	Car rental
Beaches	Commissary
Beachside bar	Disco
Beauty salon	Meeting rooms

Pharmacy
Private banquet rooms
Shopping arcade (duty free)
Snack bar, grill
Swimming pools (2 outdoor)

Television lounge with satellite reception
Tour desk
Water-sports center

ROOMS

The spacious guest rooms, luxury suites, and charming villas are all private and relaxing enough to help you recover from a day full of activities. There are also delightful cottages along the shore with private freshwater pools.

LUXURY LEVEL

Air-conditioning
Concierge
Laundry service (extra)
Maid service
Mini-bar

Phone in room
Porter service
Refrigerator in room
Room service for all meals

FOOD & DRINK

The Seagrape Terrace Restaurant treats guests to a variety of Caribbean dishes. Special children's dinners are available from 5:00 P.M. to 7:00 P.M. The Sugar Mill Restaurant offers open-air dining for lunch and dinner overlooking the golf course. Room service is available for all meals, with night owl service until midnight during the winter months.

PRIVACY & RELAXATION

The spacious grounds ensure that you can find a place to hide with the company of a good book or someone special.

SHOPPING

The Half Moon Club features a shopping arcade complete with duty-free shops on the premises.

HONEYMOONERS

This resort is great for honeymooners who want to spend a luxurious moment before returning to the hustle and bustle of everyday life. Because of staff presence, suites offer much more privacy than villas.

SINGLES

For those of you who want to meet that special someone or simply meet and enjoy interesting people, you can do so at the manager's cocktail party or at any of the many activities available for your enjoyment. This is not, however, a place to go wild.

CHILD APPEAL

The Half Moon Club is probably the best choice of all the Elegant Resorts for taking a vacation with children. Although there are no special programs or activities designed especially for the younger set, there is still plenty to do. Kids will love building mammoth sand castles on the white sand beaches or splashing in the private freshwater pools. Baby-sitters and cribs are available for children under 6.

NUTS & BOLTS

BOOKING INFORMATION: See introduction, page 95.

CONTACT INFORMATION

P.O. Box 80
Montego Bay, Jamaica
809-953-2211

DEPOSITS/REFUNDS: All the Elegant Resorts require a three-night deposit. Penalties apply for reservations cancelled within 14 days in the summer and 28 days in the winter. Cancellations for Christmas and New Year's must be made by November 15. All resorts except Tryall charge a one-night penalty if deadlines are missed. Tryall charges three nights as a penalty, and charges a minimum of $50 for all cancellations.

HANDICAP ACCESSIBILITY: None.

SIZE: 400 acres.

NUMBER OF ROOMS: 61 suites, 99 rooms, 36 villas.

TRAVEL TIME FROM AIRPORT: 10 minutes (Sangster International Airport in Montego Bay).

ROUND HILL

Type of vacation: **Resort**
Target market: **Couples, families, singles, all ages**
Location: **Montego Bay, Jamaica**
All-inclusive cost per week: **$1,400 to $2,250 plus airfare**

RATINGS

Value: 💲💲💲

Fun quotient: 🌴🌴🌴

Honeymoon suitability: ❤️❤️❤️

Singles meeting ground: 💃🕺

Child appeal: 🍦🍦

Management professionalism: ☎️☎️☎️☎️

Service: 💡💡💡

Food: 🦞🦞🦞

THE REAL STORY

Nestled on Jamaica's north coast, ten miles west of Montego Bay, lies Round Hill, set on a lush green peninsula. The adjectives *cozy* and *private* best describe the grounds. This resort provides an extraordinary level of personal service through its maids, gardeners, and private villa staff. For many people, one of the most appealing characteristics of Round Hill is its leisurely atmosphere. If you were to go on a whirlwind tour of the world, Round Hill would be the relaxing place to end your trip.

INCLUDED

Accommodations	Food
Activities	Sports
Child-care facilities	Taxes
Drinks	Tips
Entertainment & dancing	Transfer to and from airport

ACTIVITIES, SPORTS & EXCURSIONS

Round Hill offers golf and tennis, but most activities are geared toward a restful and cultural experience. The sports enthusiast may find the desired activities here; the fanatic probably will not. On-site tennis is convenient and pleasant. Golf can be played at area courses, not at the resort, which can make transportation a problem.

ACTIVITIES

Barbecue and bonfire on the beach	Nightly music
Culture	Piano bar
Dancing	Shopping (duty free)
Entertainment/shows	Sunbathing
	Television/VCR

SPORTS

Golf (3 championship courses)	Swimming (1 pool and private beach)
Horseback riding	
Sailing	Tennis (5 all-weather courts)
Shopping (duty-free boutique)	Waterskiing
	Windsurfing

NIGHTLIFE & ENTERTAINMENT

One of the most appealing characteristics of Round Hill is the resort's easy, elegant sociability. Guests can gather for cocktails in the main bar around the piano bar or meet at the weekly bonfire and beach barbecue. You will hear nightly music during dinner and for dancing afterward.

AESTHETICS & ENVIRONMENT

The bucolic, peaceful environment of Round Hill calms the soul. The lush foliage makes all seasons feel like spring.

FACILITIES

Audio-visual equipment	Beauty salon
Bars	Commissary
Beaches	Cribs

Exclusive boutique
Meeting rooms
Nannies

Piano bar
Swimming pool

ROOMS

The Pineapple House offers 36 private rooms, each with a breathtaking view of the blue Caribbean. The privately owned villas house two to four separate suites, many with their own swimming pools and separate staff.

LUXURY LEVEL

Concierge
Laundry service (extra)
Maid service

Phone in room
Porter service
Room service

FOOD & DRINK

The Georgian Colonial Dining Room serves Continental cuisine with Jamaican specialties. There is a weekly beach barbecue and gala night. Breakfast is served in your room or villa and lunch on the al fresco dining terrace.

PRIVACY & RELAXATION

Guests find privacy on secluded beaches and in quiet gardens. Villa residents can even relax around their own pools.

HONEYMOONERS

Honeymooners may find the presence of the villa staff an intrusion on privacy.

SINGLES

For those of you who want to meet that special someone or simply meet and enjoy interesting people, you can do so at the manager's cocktail party or any of the many activities available for your enjoyment.

CHILD APPEAL

Round Hill and Half Moon clubs are probably the best Elegant Resorts to choose if you want to bring children. However, the resort does not accept children under four.

NUTS & BOLTS

BOOKING INFORMATION: See Introduction, page 95.

CONTACT INFORMATION

P.O. Box 64
Montego Bay, Jamaica
809-952-5150

HANDICAP ACCESSIBILITY: None.

PACKING: Casually elegant. For Saturday galas, black tie or jacket and tie is requested. All other nights are informal.

SIZE: 98 acres.

NUMBER OF ROOMS: 27 privately owned villas; 36 rooms in Pineapple House.

TRAVEL TIME FROM AIRPORT: 12 minutes.

All rates per person, based on double occupancy for a seven-night stay.

Always ask if any special packages, promotions, or airfare discounts are in effect before booking.

All vacations described in this guide can be booked through any competent travel agent; we advise you to do so.

See the general introduction and area introductions for more details.

TRYALL GOLF, TENNIS, AND BEACH CLUB

VITAL FEATURES

Type of vacation: **Resort**
Target market: **Couples, families, singles, all ages**
Location: **Montego Bay, Jamaica**
All-inclusive cost per week: **$1,400 to $2,250 plus airfare**

RATINGS

Value: 💲💲💲

Fun quotient: ⛱️⛱️

Honeymoon suitability: 🖤🖤🖤

Singles meeting ground: Not applicable

Child appeal: 🍦🍦

Management professionalism: ☎️☎️☎️☎️

Service: 💡💡💡

Food: 🦞🦞🦞

THE REAL STORY

At Tryall, you can experience the life of a British colonial lord. This magnificent estate is secluded among the 2,200 acres of towering palms, bougainvillea, flowering trees, and gardens. The resort's opulence centers on the historic Great House, open to all guests. For privacy, you can retreat to a spacious room or villa.

The heart of Tryall's unique experience beats with the villas. There, a private staff caters to your family. You can also relax by your own private pool. Combine the luxury of a staffed second home with

104

the opulence of a super-rich life-style. While the hotel offers the all-inclusive, golfing parents will love the course, leaving the kids to frolic under the supervision of the villa staff.

INCLUDED

Accommodations
Activities
Child care (villa staff)
Drinks
Entertainment & dancing
   (winter)
Food

Sports
Sports instruction
Taxes
Transfer to/from airport

ACTIVITIES, SPORTS, & EXCURSIONS

ACTIVITIES

Dancing (winter)
Entertainment/shows
Glass-bottomed boat

Music
Sunbathing

SPORTS: Tryall has tremendous recreational appeal. There are six all-weather Laykold tennis courts, two of which are lighted for night play. The incredible 18-hole championship golf course will probably make it impossible for the golf lover to leave. It is the home of Shell's Wonderful World of Golf and the PGA/LPGA Mazda Championship. In case your partner is the golf lover and you are not, do not despair. The views from the sixth fairway and the tanning rays are enough to make you keep your head up, even while teeing off.

Deep-sea fishing
Golf
Sailing (Sunfish)
Scuba

Snorkeling
Swimming pools
Tennis
Windsurfing

NIGHTLIFE & ENTERTAINMENT

There are a total of four lounges at Tryall. Nightly entertainment is featured on the terrace.

AESTHETICS & ENVIRONMENT

The Tryall grounds are orderly and well manicured—in the British tradition.

Audio-visual equipment
Bars
Beaches
Commissary on-site

Concierge
Golf
Golf lessons
Meeting rooms

Shopping	Tennis
Swimming pools	Tennis lessons
Television with satellite reception	

ROOMS

Unique among all-inclusive resorts, Tryall offers 40 villas, each individually decorated with its own private pool. In addition, every villa is staffed with a cook, chambermaid, laundress, and gardener. The other, more traditional hotel rooms also reflect the demands of well-traveled guests.

LUXURY LEVEL

Laundry service (extra)	Porter service
Maid service	Room service
Phone in room	

FOOD & DRINK

The Tryall Golf, Tennis, and Beach Club offers a variety of delicious choices. The Great House Dining Room, overlooking the Caribbean and Montego Bay, offers a variety of Continental and local cuisine. It is open for breakfast and dinner. You can have lunch by the sea at the Beach Café, or swim for a drink at the poolside bar.

PRIVACY & RELAXATION

Tryall's individually decorated guest rooms offer a choice of breathtaking views of the beautiful grounds. The villas are secluded, but the attentive staff is always present.

SHOPPING

For those who want to browse around in a nearby store, there is a commissary on-site. For the hard-core shoppers, stroll a little farther to a street vendor or bazaar and feast on a host of colorful handmade crafts and straw goods.

HONEYMOONERS

The beautiful, colorful surroundings are the perfect backdrop for a very romantic holiday.

SINGLES

Come here only to relax. You won't find a regular supply of singles of the opposite sex.

CHILDREN

The Tryall Golf, Tennis, and Beach Club is a good resort for children. The living quarters are very spacious and every villa is supplied with staff to cater to your family's every need. Although there are no special programs or activities designed for the younger set, children ages six to twelve should be happy in the pool.

NUTS & BOLTS

BOOKING INFORMATION: See introduction, page 95.

CONTACT INFORMATION

Sandy Bay Post Office
Montego Bay, Jamaica
809-952-5110

PACKING: Wear sports attire throughout the day. After 6:30 P.M., gentlemen are required to wear sports jackets with or without ties. Ladies don cocktail attire. Whites on tennis courts is required.

SIZE: 2,200 acres.

NUMBER OF ROOMS: 52 plus 40 villas.

TRAVEL TIME FROM AIRPORT: 15 minutes (Sangster International Airport in Montego Bay).

JACK TAR VILLAGE
RESORTS INTRODUCTION

Jack Tar villages offer a very easy vacation: easy on the wallet, easy on the mind, and easy to take. They appeal to the budget-minded tourists, or to the person who happens into one of the tourist agencies owned by the same parent company. They also sell blocks of rooms to wholesalers who package their rooms with charter flights, keeping prices low.

Jack Tar Village Resorts knows what makes an all-inclusive: wallet-free vacations, a plethora of activity choices, and a warm location close to water. Perhaps more than just about anyone, it pushes the all-inclusive nature of its resorts—right on the front cover of its brochures. With the air component, the trip really does include almost everything in the base price.

Jack Tar resorts usually have amenities commensurate with the price that they charge. They try to offer the same activities and sports as many of the more expensive all-inclusives. Our experience was that they usually come up short. In our opinion their facilities don't match those of the other resorts because they tend to have less support staff, fewer maintenance workers, and less equipment. The resorts also seem to have a slightly lower quality of food than some other all-inclusives.

After reviewing over 100 resorts, the best of which are in this book, we firmly believe that Jack Tar villages have a deserved place in the sun. Budget-minded travelers should consider these tours.

Despite apparently exaggerated brochure claims about the luxury of its resorts, Jack Tar Village Resorts does offer a full all-inclusive package, usually sold with air travel packaged by its sister company, Adventure Travel USA, that is a reasonable value. Most guests that we encountered were satisfied, and some said that they would return. The clientele appears willing to overlook the resorts' shortcomings because of the comparatively low price and the number of amenities that are included.

Unlike the pictures in the brochures, you rarely find a young, vibrant crowd.

The Jack Tar Village Resorts seem to be geared to middle-aged gamblers. We suspect that many of the guests would have gone to Las Vegas, but they wandered into an affiliated agency and the agent sold them this package.

Some Jack Tar villages occupy nice properties; others, such as

108

Montego Bay and St. Kitts, have some location problems, but still have the potential to be truly wonderful clubs. The management seems to possess the correct checklist of what needs to go into an all-inclusive. We truly hope that the owners will upgrade their villages to the standards that will elevate their offerings from inexpensive to true value.

Note: The management of Jack Tar Village Resorts chose not to cooperate with the writers of this book. Although we have tried to be honest and unbiased, because they did not cooperate, we were unable to obtain some information that would have helped us complete the reviews more fully.

GENERAL INFORMATION FOR ALL JACK TAR RESORTS

Listed below are the Jack Tar villages reviewed in this book and their locations.

Montego Bay: Jamaica
Royal St. Kitts: Caribbean—St. Kitts

BOOKING INFORMATION: All of the Jack Tar resorts can be booked through your travel agent or directly with:

Jack Tar Village Resorts
1314 Wood Street
Dallas, TX 75202
800-527-9299

CONTACT INFORMATION

Jack Tar Village
P.O. Box 144
Montego Bay, Jamaica, W.I.
809-952-4341

DEPOSITS/REFUNDS: If you book directly, JTV requires a 1-night deposit within 10 days of reservation. Full payment is due within 30 days. Cancellation penalties apply within 7 days of your trip. From 4 to 7 days, they take 1 night's charge. Three days or less costs 2 nights. No-shows get no refund. The package tour companies have their own policies.

RESERVATION SCHEDULE: The winter season tends to book up months in advance with few cancellations. Rooms are reserved by different wholesalers, so if Jack Tar is booked, call several tour operators to see if any have rooms.

STAFF SUPPORT & SERVICE: The resort staff ranged from eager and courteous to indifferent and rude. The Texas booking agents are very friendly and helpful.

JACK TAR VILLAGE, MONTEGO BAY

VITAL FEATURES

Type: **Resort**
Target market: **Couples, families, singles**
Location: **Montego Bay, Jamaica**
All-inclusive cost per week: **$1,050 plus airfare (air packages available through travel agents)**

RATINGS

Value: 💲💲💲

Fun quotient: 🏖️🏖️🏖️

Honeymoon suitability: 🖤🖤

Singles meeting ground: 🧍

Child appeal: 🍦🍦

Management professionalism: ☎️☎️

Service: 💡💡💡

Food: 🦞🦞

THE REAL STORY

Jack Tar Village lies right in the middle of all the beach action of Montego Bay. In some ways, it offers the advantages of an all-inclusive with the excitement of the city. The compound has a private beach and grounds that are open to guests only. Guests wear a photo ID badge, which lets the staff know that they are entitled to eat, drink, and participate in the activities. Just outside the gate, the real

Jamaica beach town presents itself, with shops, clubs, local restaurants, and the straw market.

The resort itself was marred by shoddy maintenance at the time of our visit in early 1989. For example, the tiles in the dining room appeared cracked, chipped, or missing. The guest rooms looked worn and the common areas needed renovation as well. In our opinion, all the furniture would have been discarded long ago by any of the SuperClubs or Sandals resorts.

Do the guests care about the apparent lack of maintenance? In most cases they were just happy to be in Jamaica on a vacation that they could afford. The ones we met said that they were having a great time just lying out on the soft sand, drinking cold libations, and enjoying the weather. Many also enjoyed the proximity of the town.

The on-site activities directors exude energy and concern for the guests. The resort lacked the deluxe sports facilities available at other clubs, but again, guests did not seem to care much. JIV does not seem to draw the sports fanatic crowd. Guests just want to relax, play a few games of volleyball and water polo, or take out a sailboat now and again.

The beach at Jack Tar is divided into two parts. The larger portion is held in by a seawall (you climb down a ladder into the water), while the shorter section, used to launch sailboats, slopes down into the sea. The walled beach is too deep for wading but is better for swimming. A couple of anchored floats give swimmers a good destination where they can hang out and catch some rays.

INCLUDED

Accommodations	Sports
Activities	Taxes
Airfare (very often)	Tips
Drinks	Tours
Food	Transfer to and from airport

VALUE

The quality of Jack Tar does not compare to that of the Sandals or SuperClubs resorts. If you can't afford one of those resorts, you might find JTV a good deal. This is especially true if you get a super deal on an air/land package. However, if you plan to scuba dive, the extra charges will bring you over what you would have paid at one of the better resorts that include it.

ACTIVITIES, SPORTS, & EXCURSIONS

Activity directors offer plenty to do for those who desire physical activities. They will also organize games on an ad hoc basis. Interest varies from week to week. In general, JTV guests just want to relax, and they are left alone to do just that. Many of the more spirited souls seek their adventures off the resort, using the village for meals and sports.

The following activities are offered, if guests show sufficient interest. A daily activity sheet lets you know what is available.

ACTIVITIES

Arts & crafts	Mixology classes
Dancing	Movies
Entertainment/shows	Sunbathing

At extra cost, the tour desk will arrange a ride on a glass-bottomed boat.

SPORTS: Abundant water sports are offered on the premises or five minutes away via shuttle bus. Sailing, windsurfing, and waterskiing can be done in unlimited quantities. Guests can borrow snorkeling equipment to view nearby reefs. Instructors teach scuba diving, but the actual diving trips and equipment rental costs are extra.

Aerobics/exercise classes	Swimming
Badminton	Tennis
Bicycles	Volleyball
Sailing (Sunfish)	Waterpolo
Shuffleboard	Waterskiing
Snorkeling	Windsurfing

ITINERARY & DAILY SCHEDULE

Guests usually come on a one-week package tour. The activities and menus follow the weekly cycle.

Rooms are booked in packages or by the night. The proximity to the airport makes this an easy place to come to for a long weekend.

NIGHTLIFE & ENTERTAINMENT

After dinner, guests may gain free entry into an adjacent nightclub, which is also open to the public. Vouchers buy drinks at the bar. The mix of tourists with a few locals at the club provides a fairly unique atmosphere for an all-inclusive. It also gives singles a chance to meet tourists who are not staying at JTV.

AESTHETICS & ENVIRONMENT

The internal layout lends itself well to the all-inclusive concept. The dining room provides a perfect example of the potential of Jack Tar's Montego Bay resort. The large, airy room overlooks the water, beach, sunbathers, and boat traffic. Truly romantic. Similarly, the guest rooms are generally well laid out, and some have good views, but they are in need of a little freshening up.

FACILITIES

Bank	Entertainment coordinators
Bars (3)	Gift shop
Beaches	Medical station
Beauty salon	Safety-deposit box
Casino	Snack bar, grill
Concierge	Swimming pool
Disco	Water sports center

ROOMS

All the rooms have air-conditioning and the oceanfront rooms have great views. The rooms themselves provide all the essentials necessary for comfort. The furniture and maintenance are comparable to those in a budget beach hotel in the States.

LUXURY LEVEL

Air-conditioning	Maid service
Clock	Phone in room
Laundry service (extra)	Porter service

FOOD & DRINK

The resort serves tasty food of reasonable quality. The wide selection and almost unlimited quantities (you can order seconds) will give you all you need or want. Wine is served with dinner, and you can always bring your drinks from the bar. The service staff does a good job of keeping people happy. Authentic Jamaican "jerk" chicken and pork, not found in any tourist restaurant or resort, lies just outside the resort. The beach bar serves tropical drinks, sodas, and beer. Just show your ID and you can get as much as you want.

STAFFING & SERVICE

The Texas booking agents are extremely helpful. The on-site staff display typical Jamaican traits of warmth and congeniality, although they work at a fairly lethargic pace.

PRIVACY & RELAXATION

Jack Tar provides an oasis in the middle of Montego Bay. Here, the only noises you hear are the waves and the ocean breeze. There is no irresistible push to get involved in activities and sports.

SHOPPING

The resort is located in the middle of a long shopping strip. The stores sell jewelry, coffee, T-shirts, and other souvenirs. The mini straw markets in the back alleys often have the nicest art and woven goods at the best prices. Jack Tar's location gives you ready access to all this. In addition, there is a gift shop just outside the gate that, while offering good prices, has rather dull merchandise.

HONEYMOONERS

Couples on tight budgets might find this a good alternative. The management will arrange a wedding, but with less finesse than some of Jamaica's other resorts.

SINGLES

While not geared toward singles, Jack Tar provides a good vacation for them. If the ratios on the resort don't go your way, you aren't stuck. All of the nightlife of Montego Bay is open to you, including the adjacent nightclub, which will give you cover and drinks for free.

CHILD APPEAL

There are no special areas or supervised activities for kids.

NUTS & BOLTS

BOOKING INFORMATION: See Jack Tar introduction, page 109.

CONTACT INFORMATION

Jack Tar Village
P.O. Box 144
Montego Bay, Jamaica, W.I.
809-952-4340

CURRENCY: The front desk will change your U.S. or Canadian dollars into Jamaican dollars.

DEPOSITS/REFUNDS: See Jack Tar introduction, page 109.

HANDICAP ACCESSIBILITY: The resort has ramps and elevators, but there are no rails in the bathrooms.

PACKING: The dress is very casual. There is only a "no shorts or tank tops" policy for dinner.

RELIGIOUS SERVICES: Nearby.

RESERVATION SCHEDULE: See Jack Tar introduction, page 109. The winter season tends to book up months in advance with few cancellations. Rooms are reserved by different wholesalers, so if Jack Tar is booked, call several tour operators to see if any have rooms.

NUMBER OF ROOMS: 128.

NUMBER OF EMPLOYEES: Not available.

SPENDING MONEY: You need very little. A few hundred dollars could buy several very nice pieces of art.

Cost Worksheet

	High Season[1]	Off-Season[2]
Accommodations		
(7 days)[3]	$1,050	$980
Food	incl.	incl.
Drinks	incl.	incl.
Departure tax	$10	$10
Sports	incl.	incl.
Airfare (packages with airfare are often available)	_____	_____
Sight-seeing		
Tips	incl.	incl.
Additional & sports[4]		
Souvenirs	_____	_____

[1] High season dates: Christmas to Easter
[2] Off-season dates: Easter to Christmas
[3] Premium for single person: $190 per night (high season), $1,330 per week (high season); $180 per night (off-season), $1,260 per week (off-season).
[4] Offered for extra charge: laundry service; nighttime baby-sitting, $3 per hour; scuba, $30 per dive, including equipment.

SANDALS CLUB RESORTS INTRODUCTION

THE REAL STORY

Five Sandals Club resorts rest along the shores of Jamaica—three in Montego Bay and two new resorts in Negril and Ocho Rios. Each accepts only couples, but the feel differs at every location. The following reviews describe the general concept and the unique atmosphere of the three Montego Bay Sandals: Carlyle on the Bay, Montego Bay, and the Royal Caribbean. Workers were reportedly putting the finishing touches on the Negril resort at the time this book went to press.

Sandals is designed, run, and marketed for couples—male and female pairs only; all attract a high percentage of honeymooners. Other guests come to celebrate anniversaries, to renew their vows, or to get married. Some just come to enjoy life. The couples concept allows busy people to spend time together in an atmosphere away from children, telephones, and other constant interruptions.

Guests range in age from young twenties to seventies, with the majority of people in their mid-twenties. Couples in their thirties, forties, fifties, and sixties will find plenty of company, along with ample activities geared to them. Older couples frequently come in groups. Repeat guests often bring friends with them.

Montego Bay and Royal Caribbean guests enjoy full reciprocal use of the resorts. The properties are geographically close, and a shuttle bus will take you between the two. It runs only during the day, but an evening taxi ride between the two only costs a few dollars. You probably won't want to commute, but you may wish to see what the other campus is like. Guests at the lower-priced Carlyle property do not have the same privileges because, as one manager said, "Everyone would pay the low rates here and spend all their time at the other resorts."

ACTIVITIES, SPORTS, & EXCURSIONS

Playmakers, the friendly young Jamaican staff, organize sporting events and activities. They create the theme nights, such as Buccaneers and Wenches, Grecian Night, Formal Night, a beach party, and a King Neptune celebration. Sports competitions range from water volleyball to boccie (lawn bowling). Other popular activities include drinking, dancing (including reggae dancing lessons), card games, and talent shows.

116

Jason's Tips:

On talent night, the band will back you up and make you sound like a professional. Ask in advance and they'll make a video tape of you with your own calypso or reggae band. Customary taxi rates from the resort into town and to other destinations are posted, but you must bargain for your fares. Fix the cost in advance or you are begging for a fight at the end.

ITINERARY & DAILY SCHEDULE

Activities are structured but optional. No one will come to your door and drag you to an event. You can miss a lot if you don't look around and seek out the fun.

Sandals gives bottles of inexpensive champagne to those guests celebrating an anniversary; if you want a special bottle, bring it from home. Birthday girls and boys get a cake.

NIGHTLIFE & ENTERTAINMENT

Each Sandals resort has nightly entertainment. Montego Bay and Royal Caribbean have A. J. Brown, a dynamic singer who is touted as Jamaica's number-one cabaret act. The Carlyle has smaller, more mellow, bands that fit with its size.

FOOD & DRINK

The food at the resorts tends to be similar. You choose your own breakfast and dinner from a large and varied display. A waiter then takes your plates to a table. You get your own drinks at the bar and bring them up to the table. Many of the employees eat in the same dining room as the guests. These include Playmakers, administrative personnel, and PR folk. This adds to the experience.

STAFFING & SERVICE

Natives joke about "Jamaican time," which means anytime from 10 minutes to half an hour after an event is scheduled. The Sandals staff, however, get meals and events together promptly at the appointed time. They are extremely friendly and well trained. Almost everyone on-staff is Jamaican. Management strongly encourages staff loyalty by such policies as helping them buy houses, for example. Many of the employees worked at other places first, then came to Sandals for the pay and benefits.

Management really stresses service. It is sometimes slow, by American standards, but is almost always friendly. In general, management can be given high marks for its professionalism. An example of this is the way that it reconfirms your departing flight. If it is running late, they keep you at the resort, feed you, and entertain you until your plane is ready to take off. Sometimes couples are offered a hospitality suite to shower in after swimming during a flight delay.

HONEYMOONERS

Nothing special is done for honeymooners because they comprise the majority of the guests. Still, these are special places to spend a honeymoon.

WEDDINGS

Many people choose to get married at Sandals. Sandals Royal Caribbean has hosted over 250 weddings in two years, while Montego Bay boasts of over 500 in seven years. By having a small service at the beginning of their honeymoon, couples save the hassle and expense of a big wedding, and go home with memories of having been married on a beautiful tropical island.

You can pick your spot from several beautiful gardens; some couples even get married at sea. If you are Catholic, you need a letter from your priest back home. If this is a second marriage, be sure to bring divorce papers. If one or both of you are widowed, you need the proper death certificate. A wedding package at Sandals costs $150 (U.S. currency) and includes the following:

Document processing	1 picture
Minister	Videotape
Wedding cake	Witnesses
Champagne	

NUTS & BOLTS

BOOKING INFORMATION: Any travel agent can book you. They can usually get you good air/land rates. For further information on a particular resort or to obtain a brochure, call the following:

Unique Vacations
7610 S.W. 61 Avenue
Miami, FL 33143
305-284-1300
800-327-1991

DEPOSITS/REFUNDS: Full payment is due 30 days prior to scheduled arrival day. For a refund, reservation cancellations must be received 21 days prior to your scheduled arrival day. If you are not happy (highly unlikely) they'll try to accommodate you at another Sandals resort.

PACKING: Sandals. You will wear these most of all. Bring one set of nice clothes. In Jamaica, formal means long cotton pants and a collared shirt for men. Women need no more than a nice sundress, but some break out the leather skirts in anticipation of a night in the disco. Whether or not you are married, Sandals is a honeymoon. It's OK to dress for your significant other. You can also walk around barefoot most of the time. Sandals has tennis rackets, scuba equipment, and other sports paraphernalia. If you want to bring your own, do so. They'll lend you what you don't have. Other items to bring include mosquito spray (we recommend 100 percent deet for guaranteed protection) and a cassette player for beach and pool use.

RESERVATION SCHEDULE: Rooms for the winter tend to sell out quickly. Space is easier to get in the summer and during the off-season.

All rates per person, based on double occupancy for a seven-night stay.

Always ask if any special packages, promotions, or airfare discounts are in effect before booking.

All vacations described in this guide can be booked through any competent travel agent; we advise you to do so.

See the general introduction and area introductions for more details.

SANDALS CARLYLE ON THE BAY

VITAL FEATURES

Type of vacation: **Resort**
Target market: **Couples**
Location: **Montego Bay, Jamaica**
All-inclusive cost per week: **$1,395–$1,495 plus airfare**

RATINGS

Value: 💲💲💲💲💲

Fun quotient: 🏖️🏖️🏖️🏖️🏖️

Honeymoon suitability: ❤️❤️❤️❤️❤️

Singles meeting ground: Not applicable

Child appeal: Not applicable

Management professionalism: ☎️☎️☎️☎️☎️

Service: 💡💡💡

Food: 🦞🦞🦞

THE REAL STORY

Have you ever known a person who lived in the suburbs but always identified with his first city apartment? "No, it wasn't spacious, luxurious, or in the swankiest neighborhood. But it had character and I had the best time of my life there." Carlyle on the Bay will leave you with those type of memories.

The Sandals resort in downtown Montego Bay should really be called Carlyle-across-the-street-from-the-Bay because you have to cross a public street to get to the water. "No problem," as the

Jamaicans would say. The fact that the resort does not have its own beach allows guests to experience Sandals at quite a reduced rate. Although it's somewhat of a stepchild, Carlyle has the charm, feel, and, above all, the spirit of Sandals.

Carlyle offers an urban Jamaican experience. It is located in the middle of all the action of Montego Bay. This small hotel offers an intimacy not found at big resorts. The manager will get to know you within the first day, you will get to know the bartender within the first hour, and in less than a week all the guests become friends with each other.

The small size of Carlyle only applies to the number of rooms and the acreage of the common space. The rooms are ample, and most overlook the courtyard; some have a breathtaking view of the bay.

And the spirit! This is the place to reclaim that spring break atmosphere dulled by a few years or decades on the job. The scene at the bar may remind you of a continuous Christmas party. If you do not want that much revelry, you can escape the noise. In that case, Carlyle becomes a very good, full American plan hotel, which includes all sports and more.

What Sandals Carlyle on the Bay loses by not having its own beach it makes up for in efforts and contortions to provide all the features found in its big sister resorts. It shuttles guests to Doctor's Cave Beach, a semiprivate beach that is one of the best known on the island. It has a little water sports shack across the way that handles all the water sports. On the grounds, it has set up a dry-land beach, complete with a volleyball net.

The bar service at Carlyle exceeds that of most other resorts. The guests quickly come to know and love the bartenders, who are quick, fun, and efficient. The bartenders' specialty drinks are posted on a board, and a lot of people feel compelled to try them all. Why not? They're free.

Any couple from their early twenties on up will have plenty to do and will feel welcome. There are lots of water sports and fountains of booze. A lot of young honeymooners come here for that reason, but older couples will enjoy it too.

INCLUDED

Accommodations
Activities
Airfare
Cigarettes
Drinks
Entertainment & dancing
Food
Room service

Snacks, anytime
Sports
Sports instruction
Taxes
Tips
Transfer to and from airport
Wine with dinner

ACTIVITIES, SPORTS, & EXCURSIONS

Aerobics/exercise class
Badminton
Croquet
Horseshoes
Kayaks/canoes
Pedal boats
Ping-Pong

Sailing (Sunfish)
Shuffleboard
Snorkeling
Tennis (lighted for night play)
Volleyball
Water polo
Windsurfing with instruction

Carlyle on the Bay has a full water sports center except for scuba diving. Across the street from the resort, a water sports hut provides guests with Windsurfers, sailboats, and kayaks. The swimming is done at Doctor's Cave Beach, which is accessible by shuttle or on foot.

Parasailing and jet skiing are offered at a neighboring public beach. Jet skiing costs $35 (U.S. currency) per half hour. Local entrepreneurs also offer waterskiing.

ACTIVITIES

Arts & crafts
Board games
Culture/music/language
    classes
Dancing

Entertainment/shows
Glass-bottomed boat
Movies (2 times daily from
    satellite TV)
Subathing

Other popular activities include reggae dancing lessons, sports competitions such as water polo, and fun games such as boccie.

A player's lounge has constant games of bridge, cards, dominos, and the like. A giant-screen TV is hooked up to a satellite dish. This serves the truly devoted "couch plantains."

EXCURSIONS: For information on excursions, see the Jamaica Introduction and the section on Sandals Montego Bay (pp. 77–78 and 128–129).

ITINERARY & DAILY SCHEDULE:

Guests are accepted on Fridays through Mondays only. A staff member conducts an orientation every day at 5:00 P.M. Attendance is highly recommended so you'll know what's going on.

You may sign up for less than a week in the off-season only. Most North Americans come on the weekend and stay for a week.

NIGHTLIFE & ENTERTAINMENT

The after-dinner entertainment includes active games, dress-up theme nights, and entertainment. The entertainment is geared to the personal size of Carlyle. For example, you would have a small combo here rather than a nightclub act.

AESTHETICS & ENVIRONMENT

Carlyle has the feel of an intimate inn. The rooms are air-conditioned and good-sized. They are decorated very tastefully and are well maintained. The bathrooms are new, as is the furniture. All rooms have air-conditioning, most of them have ceiling fans.

FACILITIES

Bank	Entertainment coordinators
Bars	Gift shop
Beaches	Hot tub
Beauty salon	Medical station
Concierge	Piano bar
Disco	Swimming pools

ROOMS

The rooms are decorated Caribbean style, with twin or queen-size beds. Standard rooms on the ground floor have no patio, but they overlook the pool. The second and third floors have standard and deluxe rooms with balconies and either an ocean or a pool view.

LUXURY LEVEL: Air-conditioning, maid service, porter service, room service.

FOOD & DRINK

Sandals's price includes all you can eat and drink. The hotel serves three meals a day, plus hot dogs and hamburgers at a snack bar.

Guests take their own breakfast and lunch from a large and varied buffet. The chefs do a good job preparing American, Continental, and Jamaican fare. The fish is fresh and the island-grown fruit ripe and sweet.

Dinner is served in a restaurant. In a former life, the restaurant was open to the public and won awards from food critics. It now functions as the dining room for Carlyle, which serves sit-down dinners. The food earns good reviews, although the selection and quality are slightly lower than at the other Sandals resorts.

A rathskeller-type bar adjoins the restaurant. Guests belly up to the bar for a nightly bonding and bombing exercise. The bartenders take care of them very well. An outdoor bar serves the pool and lawn loungers very well.

STAFFING & SERVICE

The staff does a great job of keeping the guests happy. Everyone on-staff, including the general manager, makes an effort to get to know all the visitors. The personal touch adds to the overall experience.

PRIVACY & RELAXATION

Your relaxing will all be done in the resort, which is quite calm during the day. The public beach tends to fill up with Jamaican traders who think nothing of interrupting your nap or reading to sell you a joint or just to talk.

SHOPPING

A small on-site gift shop sells sundries. Craftspeople come into the resort to sell their wares. Right outside the gate, shops and stands sell practically all the goods that can be found in Jamaica. If you like to shop, Carlyle on the Bay offers more opportunities than most of the other all-inclusives, because you can leave the resort anytime you like and be in the middle of the shopping district in minutes.

HONEYMOONERS

Carlyle now only accepts couples. (They used to take singles and children.) A lot of honeymooners on a tight budget come here because you get a quality all-inclusive package for a lot less than at the other Sandals resorts.

NUTS & BOLTS

BOOKING INFORMATION: See the Sandals Club Resorts Introduction, page 118.

CONTACT INFORMATION

Sandals Carlyle on the Bay
P.O. Box 412
Montego Bay, Jamaica, W.I.
809-952-4140

DEPOSITS/REFUNDS: Full payment is due 30 days prior to scheduled arrival day. For a refund, cancellation of a reservation must be received 21 days prior to scheduled arrival day. If you are not happy (highly unlikely), they'll try to accommodate you at another Sandals resort.

HANDICAP ACCESSIBILITY: None.

SIZE: 3 acres.

NUMBER OF ROOMS: 52.

MAXIMUM NUMBER OF GUESTS: 100.

ARRIVAL AIRPORT: Sir Donald Sangster International Airport in Montego Bay.

TRAVEL TIME FROM AIRPORT: 15 minutes.

SPENDING MONEY: You could get by with only the $8 departure tax, but it's best to bring some money for souvenirs and a tour or two. It's hard to pass those shops every day without buying something.

Cost Worksheet	High Season[1]	Off-Season[2]
Accommodations (7 days)	$698–$748	$658–$725
Food	incl.	incl.
Drinks	incl.	incl.
Departure tax	8	8
State tax	none	none
Hotel tax	none	none
Sports	incl.	incl.
Airfare	_____	_____
Sight-seeing		
Tips	none	none
Additional sports		
Souvenirs	_____	_____

[1] High season dates: January 1 to March 30
[2] Off-season dates: March 31 to December 21

SANDALS MONTEGO BAY

Type of vacation: **Resort**
Target market: **Couples only (heterosexual)**
Location: **Montego Bay, Jamaica**
All-inclusive cost per week: **$1,000 plus airfare**

RATINGS

Value: 💲💲💲💲

Fun quotient: 🏝️🏝️🏝️🏝️🏝️

Honeymoon suitability: ♥♥♥♥

Singles meeting ground: Not applicable

Child appeal: Not applicable

Management professionalism: ☎☎☎☎☎

Service: 💡💡💡

Food: 🦞🦞🦞🦞

THE REAL STORY

Sandals Montego Bay is like summer camp for adults. Life revolves around activites, sports, games, merriment, and social life. The large size of the resort and its centralized nature focus people's attention on the activities. Playmakers organize enthusiastic guests into all sorts of competitions. Water sports personnel give instructions in individual sports such as waterskiing and windsurfing. Couples can be found everywhere, paddling kayaks, sailing Sunfish, and as scuba buddies. "Hello Mudda, Hello Fadda . . ."

While the facilities, sports, and activities may look identical to those at the other Sandals resorts, the feel here differs somewhat. People tend to be more outgoing, and competitive, and more in-

126

volved in group activities. Playmakers award miniature leather sandals, which any Sandals veteran recognizes as medals of honor. Crowds of people step up to compete in the games. Does this sound overly strenuous? Naw. Most people keep the fun in perspective. For every grunt of physical exhaustion, you are bound to hear five chuckles.

The 1,700-foot beach accommodates all the guests comfortably, although it sometimes seems crowded because so much activity is going on. Near the water sports center, boats constantly come and go. Farther down, full teams vigorously play volleyball.

Meals and nighttime activities offer a highly engaging experience. Many guests party as hard as they play sports. The Playmakers constantly keep things going, whether the activity is a toga party or A. J. Brown entertaining the guests (and getting them onstage).

With all the activity, can you relax at Sandals Montego Bay? Of course. A long promenade along the coral coast, a lounge chair, or an underwater seat in the pool offer places to hang out. At the far end of the beach, the lounge chairs become more spread out. Here you can just relax in the sun. But make no mistake, when you go to the dining room for your next meal, you'll be right back in the middle of the fun.

Is this a place where former guests would return? They used to offer a free trip after ten visits, but management stopped that practice because too many people qualified.

As do the other Sandals resorts, Montego Bay accepts adult couples only. You'll find singles only on the tennis courts.

INCLUDED

Accommodations	Snacks anytime
Activities	Sports
Airfare	Sports instruction
Cigarettes	Taxes
Drinks	Tips
Entertainment & dancing	Transfer to and from airport
Food	Wine with dinner
Room service	

VALUE

The quantity of activities, food, drinks, and, most important, spirit, makes Sandals Montego Bay an excellent value.

ACTIVITIES, SPORTS, & EXCURSIONS

ACTIVITIES

Arts & crafts	Culture/music/language
Board games	classes

Dancing
Entertainment/shows
Movies

Nude sunbathing
Sunbathing

SPORTS: All the beach personnel are trained as lifeguards, and they tend to get upset if you venture out too far. Formal instruction for the water sports is thorough and competent.

Dive masters take guests to colorful reefs. They run a tight ship that emphasizes safety. The dives are shallow, none over 35 feet. Certified divers and resort course graduates dive together. Several different reefs offer varied underwater terrain. There is a well-run resort course, but it will not get you true certification. The dive instructors are PADI-certified dive masters and instructors, and they will really scrutinize your instruction and dive log.

Divers should register at the scuba desk immediately, because the staff has to check you out the day before you can dive. This is at 2:00 P.M. Don't miss it or you miss a day. This is especially important for people on a three-to-four-day stay.

Group sports lessons are held daily at set times. For individual tennis lessons, make reservations with the pro in advance.

The swimming pools, solar heated to a soothing 85 degrees, are well shaped for laps.

The health club is set up for serious workouts with universal machines and some free weights. It's not tempting enough to make you want to start a program, but you can use it to keep up.

Specialty aerobics classes include "dancersice," "Aquasice," and "joggersice." Other people seem content to spend their weekend involved in "drinkersice," "eatersice," "fantasice," and "romantisice." If you want to "golfersice," your greens fees at a nearby club are covered.

Parasailing and jet skiing are offered for additional cost at a neighboring public beach. Jet skiing costs $35 (U.S. currency) per half hour. There are enough activities to do without them, including waterskiing.

Aerobics/exercise classes
Badminton
Basketball
Croquet
Golf
Horseshoes
Kayaks/canoes
Pedal boats
Ping-Pong
Racquetball
Sailing (Sunfish)

Scuba
Scuba resort course
Shuffleboard
Snorkeling
Swimming
Tennis
Volleyball
Water polo
Waterskiing
Weightlifting
Windsurfing

EXCURSIONS: The following are offered at extra cost; for descriptions, see the Jamaica Introduction (pp. 77–78).

Catadupa Chu Chu village tour
Catamaran cruise to Montego Bay
Kingston
Negril by boat, air, or bus (a long ride), with a stop at Rick's Café
Ocho Rios for shopping and stop at Dunn's River Falls; you get to
    see some Jamaican towns on the way (full day)
Rafting trips (45–60 minutes)
Shopping trips to Montego Bay (half day)
West Coast to Negril
Plantation tours with optional hot-air balloon ride
Horseback riding on beach
Deep-sea fishing
Evening on a riverboat Sunday–Thursday

Guests at the hotel love the *Mary-Ann* "fun cruise." The operators give a guided tour of spectacular coral reefs for snorkeling. An on-board reflexologist administers foot massages. The open bar keeps the liquid flowing in the boat almost as fast as it flows by outside.

ITINERARY & DAILY SCHEDULE

Guests can check in from Fridays through Mondays only. A staff member conducts an orientation every day at 5:00 P.M. Attendance is highly recommended so you'll know what's going on.

Playmakers run events on a weekly schedule, as follows:

Sunday—Formal Night (no shorts at dinner)
Monday—Beach Party Night
Tuesday—Pirates Night
Wednesday—Jamaica Night/Reggae Night
Thursday—Nautical Night
Friday—Toga Night
Saturday—Rock & Roll Night

NIGHTLIFE & ENTERTAINMENT

The after-dinner entertainment varies among active games, dress-up theme nights, and entertainment.

The disco stays open until the last person has left, so it often pulses very late into the night. It has the lights and beat that you would expect of an international disco. Some people pack it in early for a jump on the romancing, but if you want to party hard until 2:30 you're likely to find company.

AESTHETICS & ENVIRONMENT

Sandals opened in November 1981. The resort was renovated at that time, and has been constantly improved since. The bathrooms are new, as is the furniture. All rooms have air-conditioning and most have ceiling fans.

FACILITIES: There are two TV sets for your use in the hotel. Both are hooked up to a satellite dish so you can see some great movies. Sandals Montego Bay has a large and well-stocked gift shop. It's a little more expensive than the outside markets, but you will find quality items without crowds and obnoxious street vendors. Shopping in the gift shop is duty free.

Bank	Entertainment coordinators
Bars	Gift shop
Beaches	Hot tub
Beauty salon	Medical station
Concierge	Piano bar
Disco	Swimming pools (2)

ROOMS

The rooms here vary from ordinary hotel rooms to elegant, spacious private suites. Most rooms overlook the water. Your choice should depend on your budget and how much time you think you will spend in the room. Romantic couples with cash would do well to get the upgrades, but all rooms have king-size beds and all enjoy the same meals and water sports.

Standard: Large room located above the dining room. Side view of ocean, ceiling fans. Budget way to go.

Superior: Original wing of hotel, with balcony or patio overlooking coral beach, hot tubs, and trees.

Deluxe: Newer version of superior rooms.

Deluxe beachfront: Balconies or patios facing water. Central location.

Junior villas: Detached duplex on quiet side of beach. Recently built. Very charming.

One-bedroom villa suite: The perfect honeymoon cottage.

LUXURY LEVEL

Air-conditioning	Phone in room
Clock	Porter service
Hair dryer	Radio
Laundry service	Television in room
Maid service	

FOOD & DRINK

Sandals's price includes all you can eat and drink. There are three meals a day, plus hot dogs and hamburgers and a self-serve fruit bar around the clock.

Guests take their own breakfast and lunch from a large and varied buffet. The chefs do a good job preparing American, Continental, and Jamaican fare. The fish is fresh, and the island-grown fruit is ripe and sweet.

Dinner is served in a small candlelit dining room or on an outdoor terrace lit with street lamps and lights in the trees. Waiters serve dinner at two seatings. The manager collects fine wines and keeps threatening to upgrade the wine served to guests, which presently compensates for quality with quantity.

The Oleander Deck Restaurant serves authentic Jamaican dishes such as pepper pot soup and escovitched kingfish. You must make reservations in advance. Try to make them very soon after you check in, because seating is very limited.

Four bars mix libations that keep your insides cool. The bars also tap kegs of Red Stripe, a Jamaican beer that may become your best friend.

PRIVACY & RELAXATION

It's easy to slip away to the quiet side of the beach, lounge in one of the six Jacuzzis, or swim out to the tanning buoy. But you're likely to see at least a few other people.

If you sleep away the week, you might feel as if you're missing something. You *could* come here for sheer relaxation, but you'd be missing the point.

Sandals Montego Bay's proximity to the airport boosts its noise level somewhat. The staff turns lemons into lemonade by encouraging everyone to wave to the planes—all five fingers! They also request that men kiss their women, and it makes the frequent aerial passings quite fun.

SHOPPING

Seagoing merchants peddle conch shells (some made into horns), beaded necklaces, and just about anything else that you desire. They will also braid your hair at cut-rate prices.

Sandals Montego Bay has a store worth noting for its fashions. Pitagail, the manager, really has an eye for beauty, and the selection is terrific. Ask for her help.

Wander into town to bargain for your souvenirs. That's part of the culture. The shops across from Doctor's Beach offer some nice things. The legitimate stores have the latest selection in reggae tapes.

A resort photographer wanders around snapping pictures of the guests. If he catches you making a kill shot at volleyball, you'll treasure the photo forever.

HONEYMOONERS

Sandals Montego Bay offers a super fun vacation. If that's what you want for your honeymoon, you won't find a better place. Many people would agree with you—because the resort is crawling with newlyweds.

NUTS & BOLTS

BOOKING INFORMATION: See the Sandals Club Resorts Introduction (p. 118).

CONTACT INFORMATION

Sandals Montego Bay
P.O. Box 100
Montego Bay, Jamaica, W.I.
Telephone: 809-952-5510

HANDICAP ACCESSIBILITY: None.

SIZE: 19 acres.

NUMBER OF ROOMS: 234.

MAXIMUM NUMBER OF GUESTS: 468.

TRAVEL TIME FROM AIRPORT: 10 minutes.

SPENDING MONEY: Bring a little extra money for tours and shopping.

Cost Worksheet		
	High Season[1]	*Off-Season*[2]
Accommodations		
(7 days)	$998–$1,148	$913–$1,018
Food	incl.	incl.
Drinks	incl.	incl.
Departure tax	8	8
State tax	none	none
Hotel tax	none	none
Sports	incl.	incl.
Airfare	_____	_____
Sight-seeing		
Tips	incl.	incl.
Additional sports		
Souvenirs		

[1] High season dates: January 1 to March 30
[2] Off-season dates: March 31 to December 21

SANDALS ROYAL CARIBBEAN

VITAL FEATURES

Type of vacation: **Resort**
Target market: **Couples only (male and female pairs), early twenties and older**
Location: **Montego Bay, Jamaica**
All-inclusive cost per week: **$1,000 plus airfare**

RATINGS

Value: 💲💲💲💲💲

Fun quotient: ⛱⛱⛱⛱

Honeymoon suitability: ❤❤❤❤❤

Singles meeting ground: Not applicable

Child appeal: Not applicable

Management professionalism: ☎☎☎☎☎

Service: 💡💡💡💡

Food: 🦞🦞🦞🦞

THE REAL STORY

Sandals Royal Caribbean has created the perfect environment for couples in love. Low colonial architecture, rooms with calm views of the ocean, and spacious, landscaped grounds beget a regal ambience. An active atmosphere allows as much motion as you like, but none that interferes with private moments. Room service for breakfast allows you to continue if you don't want to surface.

The campus of Sandals Royal Caribbean recalls Jamaica's British colonial past. A columned portico leads into a marble entryway. The royal feeling continues throughout, employees address guests as

133

lords and ladies, and afternoon tea comes on a cart with finger sandwiches. Small stretches of beach, parcels of lawn, intimate hot tubs, and a private island offer couples plenty of time alone. The ratio of facilities to guests is uncommonly large. It won't make you feel like Princess Di and Chuck, but you can sun without being bothered by paparazzi.

As with the other Sandals resorts, Royal Caribbean Playmakers organize all sorts of daytime sports and nighttime activities. Many people choose to participate, some quite competitively. A "Royal Tournament" features beach games, raft relays, and the like. There are also lawn games, patois (Jamaican dialect) lessons, reggae dance classes, and competitions for best tan, best chest, and so forth. You can test your pedal boat skills at the aquafest.

The Playmakers will also entertain the guests, and are always available to play a game of Ping-Pong or get up a game of volleyball. (Get a *real* job, right?) They won't drag you out of your lounge chair, however, and there is no pressure to join group activities.

Theme nights keep people entertained after dinner. Buccaneers' Night includes a parade, which varies in look and tone from Toga Night. One night a week, everyone goes out to the island for a barbecue and calypso dance contest, and to watch a woman who dances on broken bottles (unlike people at a college pub, this woman doesn't wear shoes). At the beach party, you get to play games, try limbo, team up for competitions. Friday is Formal Night, with a show.

The crowd here tends to be less intense than that at Sandals Montego Bay. Perhaps this goes with the resort's smaller number of rooms. It does not have Montego Bay's New York pace. Toga parties don't have the same risqué factor. Some people just swim up to the pool bar, find an underwater seat, and park there for the week.

If the other Sandals has rooms, you may switch over. But guests rarely do.

INCLUDED

Accommodations	Snacks anytime
Activities	Sports
Airfare	Sports instruction
Cigarettes	Taxes
Drinks	Tips
Entertainment & dancing	Transfer to and from airport
Food	Wine with dinner
Room service	

VALUE

The quality of the whole package makes Sandals an excellent value.

ACTIVITIES, SPORTS, & EXCURSIONS

ACTIVITIES: In addition to water sports and tanning, popular activities include drinking, board games, TV watching, nightly entertainment, dancing, and sports competitions including water polo and games such as boccie. The player's lounge constantly has games of bridge, cards, dominos, and the like in progress.

Arts & crafts
Board games
Culture/music/language
    classes
Dancing

Entertainment/shows
Glass-bottomed boat
Nude sunbathing
Sunbathing

SPORTS: Sandals's private cove is a great protected area for learning to sail or windsurf. About one third of the cove is too shallow to use, and the rest is too small to really get going on if you are adventurous. The lifeguards get nervous if you go out too far and they will come get you.

The free-form pools lend themselves to splashing and to paddling to the pool bar. Formal instruction for the water sports is thorough and competent. The equipment and instruction are more geared to the beginner. There is no shortage of equipment, but it's a little worn. For free tennis lessons, make reservations with the pro one day in advance. Golfers can tee off to their heart's content. Greens fees are included in the price; only the mandatory cart rental costs extra.

Dive masters take guests to colorful reefs. They run a tight ship that emphasizes safety. The dives are shallow, none over 35 feet. Certified divers and resort course graduates dive together. There are several different reefs, so the underwater terrain is varied. A well-run resort course is offered, but it will not get you true certification. The dive instructors are PADI-certified dive masters and instructors. They really scrutinize your instruction and your dive log. Divers should register at the scuba desk immediately, because the staff must check you out the day before you can dive. This is at 2:00. Don't miss it or you miss a day. This is especially important for people on a three-to-four-day stay.

Parasailing and jet skiing are offered for additional cost at a neighboring public beach. Jet skiing costs $35 (U.S. currency) per half hour. There are enough activities to do without them, including water skiing.

Badminton	Pedal boats	Swimming
Basketball	Ping-Pong	Tennis
Croquet	Sailing (Sunfish)	Volleyball
Golf	Scuba	Water polo
Horseshoes	Scuba resort course	Waterskiing
Jogging trail	Shuffleboard	Weightlifting
Kayaks/canoes	Snorkeling	Windsurfing

EXCURSIONS: The following are offered at extra cost; for descriptions, see the Jamaica Introduction (pp. 77–78).

Cataduppa Chu Chu village tour
Catamaran cruise to Montego Bay
Kingston
Negril by boat, air, or bus (a long ride) with a stop at Rick's Café
Ocho Rios for shopping and a visit to Dunn's River Falls; you get to
    see some Jamaican towns on the way (full day)
Rafting trips (45–60 minutes)
Shopping trips to Montego Bay (half day)
West Coast to Negril
Plantation tours with optional hot-air balloon ride
Horseback riding on beach
Deep-sea fishing
Evening on a riverboat Sunday–Thursday

Guests at the hotel seem to love the *Mary-Ann* "fun cruise." The operators give a guided tour to spectacular coral reefs for snorkeling. An on-board reflexologist administers foot massages. An open bar keeps the liquid flowing in the boat almost as fast as it flows by outside.

ITINERARY & DAILY SCHEDULE

A staff member conducts an orientation every day at 5:00 P.M. Attendance is highly recommended so you'll know what's going on.
    Playmakers run events on a weekly schedule, as follows:

Monday—Buccaneer's Night
Tuesday—Grecian Night
Wednesday—Island Carnival
Thursday—Beach Party
Friday—Regency Evening (formal night with a show)

The weekends tend to be "chillin'" times when guests arrive and decompress, or depart. If you seek to relax, then a long weekend is a good time to come. If you are looking for a whirlwind of activity, then plan to stay for a week, or limit your short stay for the weekdays. Sandals Montego Bay offers a higher level of activity.
    Most people come during weekdays, although guests may arrive any day. Activities are scheduled from weekend to weekend. If you would like to make friends with other couples, this is the way to do it.

NIGHTLIFE & ENTERTAINMENT

The after-dinner entertainment varies among active games, dress-up theme nights, and entertainment.
    The disco goes until the last person has left. The disco at Sandals

Royal Caribbean has the lights and beat that you would expect of an international disco. It is adequately sized to accommodate those who are interested, which varies from week to week. In general, you won't find the hell-bent, party-all-night types here. A lot of people go for late-night swims . . . up to the pool bar. The snack bar is also open late.

AESTHETICS & ENVIRONMENT

The word *charming* describes the Royal Caribbean better than does *luxurious*. The features are not plush, but the resort lacks nothing. It is a bit older than some, but it has character and is extremely well maintained.

Even at 100 percent capacity, the resort feels half empty. There are always plenty of dining tables, empty hammocks slung between trees, splashing spaces in the pools, and lounging spots on the beaches. People queue up only for the waterskiing boat. A flock of peacocks, peahens, and pea chicks wanders around the lawns. They like to perch on the walls surrounding the patios.

The naturally calm bay waters are further protected by a system of jetties and sandbars, which makes a private area for swimming, waterskiing, sailing, and the like. One hundred yards offshore is a little private island, site of a weekly party and, unofficially, the place for private nude sunbathing.

The beautiful dining room is done in British colonial style and is lined with French doors opening to an ocean view. Jamaican art graces the walls of all the common areas.

There are two free-form pools, a large one with a swim-up bar, and a smaller private one. Neither is good for doing laps, but both are large enough for frolicking.

The rooms here complement the natural terrain. No building rises higher than two stories. The first floors all have porches; the top floors, balconies.

FACILITIES

Bank	Hot tub
Bars (4)	Medical station
Beaches	Piano bar
Beauty salon	Snack bar, grill
Concierge	Swimming pools (2)
Disco	Tour desk
Entertainment coordinators	Water-sports center
Gift shop	

Four bars keep refreshments at hand: a beach bar; a piano bar for cocktail hour; a disco bar, which stays open as long as you can stand; and a pool bar. Next to the east pool is also a little cart of drinks. The lawn, pools, and physical facilities are well-groomed and well-maintained.

The biggest contribution made by the health club is that it gets you away from the bars and buffets. It is located in an open-air, shaded setting, away from the wind, but is too hot for a workout except during the morning. Also, it is not equipped with all the modern machines. It does have a sauna, but that seems redundant in Jamaica. Few people seem interested in the health club facilities.

ROOMS

Decorated in pastel, all the rooms have a king-size bed and high ceilings with powerful paddle fans that keep fresh, sea-scented air moving around. It's more refreshing than air-conditioning, and the fans fit in nicely with the colonial architecture.

For all their common charm, the rooms here vary a fair amount. All have private patios or balconies and Jamaican furnishings. The least and most expensive differ in price by about $550 per week. All of the guests eat the same food and use the same facilities. Still, the room service option and the honeymoon nature of the hotel should make room selection important for some couples. The room choices are as follows:

Standard: Located closest to the lobby. In the middle of things. No
    ocean view.
Lanai: Between the tennis courts and main entrance. No ocean
    view but away from the foot traffic flow.
Superior: Close to the lobby and action.
Deluxe: Overlooks main lawn or a small pool. A room overlooking
    the east pool, in this class, may offer the best combination of
    privacy and price because you are close to the small beach and
    small pool, yet out of the main traffic flow.
Deluxe beach: Right on the beach. The extra hundred is worth it,
    because with the view—the water, the boats, the private island,
    and the romantic atmosphere—you probably will want to
    spend a fair amount of time in your room, on the porch . . .
    well, you get the idea.
Junior suite: For that once in a lifetime splurge. It has a private
    sitting room. You can keep the curtains open to the view and
    still have complete privacy. The same applies to the balcony.
    Extravagant. Bright and cheery, this is the type of room that
    you could lounge around in, spending languid moments. You
    won't be able to justify the expense, but you'll make memories
    here.

In general, the first-floor oceanfront rooms have patios with direct access to the beach. The second-floor rooms have a tad better view and breeze. The cost is the same.

LUXURY LEVEL

Air-conditioning	Phone in room
Clock	Porter service
Hair dryer	Radio
Laundry service	Room service
Maid service	Television in room

FOOD & DRINK

You'll never go hungry. Sandals could outfeed a cruise ship. Add the unlimited drink element and you've got the best deal since you were a kid.

If you bring a ravenous appetite to a meal, you can order seconds, thirds, as many entrées as you want. This includes lobsters, steaks, whatever. The gluttony wears thin after the first couple of days. Pace yourself, and eat according to the amount of activity that you do. Then you'll feel fine.

The hearty American-style breakfast includes eggs, bacon, cereal, omelets, juice, and more, with a few local specialties such as mangos and blue mountain coffee added. A Continental breakfast can await you in the morning if you wish. The lunch buffet features meat, seafood, local specialties, sandwiches, salad, and the like. Breakfast and lunch have tropical fruit, mangos, papayas, cantaloupes, watermelons, and other—unrecognizable, but equally fresh—fruit.

The dress for breakfast and lunch is very informal, with shirts for men and shoes for all optional.

The dinner menu offers several choices of fresh fish, seafood, and meat, often from French, Italian, or Jamaican cuisine Americanized. Jamaican specialties are available with some of the spicy punch missing. They'll add it if you ask. The food is pretty good, but not first-class. The dessert table is huge, with cakes, flan, and rice puddings; it's quite good and very extensive.

The chefs make a seven-course Jamaican cuisine dinner for a maximum of 20 people per sitting. They offer this on Fridays, Saturdays, Sundays, and Tuesdays. Sign up early and chow down.

A beachfront snack bar serves burgers, fries, fruit, and drinks in the afternoons and late evenings. The pool bar has a heated case ready with Jamaican meat pies and other native snacks.

PRIVACY & RELAXATION

Sandals Royal Caribbean offers plenty of corners for two, and room service always offers the option of dining alone. Of the three Montego Bay Sandals resorts, Royal Caribbean offers the quietest atmosphere and the most places to lounge. Hammocks swing between the palms of the gardens. On the beach and at the pools, Playmakers organize activities for those who want to partake. They usually get enough people to have fun, but do not push the others. If you are sports oriented, you can go all day. Other people just hop between the bars. This can be a great place to come to if you are looking for some quiet and like to read books while looking over the ocean.

SHOPPING

Seagoing merchants peddle conch shells (some made into horns), beaded necklaces, and just about anything else that you desire. They will also braid your hair at cut-rate prices.

The gift shop sells some of the same merchandise found in town, from trinkets to fashion, at hotel prices. It is fairly small, however. Sandals Montego Bay has a store worth noting for its fashions. Pitagail, the manager, really has an eye for beauty, and the selection is terrific. Ask for her help. Wander into town to bargain for your souvenirs.

The resort photographer takes portraits that are truly first rate in terms of composition. You can expect to get several that are album quality. At $6 per shot, the price is quite reasonable.

HONEYMOONERS

The physical layout, activities, and couples-only nature of Sandals make it ideal for a honeymoon. The little nooks, lawns, beaches, and pools lend themselves to snuggling in twosomes. Even at full capacity, the place only seems half crowded. Here you can always find a pool, hammock, or beach where you can be alone.

Without exception, the honeymooners that we encountered were convinced that they had made the right choice of honeymoon destination. The only faint gripe we heard was from one young bride who wished that they had rented an oceanfront suite.

Private balconies and large rooms overlook gentle ocean views of boats anchored in the harbor and off the private beach. Sandals Royal Caribbean remains one of the few resorts that offer room service. People tend to wake with the sun, but you don't have to get out of your bed until lunch.

NUTS & BOLTS

BOOKING INFORMATION: See the Sandals Club Resorts Introduction (p. 118).

CONTACT INFORMATION

Sandals Royal Caribbean
P.O. Box 167
Montego Bay, Jamaica, W.I.
Telephone: 809-953-2231

HANDICAP ACCESSIBILITY: No special facilities, but doors are wide enough for wheelchair access.

RELIGIOUS SERVICES: None are offered on the property.

SIZE: 10 acres.

NUMBER OF ROOMS: 170.

MAXIMUM NUMBER OF GUESTS: 340.

TRAVEL TIME FROM AIRPORT: 10 minutes.

SPENDING MONEY: Bring money for souvenirs and tours.

Cost Worksheet

	High Season[1]	Off-Season[2]
Accommodations		
(7 days)	$998–$1,148	$913–$1,018
Food	incl.	incl.
Drinks	incl.	incl.
Departure tax	8	8
State tax	none	none
Hotel tax	none	none
Sports	incl.	incl.
Airfare	_____	_____
Sight-seeing		
Tips	incl.	incl.
Additional sports		
Souvenirs	_____	_____

[1] High season dates: January 1 to March 30
[2] Off-season dates: March 31 to December 21

SUPERCLUBS
INTRODUCTION

THE REAL STORY

The SuperClubs of Jamaica offer a range of resorts on Jamaica's sandy north shore. Each of the four resorts caters to a different demographic group, and each has a unique personality. The marketing department jokes that singles meet at Hedonism II, get married at Couples, celebrate their anniversaries at Jamaica Jamaica, and bring their kids to Boscobel Beach. Considering the consistent quality of the resorts, and the wide range of activities that they offer, you could easily follow that scenario and not get bored.

Even though each of the SuperClubs has a different character, they share certain traits. They all come close to offering a completely all-inclusive vacation. If you wanted, you could wine, dine, tour, sport, and party without spending anything other than the departure tax. All scuba diving, sports lessons, and equipment come with the package. The management pays meticulous attention to every detail, including food quality, grounds and facilities maintenance, and decoration. The staff exudes warmth and personality.

 Jason's Tips:

The cooks or buffet staff will spice your food as their mother would prepare it, but the Jamaican food at the resorts is no substitute for absolutely authentic "jerk" chicken or pork found in Ocho Rios.

With advance notice, the chefs will try to accommodate any dietary restrictions, including low cholesterol, low calorie, vegetarian, and kosher.

NUTS & BOLTS

BOOKING INFORMATION: Book through your travel agent. Several tour wholesalers have air/land packages at special rates.

DEPOSITS/REFUNDS: If you decide that the SuperClub that you selected does not meet your expectations, you may transfer to any of the other SuperClubs if it has room. The excellent food, service, amenities, and activities make this unlikely. If, however, you want a more romantic atmosphere, you would go to Couples. If you want more singles or rowdiness, try Hedonism II. Late teenagers may find more companionship at Boscobel Bay. Those seeking a cultural experience mixed with an active life-style will choose Jamaica Jamaica.

Check with your travel agent to find out the deposit and refund policy of the air charter company involved. Also, make sure that the charter company has insurance, an escrow arrangement with a bank, or some other plan to safeguard your money.

All rates per person, based on double occupancy for a seven-night stay.

Always ask if any special packages, promotions, or airfare discounts are in effect before booking.

All vacations described in this guide can be booked through any competent travel agent; we advise you to do so.

See the general introduction and area introductions for more details.

BOSCOBEL BEACH

VITAL FEATURES

Type of vacation: **Club**
Target market: **Families with children, single parents or grandparents with children**
Location: **Oracabessa, Jamaica (near Ocho Rios)**
All-inclusive cost per week: **$2,000 (for a family of four) plus airfare**

RATINGS

Value: 💲💲💲💲💲

Fun quotient: ⛱️⛱️⛱️⛱️⛱️ ⛱️⛱️⛱️
(children)   (adults)
Honeymoon suitability: Not applicable

Singles meeting ground: 👤👤👤👤👤

Child appeal: 🍦🍦🍦🍦🍦

Management professionalism: ☎️☎️☎️☎️

Service: 💡💡💡

Food: 🦞🦞🦞

THE REAL STORY

Boscobel (rhymes with Taco Bell) caters to families with children. Management understands what children want and what parents need. And it provides just that. More than just tolerating children, the staff treat them as special guests. Because two children under age 14 stay free when sharing a room with adults, this vacation becomes fairly economical for a family.

Located close to Ocho Rios on the northeast coast of Jamaica, this resort seems to be carved out of the mountainside. *Boscobel* means "beautiful garden" in old Spanish, and the resort lives up to its name, offering breathtaking views of the beach and water from almost everywhere. Guards patrol the compound, making sure that no unauthorized person enters or leaves. Children have the freedom to choose their own activities, and parents can rest assured that their offspring are safe. The all-inclusive concept works exceptionally well for children, because they can get something to eat or participate in a sport without having to bug their parents for money or a ticket. It also gives parents time off alone and undisturbed. Also, parents are rarely put in the position of having to say no, because the children's safety is guarded by the club staff. For children under 16, there are enough others their age to allow them to form friendships.

The hotel provides activities and supervision for infants to adults—and everyone in between. Children have care, sports, and food. Adults can participate in sports, with or without their kids, or can relax by the pool. Quality family time can be found at dinner or in the evenings, *if* you can tear your kids away from their group of friends.

Boscobel's "country club by the sea" slogan seems appropriate. There are four excellent tennis courts. You must ride 30 minutes to get to the golf course, which is located at one of the other SuperClub properties, Jamaica Jamaica, but it is set by the water, and the ride is fairly enjoyable. Boscobel is a good choice for duffers with kids, whether or not they want to take them out onto the links, since all greens fees are included.

Think of Boscobel as a summer camp that you can share with your kids.

INCLUDED

Accommodations	Sports
Activities	Sports instruction
Child care	Taxes
Cigarettes	Tips
Drinks	Tours
Entertainment & dancing	Transfer to and from airport
Food	Wine with dinner

 Jason's Tips:

You can maximize the return on the airfare by leaving the Boscobel campus to experience Jamaica. The Meet the People program offers your best opportunity to turn this trip into a cultural and educational experience. See the Jamaica Introduction (pp. 76–77) for details.

VALUE

Other vacations may cost less, but you'd be hard-pressed to find one offering better value. The policy that allows kids to stay free makes the stay fairly economical.

ACTIVITIES, SPORTS, & EXCURSIONS

FOR KIDS AGES 3–5

Arts & crafts
Beach games
Glass-bottomed boat ride
Mousercise
Nature walk/pony rides
Picnic
Quiet time

Reggae dance classes
Sandcastle contest
Story time
Talent show
Toys
Treasure hunt

FOR KIDS AGES 6–12

Arts & crafts
Beach games
Bicycle tours
Computer games
Donkey ride
Glass-bottomed boat tours
Hat making
Hopscotch-limbo lessons
Indoor games
Movies in room
Patois classes

Ping-Pong
Pool games
Pool table
Reggae dance classes
Scavenger hunt
Shell hunting
Talent/fashion show
Tennis lessons
Television
Video games

FOR TEENS

Cricket
Movies in room
Photo exposition
Picnic
Ping-Pong

Pool table
Pool olympics
Sailing clinic
Television/movies
Tennis clinic

FOR ADULTS

Board games
Mixology classes
Patois classes

Reggae dancing lessons
Television/movies

FOR FAMILIES

Arts & crafts
Board games

Culture/music/language
    classes

Dancing
Entertainment/shows
Glass-bottomed boat tours

Movies
Tours

SPORTS

Aerobics
Bicycles
Cricket
Golf
Jogging trail
Kayaks
Kite flying
Pedal boats
Pool olympics
Sailing (Sunfish)

Scuba
Snorkeling
Soccer
Swimming (lap pool)
Tennis (4 lighted courts)
Volleyball
Water polo
Weight room (Nautilus and
    free weights)
Windsurfing (Mistral School)

EXCURSIONS

Dunn's River Falls (nominal
    entrance fee plus tip for
    guide)
Kingston visit (extra)

Ocho Rios shopping excursion
Prospect Plantation & White
    River Gorge
River rafting trip (extra)

ITINERARY & DAILY SCHEDULE

Arrivals are accepted every day of the week. Sunday is Caribbean
Night, the highlight of the week.

NIGHTLIFE & ENTERTAINMENT

After dinner, a nightclub singer or native dancers present family
entertainment. The limbo dancers and fire-eaters capture the attention of young kids and adults. All this leaves the teens a bit restless
(but what doesn't?). A kids' disco plays songs early in the evening. At
eleven, it spins records for late teens and adults. A piano bar is
restricted to adults only. The evenings, which are usually cool and
clear, lend themselves to after-dinner strolls.

AESTHETICS & ENVIRONMENT

Boscobel looks like a Florida resort that you might see in a 1950s
vintage movie. Built in a horseshoe shape overlooking the water,
boardwalks connect the lanai rooms. Junior suites overlook the pool
and the water. The circular dining room, used for night dining, has a
high arched opening that leads to an outdoor terrace and a view of
the ocean.

In general, staff members do an excellent job of maintaining the common areas. The management constantly replaces the carpeting and furniture in rooms that seem, to the nonhotelier's eye, spartan, sturdy, and childproof.

FACILITIES

Bank	Medical station
Bars	Piano bar
Beach	Pool
Beauty salon	Safety-deposit box
Disco	Snack bar and grill at beach
Gift shop	Water-sports center
Hot tubs	

ROOMS

For two people, or two plus a small child in a crib or a rollaway bed, the Upper Lanai rooms are better than the Lower Lanai rooms. They are larger, have an above-the-treeline view, and are away from the smoke of the beach grill.

Junior Suites can accommodate up to two adults and two children. These have double beds and a sunken living room with a fold-out couch. They also have large private balconies, which overlook the pool and the ocean. All have large, private balconies. Mountain View Junior Suites can be had for the price of the cheaper Lanai rooms. They are a bit smaller than the other Junior Suites, but recommended for families on a budget. The time you spend on your private balcony will probably be minimal anyway.

Unfortunately, the bathrooms contain no electrical outlets. The bedrooms have a desk with a mirror, but bring an extension cord for your razor or curling iron because the outlets in some rooms are far from the mirror.

LUXURY LEVEL

Air-conditioning	Porter service
Laundry service (extra)	Radio
Maid service	Refrigerator in room
Phone in room	Television in room

FOOD & DRINK

Boscobel serves American-style cuisine that will always provide something acceptable for picky eaters. Adults will probably think that the food ranges from very good to somewhat bland. Breakfast and lunch are served buffet style. Breakfast consists of all the traditional favorites—juice, cereal, eggs, pancakes, rolls. At lunch they sometimes serve tasty Jamaican specialties, along with the type of food that can be found at an American family restaurant. Included dinners feature Continental cuisine, available in a full-service setting or from a buffet. Lobsters, steaks, and ribs highlight the week, with fish, spaghetti, and chicken comprising the usual fare.

Drinks flow plentifully and can be found everywhere. Kids are served a myriad of nonalcoholic cocktails and shakes, while adults imbibe similar ones with an optional kick. Bars, which are fully stocked with name-brand liquor, serve drinks on the veranda, close to the pool, and on the beach level. A grill, also located on the beach level, serves somewhat greasy American-style fast food.

STAFFING & SERVICE

The staff does an excellent job of letting kids have fun *safely*. Its members have the mentality and temperament of good camp counselors.

PRIVACY & RELAXATION

You can be as busy or as lazy as you wish. Your kids might even ignore you once they get hooked up with some other kids and the staff.

The layout, including common decks for most rooms and the large common areas, lends itself better to child supervision than to adult privacy. Louvered room doors limit sound privacy. Room doors do not lock from the inside (this would prevent entry by children with keys).

SHOPPING

Ocho Rios offers a straw market for trinkets and crafts. Try the Ocean Center for shops selling Jamaican hand-painted dresses and fashions, although you might miss the fun of haggling.

HONEYMOONERS

Unless your ideal honeymoon palace includes minimal privacy and lots of kids, go somewhere else.

SINGLES

This is not the place for swinging singles, although it may be just right for single parents.

CHILD APPEAL

Boscobel is designed for families. Food, activities, and facilities are geared around the kids, but adults will still find plenty to do. There are better places to go if you have no kids, but no better place to go if you have them.

Following Jamaican laws and customs, guests over 15 years of age are charged as adults and are treated like adults. They may drink and participate in all activities. Our observations indicated that the freedom given young adults made them more responsible. We saw no incidence of drunkenness or rowdiness among adults of any age.

Jason's Tips:

Guests 16 years and older fall into the gap between kids and adults. Unless they come as a group and content themselves with water sports, they might feel a little out of place. Families with only high school—age and college-age children should consider going to Jamaica Jamaica.

NUTS & BOLTS

CONTACT INFORMATION

Boscobel Beach
P.O. Box 63
Ocho Rios, Jamaica, W.I.
809-974-3330
800-247-3733

HANDICAP ACCESSIBILITY: The elevator and service ramps can take you almost everywhere. Steep inclines make self-propulsion difficult.

PACKING: Go light, because you will spend 90 percent of your time in your swimsuit and flip-flops. You need one pair of rubber-soled shoes for the Dunn's River Falls tour. Casual-formal outfits are appropriate in the dining room, which means a shirt with collar and long pants for men. Women need nice summer dresses. Jackets and ties look ridiculous in this climate. Bring tennis and golf shoes if you plan to participate in these sports. An old T-shirt is recommended for diving. Leave your diving equipment, including booties, at home; warm-water gloves are optional. The water sports department provides everything. Windsurfing gloves and booties help if you have them. Sunglasses are a must.
    Laundry service is available, but is slow and very expensive. Bring enough clothing for your stay.

RELIGIOUS SERVICES: The concierge can arrange for a taxi to take you to the services of your choice. The taxi costs extra.

RESERVATION SCHEDULE: The holidays and summer months are busy. Advance booking is recommended, although rooms can often be had on short notice.

NUMBER OF ROOMS: 208.

Maximum number of guests: 416 adults, 416 children.

Travel time from airport: 1 hour 45 minutes.

Spending money: Other than the departure tax ($8 per person) and a small tip for the guide at Dunn's River Falls, you could get away with spending nothing. But you'd miss the fun of bargaining in the straw market.

Cost Worksheet		
	High Season[1]	*Off-Season*[2]
Accommodations		
(7 days)[3]	$1,250	$1,090
Food	incl.	incl.
Drinks	incl.	incl.
Departure tax	8	8
Sports	incl.	incl.
Airfare	_____	_____
Sight-seeing	incl.	incl.
Tips	incl.	incl.
Additional sports[4]		
Souvenirs	_____	_____

[1] High season dates: December 22 to April 27
[2] Off-season dates: April 28 to December 21
[3] Premium for single person: Single parents need only pay the single-person rate and are allowed up to two children free.
[4] Offered for extra charge: Nighttime baby-sitting, $3.50 per hour; massage, $30; scuba certification, $260

COUPLES

VITAL FEATURES

Type of vacation: **Resort**
Target market: **Couples**
Location: **Ocho Rios, Jamaica**
All-inclusive cost per week: **$1,000 plus airfare**

RATINGS

Value: 💲💲💲💲💲

Fun quotient: 🏖️🏖️🏖️🏖️

Honeymoon suitability: 🖤🖤🖤🖤🖤

Singles meeting ground: Not applicable

Child appeal: Not applicable

Management professionalism: ☎️☎️☎️☎️☎️

Service: 💡💡💡

Food: 🦞🦞🦞

THE REAL STORY

Couples is designed for couples: honeymooners, vacationers, anniversary celebrators, sun seekers, any male and female who want to look gaga into each other's eyes for a week or more. This SuperClub resort offers as much activity or solitude as you wish. Beauty and serenity define the grounds. Nothing here will shock you: no funky food, no unwanted noise, no unpleasant surprises. This land-based Noah's ark serves plentiful water sports, delectable shows, well-seasoned activities, and classic food. The atmosphere brings out the best in people, so you will probably make fast friends with other couples.

Don't come here for late-night wildness. You won't find a disco or a

152

toga night. Management offers a nightly show and dancing, but something about the salt air, or maybe the palms, makes couples drift off on their own. After this vacation, you should feel rested and invigorated. Depending on the activities you choose, you will also feel well fed, toned up, pampered, or all three.

We visited Couples Jamaica. Management tells us that Couples St. Lucia is very similar. The feel is much more tropical-American than Jamaican, so it could be located on any one of dozens of beautiful beaches anywhere in the world.

Couples competes directly with the four Sandals resorts, but the atmosphere here is much more serene. Less emphasis is placed on organized activities and late-night electricity, and Couples includes excursions in its base price.

The beauty remains nothing less than extraordinary, the atmosphere lush and elegant. After more than a decade of operation, Couples has attracted a loyal following of visitors who come on a regular basis. This is truly a resort that you could recommend to a friend.

INCLUDED

Accommodations	Sports instruction
Activities	Taxes
Cigarettes	Tips
Drinks	Tours
Entertainment & dancing	Transfer to and from airport
Food	Wine with dinner
Sports	

VALUE

If you can afford the price of admission, which is competitive, Couples's quality makes it a bargain.

ACTIVITIES, SPORTS, & EXCURSIONS

ACTIVITIES

Arts & crafts	Glass-bottomed boats
Board games	Mixology classes
Culture/music/language classes	Nude sunbathing
	Reggae dance lessons
Dancing	Sunbathing
Entertainment/shows	

SPORTS: Couples boasts extraordinary sports facilities. The pool has a diving board—a rarity in Jamaica. An air-conditioned sports complex surrounds the pool and includes a workout/weight gym, complete with free weights and Nautilus equipment.

Clinics are available for each sport. Even though they occur at set times, the instructors will help you anytime they have a chance.

Golfers can enjoy free greens fees at the Runaway Bay Golf Couse, 45 minutes away. Eighteen well-groomed holes plus an 18-hole putting green await you, but remember to stick your wallet in your plaid pants, because caddies, carts, and club rentals require greenbacks.

Racket sports abound. The resort has five tennis courts, three of which are lighted. New Yorkers love the one-wall handball court. A squash pro conducts daily clinics and gives individual lessons in the air-conditioned squash courts.

The basic horseback ride goes slowly enough for tourist riders, so have no fear if your equestrian experience is limited to watching "Mr. Ed" reruns. The horses amble through the beautiful countryside, where you will see tropical foliage and hilltop views of the ocean. The resort also has a jumping course for serious riders.

The water sports instructors are extremely safety conscious and helpful. Accredited diving instructors (PADI) offer resort and full-certification courses. The windsurfing teachers maintain a Mistral School. At Couples, the kayaks are, of course, built for two. Sunfish and catamarans are available to sailors and those who would like to learn.

 Jason's Tips:

If you are a good rider, talk to the riding supervisor. You may qualify for a 2½-hour trail ride.

SPORTS

Aerobics/exercise classes	Snorkeling
Bicycle	Squash
Golf	Swimming
Handball	Tennis
Horseback riding	Volleyball
Jogging trail	Water polo
Kayaks/canoes	Waterskiing
Sailing	Weight room
Scuba	Windsurfing
Scuba resort course	

Jet skiing and parasailing are available outside the resort for extra cost.

EXCURSIONS: Couples includes several tours in the base price. A two-masted schooner takes guests, buccaneer style, to Pigeon Island. Resort buses also take guests into Ocho Rios for shopping excursions, to Dunn's River Falls (you pay only the nominal entrance fee), to Prospect Plantation, and to White River Gorge. Each tour is worthwhile.

The following trips are offered for an extra charge: Kingston, rafting trips, and a catamaran ride.

ITINERARY & DAILY SCHEDULE

Arrivals are accepted on Friday, Saturday, Sunday, and Monday only.

NIGHTLIFE & ENTERTAINMENT

The night starts with a multicourse candlelit dinner. Afterward, a nightclub act or native show performs on the veranda. The resident band usually starts the night's dancing off with a few slow songs and then feels out the crowd to see if it wants to pick up the pace. The band retires early. Couples can then go to the piano bar for snuggling, sing-alongs, or dancing. This bar offers highballs only, so no whirling blender spoils the atmosphere.

AESTHETICS & ENVIRONMENT

From the moment you arrive at the front entryway, you realize that you are someplace special. The architecture and carefully manicured grounds are stately and calming. Flowers line the veranda and the front lawn. Tropical plants grow everywhere, inside and out. Everything is well conceived and orderly. The hotel complements the natural beauty of the beach and reef; all furniture blends well with the feel of the buildings. During our visit, management showed us plans to refurbish cottages, although they looked almost new. The attention to every detail shows.

The 800-foot beach boasts toe-wiggling-soft sand. A natural reef protects the beach from waves, guaranteeing calm swimming and boating waters. An island 200 yards offshore offers a location where your no-wallet vacation can become no pockets . . . or pants . . . or swimsuit. The island offers not only sun but shady gazebos with hammocks for two.

FACILITIES

Bank	Hot tubs (2)
Bars	Medical station
Beach	Piano bar
Beauty salon	Safety-deposit box
Concierge	Swimming pool
Entertainment coordinators	Water-sports center
Gift shop	

ROOMS

All the rooms have king-size beds and beautiful decor. Go for the ocean view. It's only a few dollars more, and you'll want to spend time on the very private balcony. The fourth-floor rooms have the most style, with parquet entrances, angled walls, and triangular bathtubs. If you desire more space, rooms 203, 204, 205, 303, 304, and 305 are the largest.

The villas off the front lawn have two large bedrooms—each with its own bath—a living room, and a kitchenette with refrigerator. The living rooms and bedrooms have vaulted ceilings with wooden beams and paddle fans. These villas are promoted for two couples. Unless you love to play cards together, this is an acceptable option, but not the best.

LUXURY LEVEL

Air-conditioning	Porter service
Hair dryer	Radio
Laundry service (extra)	Refrigerator in room (in the
Maid service	garden rooms only)

At Couples, *not* having a television or phone in the room is viewed as a luxury.

FOOD & DRINK

Couples serves Continental cuisine expertly prepared by a French chef. Traditional food—steak, lobster, pasta, chicken—arrives on the table year-round. In the winter, the chef prepares more creative "nouvelle cuisine." The elegant dining room hosts a nightly sit-down five-course affair. It will seat you with other couples unless you request a table for two. A barbecue party replaces the formal dinner once a week.

Breakfast features a buffet line for juices, fruit, and cereal. A hot entrée, such as eggs Renais, a Rice Krispies waffle, or an omelet, is brought to the table along with a basket of freshly baked breads and rolls.

If you can eat any more food between breakfast and dinner, the luncheon buffet offers a wide array of entrées, salads, fruits, and desserts.

STAFFING & SERVICE

Management displays a pride in Couples that borders on chauvinism. It treats any request very seriously. Don't hesitate to contact the staff with requests.

Jason's Tips:

Anniversaries and birthdays can be celebrated at no extra cost. Let an organizing staff member know at least one day in advance. They expertly and romantically arrange weddings.

PRIVACY & RELAXATION

You can be as busy or as lazy as you wish. The atmosphere does not lend itself to a flurry of activity. Guests socialize quite a bit, but private moments are respected. Privacy can be found on the island, where you tan all over. Or take a stroll on the front lawns. Or find a nook in the piano bar. Or escape public view while lying on a hammock for two in a gazebo. Here, the guest room balconies are super private, so at night you can stargaze, listen to the ocean, and, you know . . .

SHOPPING

Ocho Rios offers a straw market for trinkets and crafts. Try the Ocean Center for shops selling Jamaican hand-painted dresses and fashions, although you might miss the fun of haggling. The gift shop has a lot of souvenirs, including Jamaican Tia Maria and handiwork. The selection of T-shirts is wide, and the price is only about 20 percent more than you would pay after haggling in Ocho Rios. Be sure to bring back some shirts with Couples's controversial logo. They are available only at the gift shop and are unique enough to be remembered.

HONEYMOONERS

Couples is far from any hustle or bustle, and it is hard to imagine a place more romantic. It was designed for honeymoons. Keep this in mind if you are wild partiers and wish to continue this on your honeymoon—and look elsewhere. Couples offers lots of opportunities for people to enjoy each other. Come here to get to know the one you love.

While many resorts offer weddings, Couples seems to be the Las Vegas of the Caribbean in that it does lots of weddings, sometimes several a day. It's easy to understand why people choose this resort. Marriages are free, including the minister and license. (Optional extras include flowers, $30; videotape, $120; and 24 photographs, $100.) The lawn is ideally set up, with a bridal runway and latticed reception area. Management does an exceptional job taking care of the details. The photographers make use of natural photo situations, for example, the couple on the beach with the island in the background. Also, the hotel itself is romantic. If you choose to get married here, take your bride back to a fourth-floor room and carry her to the sunken bed. The minister mandates that the couple must spend the first two hours behind closed doors.

NUTS & BOLTS

BOOKING & CONTACT INFORMATION: Most travel agencies can book you; try to find one that can give you an air/land package. Air Jamaica tends to have the least expensive flights. Or write or call:

Couples
P.O. Box 330
Ocho Rios, Jamaica, W.I.
809-974-4271
800-858-8009

Cost Worksheet

	High Season[1]	Off-Season[2]
Accommodations (7 days)	$1,120–$1,190	$970–$1,040
Food	incl.	incl.
Drinks	incl.	incl.
Departure tax	8	8
State tax	none	none
Hotel tax	none	none
Sports	incl.	incl.
Airfare	_____	_____
Sight-seeing		
Tips	no tipping allowed	
Additional sports[3]		
Souvenirs	_____	_____

[1] High season dates: December 22 to January 12; January 13 to March 30
[2] Off-season dates: June 30 to August 31. Regular season dates: March 31 to June 29, September 1 to December 21. The hotel offers special spring, summer, and fall rates that bottom out in September.
[3] Offered for extra charge: Golf cart, caddy fees

HANDICAP ACCESSIBILITY: The rooms and public facilities are wheelchair accessible, and the staff will help you overcome any difficulties.

PACKING: Casual dress prevails at all times. See the Jamaica introduction for specifics.

RELIGIOUS SERVICES: Management will make arrangements for you to take a taxi to nearby Christian churches.

RESERVATION SCHEDULE: Couples's occupancy rate runs over 90 percent year-round; it's completely booked during the high season and the spring honeymoon season. Flights can also be hard to come by from some locations. Make reservations as far in advance as possible.

SIZE: 10 acres.

NUMBER OF ROOMS: 152, which accommodate exactly 304 persons at full occupancy, which is the normal condition.

NUMBER OF EMPLOYEES: 250.

TRAVEL TIME FROM AIRPORT: 1 hour 30 minutes.

SPENDING MONEY: You'll need extra money for tours and souvenirs.

HEDONISM II

VITAL FEATURES

Type of vacation: **Resort**
Target market: **Singles, couples, families with members over 16
    years, heathens!**
Location: **Negril, Jamaica**
All-inclusive cost per week: **$1,000 per person plus airfare to
    Montego Bay**

RATINGS

Value: 💲💲💲💲💲

Fun quotient: 🏖🏖🏖🏖🏖

Honeymoon suitability: ❤❤❤

Singles meeting ground: 🧍🧍🧍🧍🧍

Child appeal: Not applicable

Management professionalism: ☎☎☎☎☎

Service: 💡💡💡

Food: 🦞🦞🦞🦞

THE REAL STORY

"Seventy-three lunchtime spins, and the old soldier still didn't
win." This statement demands an explanation. A lunchtime spin, as
any veteran of Hedonism II would know, is a game played at midday,
six days a week. To have participated in 73 of them one would have
had to have made over 12 week-long journeys to Hedonism II. The
old soldier (at the advanced age of 33) hoped that his dozen or so
previous trips would win him the prize for the most visits. The
winner, however, had come 14 times in the decade-plus history of the
club. One guest comes for three months at a time, twice a year.
Hedonism II engenders this type of fanaticism.

Hedonism keeps its converts because it exemplifies active fun, primarily in sports and games. There are superb tennis and squash courts, a basketball court, and water sports galore. To keep the tanned body toned, a gym features free weights and the full spectrum of Nautilus equipment. Each of the athletic facilities has competent and available instructors. If you go with the goal of improving your tennis game you can take two tennis lessons a day. During September, Hedonism II conducts Pro Sports clinics in windsurfing, squash, weightlifting, and tennis. Guest instructors include top professional and Olympic champions.

As good as the competitive sports are, many guests regard them as being secondary to "other pursuits." A returning guest usually brags about the indoor sports or the risqué activity at Toga Night. Continual games offer activities for sports devotees and couch potatoes alike. Lunchtime spins, for example, include reggae lessons, orange passing (neck-to-neck), and balloon popping (the balloons being strategically located inside swimsuits). The staff facilitates merriment, quick acquaintances, and friendships.

Hedonism II has earned its reputation as a resort that does not sleep. Early morning sports fanatics tromp the tennis and squash courts. Activities continue all day. The evening offers entertainment, then time to wade in the ocean surf or bubble in one of the hot tubs (clothing optional). The disco pulses until five in the morning. From the bar you can see the underwater activities in the pool. Typical guests spend three days partying wildly, probably without sleep, then grope for their rooms to get some rest.

People often compare Hedonism II with Club Med. Many diehards have tried both resorts. They return to Hedonism II for a few reasons: the staff speaks English, admission includes all drinks, and ganja is readily available.

The Hedonism II experience can be anything that you want: sports clinic, fraternity party, singles bar, honeymoon heaven, or a combination of the above. Its motto states that pleasure comes in many different forms.

The ratio of single males to females varies weekly and is hard to predict, but usually averages about 50–50. Quite a few couples come as well, especially during the New Year's and Christmas weeks. If you come looking for romance, you might be successful. If you seek fun, you won't go home disappointed.

INCLUDED

Accommodations	Sports
Activities	Taxes
Cigarettes	Tips
Drinks	Tours
Entertainment & dancing	Transfer to and from airport
Food	

VALUE

Quality is very high. The price truly covers everything.

ACTIVITIES, SPORTS, & EXCURSIONS

ACTIVITIES

Arts & crafts	Horseback riding
Board games	Movies
Culture/music/language classes	Nude sunbathing
	Sunbathing
Dancing	Underwater vision boat
Entertainment/shows	

SPORTS: The sports facilities here are world-class: air-conditioned squash courts, a fully equipped gym with free weights and Nautilus, six lighted tennis courts, and all the water sports that you could imagine. Clinics are available for each sport at set times. Instructors are usually helpful and always safety conscious. Diving instructors offer a free resort course that allows guests to dive at the SuperClubs resorts.

Aerobics/exercise classes	Squash
Basketball	Swimming
Bicycles	Tennis
Horseback riding	Volleyball
Jogging trail	Water polo
Sailing (Sunfish)	Waterskiing
Scuba	Weightlifting
Scuba resort course	Windsurfing
Snorkeling	

Other water sports offered by independent operators outside the gate for extra cost include catamaran rides, jet skiing, and parasailing.

EXCURSIONS: There's a bus trip to Rick's Café to watch the sunset ($5). Mopeds can be rented outside the gate ($15 a day after bargaining).

ITINERARY & DAILY SCHEDULE

Guests arrive every day of the week, although most come on the weekends; the club biorhythm keeps pulsing that way.

NIGHTLIFE & ENTERTAINMENT

If you started reading this category first, Hedonism II could be the place for you. There are bars, dancing, and hot tubs, and anything that you could fantasize happens here.

AESTHETICS & ENVIRONMENT

Located on Negril's famous seven-mile beach, Hedonism II occupies a beautiful 22-acre compound. The resort is surrounded by cliffs, woods, and parkland. The horseback tour explores these plus the pristine beaches of Bloody Bay.

The grounds remain true to the trademark of all the Jamaican SuperClubs: immaculate. The beach sand is hard, reminiscent of Daytona Beach in Florida. It makes a firm surface for walking or running (you can also go barefoot or use running shoes). The nude beach is less inviting, as it has coral on the bottom.

FACILITIES

Bank (money changer)
Bars (4, including a nude bar)
Beaches
Beauty salon
Concierge
Disco
Entertainment coordinators
Gift shop

Hot tub (2, 1 nude & 1 prude)
Medical station
Piano bar
Safety-deposit box
Snack bar, grill
Swimming pool
Tour desk
Water-sports center

ROOMS

Picture yourself lying on your bed after a day in the sun. That's not hard at Hedonism II, because the ceilings are mirrored. These are not red-velvet-style tacky rooms, but well-appointed, tastefully decorated, and color-coordinated ones. They just happen to have large mirrors. Rooms come with a king-size bed or two twins. Storage is limited to two small drawers per person, plus hanging wardrobe space. Nothing resembles a formal night here, so two drawers should be able to hold your clothes plus the souvenirs that you buy.

You can request rooms overlooking the nude beach.

LUXURY LEVEL: Air-conditioning, laundry service (extra), maid service, porter service.

FOOD & DRINK

Good and plentiful. The chefs prepare a tasty buffet for all three meals. In addition, snacks are offered during the cocktail hour and at the midnight buffet. Hedonism II serves a combination of Continental and toned-down Jamaican dishes. With the plentiful selection of main courses, salads, and desserts, you should be satisfied at every meal; food is tasty but not gourmet.

Libations are offered at four bars, including Bare Bottom's, at the nude beach, and Cheryl's Pub, the piano bar.

STAFFING & SERVICE

Management is eager to please and responsive. You may contact the activities coordinators or the general management of the hotel with any concerns; the professional, on-site staff is very helpful.

Don't come here for service in the traditional sense. The staff does a good job keeping the mob amused, in check, and well lubricated. Drinks sometimes arrive slowly at the bar. All the meals are served buffet style, with water poured at the table. The dining room staff is very efficient.

PRIVACY & RELAXATION

Couples have private rooms. Management pairs singles with room-mates. The grounds are big enough to give you private space. The atmosphere lends itself to constant socializing.

Sleep is practically nonexistent for some party animals. You can find some quiet sleeping time between the hours of 5:00 A.M. and 7:00 A.M., when the disco closes and breakfast begins, but don't expect to come here for a soothing vacation.

SHOPPING

A number of stands outside the resort sell art, T-shirts, and trinkets. The gift shops at the resort offer the same in a cleaner, less pressured atmosphere. If you stay active in the games, you could win enough bottles of Tia Maria and rum to supply the folks back home.

HONEYMOONERS

If you are looking for sun, sports, beaches, and activities, with the possibility of a wild party, this is the place. If you and your significant other want some quiet time alone, the Couples resort would probably be more appropriate. The atmosphere at Hedonism II also lends itself to other people sometimes hitting on your spouse.

SINGLES

This is heaven for singles.

NUTS & BOLTS

BOOKING & CONTACT INFORMATION: Most travel agencies can book you, and should be able to get you an air/land package. Air Jamaica tends to have the least expensive flights. Often groups book space at preferential rates. Specialty organizations offer packages for like-minded groups. For example, Lifestyles, a company that caters to "swinger" couples, organizes special tours.

Hedonism II
P.O. Box 25
Negril, Jamaica, W.I.
800-858-8009
516-868-6924
809-957-4201 (Jamaica)

HANDICAP ACCESSIBILITY: None.

PACKING: You will spend 90 percent of your time in your swimsuit
and flip-flops, so pack light. Bring jeans and boots (tennis shoes will
do) for horseback riding. Sunglasses are essential.

Leave your jewelry at home. You'll need your neck for your room
key and your hands for drinks. If there is something you must bring,
leave it in the club's safety-deposit box.

Veterans of the nude beach bring their own water floats. The coral
ocean floor makes floating the preferred way to spend the day.

Cost Worksheet		
	High Season[1]	*Off-Season*[2]
Accommodations[3]		
(7 days)	$955	$910
Food	incl.	incl.
Drinks	incl.	incl.
Departure tax	8	8
State tax		
Hotel tax		
Sports	incl.	incl.
Airfare	_____	_____
Sight-seeing	incl.	incl.
Tips	incl.	incl.
Sports		
Souvenirs		
Extra[4]	_____	_____

[1] High season dates: December 15 to May 15
[2] Off-season dates: May 16 to December 14
[3] Premium for single person: Single supplement $50 per night.
[4] Offered for extra charge: beauty salon, gift shop (great stuff), massage
($30).

RELIGIOUS SERVICES: None.

RESERVATION SCHEDULE: The busy winter season usually fills up early. Airplane space to Jamaica can often be hard to book. Advanced booking is recommended.

SIZE: 22 acres.

NUMBER OF ROOMS: 280.

MAXIMUM NUMBER OF GUESTS: 560

TRAVEL TIME FROM AIRPORT: 1 hour 45 minutes.

SPENDING MONEY: You could bring nothing but the departure tax and get by, but $150 will do you for a trip to Rick's, a day's moped rental (to see the town), and souvenirs.

JAMAICA JAMAICA

VITAL FEATURES

Type of vacation: **Resort**
Target market: **Couples, singles, families, 16 years and above**
Location: **Runaway Bay, Jamaica**
All-inclusive cost per week: **Approximately $1,100 to $1,300 (if you shop around you should get an air/land package for that)**

RATINGS

Value: 💲💲💲💲💲

Fun quotient: ☂☂☂☂☂

Honeymoon suitability: ♥♥♥♥

Singles meeting ground: 👤👤

Child appeal: Not applicable

Management professionalism: ☎☎☎☎☎

Service: 💡💡💡💡💡

Food: 🦞🦞🦞🦞

THE REAL STORY

Have you ever said to yourself, "All-inclusives, yech. I want a real cultural experience. I don't want to hang out with a bunch of other gringos/haoles/yankees/(insert pejorative term of your choice here)"? But your other half hears the stories, looks at the brochures, and thinks it might be a great time. "Jamaica Jamaica, the Hotel" may be for you.

The brochure says it best: "Come touch the Jamaica in Jamaica." This SuperClubs resort truly offers a chance to combine your resort vacation with a cultural experience. No, a week's stay here does not resemble a term in the Peace Corps or a trek through the Andes. But

167

you do get to sample Jamaican food, art, language, geography, and above all, climate. Here, you live like an (enlightened) British aristocrat on vacation at his plantation. And if you make the effort to get to know some of the staff people, or take advantage of the Meet the People program (see the Introduction to Jamaica, pp. 76–77), you can combine relaxation and enrichment in your vacation.

Jamaica Jamaica exudes a lighthearted, party atmosphere that is oriented toward activity. Loudspeakers play music during lunch and dinner. All sorts of activities involve the guests. Highlights of the week include Jamaica Night and Pirates Night, each with participatory costumes and games. You have to look hard to find people who don't dress up. Go someplace else if you're looking for a week of quiet relaxation. Jamaica Jamaica reflects not only the culture but also the spirit of the island.

The activity continues on to the beach, where the resort offers more sports and games than you knew existed. Learn to scuba dive, windsurf, sail, or just float in the glass-bottomed boat. The staff constantly organizes other games such as cricket and beach volleyball.

Jamaica Jamaica accepts guests 16 years of age and older. There tend to be a lot of guests in their late twenties, thirties, and forties, but those older or younger would feel comfortable here too. This resort ideally suits couples who are active, both in sports and activities, and families with college-age children. It also accepts couples of the same sex and singles, who can agree to be matched with someone or pay a singles supplement.

INCLUDED

Accommodations	Sports
Activities	Sports instruction
Cigarettes	Taxes
Drinks	Tips
Entertainment & dancing	Tours
Food	Transfers to and from airport

VALUE

The number of activities and the quality of the experience make Jamaica Jamaica an excellent value. Stay here one week and you'll want to come back. Stay two and you'll be busy trying different things the whole time.

ACTIVITIES, SPORTS & EXCURSIONS

ACTIVITIES: The activities are almost too numerous to list. The carriage ride and the bicycle tour take you through similar routes in the "Jamaican Riviera." You travel through a neighborhood of grand homes including, among others, the one belonging to the owners of SuperClubs. The bicycle tour travels at a leisurely pace; the carriage ride, complete with chilled wine, adds an elegant touch to the week. Both trips are worthwhile.

Reservations for the carriage ride can be made only on the day you wish to go, so sign up early. Most activities here start on time. Show up ten minutes in advance for the trips and activities, or you might be left behind.

Arts & crafts	Movies
Beach party	Nature walk
Board games	Nude sunbathing
Croquet	Patois classes
Culture/music/language classes	Ping-Pong
	Pool table
Dancing	Reggae dance lessons
Donkey ride	Scavenger hunt
Entertainment/shows	Skittle pool
Goat racing	Story time
Horse-and-carriage ride	Sunbathing
Kite flying	Video games
Mixology classes	

SPORTS: The resort offers a full complement of water and land sports. Jamaica Jamaica lies next to the SuperClubs golf course. Anyone planning to do a lot of golfing may want to stay here, as it offers the best access to the links, unlimited use, and no greens fees. You need only pay for the mandatory golf cart rental. Keep in mind, however, that the afternoon sun can be brutal, and humidity becomes a factor when you get away from the water.

The scuba instructors teach a free resort course for noncertified people who want to dive, or will give you a certification course for $250. The weight room is equipped with Nautilus equipment and free weights.

Aerobics/exercise classes	Snorkeling
Bicycles	Swimming (lap pool)
Golf	Tennis
Jogging trail	Volleyball
Kayaks	Water polo
Sailing	Weight room
Scuba	Windsurfing (Mistral School)

EXCURSIONS: Sailing cruise, Ocho Rios shopping excursion, Dunn's River Falls (nominal entrance fee), trip to Kingston (extra), river rafting (extra).

ITINERARY & DAILY SCHEDULE

Arrivals are accepted every day of the week. Thursday night is Jamaica Night, the highlight of the week. Dinner is served on the beach terrace, followed by games and activities on the beach. Plan to get covered with sand. Monday night is Pirates Night, with a costume competition.

Many Europeans choose to spend longer than a week at the resort. Two weeks allows a chance to experience the resort and see a bit of the island. You may want to consider combining your Jamaica Jamaica trip with a stay at Hedonism II or Couples.

NIGHTLIFE & ENTERTAINMENT

Nights at Jamaica Jamaica offer choices. The nightclub stages shows with music by the house band. The Heritage dancers move to the rhythmic beats of reggae music while the voodoo man shouts the spirits away. The limbo dancer bends under fire in ways that you won't believe. At Jamaica Jamaica native performing arts are really displayed.

Other nights, the guests get into the act, dancing reggae, wearing togas, or playing games at the beach. Afterward you can dance at the disco, which draws a lively crowd, or sing with the well-oiled crooners at the piano bar. Feel free to take a midnight stroll—the beach security is excellent.

Jamaica Jamaica is slightly wilder than Couples or the Sandals resorts, perhaps as a result of the mix of singles and couples.

AESTHETICS & ENVIRONMENT

Natural, comfortable, active: these adjectives describe the resort. You'll feel OK walking in your bathing suit or dressed with casual elegance at dinner. All the luxuries are here, but you don't have to get dressed up to enjoy them.

Music from the piano bar fills the colorful, comfortable common areas, which are decorated with a Jamaican ambience. Waterfalls surround the open, tropical lobby, which also contains a piano bar, games, and weightlifting machines. A lap pool borders the lobby. Cane chairs for two swing from the ceiling, giving couples a private, pillowed oasis in the middle of all the activity.

Jamaica Jamaica is located in Runaway Bay, between Ocho Rios and Montego Bay. Not a center of tourism, it neighbors the Super-Clubs golf course on one side and small private properties on the others. The grounds and gardens sprout lush vegetation, which the grounds crew maintains meticulously. It also keeps all the facilities clean, including the weight room and pools.

Jamaican art adorns the walls of the resort. Vibrant murals decorate the dining room. Native tapestries depict Jamaican culture. The fragrant air, mixed with the sea breeze, flows through the lobby, the terrace, and the outdoor patio of the "formal" eating area.

If you look past the low buildings to lush foliage and well-designed gardens, you know that you are in the tropics. Numerous palm trees top all other buildings, providing small umbrellas of shade on the lawn and on the beaches.

If you eschew the shade for the full sun on your skin, you will find a long stretch of beach, reputed to be the longest on the island's north shore. If you want to bronze your whole body, a portion of the beach is reserved for nude sunbathing. That stretch of sand seems to be the most popular with the European guests.

FACILITIES

Bank	Hot tubs
Bars (4)	Medical station
Beach (nude and prude)	Nightclub
Beauty salon	Piano bar
Concierge	Pools (2)
Disco	Safety-deposit box
Entertainment coordinators	Self-serve bar at nude beach
Gift shop	Water sports center

ROOMS

Management expresses pride in the hardwood furniture and Caribbean decor, but we found the guest rooms to be dark. All of them are contained in two-story, motel-style buildings, recently constructed or renovated. It looks a bit like a California garden apartment complex. As in the other SuperClubs, management is almost maniacal about maintenance.

All rooms cost the same. If you write the management in advance, you may select your room. Rooms 2100 through 2137 and 3200 through 3237 face the pool and the ocean. Ask for a second-floor room close to the beach for the best view of the water and activities. Rooms 3100 through 3137 offer proximity to the nude beach—and the most privacy, because they face a landscaped area. For the best combination and a limited water view, ask for a second-floor room near the beach.

LUXURY LEVEL: Air-conditioning, maid service.

FOOD & DRINK

The food and drink are plentiful and exotic, offering a choice of authentic Jamaican or Continental cuisine. The kitchen serves colorful, ripe tropical fruits, including papayas and mangos, at each meal, but conventional meat 'n' potato eaters will also find plenty to eat.

Breakfast and lunch are served on the beach terrace. For dinner, guests can choose between a buffet on the terrace and a full-course sit-down dinner in the dining room. The two have different menus, but each offers several choices of Continental and Jamaican dishes. (We highly recommend that you try the exotic Jamaican specialties.) In general, the food ranks with the best that you will find on the island. The resort earned our highest rating in this category, not because it competes with gourmet restaurants, but for the variety and quality of the native cuisine. The Continental food offers a good alternative when you want to touch base with something familiar.

STAFFING & SERVICE

Management is eager to please and is extremely responsive. You may contact the activities coordinators or the general management of the hotel if you have any concerns.

PRIVACY & RELAXATION

Jamaica Jamaica is the largest of the SuperClubs resorts. It doesn't have the isolated hideaways found at Couples or at Sandals Royal Caribbean; you never feel crowded, but you are rarely alone. You can escape the activity on the nude beach. Choose your room based on your need for privacy. You can be lazy at times, but if you relax too long, you may feel as though you are missing the fun.

SHOPPING

See "Ocho Rios" (p. 79) in the Jamaica Introduction.

HONEYMOONERS

Many couples do get married and/or spend their honeymoon at Jamaica Jamaica. The resort offers a full marriage package for $150 (including registration, minister, cake, champagne, flowers, and a carriage ride through the countryside).

The resort's strength lies in its common areas, ambience, and activities, not in the individual rooms and opportunities for privacy. If you like to mix with all sorts of people, not just couples, this is a great place to go.

SINGLES

Jamaica Jamaica does not actively market itself as a singles resort. A fair number of unattached people come here, but they are not noticeably on the prowl. A fair number do get together anyway.

NUTS & BOLTS

BOOKING & CONTACT INFORMATION: Try to find a travel agency that can give you an air/land package. Air Jamaica tends to have the least expensive flights. Or call or write:

Jamaica Jamaica, the Hotel
P.O. Box 58
Runaway Bay, Jamaica, W.I.
800-247-3733
809-973-2436-8

HANDICAP ACCESSIBILITY: Jamaica Jamaica is laid out on one level, but is not barrier free. Contact the resort directly for specific information.

PACKING: You will spend 90 percent of your time in your swimsuit and flip-flops (or less at the nude beach), so pack light. You need a pair of rubber-soled shoes for the Dunn's River Falls tour. Casual-formal outfits are appropriate for the dining room, which means a shirt with collar and long pants for men. Women need nice summer dresses. Jackets and ties would be ridiculous in this climate. Bring tennis and golf shoes if you plan to participate in these sports. An old T-shirt is recommended for diving (leave your equipment at home, warm-water gloves are optional). Windsurfing gloves and booties are fine if you have them, but they are not necessary. Bring two pairs of sunglasses, in case you lose one.

RELIGIOUS SERVICES: The management will call a cab that will take you to a Christian service.

Cost Worksheet		
	High Season[1]	Off-Season[2]
Accommodations		
(7 days)[3]	$1,180	$920
Food	incl.	incl.
Drinks	incl.	incl.
Departure tax	$8	$8
Sports	incl.	incl.
Airfare	_____	_____
Sight-seeing	incl.	incl.
Tips	incl.	incl.
Sports		
Souvenirs	_____	_____

[1] High season dates: December 22 to April 27
[2] Off-season dates: April 28 to December 21
[3] Single supplement (charged for private room only); $50 to $60.

RESERVATION SCHEDULE: Holiday vacations begin to fill up a year in advance, but six months should be enough notice for the high season. A few months' notice will usually suffice in the off-season.

SIZE: 22 acres.

NUMBER OF ROOMS: 238.

TRAVEL TIME FROM AIRPORT: 1 hour 5 minutes.

SPENDING MONEY: You don't need anything except the $8 departure tax. Take some money to buy art and trinkets from the locals.

TRELAWNY

VITAL FEATURES

Type of vacation: **Resort**
Target market: **Families, couples, singles, groups of all ages**
Location: **Falmouth, Jamaica**
All-inclusive cost per week: **Bargain packages available for much less than "rack" rate. These often cost less than $1,000 from New York, including airfare.**

RATINGS

Value: 💲💲💲💲

Fun quotient: ⛱⛱⛱⛱

Honeymoon suitability: ❤❤❤

Singles meeting ground: 👤

Child appeal: 🍦🍦🍦🍦🍦

Management professionalism: ☎☎☎☎

Service: 💡💡💡💡

Food: 🦞🦞🦞

THE REAL STORY

While Trelawny welcomes all, families will probably enjoy this resort most. Its PR department calls it "the exclusive resort for everyone." We don't really understand that, but we like the resort, and we love the price. There are activities and supervision for children, as well as sports and follies for adults. The relaxed atmosphere lets everyone do his own thing.

Located on eight acres between Ocho Rios and Montego Bay, Trelawny has a beautiful beach on Jamaica's fabled north shore. It offers lots of activities and big resort facilities. The bottom line makes your wallet feel good too. While sports and games come with the package, you select the meal plan that suits you best. You also pay for your drinks. This allows light eaters and light drinkers to craft budget vacations for themselves. For example, 80 percent of the guests take the two-meal plan instead of the three-meal plan. This works well for people who eat only two big meals a day on vacation, or who may be out sight-seeing in the middle of the day.

Trelawny ranks with the true all-inclusives because all guests can participate in all the activities, including water sports and lessons. Programs and games fill the day. Live entertainment and music keep the evenings hopping.

"Islanders" organize participatory games around the pool and beach. Most of these would earn a G or PG rating; any member of the family can join in. "Mini-islanders" lead the merriment for the little ones. The scuba resort course takes place at specified times several days a week. Instructors will give ad hoc individual lessons on how to windsurf, sail, or use any of the other sports equipment.

Parents can leave their children in the care of the "mini-islanders" all day if they wish. In the evening a readily available baby-sitting service will watch kids. Children's programs operate year-round. Families can play some of the games together. Many also take trips to the Ocho Rios straw market, the plantations, rafting, Dunn's River Falls, or other destinations.

Ignore the "rack" (or standard rates) at Trelawny. Nobody pays them. During the off-season (after Easter and before Christmas), holders of the Entertainment discount coupons can receive a 50 percent discount on the land portion on stays of four to seven days. (Entertainment coupon books are available for most major cities in the United States and Canada. You can obtain information by contacting Entertainment Publications, Inc., 1400 N. Woodward Avenue, Birmingham, MI 48011.) Travel agents can sometimes offer even better rates on air/land packages. During the summer, children aged 14 and under sharing their parents' room stay totally free.

While Trelawny caters to everyone, the guest composition varies somewhat during the year. The honeymoon months of May, June, August, and September attract a lot of couples. Singles come mostly during spring breaks of the United States (in February) and Canada (in March). All special holidays and summers bring mostly families.

INCLUDED

Accommodations	Food
Activities	Sports
Entertainment & dancing	Sports instruction

Transfers to and from the airport are not included, but are a part of many package deals.

VALUE

Trelawny offers all sorts of packages and discount coupons, making a vacation here truly affordable for a family. Most guests seem thrilled at the deal that they got. Entertainment two-for-one coupons and other promotions offered through travel agents make Trelawny a great value, especially during the off-season.

ACTIVITIES, SPORTS, & EXCURSIONS

Activities are often varied according to the demographic makeup of the guests.

FOR KIDS AGES 2–5

Best swimsuit competition
Block building
Cartoons
Crafts
Disco
Finger painting
Kite flying

Mousercise
Nature walks
Races
Sand castle building
Story time
Swing games

FOR KIDS AGES 6–12

Banana eating
Best swimsuit competition
Darts tournament
Disco
Fruit tasting
Hula hoop contests
Kite flying

Pepsi-drinking competition
Races
Splash & dive competitions
Supervised beach activities
Tennis clinic
Volleyball

FOR TEENS: Ask. They have programs.

FOR ADULTS

Arts & crafts
Bingo parties
Board games
Crab races
Culture/music/language
  classes
Dancing
Darts tournaments
Entertainment/shows

Fashion shows
Glass-bottomed boat
Limbo dance competitions
Reggae dance lessons
Sauna
Sports clinics & competitions
Sunbathing
Swimsuit competition

SPORTS: Trelawny has seven staff dive masters, three boats, and a shack full of equipment. The free resort course is offered three times a week. Guests may do one free scuba dive per day.

Aerobics, exercise, dancercise classes
Badminton
Basketball
Golf (discounted greens fees)
Horseback riding (extra)
Jogging trail
Parasailing (extra)
Ping-Pong
Sailing (Sunfish)
Scuba

Scuba resort course
Shuffleboard
Snorkeling
Swimming (boomerang-shaped pool)
Tennis (4 lighted courts)
Volleyball
Waterskiing
Weightlifting
Windsurfing

EXCURSIONS: Cruise on *Bamboo Prince* (extra), plantation tours, shopping trips to Montego Bay (2 times daily, cost included), Ocho Rios.

ITINERARY & DAILY SCHEDULE

Trelawny does not require a minimum stay except at Christmas and during Presidents' week in February, when a seven-night minimum applies.

Floridians often stay three to four nights. Most others come for six or seven nights. The majority of guests come from Canada. Along with the European guests, they often vacation for a fortnight.

NIGHTLIFE & ENTERTAINMENT

Trelawny offers a week's worth of nightlife on the property. After-dinner shows feature cultural events, comedians, native acts, and the usually sophisticated toga party.

In general, Trelawny offers spirited but not wild nightlife. After the show, dancing can be done at the Rum Keg Disco and Club Impact.

AESTHETICS & ENVIRONMENT

At first glance, Trelawny looks like a conventional large beach hotel. Management retrofitted it with good activities, small honeymoon cottages, a children's center, and a water sports program to make it work as an all-inclusive.

An open-air lobby and bar give Trelawny a tropical feel. The four seven-story towers let you know that this resort has quite a few rooms. Fortunately, the tasteful grounds and dispersed activities hubs keep it from feeling crowded. In general, the staff keep things well maintained and working.

FACILITIES

Bank
Bars

Beaches
Beauty salon

Children's center	Safety-deposit box
Coffee shop	Swimming pool
Disco	Tour desk
Entertainment coordinators	TV lounge
Gift shop	Water sports center
Medical station	Zoo (mini)
Pro shop	

ROOMS

Most people stay in the four towers, which are connected by breezeways. All rooms have private balconies and baths, with ocean views from the upper floors. Superior rooms have guaranteed ocean views; if you book a standard room you'll get the best room available. Since 75 percent of the rooms have an ocean view, you can expect to get an ocean view during the summer months, which have traditionally low occupancy.

One-story cottages have easy access to the beach and all the activities. These accommodations, which actually consist of large, single-room town houses, connect for families and groups. Honeymooners get ocean-view rooms as a matter of right, and cottages if available.

Rooms have king-size and double beds. Up to two children may stay in their parents' rooms on cots. Some rooms have two double beds.

LUXURY LEVEL

Air-conditioning	Porter service
Laundry service (extra)	Radio
Maid service	Refrigerator in room (on
Phone in room	request)

FOOD & DRINK

Trelawny offers early dinners for kids. The whole family can eat at the same time, or parents can choose to eat later. Guests can eat in the indoor or outdoor dining rooms or in the coffee shop.

For breakfast and dinner, the menu is the same if you eat outdoors or in the Jamaica Room. Breakfasts are served buffet style. You can take juices, Continental items, and sample the two Jamaican entrées. Dinners also offer Continental and Jamaican food, varied with theme nights, including barbecues and specialties. Two or three nights a week you are offered sit-down service for dinner. Typical entrées include various dishes of beef, poultry, fish, and lobster. Fresh fruits and vegetables come with every meal.

Alcoholic beverages are reasonably priced, and happy hours offer many two-for-one specials. New arrivals are treated to a welcome party with free rum bamboozles.

STAFFING & SERVICES

The staff take good care of all the guests, especially the kids.

PRIVACY & RELAXATION

People come to relax. You won't find a busy atmosphere or be pushed to get involved. Since Trelawny caters to a wide range of age groups, it lets you find your own activity level.

Parents can put their children in the care of the "islanders" when they want to slip off alone. Baby-sitters allow them to enjoy the nightlife.

SHOPPING

The Bamboo Village shopping area, a collection of merchants in huts, is located next to the hotel grounds. Bloomingdale's has no plans to open a store here.

HONEYMOONERS

Trelawny offers a special honeymoon package. It includes the following items: ocean-view room; breakfast and dinner daily; honeymoon dinner with wine and wedding cake; goodies including fruit basket, liqueur, T-shirts, champagne, and a $100 return gift certificate; all games and sports; and one horseback ride for two.

A marriage package includes all the legal necessities: a minister, champagne, flowers, and a wedding cake. A special gazebo is used for weddings.

SINGLES

While it could not be called a singles resort, it actively recruits unmarrieds who want to relax. Trelawny appeals to subdued singles or single women who don't want to be nagged. It is also perfect for families with young adult children or single parents.

CHILD APPEAL

Trelawny has created a wonderful place for kids. The private grounds provide security and most times of the year children will have many pals to play with. During the Christmas, Easter, and summer vacation holidays, special children's programs provide additional entertainment.

NUTS & BOLTS

BOOKING INFORMATION: Reservations can be made through travel agents and tour companies. They'll give you much better rates than the resort will directly. If your travel agent balks at working with people who use the Entertainment card (see "The Real Story," p. 176) find another. For information, contact Trelawny's sales and marketing department.

65 West 54th Street
New York, NY 10019
212-397-0700

CONTACT INFORMATION

Trelawny
P.O. Box 54
Falmouth, Jamaica, W.I.
809-954-2450

DEPOSITS/REFUNDS: Confirmed reservations require a 3-night deposit per person. The balance is due 21 days prior to your arrival at the hotel. If reservations are made within 21 days of arrival, full payment is due immediately.

Deposits will be refunded if cancellations are received no later than 21 days prior to arrival in the winter season and 10 days prior to arrival in the summer season. All deposits are forfeit if you cancel within the 21 days. A verified death in the family or illness preventing travel is a reasonable cancellation excuse and will get your money back within the 3-week limit.

HANDICAP ACCESSIBILITY: Ramps but no handicap bathrooms.

PACKING: The dress is Jamaican casual. Bring several swimsuits and a strong sunscreen.

RELIGIOUS SERVICES: Ask concierge.

RESERVATION SCHEDULE: For Christmas and Presidents' Week, you'll need reservations six months in advance. The rest of the year, one month's notice should do.

SIZE: 8 acres.

NUMBER OF ROOMS: 350.

MAXIMUM NUMBER OF GUESTS: 700.

NUMBER OF EMPLOYEES: 500.

FUTURE PLANS: Renovation planned for 1990.

TRAVEL TIME FROM AIRPORT: 30 minutes (Sangster International Airport in Montego Bay).

Transfers are not included in the base price, but they may be purchased from independent companies at the airport for an additional $30 (U.S.) (for one to four persons) each way. The resort is 23 miles from the airport. Most tour operators include transfers in their packages.

Cost Worksheet

(Intentionally left blank. Fill out with your travel agent based on available deals.)

	High Season[1]	Off-Season[2]
Accommodations (7 days)[3]		
Food		
Drinks		
Departure tax	$8	$8
Sports		
Airfare	_____	_____
Sight-seeing		
Tips		
Additional, sports[4]		
Souvenirs	_____	_____

[1] High season dates: Christmas and Presidents' Week
[2] Off-season dates: After Easter, before Christmas
[3] Premium for single person: Depends on tour operator
[4] Offered for extra charge: Baby-sitting? No problem. It costs $2.50 per hour for the first three hours, and $1.50 per hour after that. Scuba certification costs $150 (a bargain). You must stay for one week.

St. Kitts

BANANA BAY BEACH RESORT

VITAL FEATURES

Type of vacation: **Resort**
Target market: **Couples, families**
Location: **St. Kitts, West Indies**
All-inclusive cost per week: **$840**

RATINGS

Value: 💲💲💲

Fun quotient: 🌴🌴🌴🌴

Honeymoon suitability: ❤❤❤❤❤

Singles meeting ground: 👤

Child appeal: 🍦🍦

Management professionalism: ☎☎☎☎

Service: Not applicable

Food: Not applicable

THE REAL STORY

Distinctive beauty in a rare Caribbean wildlife setting distinguishes the Banana Bay Beach Resort. The low-rise hotel complex practically disappears when set against the grandeur of the mountains. St. Kitts Island is shaped like a whale. Banana Bay is located on the fluke, and is accessible only by four-wheel-drive vehicle or by boat.

The resort defines its isolation and tranquillity by what it doesn't have: no phones, no TV, no letter carrier, no concrete pool, and no nightclub. If you like to camp and hike, this is the place. The small number of guests makes you feel as if you own the beach (except for one day every two weeks when the Windjammer ship *Polynesia* drops off her passengers). Banana Bay has the feel of a nature preserve. After a short penetration into the woods, you can hear the birds chirping and the monkeys chattering. At extra cost, management will arrange for a nature safari by four-wheel-drive vehicle. Even better, you can hike.

You won't find wild nightlife or a pulsating beat here, although a few nights out on the town can be had a short drive or boat ride away.

We liked Banana Bay so much that we stretched the all-inclusive rules to include it in this book. The price of the room includes breakfast and dinner only. Guests must buy their own lunches and drinks at the beach bar. Limited water sports are included; instruction costs extra.

INCLUDED: Accommodations, food (modified American plan), sports (some), transfer to and from airport.

VALUE

This is a very specialized vacation offering. If you value privacy and quiet more than activities—and think it's worth paying to stay at a small place—you will find Banana Bay worthwhile.

ACTIVITIES, SPORTS, & EXCURSIONS

ACTIVITIES

Arts & crafts
Board games
Culture/music/language
    classes
Entertainment

Movies
Nude sunbathing
Sunbathing
Underwater vision boat

SPORTS: Banana Bay Beach Resort brags that it has "no concrete surrounding a pool of chemical water, just a gorgeous beach lapped by crystal clear blue-green water . . ." The calm bay waters really do lend themselves to easy swimming, windsurfing, sailing, and waterskiing. Even the most apprehensive swimmer will feel comfortable in these shallow waters.

Sports instruction costs approximately $8 an hour extra.

Deep-sea fishing (extra)
Golf (extra)
Hiking
Jogging trail
Pedal boats
Sailing
Scuba (extra)

Snorkeling
Swimming
Tennis
Water polo
Waterskiing (extra)
Windsurfing

EXCURSIONS: At an extra cost the resort can arrange scuba diving, deep-sea fishing, and island tours. Trips to St. Kitts' compatriots on Nevis can also be arranged. Put on your hiking boots to explore the island on your own.

ITINERARY & DAILY SCHEDULE

There are no schedules to follow at Banana Bay. You go with the wind, and the gentle Caribbean breeze won't move you very fast.

NIGHTLIFE & ENTERTAINMENT

Banana Bay provides an intimate setting with quiet porches lit by the moon and stars. If you desire a more dynamic experience, the boat will ferry you to Ocean Terrace Inn in the capital of Basseterre. There you can dine at the Fisherman's Wharf Barbecue Restaurant and Bar. Don't worry about catching the boat back, Ocean Terrace will put you up for the night if you make arrangements before leaving Banana Bay.

AESTHETICS & ENVIRONMENT

Roam with a view. Mountains and water completely surround the small hotel. Just two miles across the turquoise water lies Nevis, the sister island to St. Kitts.

Coconut palms line two of the world's loveliest beaches made of coral and white sand. Swaying in a hammock above the white sand, with a view of the calm water and the wooden pier topped by a gazebo, you may daydream—complete tranquillity.

FACILITIES

Bars
Beaches
Concierge

Snack bar, grill
Tour desk
Water-sports center

ROOMS

There is only one classification of rooms at Banana Bay. All of the rooms have an ocean view and a private bath. The rooms are cooled by trade winds and ceiling fans, which usually suffice (but not always).

LUXURY LEVEL: Laundry service (extra), maid service.

FOOD & DRINK

Banana Bay serves home-style Caribbean breakfasts and dinners in a dining room that resembles your favorite out-of-the-way place. A bar sells drinks before dinner; wine with dinner costs extra. We did not visit the resort during mealtime, but wonderful aromas wafted out of the kitchen.

The Booby Bird Beach Bar serves lunches and drinks, which cost extra. Guests are a captive market.

STAFFING & SERVICE

Banana Bay and Ocean Terrace Inn are small, family-owned and -run resorts. The care and warmth of the staff shows in their attitude and the quality of the experience.

PRIVACY & RELAXATION

The isolated nature of the resort and the long stretch of beach for the relatively few guests give you the feeling of privacy. Often you can have the beach to yourself or spend the day roaming through the hills without encountering anybody else. Numerous hammocks, terraces, and the great house give you places on the property to be alone. Here, you've got nothing but time.

SHOPPING

Banana Bay is more of a shell-searching haven than a place for the shopping mall maven.

HONEYMOONERS

If you seek a romantic place to be alone, look no further. This retreat may also be the perfect place to become reacquainted with your mate for a second honeymoon.

SINGLES

The isolation and secluded environment that appeals to couples may drive singles crazy.

CHILD APPEAL

Small children might like this as well as any other beach, although parents will probably find the support services to be lacking. Preteens and teens require more activities and companionship than are offered here. Overall, this is a better place to visit when you can leave the kids at home.

NUTS & BOLTS

Booking information

U.S. representatives:
American/Wolfe International
6 East 39th Street
New York, NY 10036
800-223-5695

Canadian representatives:
International Reservations
  Worldwide
842 York Mills Road
Don Mills, Ontario M3B 3AB

Contact information

Banana Bay Beach Resort
  and Ocean Terrace Inn
P.O. Box 65
St. Kitts, West Indies
809-465-2754/4121

Currency: American dollars, credit cards, and traveler's checks are accepted on the island.

Customs/duty: Standard U.S. and Canadian customs and duties apply.

Deposits/refunds: To confirm reservations a three-night deposit is required. Your deposit will be returned if you cancel 30 days prior to departure date.

Electricity: 110 volts 60 cycles.

Handicap accessibility: None.

Packing: Bring hiking boots and socks. Long cotton pants help in the brush. Casual and beach dress prevail, although presentable slacks and shirt or sundress are required for dinner. Cool evenings often dictate a sweater or light jacket. Mosquito repellent will make your treks more pleasant. High-power binoculars will help you spy on wildlife.

Religious services: None are offered on the property.

Reservation schedule: In the high season, the hotel is starting to fill up well in advance. Off-season, you can make last-minute plans if you have to.

Number of rooms: 20.

Maximum number of guests: 40.

TRAVEL TIME BY AIR

Chicago: **5 hours 58 minutes**
Los Angeles: **7 hours 10 minutes**
New York: **4 hours 45 minutes**
Toronto: **7 hours 30 minutes**

ARRIVAL AIRPORT: Golden Rock Airport.

TRAVEL TIME FROM AIRPORT: You must take a 5-minute taxi ride to the Ocean Terrace Inn. From there Banana Bay's shuttle boat will ferry you to Banana Bay. It takes 45 minutes.

VISA/PASSPORT REQUIREMENTS: U.S. and Canadian citizens will need proof of citizenship.

Cost Worksheet	High Season[1]	Off-Season[2]
Accommodations		
(7 days)[3]	$840	$630
Food (lunches)	50	50
Drinks	70	70
Departure tax	8	8
Sports	incl.	incl.
Tips[4]		
Taxes[4]		
Airfare	_____	_____
	$1,136	$886
Sight-seeing		
Tips		
Additional sports		
Souvenirs	_____	_____

[1] High season dates: December 16 to April 15
[2] Off-season dates: April 16 to December 15
[3] Premium for single person: $200 per night in high season and $180 per night in off-season.
[4] Essential extras: Approximate tips, 10% added to bill; taxes: 7%

JACK TAR VILLAGE ROYAL ST. KITTS

VITAL FEATURES

Type: **Resort**
Target market: **Couples, families, singles**
Location: **Basseterre, St. Kitts**
All-inclusive cost per week: **$1,050 (packages often include airfare)**

RATINGS

Value: 💲💲💲

Fun quotient: ⛱⛱⛱

Honeymoon suitability: 🖤🖤

Singles meeting ground: 🧍

Child appeal: 🍦🍦

Management professionalism: ☎☎

Service: 💡💡💡

Food: 🦞🦞

THE REAL STORY

Jack Tar Village Royal St. Kitts occupies the same low-end all-inclusive market niche of the other Jack Tar resorts. When purchased with airfare arranged by JTV's wholesaler, Adventure Tours, a vacation here offers an inexpensive way to get to a warm climate. This chain appeals to the budget conscious and to those who aren't looking for anything different from what they would find in a warm Stateside resort. It provides a relatively cheap sun fix for someone who likes to gamble, despite facilities that we felt were mediocre and maintenance that we thought was poor.

189

Jack Tar Village Resorts has the only legitimate gaming house in town. It forms the centerpiece of the chain's Royal St. Kitts Resort & Casino. A lot of the guests do come to tempt lady luck. Jack Tar keeps them fed, drinking, and entertained. For the most part, they get what they come for. If you were to change the signs at the airport and the hotel to read "Bahamas," we doubt if many of the guests would notice or care.

Devoid of its own beaches, but close to those facing the Atlantic and the Caribbean, Royal St. Kitts tries hard to compensate by shuttling guests to the two shores. It has set up a bar on the Atlantic beach and its guests have use of a water sports center on the Caribbean. A private bar and snack shack charges for drinks and food. On the property, a sunning deck surrounds a large pool. In practice, most guests stay on the property near the grill and bar. During a vacation, few people want to take buses to a beach or desire to commute between their Windsurfer and the place to get a drink.

Royal St. Kitts looks good on paper. It has everything. It's all included in the price, except gambling debts, of course. It satisfies many customers, especially those who haven't traveled much.

INCLUDED

Accommodations	Sports
Activities	Taxes
Airfare (very often)	Tips
Cigarettes	Tours
Drinks	Transfer to and from airport
Food	

VALUE

Jack Tar offers a lot of "thud" for the buck. If you were to make a checklist and compare it to similar trips, it would appear to be a good deal. In many ways it really is. Remember that this is a budget vacation and you're not getting a lot of quality in facilities, food, or activities. If you desire little more than a warm place to gamble and drink, this might be an acceptable choice.

ACTIVITIES, SPORTS, & EXCURSIONS

The activities are not very well organized and seem to be done on an ad hoc basis.

ACTIVITIES

Arts & crafts	Movies
Board games	Sunbathing
Dancing	Underwater vision boat (extra
Entertainment/shows	cost through tour desk)
Mixology classes	

Sports: The public beach has a water sports center that is available to Jack Tar guests. The equipment is in good repair, but there isn't a whole lot of it.

Aerobics/exercise classes	Shuffleboard
Badminton	Snorkeling
Bicycles	Swimming
Fishing	Tennis
Golf	Volleyball
Horseback riding	Water polo
Pedal boats	Waterskiing
Sailing (Sunfish)	Windsurfing

ITINERARY & DAILY SCHEDULE

Guests usually come on a one-week package tour. The activities and menus follow the weekly cycle, so you'll get all Royal St. Kitts has to offer during your seven-day stay.

NIGHTLIFE & ENTERTAINMENT

After-dinner shows feature native fire-eaters, limbo dancers, and local songs. An outdoor stage allows you to enjoy the evening air. After dinner, dancing draws a healthy crowd up to the stage. A lot of people spend their time in the casino or slumped in chairs watching cable television. Theme nights include a toga party, dance contest, and guest talent show.

AESTHETICS & ENVIRONMENT

Unfortunately, Jack Tar at St. Kitts suffered from inattention to maintenance when we were there. The front entrance is modern and clean, but its tile floors were chipped and cracked. The lawns were fairly unkempt, with only few scattered blades of grass. The village is a self-enclosed compound; the management has done an admirable job of creating a resort atmosphere using canals and a swimming pool, overlooking a lagoon. Still, you are isolated from the incredible natural beauty of the island.

FACILITIES

Bank	Gift shop
Bars	Medical station
Beaches	Piano bar
Beauty salon	Safety-deposit box
Casino	Snack bar, grill
Concierge	Swimming pool
Disco	Water sports center
Entertainment coordinators	

ROOMS

All rooms have balconies or verandas. Some of the upper-floor rooms have views. They are fitted with double or king-size beds. Our biggest rap against Jack Tar remains the careless maintenance. The rooms at Royal St. Kitts, for example, have several different kinds of tile that don't match. The furnishings are spartan but adequate. We certainly had to wonder why beautiful real estate looked like rent-controlled property. In our opinion, Royal St. Kitts desperately needs a full-scale renovation. While guests come here for a good deal, we feel they deserve better.

LUXURY LEVEL

Air-conditioning	Porter service
Clock	Radio
Laundry service (extra)	Room service
Maid service	Television in room
Phone in room	

FOOD & DRINK

All the food is standard American fare. It's plentiful and caters to the palate of Middle America. There are also a few Americanized St. Kittian dishes.

An open-air coffee shop and the pool grill serve that occasional snack. Bars located at the pool and the Atlantic beach satiate the Caribbean thirst.

STAFFING & SERVICE

At the resort we were treated in a way that alternated between indifference and rudeness. On the other hand, the Texas booking agents could not have been more friendly. The St. Kittians tried to be helpful, but didn't seem to have their act together.

PRIVACY & RELAXATION

The resort has two main central areas: the outdoor stage area and the lobby, which focuses on the casino, entrance, and television room. The lack of private beaches and the large number of rooms for the moderate-size grounds make it hard to find any private space. As most of the pool and canal areas are brightly lit, it is hard to find a dim, romantic path for a stroll.

SHOPPING

Several gift shops on the premises offer sundries and trinkets to bring home. The batik factory, accessible by optional tour, tie-dyes fabrics using the lost-wax technique. The fabrics cost about double what you'd pay for them in the South Pacific, but less than in the

States. The factory promotes the batik as works of art and unusual pieces of clothing. It does offer a long piece of cloth that can be folded many ways to be used as a beach cover-up, dress, and hair wrap. Straw market vendors sell Caribbean crafts and art, along with T-shirts, straw hats, and trinkets.

HONEYMOONERS

If you are counting pennies, Jack Tar may be able to arrange a good charter flight and land package. If you stay at another place on the island, Jack Tar will sell you a night pass that will allow you to eat, drink, dance, and see the show. Gamblers can enter the casino directly without a pass.

SINGLES

You probably won't find many prospects here.

CHILD APPEAL

We suspect that kids would be fairly bored. There are dozens of better choices.

NUTS & BOLTS

BOOKING INFORMATION: See Jar Tar Introduction in the Jamaica section, page 109.

CONTACT INFORMATION

Jack Tar Village
P.O. Box 406
Frigate Bay, St. Kitts, W.I.
809-586-3557

CURRENCY: If you don't possess Texas black gold (if you did you wouldn't come here) the front desk will change your American and Canadian dollars for Eastern Caribbean Units.

DEPOSITS/REFUNDS: See Jack Tar introduction in the Jamaica section, page 109.

HANDICAP ACCESSIBILITY: Difficult.

PACKING: The dress is very casual.

RELIGIOUS SERVICES: Nearby.

RESERVATION SCHEDULE: The winter season tends to book up months in advance with few cancellations.

NUMBER OF ROOMS: 247.

NUMBER OF EMPLOYEES: Not available.

TRAVEL TIME BY AIR

Chicago: **8 hours**
Los Angeles: **12 hours 40 minutes**
New York: **5 hours**
Toronto: **8 hours 40 minutes**

ARRIVAL AIRPORT: Golden Rock Airport.

TRAVEL TIME FROM AIRPORT: 15 minutes.

Cost Worksheet

	High Season[1]	Off-Season[2]
Accommodations (7 days)[3]	$1,050	$980
Food	incl.	incl.
Drinks	incl.	incl.
Departure tax		
Sports	incl.	incl.
Airfare	_____	_____
Sight-seeing		
Tips	incl.	incl.
Additional sports		
Souvenirs		
Extra[4]	_____	_____

[1] High season dates: Christmas through Easter
[2] Off-season dates: After Easter to before Christmas
[3] Premium for single person: $1,260 per week
[4] Offered for extra charge: Baby-sitting at night, $2 to $3 per hour

The U.S. and British Virgin Islands

INTRODUCTION

Situated just 60 miles east of Puerto Rico, the Virgin Islands enjoy a Caribbean climate and close proximity to the continental United States. License plates in the U.S. Virgin Islands claim the islands are "American Paradise." It's true. The Virgin Islands are the stuff postcards are made of. They're rich with white sand beaches, uninhabited cays, clear aquamarine waters, and gentle seas. Every year more vacationers, sailors, divers, and sun worshipers discover the islands.

Modern tourists aren't the first folks to appreciate the islands. Throughout time the location and physical makeup of the islands have influenced their history. Since the first inhabitants arrived in seafaring canoes, the islands have provided a strategic location for surveying the rest of the Caribbean. The islands lie in the middle of the archipelago of islands that stretches from Venezuela to Florida. The Spanish first used them as a staging point for their transatlantic fleets. Later the same islands sheltered pirates and privateers who plundered the rich Spanish galleons. Eventually the riches stopped flowing from the Americas and the settlers in the Virgin Islands turned to agriculture.

By the late 1660s, large plantations were thriving. The colonists satisfied the intense demand for labor by importing slaves from

Africa. Time went by peacefully until the 1700s, when drought, hurricanes, and the American Revolution shook the islands. Piracy began again, and the slaves began to revolt. By the mid-1800s the slaves were free and most whites had fled the islands. The Virgin Islands slept quietly for the next hundred years, waking up briefly to watch the Danes transfer territorial ownership of their islands to the United States in 1917. Finally, in the 1960s, the location and physical makeup of the islands played their latest hand as tourists spread the word about the Virgin Islands.

For now the islands remain largely unspoiled by commercial development. Quiet and peaceful, they offer a place where visitors can vacation in the sun and surf without the crowds and intensity of the larger Caribbean islands. The Virgin Islands are truly treasured islands.

The same factors that make the Virgin Islands such a popular vacation destination prompted several all-inclusives to locate there. The U.S. and British territories have natural beauty, a favorable climate, and the familiar English language. In the all-inclusive resorts, everything is even easier.

U.S. VIRGIN ISLANDS

ST. CROIX: St. Croix is the largest and farthest removed of the Virgin Islands. Located 35 miles south of St. Thomas, the 84-square-mile island maintains a comfortable balance between the development of St. Thomas and the natural beauty of St. John. St. Croix boasts an airport, a deep-water port, and all the niceties of town, yet it also has a mountainous rain forest, wide verdant fields, and a desertlike east end. The entire island retains a strong sense of history that can be seen in the streets, the structures, and the ruins of the old sugar plantations. The two major towns, Frederiksted and Christiansted, have decidedly different styles. The smaller Frederiksted has a Victorian flavor and the more developed Christiansted shows a strong Danish influence.

Frederiksted is located on the west end of St. Croix, some 17 miles from Christiansted. Although nineteenth-century architecture dominates the town, Frederiksted traces its roots back to the construction of Fort Frederik in 1760. The earlier Danish structures were burned down in 1878 when labor riots sparked a fire. Rebuilt after the blaze, the town took on its present gingerbread colonial appearance. The Victorian-style buildings and tree-lined streets of the main shopping district begin literally at the edge of the pier. Most of the historic sights are located within a seven-block radius. Frederiksted is a sleepy village that rests quietly until a cruise ship arrives. And even then the activity in town quiets quickly as the majority of visitors head for Christiansted.

Christiansted is perhaps the best preserved town in the Virgin

Islands. Its buildings proudly proclaim their eighteenth-century Danish heritage. Small shops and restaurants occupy the majority of historic buildings crowded along the waterfront. Open-air markets sell fresh produce. Sidewalk cafés serve hot food and cool drinks. Fort Christiansted, the Government House, the Scale House, and the Old Danish Customs House will intrigue history and architecture buffs. A half-day walking tour hits all of the town's highlights.

Tour companies, taxis, and car rental agencies provide transportation out of town. For a real look around the island, rent a Jeep and leave the pavement behind. Four-wheel up and down the rugged dirt roads, discovering abandoned plantations and windmills. To the east, cacti and other desert plants dominate the landscape. In the northwest mountains, mahogany trees, fig trees, and other jungle plants compete for space. On the west end, miles of deserted beaches mark the coast. Near the airport, the Cruzan Rum distillery is open for tours and rum tastings.

ST. JOHN: Only 5 miles away from St. Thomas, St. John suggests an alternate state. As the Kite, a bar overlooking Cruz Bay, puts it: "2,000 miles away from reality." Gone are the bustling throngs of tourists, the traffic, noise, and near-constant motion. Instead, St. John is a 19-square-mile refuge with open spaces, near-deserted beaches, and remote romantic hideaways. With no airport and no deep-water port for cruise ships, visitors must make an extra effort to reach the island. Parkland status protects two-thirds of St. John from human development. Over 5,650 acres of coastal water and 9,500 acres of beaches, hillsides, and historic ruins remain natural and unspoiled. The rest of the island is private property, with the largest landholdings belonging to the Rockefellers. Their resort, Caneel Bay, is one of the oldest and best known in the Caribbean, and is reviewed in this chapter.

Cruz Bay is the hub of St. John, the island's main town, and a port of entry for the U.S. Virgin Islands. All ferries and seaplanes dock here, and all roads start from the main harbor. The customs office is located just beyond Battery Point. Nearby are the majority of the island's shops, restaurants, and businesses. Car rental agencies offer you a chance to explore the island on your own. For a more informative trip, try a tour with one of the taxi drivers. Most drivers explain the island's human and natural history as well as point out the interesting sights. The generally humorous drivers give you a feel of the island spirit. Buses regularly run from town to the more popular beaches.

Perhaps the best way to experience St. John is to walk. Hiking trails crisscross the park, leading to mountaintop views and secret jungle hideaways. The ruins of the Annaberg sugar plantation await exploration at the north end of the island. Nearby, Trunk Bay features a marked underwater snorkeling trail. On the south shore you can see the petroglyphs, rock carvings originally attributed to the island's Indian inhabitants but now thought to have been done by African slaves. The Ranger Station in Cruz Bay, open daily from 8:00 A.M. to 4:30 P.M., provides maps, brochures, slide shows, and guided nature walks.

ST. THOMAS: St. Thomas is the most popular and most populous of the Virgin Islands. Only 4 miles wide by 13 miles long, the island packs a lot of development into a small place. St. Thomas has an airport, deep-water port, and a city providing a wide range of luxuries, yet still has room for beaches, coves, and quiet harbors. Although the island has nice resorts and beaches, many people use its busy airport and harbor as a jumping-off point to the other islands.

Compared to the other Virgin Islands, life on St. Thomas moves at a fast pace. Visitors come straight from their busy lives on the mainland and plunge into their vacations without slowing down. On St. Thomas you can do everything, from sailing, swimming, and snorkeling to shopping, sight-seeing, and spending a night on the town.

At the center of all the activity is Charlotte Amalie. Named after a Danish queen, the town is not only the largest on the island, it's also the capital of the U.S. Virgin Islands. The harbor at Charlotte Amalie offers protection from all but the most severe storms; it's been a haven for ships since the fifteenth century and its many historic buildings remain intact. The Danes permitted the sale of goods obtained by piracy as well as by honest trade, and the islanders have retained their free port status. Today, merchandise from around the world floods the duty-free stores. Shopping remains one of St. Thomas's most popular sports, even though stateside discount stores sell goods for lower prices.

Almost every day, hundreds of tourists pour off the cruise ships, determined to see the entire island while they're in port. Few get far beyond the shopping district. If you've only got a short time, try a walking tour of Charlotte Amalie. Begin at the Visitor's Center in the Grand Hotel. Then leave the waterfront and wander through the maze of narrow streets and old stone buildings rich in St. Thomas's 300-year history. If you've got more time or don't care to see Charlotte Amalie, rent a car, hail a cab, or hop a bus and head out of town. Tourist highlights include the following: Magen's Bay, a mile-long horseshoe-shaped beach well worth the minor admissions charge; Coki Beach, reputed to have the best snorkeling on the island; Coral World, an underwater observatory that gives nondivers a glimpse of undersea life; and Drake's Seat on Skyline Drive, where legend holds that Sir Francis Drake came with his telescope to look for Spanish galleons to plunder.

BRITISH VIRGIN ISLANDS

ANEGADA: Although Anegada is only 15 miles northeast of the main chain of islands, it shares few similarities with its sister Virgins. Unlike the rest of the Virgin Islands, which are mountainous and volcanic in origin, Anegada is a low coral-and-limestone atoll that belongs in the Pacific rather than the Caribbean. The highest point on the island is only 28 feet above sea level, making it difficult to spot from the sea. More than 300 ships have wrecked off Anegada. Today 138 of those wrecks are charted for diving and exploration. Although the diving and snorkeling off the island is excellent, getting to Anegada can be a bit more difficult. Most charter companies do not allow their boats in the hazardous waters around it, and there is no regular ferry service. To get there you'll need to fly on Air BVI from nearby Beef Island Airport or take a private boat. If you like long, sandy beaches and really getting away from it all, Anegada is worth the trip.

BEEF ISLAND: Beef Island was named for the cattle that settlers used to raise to feed the local population of privateers. Today, it holds the international airport, which doesn't even have beefed-up security. But there are lots of reasons for tourists to come here. Just beyond the end of the runway you'll find Trellis Bay, a protected harbor perfect for windsurfing. In the middle of the bay sits Bellamy Cay, where the British Virgin Islands Boardsailing School rents Windsurfers and offers lessons.

COOPER ISLAND: The main anchorage on Cooper Island is Manchineel Bay on the northwest side. Visit the Cooper Island Beach Club, which serves lunch, dinner, and refreshing alcoholic drinks. Swimming and snorkeling are good off the beach, and a trail to the top of the hill gives panoramic views. While hiking be sure to avoid the Manchineel trees. The trees' sap is toxic and its yellow-green apples can be deadly if eaten.

DEAD CHEST ISLAND: "Fifteen men on a dead man's chest. Yo ho ho and a bottle of rum." This small and steeply inclined island is supposedly the place where, with a single saber, 15 pirates killed each other over a bottle of rum.

GREEN CAY: Just a stone's throw beyond little Jost Van Dyke, Green Cay is a small white sand island, perfect for day visits and picnics. Excellent snorkeling can be found on the reef extending south of the cay.

JOST VAN DYKE: Named for a seventeenth-century Dutch pirate, Jost Van Dyke is a mountainous island located northwest of Tortola. The island's fame comes from two native sons. The first, Dr. John Lettsom, founded the Medical Society of London. The second, Dr. William Thornton, designed the Capitol in Washington, D.C. Jost Van Dyke remains largely undeveloped and unspoiled. Great Harbour is the only settlement of any size, having a British customs office, a school, and several restaurants and bars. Foxy's Bar on the east side of the beach is worth a visit, as is the Sand Castle bar at White Bay.

NORMAN ISLAND: Better known as Treasure Island, after Robert Louis Stevenson's famous novel of the same name, Norman Island is a must stop. The excellent natural harbor and sea caves attracted pirates who reportedly hid their treasures on the island. Explore the caves by dinghy or with snorkeling gear. You might find gold. The water is amazingly clear, with visibility between 50 and 100 feet, and the variety of sea life off the rocks is outstanding. A trail leads from the rocky beach to the island above where wild cattle roam. If you go hiking, be sure to give the cows a wide berth.

PETER ISLAND: Peter Island is accessible by private boat or by ferry from Tortola. Beaches and anchorages are plentiful, and several trails cross the island. A climb to the top of the hill on the eastern side of Peter Island Yacht Harbour offers a good panorama of Drake's Passage and a great view of Dead Chest Island. Be sure not to disturb the homeowner near Little Harbour. At one time he reportedly shot holes in the sails of boaters who littered his beach and disturbed his peace. He's more polite these days, but still requests that visitors respect his privacy.

SALT ISLAND: Salt Island derives its name from the three evaporation ponds that once provided salt for the Royal Navy. The salt is still collected by the island's few residents, who rent the island from the queen of England. Their rent is a single bag of salt paid once a year!

Most visitors to Salt Island head for Lee Bay to dive or snorkel at the wreck of the Royal Mail Ship *Rhone*, which was smashed on the rocks in a hurricane in 1867.

SANDY CAY: Laurance Rockefeller owns this island that could have served as the setting for *Robinson Crusoe*. A footpath circles the island and gives visitors a botanical tour. If the seas are calm, the snorkeling is good off a reef on the north end of the cay. The island is located east of Jost Van Dyke.

TORTOLA: Tortola is the largest and most populous island in the British Virgin Islands. Split down the middle by a steep ridge of mountains, its shores are composed of beaches, bays, and protected coves. Most of the island has returned to wilderness since the days of the sugar plantations. After witnessing the rapid commercialization of St. Thomas, Tortola's residents have taken a go-slow attitude toward development. They want to promote their island's beauty without ruining it. Most of the island's population resides in Road Town, capital of the British Virgin Islands. The rest of Tortola's inhabitants live in the towns of East End and West End or in residences scattered about the island.

Road Town is the only sizable town on the island. Spaced out around Road Harbour, the town spreads predominantly eastward from the customs dock. The customs office also serves as the British Virgin Islands tourist office, providing informative pamphlets on the island. Nearby, many old buildings show off their West Indian charm while dozens of shops along the main street offer everything from suntan lotion to English bone china. The usual group of taxis and buses wait to take you to any island destination.

If you want to drive in the British Virgin Islands, rent a car in Road Town. Tortola is the only island large enough to get your money's worth out of a vehicle. The roads into the center of the island are steep, with hairpin turns and precipitous drop-offs. Don't let them scare you though. The views are stupendous. If you're going to rent a car, make a day trip out of it and tour the island. Head west out of town along the Caribbean toward West End and Soper's Hole. West End is less a town than a group of pastel buildings, a customs office, and a dock where ferries leave for the U.S. Virgin Islands. North of town on the Atlantic side begins a succession of beaches that ends at Cane Garden Bay, a photogenic beach with protected waters, palm trees, and a sweeping arc of sand. Farther north lies Brewer's Bay and the remains of a rum distillery. From there head inland to the trailhead up to Mount Sage. At 1,710 feet, this mountain is the highest in the Virgin Islands. To the east of Road Town are many bays and islets, including Beef Island, which is connected to Tortola by a bridge.

VIRGIN GORDA: Columbus named the island "Fat Virgin" because from seaward it resembled a fat woman lying on her back. Virgin Gorda is the second largest and second most populous of the British Virgin Islands. At one time it served as the capital of the British Virgin Islands with a population of 8,000. Today only 1,500 people live on the island, most of them in Spanish Town.

Virgin Gorda is approximately ten miles long with flat ground in the south and mountains in the center and to the north. All parts of the island above 1,000 feet are protected as national parkland. Virgin Gorda Peak, the highest point on the island, has an observation tower accessible by road through the park. At the north end of the island lies North Sound, a large protected bay perfect for sailing, swimming, and snorkeling. The Bitter End Yacht Club, reviewed in this section, is located here. Another all-inclusive resort on Virgin Gorda is the RockResort Little Dix Bay, also reviewed in this section.

On the south end of the island are the baths, Virgin Gorda's pre-eminent tourist attraction. Granite boulders larger than houses tumble onto the beach and into the sea. Enter the caves between the rocks and discover private swimming grottoes. The combination of cool rocks, surging waves, and shafts of sunlight fosters a feeling of euphoria. Go early to avoid the crowds and to allow yourself lots of time for exploration. This is one spot you won't want to miss.

NUTS & BOLTS *(for all of the Virgin Islands)*

CONTACT INFORMATION

The United States Virgin Islands Division of Tourism

St. Croix:
Box 4538
Christiansted, St. Croix,
    USVI 00820
809-773-0495

Frederiksted Customs House
Stand Street
Frederiksted, St. Croix,
    USVI 00840
809-772-0357

St. John:
Box 200
Cruz Bay, St. John, USVI
    00830
809-776-6450

St. Thomas:
Box 6400
Charlotte Amalie,
    St. Thomas, USVI 00801
809-774-8784

Chicago:
Suite 1003
343 South Dearborn Street
Chicago, IL 60604
312-461-0180

New York:
1270 Avenue of the Americas
New York, NY 10020
212-582-4520

Los Angeles:
3450 Wilshire Boulevard
Los Angeles, CA 90010
213-739-0138

The British Virgin Islands Tourist Board

Tortola:
Box 134
Road Town, Tortola, BVI
809-494-3134

San Francisco:
1686 Union Street
San Francisco, CA 94123
415-775-0344

New York:
370 Lexington Avenue
New York, NY 10017
212-696-0400
800-835-8530

Toronto:
801 York Mills Road
Don Mills, Ontario, Canada,
M3B 1X7
416-283-2235

Customs/duty: Travelers returning to the United States directly from St. Thomas or St. Croix are subject to U, S. customs inspection, usually at the airport before boarding the plane. If you are returning via Puerto Rico you will go through customs in San Juan.

Travelers in the U.S. Virgin Islands enjoy special discounts on customs duty. All U.S. residents are allowed to bring $800 worth of merchandise to the mainland every 30 days. This amount is double the $400 limit from other Caribbean islands. Items made in the U.S. Virgin Islands (mostly potent rum and handicrafts) are considered tax-exempt and are not included in the $800 duty-free allowance.

Upon entering the British Virgin Islands, visitors must fill out tourist information cards. The first part of the card is collected when you enter and the second half is taken when you leave. Keep it in a safe and readily accessible location. Luggage is subject to inspection upon both entry and exit.

Visitors returning to the United States from the British Virgin Islands are allowed to return with the standard $400 worth of merchandise, one carton of cigarettes, and one liter of liquor. Items made in the British Virgin Islands are not included in the duty-free allowance.

Entry/exit taxes: There are no entry or exit charges in the U.S. Virgin Islands, but "the British are charging, the British are charging." When leaving the British Virgin Islands, a departure tax of $5 per person if by air and $3 if by sea is assessed.

Currency: Both the United States and British Virgin Islands use U.S. currency.

Driving: A trivia question asks where, in the United States, do people drive on the lefthand side of the road. (Your old Aunt Mildred in Omaha doesn't count.) The answer is . . . the U.S. Virgin Islands. The confusion mounts for everyone, because while the cars are American lefthand drive, the roads are driven British style. The roads tend to be curvy and narrow, and the residents reckless. Forget your instincts and follow the traffic.

Electricity: All the Virgin Islands use 110 volts 60 cycles; the same as in the United States.

DIVING AND SNORKELING IN THE VIRGIN ISLANDS

Buck Island National Monument: The only underwater national monument in the United States, Buck Island is a snorkeler's mecca. A 30-minute underwater trail along the 2,000-yard barrier reef offers spectacular views of coral, sea urchins, starfish, and brilliant tropical fish. On the island itself frigate birds, pelicans, and dozens of other species of birds entertain the sunbathers and picnickers. Tour operators and private charters regularly make the two-mile crossing from St. Croix. Visitors are allowed onshore from 8:00 A.M. to 5:00 P.M.

The Wreck of the R.M.S. *Rhone*: In 1867 the Royal Mail Ship *Rhone* was caught in a late-season hurricane and smashed against the rocks off Salt Island. It sank rapidly. Today the wreck lies beneath 30 to 80 feet of water and is a British Virgin Islands national park. One of the most popular dive sites in the Caribbean, the wreck of the *Rhone* served as a set for the underwater scenes in the movie *The Deep*. Scuba divers can enter the old engine room and clearly see the parts of the old ship strewn across the ocean floor. Although the site is best explored by diving, the water is clear enough that snorkelers can enjoy the view as well.

LANGUAGES: English is all you need. Black islanders often talk among themselves in Patois, a Caribbean dialect, but they speak American English as well.

PACKING: Casual clothing rules. Most of the time you'll wear a bathing suit or shorts. However, be sure to bring a shirt or top for a trip into town because the Virgin Islands code requires that no one appear "within town limits in bathing costume or similarly abbreviated attire." For a night on the town, men may want to wear khaki or cotton pants and polo shirts; women prefer casual skirts or dresses. Up-scale resorts such as Caneel Bay dictate a jacket and tie for men and a cocktail dress or similar attire for women. All visitors should bring the following: a light jacket or sweatshirt for cool evenings and air-conditioned spaces, comfortable walking shoes, beach wear, and a camera. An umbrella might be useful, but since rainstorms rarely last longer than half an hour you can probably get by without one.

VISA/PASSPORT REQUIREMENTS: In the U.S. Virgin Islands, Americans and Canadians need only proof of citizenship. All other nationalities face the same requirements as in other parts of the United States. The British Virgin Islands prefers valid passports, but U.S. and Canadian citizens can use a birth certificate or voter's registration card. People of other nationalities must present passports.

RELIGIOUS SERVICES: Most islands have Catholic and Protestant communities. The houses of worship tend to be small, intimate, and quaint. Visitors are always welcome. Many islands also have synagogues.

RENTAL CARS: Rental cars are an ideal way to explore the islands on your own, but you'll pay for the privilege. Rates start between $35 and $40 per day for a Jeep or compact. Mileage is usually unlimited (how far can you really go?), but you pay for gas.

SHOPPING: If you walk a block or two beyond the tourist traps, you can sometimes find good prices for handmade goods and other island specialties. Be sure to check the discount prices at home before looking for bargains on photographic equipment, perfumes, china, and other items. Shopping selection in the British Virgin Islands is more limited than in the U.S. Virgin Islands, but prices are good on British imports.

TELEPHONES: All the Virgin Islands use the Caribbean area code (809). The U.S. Virgin Islands has decent phone service and direct dialing to the continental United States and the rest of the world. Pay phones cost 25 cents for each five-minute local call. The British Virgin Islands also has direct dialing, but the phone service is not as good as in the U.S. Virgin Islands. Wrong numbers are not uncommon—nor are lost coins.

TIME: The Virgin Islands are all on Atlantic Time all year. In the winter, the Virgin Islands are one hour ahead of U.S. Eastern Standard Time. When the mainland is on Daylight Savings Time, Eastern Standard Time and Atlantic Time are the same.

TRAVEL TIME: All travel times are based on nonstop flights and do not include time between connecting flights.

To St. Thomas:

Chicago: **5 hours 37 minutes**
Los Angeles: **8 hours 5 minutes**
New York: **3 hours 35 minutes**
Toronto: **7 hours 7 minutes**

To St. Croix:
Chicago: **5 hours 7 minutes**
Los Angeles: **7 hours 35 minutes**
New York: **4 hours 3 minutes**
Toronto: **6 hours 35 minutes**

To Tortola:
Chicago: **4 hours 58 minutes**
Los Angeles: **7 hours 45 minutes**
New York: **4 hours 15 minutes**
Toronto: **6 hours 37 minutes**

VACCINATION REQUIREMENTS: None.

BITTER END YACHT CLUB

VITAL FEATURES

Type of vacation: **Resort and yacht club**
Target market: **Anyone over the age of 6 who enjoys sailing or
    water sports**
Location: **North Sound, Virgin Gorda, B.V.I.**
All-inclusive cost per week: **$500 summer, $1,000 winter**

RATINGS

Value: 💲💲💲💲

Fun quotient: 🏖️🏖️🏖️🏖️

Honeymoon suitability: ❤️❤️❤️

Singles meeting ground: 🚹🚺🚹

Child appeal: 🍦🍦

Management professionalism: ☎️☎️☎️☎️☎️

Service: Not applicable

Food: Not applicable

THE REAL STORY

There is something intriguing about the Bitter End Yacht Club.
The name stirs up an image of a sailor bent furiously over the wheel
of his vessel, wind and waves ripping at his foul weather gear, yelling
over the roar of the sea, "We'll make it to the bitter end!"

To get an idea of the Bitter End Yacht Club, imagine the same
sailor hours later, lounging by a beautiful pool in his bathing suit, a
martini in one hand and a best-seller in the other. Don't get the
wrong idea. The Bitter End caters to diehard sailors—diehard sailors who enjoy luxury. The people there are serious about sailing,
regardless of whether they sail often or only one week per year. It's

207

not a club where the instructors rig the boat, get it going, have someone snap your picture when the wind gusts, then boot you off the bridge before the real sailing begins. You will not be pampered senselessly. If you're an experienced sailor, you do your own sailing. If you don't rank with America's Cup skippers, you are still expected to help with the rigging, furling, and bagging of the sails. You must even pump the bilge.

If you love water sports, this is the place for you. You will get a good dose of unlimited sailing, windsurfing, snorkeling, scuba diving, sculling, and swimming. Bitter End Yacht Club's fleet of over 100 boats is relatively new and maintained with care. You won't find secondhand equipment floating around.

The instructors must be newcomers to the Caribbean because the hot balmy weather has not affected them yet. They are alert and full of energy. Nick Trotter's sailing school offers a variety of courses that teach both beginners and advanced sailors. After a week of instruction, you should feel confident enough to sail in one of the regattas held here regularly.

Out of the water, you'll find yourself in a beautiful, lush resort. It's not uncommon to catch guests examining the flora to determine if it's real. You might suspect the employees of placing huge dewdrops on the flowers, prompting birds to chirp, and scattering coconuts on the ground. The club has a very polished look, similar to what you would find at a posh country club. It lacks the worn feeling that some resorts acquire from the continuous changing of guests. Recent renovations may explain why everything is still glowing. However, the changes do not affect the infectious feeling of adventure. You are met at the main dock by a pen of live sharks. They are only sand sharks, but that won't stop you from living out your Jacques Cousteau fantasies. The aquascope docked in the front of the club could be straight from a James Bond movie.

The Bitter End does not include absolutely everything in the base price, but it does offer a lot of water sports. There are several types of packages available. The Admiral's Package includes seven nights and eight days with unlimited water sports and three meals a day. You can live aboard a CA1 27 or Freedom 30 boat, in which case the Quarterdeck Club Marina will be your base. The boats receive daily maid service, fresh linens, drinking water, and ice. You have full use of all club facilities. The boats can also be put on moorings with regular skiff service. The Land-Sea Package allows you to spend three days on shore and four nights on a boat.

INCLUDED

Accommodations	Food
Activities	Most tips
Drinks (some)	Sports

Sports instruction   Wine with dinner
Tours

VALUE

This is not the kind of trip where you can leave your wallet at
home. Not everything is included. But the quality and quantity of
the boats, equipment, and instruction may be worth paying a little
extra for.

ACTIVITIES, SPORTS, & EXCURSIONS

All of the activities are well planned and professionally executed.
They won't hand you a snorkel and say, "Have fun." The *Ponce de
Leon* makes two guided snorkeling trips every day. The *Paranda*, a 48-
foot oceangoing catamaran, sails twice daily. The semisubmersible
aquascope goes out every morning and gives you a good look at
what's lurking beneath the water. Guests also have unlimited access
to the club's fleet of 100 boats.

Sports: For the first time in your life, the dreaded "course 101"
will actually be fun. The Nick Trotter Sailing School offers an "Introduction to Sailing" course. The school has seven four-hour courses
that range from basic to advanced. The instruction takes place in the
classroom and on the water. Each four-hour class costs $25.
The Bitter End offers some of the best diving spots in the Caribbean. Certified divers can venture anywhere in the North Sound on
Boston Whaler skiffs.
The well-known Kilbride Dive Team is based at the Bitter End. Its
members take people out daily on their 42-foot dive boat for half-day
excursions. It also offers a free "Discover Scuba" video. The Kil-
brides offer a three-hour PADI resort course.

Aerobics/exercise classes
Bicycles
Rowing sculls
Sailing (Sunfish, Lasers, Lasers II, Rhodes 19s and J-24s)
Scuba
Scuba resort course
Snorkeling (you must have your own mask and snorkel, swim fins
    and ski belts are free)
Swimming (odd shape prevents laps)
Windsurfing (school)

Excursions: The *Prince of Wales* sails four times a week and visits
Anegada, Horseshoe Reef, Dog Island, and the baths. These full-day
trips are included with the Admiral's Package. Order a picnic lunch
the night before.

ITINERARY & DAILY SCHEDULE

Here is an example of daily diving, excursions, and activities:

11:11—*Prince of Wales* trip to the baths
13:00—*Paranda* day sail to Dog Island
15:55—*Ponce de Leon*, snorkeling
17:00—*Paranda* sunset sail
17:17—Kilbride Dive Team
19:29—Manager's cocktail party and buffet
21:00—Aerobics class

NIGHTLIFE & ENTERTAINMENT

Most of the guests awaken and retire early. In the morning, you won't find many bleary-eyed zombies trying to find the coffee machine. That life-style does not jibe with sailors who must ride the winds or divers who breathe from tanks. You may see an occasional villa filled with people loudly enjoying themselves well into the evening, but no discos or lounges instigate rowdiness.

AESTHETICS & ENVIRONMENT

You almost expect Mr. Rourke to step out of one of the carts and say, "Welcome to Fantasy Island." The club is breathtaking. The chalets, perched on the side of the mountain, dramatically overlook the ocean. The dining rooms, reception center, sailing school, and other facilities sit along one strip of level ground that runs parallel to the ocean. This makes all common areas easily accessible.

Bitter End guests travel in three types of "people movers": chauffeur-driven carts, a "hillevator," and shuttle boats. You may scoff at the movers, but after the third time you climb the side of a mountain to reach your villa, you will gladly welcome the chance to be moved by some mechanical force.

The Bitter End is a self-contained club. You feel as though you're in a little village, far away from everything, even reality. Visiting yachts form the only outside traffic.

FACILITIES

Bars
Beaches
Concierge
Conference center
Entertainment coordinators
Gift shop
Medical station
Safety-deposit box
Snack bar, grill
Swimming pool
Water sports center

ROOMS

The land-based rooms at the Bitter End blend with the natural beauty of the land. The luxurious hillside chalets have marble baths and airy garden showers with open glass panels that allow a breeze to come sweeping in. The beachfront villas are quite acceptable, but they lack the elegant touches of the chalets. All chalets and villas have decks or verandas with spectacular views.

LUXURY LEVEL

Air-conditioning (chalets)	Phone in room
Clock	Porter service
Laundry service (extra)	Radio
Maid service	Room service

FOOD & DRINK

The Clubhouse Grille serves breakfast and lunch by the pool. For dinner, guests choose between the Clubhouse Steak and Seafood Grille and the English Carvery in the Pavilion. The Bitter End will prepare picnic lunches for those going on day-long excursions.

STAFFING & SERVICE

The sailing staff is young and full of energy. All of the employees, except the sailing instructors and managers, are residents of Virgin Gorda.

PRIVACY & RELAXATION

The pool provides the perfect escape. During the day, most people are involved in water sports, leaving the pool empty. The deck overlooks the ocean. Breakfast, lunch, and cocktails may be enjoyed poolside.

SHOPPING

The gift shop on the property sells a variety of knickknacks. It has shelves lined with bottles that, supposedly, washed onto the shore from the mysterious past. They seem to be a hot item. A regularly scheduled launch service will take you to the Virgin Gorda Shopping Center.

HONEYMOONERS

This club would be good for honeymooners who know each other well. There is so much to do at the Bitter End that you might see each other only rarely during the day.

SINGLES

This is not the best place for singles. It attracts mostly couples and families.

CHILD APPEAL

In the summer, Bitter End gives sailing lessons geared to children. Kids also dine with the captains. Children are seldom seen during the winter months, and there are no special organized activities for them. Kids may participate in all the water sports with parental supervision.

NUTS & BOLTS

BOOKING INFORMATION

The Bitter End Yacht Club International Inc.
875 North Michigan Avenue
Chicago, IL 60611
800-872-2392
312-944-5855

CONTACT INFORMATION

Bitter End Yacht Club
North Sound, Virgin Gorda, BVI
809-494-2746

DEPOSITS/REFUNDS: A three-night deposit is required to guarantee any reservation. It is applied to the first, second, and last nights. Deposits are refundable only on cancellations received prior to October 1 for winter and holiday seasons, or 30 days prior to arrival date for all other seasons.

HANDICAP ACCESSIBILITY: None.

PACKING: You won't need to pack anything fancy. Men wear walking shorts or slacks for dinner, and women can wear anything but a bathing suit or shorts.

RESERVATION SCHEDULE: Book four to six months in advance for the winter months and 60 days in advance for the summer.

NUMBER OF ROOMS: 81 rooms, 11 yachts.

MAXIMUM NUMBER OF GUESTS: 250.

NUMBER OF EMPLOYEES: 200.

FUTURE PLANS: New cottages are under construction.

ARRIVAL AIRPORT: Beef Island Airport, Tortola.

TRAVEL TIME FROM AIRPORT: The Bitter End provides ferry service from the airport. The trip takes about 30 minutes.

SPENDING MONEY: You will need to bring a substantial amount of spending money. The average person signs for $225 in drinks and other services.

Cost Worksheet	High Season[1]	Off-Season[2]
Accommodations (7 days)[3]	$945–$1,285	$485–$647
Food	incl.	incl.
Drinks		
Departure tax	$5	$5
Sports	incl.	incl.
Airfare	_____	_____
Sight-seeing	incl.	incl.
Tips	$9 per person per day, plus extra for the sailing staff	
Additional sports[4]		
Souvenirs	_____	_____

[1] High season dates: January 21 to March 21
[2] Off-season dates: April 9 to November 17, Shoulder season dates: December 18 to January 20, March 25 to April 8
[3] Premium for single persons: Special rates for singles vary with seasons
[4] Offered for extra charge: scuba resort course, $75

CANEEL BAY

VITAL FEATURES

Type of vacation: **Resort**
Target market: **Couples in their thirties through sixties, families with older children and teens**
Location: **St. John, U.S. Virgin Islands**
All-inclusive cost per week: **$1,382–$2,012 per person plus airfare**

RATINGS

Value: 💲💲💲💲💲

Fun quotient: 🏝️🏝️🏝️

Honeymoon suitability: ❤️🖤❤️🖤🖤

Singles meeting ground: 👫

Child appeal: 🍦🍦🍦

Management professionalism: ☎️☎️☎️☎️☎️

Service: 💡💡💡💡

Food: 🦞🦞🦞🦞🦞

THE REAL STORY

Laurance Rockefeller is a man of vision as well as money. He first discovered Caneel Bay in 1952 when it was little more than an overgrown sugar plantation. In fact, most of St. John was then a jungle, with no electricity, fresh water, or modern conveniences. What a perfect place, he decided, to create a resort where he could vacation in complete comfort. Now more than 30 years later, his vision attracts visitors to one of the most remarkable all-inclusive resorts in the world.

The Caneel Bay RockResort rests among 171 acres of natural splendor. The well-groomed grounds roll gently from the interior

214

hills to the sea. Clusters of sea grapes, hibiscus, and bougainvillea punctuate the sweeping views. Coconut palms and mangroves shade the beaches. Cactus plants surround the ruins of the old sugar mill. Designed to soothe and satisfy its viewers, the landscape shelters and screens the guest rooms and other resort facilities. Soft lights line the paths at night. The entire resort radiates a natural, understated elegance.

But an impressive landscape isn't all that Caneel Bay offers. The service and food are first-rate, as are the facilities. The rooms are decorated in bare woods and natural woven fibers. Large picture windows open to views of tropical gardens and white sand beaches. In spite of its modern conveniences, the resort maintains an old-fashioned, sumptuous atmosphere.

At Caneel Bay you can't help but relax. No phones ring. No announcements interrupt the calm. You set your own pace. You can simply enjoy the afternoon in a hammock in the shade, or indulge in the numerous activities. The resort features seven beaches, tennis courts, a swimming pool, and an assortment of water sports. A calypso band performs after dinner, and bartenders serve tasty tropical libations. Whatever you choose to do during your vacation, you'll go home feeling satisfied and planning the next visit.

INCLUDED

Accommodations	Sports
Activities	Sports instruction
Entertainment & dancing	Tours
Food	Transfer to and from airport

VALUE

The resort offers a quality vacation for people who appreciate the finer things in life and are willing to pay for them. You'll get your money's worth out of your stay at Caneel Bay.

ACTIVITIES, SPORTS, & EXCURSIONS

While there is plenty to do on an individual basis, the resort offers visitors a limited choice of planned social activities. Organized activities include round-robin tennis tournaments, rum tastings, a kitchen tour, and the manager's weekly cocktail reception.

ACTIVITIES

Board games	Movies
Dancing	Sunbathing
Entertainment/shows	

SPORTS

Aerobics	Scuba resort course (extra)
Aquacise	Snorkeling
Bicycles	Swimming (pool and ocean)
Horseback riding	Tennis
Jogging and hiking trails	Volleyball
Sailing	Windsurfing
Scuba (extra)	

EXCURSIONS: If for some reason you can't find enough to do among the resort's beaches, trails, fields, ruins, and recreational activities, Caneel Bay will send you on one of its many excursions. Don't worry about missing meals while you're away. The kitchen supplies box lunches for all adventures.

The resort provides a number of boating activities from sunset cocktail cruises to day sails around the island. The *Buccaneer* ferry cruise serves lunch at Francis Bay and stops for snorkeling on nearby reefs. Special diving trips take scuba enthusiasts to the wreck of the *Rhone* and other popular dive sites. Equipment and instruction are available.

Plenty of excursions await those folks who prefer to stay on land. Virgin Islands National Park surrounds the resort and awaits exploration. Self-guided trails leave directly from Caneel Bay. Ranger-guided tours to Reef Bay reward hikers with a look at petroglyphs made by early island inhabitants. One such glyph forms the Caneel Bay logo.

If walking is too slow, rent a Jeep from the activities desk and explore the island. Steep and winding roads pay off with panoramic views of Drake's Passage and the surrounding islands. Taxis provide sight-seeing tours for people who don't feel comfortable driving on the left side of the road. The ferry to Little Dix Bay costs $25 each way; to Cruz Bay, for shopping, $4; and to St. Thomas it's free.

ITINERARY & DAILY SCHEDULE

Your time is completely your own. Greet the dawn and be the first one at the beach, or sleep away the morning. Room service serves breakfast until 10:00 A.M. Meals are the only schedule you'll have to meet.

NIGHTLIFE & ENTERTAINMENT

Caneel Bay has no stage shows, discos, or casinos. It does feature live music and dancing at night, but things tend to be quiet in the evenings. Nightlife in Cruz Bay is not far off, if you are looking for something more lively.

AESTHETICS & ENVIRONMENT

Few resorts are as aesthetically pleasing as Caneel Bay. The architecture blends harmoniously with the environment rather than interrupting the flow of the land. The low-profile buildings are spacious and airy. Ceiling fans circulate the fresh scents of numerous tropical flowers. The resort fosters a quiet, casual atmosphere, conducive to rest and relaxation.

FACILITIES

Bars
Beaches
Concierge
Gift shop
Medical station
Piano bar

Rental cars
Safety-deposit box (in room)
Snack bar
Swimming pool
Water-sports center

ROOMS

Natural fabrics and woods combine with wicker chairs, ceramic tiles, and ceiling fans to give a tropical flavor. Large picture windows open onto a private terrace with lawn furniture. The Premium rooms on Scotts Beach feel most secluded, but all 171 guest cottages provide privacy and great views.

LUXURY LEVEL

Ceiling fans
Hair dryers (on request)
Laundry service (extra)
Maid service

Porter service
Refrigerator in room (on request)
Room service (breakfast only)

FOOD & DRINK

The food is both sumptuous and copious. Specialties range from cold fruit soups and salmon mousse for lunch to dinners of charcoal-grilled fish and lobster. Meals can be enjoyed in the more formal Turtle Bay Dining Room or on the open-air Beach Terrace with no walls between you and the sea.

The head chef pleases even the most discriminating palates. He and his staff try to accommodate special diets. The high standards of the cuisine are equaled only by the quality of the resort's service staff. Waiters cater to all your needs. Bartenders administer "thirst aid" all day in each of the lounges and on the Beach Terrace. On Wednesdays special rum tastings and drink-mixing demonstrations are featured.

Two restaurants serve Continental and full breakfasts. Room service also delivers breakfast to those too indolent to make the walk to the dining room. Lunch can be ordered from the menu or dished up buffet style. All three restaurants produce a bountiful selection of fruits, salads, soups, sandwiches, and meats. Box lunches await those who engage in off-resort excursions. Guests who stay on the property can get tea and pastries every afternoon from the Turtle Bay Lounge.

Eight-course events tantalize your senses and erode your will-power. Appetizers include Jamaican duck liver pâté, grilled polenta with Littleneck clam rolls, and traditional shrimp cocktails. Entrées range from grilled lamb to Peking-style duck, to grilled marinated rabbit with wild mushroom ravioli. Fresh seafoods also make up a good portion of the menu with dishes such as scallops, lobster with caviar, and blue crabs with whiskey.

The Sugar Mill Restaurant features a buffet cookout. Limited space is available, so be sure to make a reservation. The Turtle Bay Dining Room offers two seatings by reservation only. Jackets are required. None of the restaurants or lounges permits shorts after 7:00 P.M. Limited seatings demand that you rotate restaurants without eating in the same one for two nights in a row. Dinner reservations for Turtle Bay and the Sugar Mill must be made a day in advance. Room service orders have to be placed the night before. Checks come for signature after each meal. Gratuity is at your discretion.

STAFFING & SERVICE

Caneel Bay is an exemplary resort. The quality shows in everything, from the splendid food and friendly service to the large, comfortable rooms and magnificent grounds. The staff reflects the resort's approach completely.

PRIVACY & RELAXATION

The open spaces and strategic landscaping of the resort ensure that active guests will not disturb those who prefer quieter pursuits. The rooms and adjoining patios provide privacy, as do the numerous walks and paths. Plenty of quiet places await those willing to wander through the trees and fields.

SHOPPING

The resort gift shop features some very nice souvenirs. Be sure to save some time and liquidity to take advantage of St. Thomas's world-famous shopping.

HONEYMOONERS

Caneel Bay offers some nice extras for honeymooners. Newlyweds get a Tiffany picture frame, a complimentary bottle of champagne, and a 1½-hour cruise. Caneel Bay management says it gets over 1,000 honeymooners a year. Long strolls on the beach or beneath the trees and open-air sunset dinners lend a romantic flair to the vacation. Room service for breakfast is also quite popular with newlyweds who aren't ready to leave their rooms in the morning.

SINGLES

Although Caneel Bay attracts a strong percentage of families and couples, midlife singles do come with friends of the same sex. Who knows what romance might await?

CHILD APPEAL

Caneel Bay has no special children's activities, but kids can use the adult facilities. Older kids will find plenty to do, but younger ones may get bored. Children under 8 years of age are not permitted.

NUTS & BOLTS

BOOKING & CONTACT INFORMATION

Caneel Bay
P.O. Box 720
Cruz Bay, St. John, U.S. Virgin Islands 00830
809-776-6111
800-223-7637

DEPOSITS/REFUNDS: Caneel Bay requires a 3-day deposit to confirm reservations. The amount is due within 14 days of the reservation request. Refunds are paid only if written notice is received at least 28 days before the arrival date.

ELECTRICITY: 100 volts 60 cycles, same as in the United States.

HANDICAP ACCESSIBILITY: Caneel Bay can make special provisions if you give them notice. The resort has rather hilly terrain, and some distance separates the buildings. There are a few steps, but not an excessive amount. The lounge and beach terrace have ramp access.

PACKING: In the evening, gentlemen wear jackets. Semiformal attire is suggested for women. Be sure to pack some good hiking/walking shoes for exploring the national park. Bring your own mask and snorkel, unless you feel like sharing community property.

RELIGIOUS SERVICES: The resort holds interdenominational service on Sundays. St. Thomas has a synagogue and Catholic and Protestant churches. St. John has several churches as well. Transportation can be arranged.

RESERVATION SCHEDULE: Reservations should be made a year in advance. The average stay lasts seven to ten days, although the length of stay is flexible. During the Christmas season (December 23 to January 2) Caneel requires guests to stay a minimum of ten days. Many guests combine a stay at Caneel with a visit to one of the other RockResorts.

SIZE: 171 acres, plus 5,000 acres of surrounding Virgin Islands National Park.

NUMBER OF ROOMS: 171 guest villas.

MAXIMUM NUMBER OF GUESTS: 513.

NUMBER OF EMPLOYEES: 552.

Cost Worksheet		
	High Season[1]	*Off-Season*[2]
Accommodations		
(7 days)[3]	$2,765–$4,025	$1,925–$2,765
Food	incl.	incl.
Drinks		
Departure tax	none	none
State tax	7½%	7½%
Hotel tax	none	none
Sports	incl.	incl.
Airfare	_____	_____
Sight-seeing		
Tips		
Additional, sports[4]		
Souvenirs	_____	_____

[1] High season dates: December 20–April 16
[2] Off-season dates: June 1 to October 31. Shoulder season dates: April 17 to May 31, November 1 to December 19
[3] Premium for single person: $380
[4] Offered for extra charge: scuba certification (resort course), $65; massage, $35.

TRAVEL TIME: Guests arriving at the St. Thomas airport should report to the Caneel Bay Lounge at the airport, where transportation via taxi can be arranged to Caneel Bay ferries. Private ferries leave for Caneel Bay periodically throughout the day, and guests ride free of charge. Public ferries leave from Charlotte Amalie and Red Hook. One-way charges are $12 and $9 respectively. The trip from St. Thomas to St. John takes about 30 minutes.

SPENDING MONEY: Bring enough money for tips, drinks, shopping in St. Thomas.

All rates per person, based on double occupancy for a seven-night stay.

Always ask if any special packages, promotions, or airfare discounts are in effect before booking.

All vacations described in this guide can be booked through any competent travel agent; we advise you to do so.

See the general introduction and area introductions for more details.

LITTLE DIX BAY

VITAL FEATURES

Type of vacation: **Resort**
Target market: **Mature crowd (and a few yuppies)**
Location: **Virgin Gorda, Virgin Islands**
All-inclusive cost per week: **$1,837 plus airfare**

RATINGS

Value: 💲💲💲💲

Fun quotient: 🏝️🏝️🏝️

Honeymoon suitability: ❤️❤️❤️❤️

Singles meeting ground: 👫

Child appeal: 🍦

Management professionalism: ☎️☎️☎️☎️☎️

Service: 💡💡💡💡💡

Food: 🦞🦞🦞🦞

THE REAL STORY

Many cruises and resorts arrange for the guest's transportation from the airport. Often this consists of a harried-looking person awkwardly holding up a cardboard sign with the name of the resort written in Magic Marker, around which hordes of uncertain tourists swarm. At Little Dix Bay, however, both the hosts and the guests emit an aura of ease and confidence. There are no signs of amateurism at Little Dix Bay or, for that matter, at any of the Rock-Resorts. It is obvious that for these guests, vacations are a pleasant and frequent occurrence, rather than a risky enterprise undertaken only once every ten years or so.

Laurance S. Rockefeller has an uncanny knack for discovering the most beautiful spots in the Caribbean, acquiring the land, and then creating a RockResort on the property. The three RockResorts in the Caribbean are carefully designed with the environment in mind. They appear to melt effortlessly into the landscape. The resorts eventually become synonymous with the island on which they are located, making it impossible to recall the island without thinking of the resort.

Little Dix Bay is nestled along a half-mile crescent-shaped beach. In the tradition of all RockResorts, it refrains from boxing, bundling, balling, or hedging the natural landscape; instead, it encourages Mother Nature to do the decorating. Mahogany and flowering trees surround the sloping lawns, creating a natural wall around the resort. The profusion of wild growth inside the wall is staggering.

Little Dix Bay is as warm and welcoming as it is posh. After 20 years of operation, the resort has acquired a fiercely dedicated clientele. Many guests come at the same time each year and expect to vacation together.

Management likes to tell the story of the time when Dick Cavett, a frequent guest, brought Muhammad Ali to Little Dix. "The champ" summed up his thoughts on the resort by saying, "Hey, man, this is paradise."

INCLUDED

Accommodations	Sports
Activities	Sports instruction
Entertainment & dancing	Taxes
Food	Tips
Island picnic	Transfer to and from airport

VALUE

A RockResort vacation is as high in value as it is in price. There are a number of special packages available from April to December, when rates are lower than during the regular season.

ACTIVITIES, SPORTS, & EXCURSIONS

Planned activities are limited and the pace is relaxing. Little Dix provides a Boston Whaler taxi that will take you to seven Virgin Gorda beaches or to the baths, a series of giant boulders shielding deep, clear pools. The concierge distributes a list of things to do on the island.

ACTIVITIES: Music/dancing, movies, sunbathing, weekly horticultural tours.

SPORTS: The Virgin Gorda Yacht Harbor, owned by Little Dix Bay, is home to 120 boats. Many of the vessels are available to guests for day charters. Tennis clinics are held regularly at the resort. Sailors can catch some wind in a Sunfish or a 49-foot Hinkley.

Sailing	Tennis (seven courts)
Snorkeling	Waterskiing
Swimming	

EXCURSIONS: A Boston Whaler sails to other beaches for a day outing and picnic on Thursdays.

ITINERARY & DAILY SCHEDULE

A pamphlet in your room lists all of the activities offered at the resort and those at neighboring locations. You could go the entire week without wearing a watch. There are no schedules. Activities are offered several times throughout the day.

NIGHTLIFE & ENTERTAINMENT

There is no nightlife at Little Dix Bay. Most people head to town after dinner. The Pavilion hosts an occasional impromptu party. The four interconnected Polynesian-style huts provide the perfect spot for mingling.

A steel band plays during dinner. Afterward, people relax on the terraces, go to the beach, or sit in one of the cafés.

AESTHETICS & ENVIRONMENT

The main buildings at Little Dix Bay are surrounded by open-air terraces. The open-air environment tends to make people friendly and allows them to interact freely.

FACILITIES

Bars	Gift shop
Beaches	Safety-deposit box
Beauty salon	Snack bar, grill
Concierge	

ROOMS

Hexagonal-theme rooms all face the sea. Some rest on stilts. All have patios.

LUXURY LEVEL

Hair dryer
Laundry service
Maid service

Porter service
Refrigerator in room
Room service

FOOD & DRINK

Guests enjoy three meals a day. The menu varies daily, and includes French, Continental, seafood, and other fresh dishes, often with light sauces. The food is uniformly excellent. Drinks cost extra, but the resort gets you started with a complimentary bottle of rum upon arrival.

The Sugar Mill Bar and the Pavilion Dining Room form a romantic, interconnected dining and lounge area. The Pavilion serves all three meals. The Sugar Mill serves lunch and dinner. The Oceanfront Beach House offers casual Continental breakfasts, lunches, and cocktails.

STAFFING & SERVICE

The employees are islanders who view Little Dix Bay as "their" resort. You can tell right away that they do their jobs with pride.

PRIVACY & RELAXATION

The resort hides in a very remote locale. No telephones or televisions disturb your peace. It's up to you to make your own fun.

SHOPPING

A gift shop on the property sells items that tend to be touristy and expensive. Go to the town to find authentic local products.

HONEYMOONERS

Little Dix Bay offers a special honeymoon vacation from April to December. The newly married couple receives a bottle of champagne and a Tiffany picture frame engraved with the Little Dix crest.

SINGLES

This is a great place to catch the rich older person of your dreams, but you may spend a lot of money waiting around for an eligible one to show up.

CHILD APPEAL

Children under the age of 8 are not allowed at Little Dix Bay. The atmosphere is quite adult.

NUTS & BOLTS

BOOKING & CONTACT INFORMATION

Little Dix Bay
P.O. Box 6313
Church Street Station
New York, NY 10249
212-765-5950
800-223-7637

Little Dix Bay
P.O. Box 70
Virgin Gorda, British Virgin
    Islands
809-495-5555
Fax: 809-495-5661

DEPOSITS/REFUNDS: A deposit equal to three nights' accommodations is required to guarantee a reservation, and is due within 14 days of the reservation request. A refund of the deposit will be made if you notify the resort of cancellation at least 28 days prior to your arrival date.

ELECTRICITY: 110 volts 60 cycles. Same as in the United States.

HANDICAP ACCESSIBILITY: None, although the staff will try hard to accommodate special needs.

Cost Worksheet	High Season[1]	Off-Season[2]
Accommodations (7 days)[3]	$1,837	$1,137
Food	incl.	incl.
Drinks		
Departure tax	$5	$5
Sports	incl.	incl.
Airfare	_____	_____
Sight-seeing		
Tips[4]		
Additional sports		
Souvenirs	_____	_____

[1] High season dates: December 20 to April 15
[2] Off-season dates: June 1 to October 31. Shoulder season dates: April 16 to May 31, November 1 to December 19
[3] Premium for single person: Double rate less $65
[4] Tips: High season, approximately $150; off-season, approximately $90

PACKING: You will need a beach wrap and sandals for daytime meals. After 6:00 P.M. gentlemen are required to don jackets; women wear semiformal evening attire.

RELIGIOUS SERVICES: None are offered on the property, but the concierge will provide you with a list of local services

RESERVATION SCHEDULE: You should book three to four months in advance for the winter months and two to three months in advance for the summer.

SIZE: 500 acres.

NUMBER OF ROOMS: 102.

ARRIVAL AIRPORT: Virgin Gorda.

TRAVEL TIME FROM THE AIRPORT: 3 minutes.

HAWAII

INTRODUCTION

A recent survey discovered that a large percentage of lottery winners spent their first prize dollars on a trip to Hawaii. The mythical lure of these islands has ingrained itself in the minds of Americans and Canadians. The fabled beaches, perfect climate, and dreams of an endless summer call people from around the world.

Many people go to Waikiki, seeking the nightlife, shops, and East-West interchange. Others avoid Hawaii altogether because their vision of the islands is obscured by the glass-and-concrete boxes that rise from the beaches of Waikiki. For them, the fiftieth state bears a closer resemblance to Miami Beach than paradise. However, if you study Waikiki's backdrop—from the clear Pacific waters to chiseled Diamond Head—you may discern that the real Hawaii exists beyond the built-up beachfront. In fact, Hawaii offers something for both people who seek urban activity and those who desire pristine beauty.

Many people view Hawaii as a once-in-a-lifetime vacation, so they try to pack a tour of all the islands into a week or two. This is like trying to see Europe in a month. You might see a lot, but you'll experience little. A far more sensible approach involves getting to know one or two locations well, then taking a few side trips or a cruise around the islands. The cruise approach will at least alleviate the burden of packing, unpacking, and arranging transportation and accommodations.

Unlike some other destinations, Hawaii offers no compelling reason to go to an all-inclusive resort. In fact, many people prefer to travel the islands at their own pace. On the other hand, three excellent resorts are well worth a visit. Each offers the guests an opportunity to enjoy Hawaii's weather, culture, and natural beauty with all the advantages that are offered by all-inclusives in general. A fourth all-inclusive, American Hawaiian Cruises, offers the tourists a chance to see a representative sample of Hawaii's diversity and spectacular landscapes. It is reviewed in the Cruises section.

THE ISLANDS

A short visit to the islands usually converts tourists to Hawaii lovers. Below are brief descriptions of the islands that you may decide to visit. Everybody seems to come back from Hawaii with his own favorite island.

HAWAII ("THE BIG ISLAND"): The home of the volcano goddess Pele, Hawaii was King Kamehameha's royal, political, and cultural center. Pele's fire still burns in Volcano National Park, where visitors climb on a landscape that was used by NASA to simulate the moon's surface. You can walk through the caldera of the active volcano right up to the crater.

The island's best beaches are found on the west coast of the island in the Kailua-Kona area. There are also archaeological remains of the homes of Hawaii's royal family. One of the world's finest all-inclusives, Kona Village, is built on the grounds of an ancient Hawaiian village.

In striking contrast to the volcanic areas, the eastern part of the island holds some of the lushest landscape on all the islands, made so by the average of 136 inches of rain that it receives each year. Botanical buffs will find the flora and fauna of this side of the island well worth exploring.

KAUAI: Kauai is the Hawaii of your dreams—and that of Hollywood movies. Created out of one volcano, the top of the island gets more rain than anyplace else on earth: 471 inches per year! The water pours down the mountain, forming spectacular waterfalls and creating lush, green scenery. At sea level, the beaches and parks are everything that you could wish Hawaii to be: warm and scenic, with waves. The drive through the countryside is equally spectacular. Lush green farms and ranches make patterns on the valley when viewed from the mountains.

Kauai is the lush, tropical Hawaii that most resembles Hollywood's version of paradise. Moviemakers used the waterfalls that run off Kauai's green mountains for the opening shots of "Fantasy Island" and the stomping grounds for Gilligan. The setting that directors often choose is Coco Palms, a resort that is reviewed later in this section.

MAUI: "Maui no ka oi," say the natives, meaning "Maui is the best." The island can certainly make a case for that claim. Maui gets more sun than the other popular islands, an incredible 350 days of the year—virtually every day that Rodney Dangerfield doesn't visit. The scenery is so beautiful that Hawaiian legend made this island the home of the demi-god Maui. Today, scarce real estate commands astronomical prices. It should surprise no one that Maui has more millionaires per capita than either Palm Springs or the French Riviera; its beauty also outshines either of these locations.

The real Maui wowie is the local marijuana, grown in the dense cane fields. Many say that it is Hawaii's most valuable cash crop. Perhaps it contributes to the carefree attitude, serenity, and sense of confidence that most islanders feel.

Boats land in Lahaina, a charming seaport that served as Hawaii's capital before Kamehameha's son moved it to Honolulu. Now, Maui welcomes two million tourists a year, second only to Oahu. Whale hunters made Lahaina a hell-raising, whoring town before the missionaries tamed it a bit. The missionaries came to do good and ended up doing very well. Their descendants now own most of the private land on the islands.

Although the whalers have left, the whales still spawn off the coast of Maui from late November to early May. Voyeurs can pull out their binoculars to get a close look as the giant creatures frolic and mate.

MOLOKAI: In Hawaiian, Molokai means "barren sea." Although the land suits ranchers and pineapple farmers well, very few tourists have discovered it. The island has many virgin beaches and one-horse towns. Development has been slow and rare.

OAHU: Oahu, meaning "gathering place," houses 75 percent of Hawaii's population and attracts the bulk of Hawaii's tourists. People come here for the beaches, the famous surfing, and the historical monuments, including Pearl Harbor.

The town of Honolulu services the state's best deep-water port, military bases, and commerce. History and architecture buffs would find the old town worth visiting even if Waikiki Beach was nowhere close by. The influence of Chinese, British, and Japanese cultures mixes with the local and American customs to produce a special blend in this modern city.

To many people, Waikiki represents overcommercialization and a warning to other islands, especially Maui. Other people find the atmosphere exciting. They stay for the shops, nightlife, restaurants, beaches, and resorts. They are willing to look past the skyscrapers to the incredible natural beauty of banana fields, the surfing beach of Waimea, and Diamond Head crater. With a little exploring, visitors can find natural beauty that ranks with the best that Hawaii has to offer.

Oahu, well known for the naval base at Pearl Harbor, is now regularly attacked by hordes of tourists. The Polynesian Cultural Center re-creates the South Pacific culture and music, although the authentic feeling is somewhat sanitized by the center's Mormon operators. It is well worth a visit. The buffet, however, is overpriced, and of fairly low quality.

Oahu has quickly become the honeymoon spot of choice for the Japanese. In fact, you may hear more Japanese spoken than English in numerous restaurants and hotels, many of which are owned by Japanese companies.

An oasis of charm and civility in Waikiki is the Moana Surfrider Hotel, a turn-of-the-century landmark. Wealthy guests who visited the island in the early 1900s stayed there. The hotel has recently been renovated into a resort that has retained the feeling of a genteel guest house. One section of the hotel is reserved for guests of Club Perillo, which we review in detail later in this part.

NUTS & BOLTS

CONTACT INFORMATION (Visitor's Information Bureaus):

State of Hawaii:
  2270 Kalakaua Avenue,
      Suite 801
  Waikiki Business Plaza
  Waikiki, HI 96815
  808-923-1811

Hawaii (The Big Island):
  Hilo Plaza, Suite 104
  180 Kinoole Street
  Hilo, HI 96721

Kauai:
  Lihue Plaza Building
  Suite 207
  3016 Umi Street
  Lihue, HI 96715

Maui:
  County Building
  200 High Street
  Wailuku, HI 96793

CURRENCY: The same Yankee dollars used elsewhere in the United States.

CUSTOMS/DUTY: The United States Department of Agriculture regulates what plants and foods you can bring on and off the islands. They often search bags. If you buy a plant, make sure that it is marked "USDA approved for export."

The following common items may not be taken off the islands: berries; cactus plants; cotton; some fresh flowers; any fruit other than pineapples, coconuts, and papayas; plants in soil; soil; sugarcane; insects; and snails.

Local custom says that Pele exacts revenge on those who take lava rock from the islands. Seeming rational people tell stories of the horrors that have afflicted people who have violated this taboo. Supposedly, the docks and post office are full of rocks that the afflicted have sent back but locals will not unload.

FESTIVALS/HOLIDAYS: All the standard U.S. holidays are used as excuses to play hookey from work. In addition, numerous local celebrations spark the local spirit. Check with the tourist bureau to find out which holidays fall during your visit.

LANGUAGES: Hawaiians speak English, but you might not recognize it as such. They often talk with a strong Pacific accent and use different expressions. "Eh brah, howzit," for example, roughly translates to "How's it going?" "Cockaroach" means to rip off, and "s'koshi" indicates a little bit or a little person.

The Hawaiian alphabet has only twelve letters, and the similarity of names often makes recognition of places difficult for the newcomer. In addition, native Hawaiian words have made it into the local language for all residents, including relative newcomers. The following list gives some commonly used words.

Hawaiian	Pronunciation	English
Aikane	Eye-kah-nay	Friend
Ala	Ah-lah	Roadway
Aloha	Ah-lo-hah	Hello/good-bye
Ewe	Eh-vah	Westerly
Hale	Hahlay	House/hut
Haole	Ha-oh-lay	Caucasian
Kai	Ki	Sea
Kamaaina	Kah-mah-aye-nah	Native
Kane	Kahnay	Man
Lanai	Lah-nye	Balcony/patio
Lua	Loo-ah	Rest room
Luau	Loo-ow	Native feast
Mahalo	Mah-hah-low	Thank you
Makani	Mah-kah-nee	Wind
Moku	Mow-koo	Ship
Pali	Pah-lee	Cliff
Puka	Poo-kah	Hole
Pupu	Poo-poo	Hors d'oeuvre
Wahine	Vah-hee-nay	Woman
Wikiwiki	Weekee-weekee	Fast/quick

PACKING: In general, the Hawaiians dress very casually. They generally avoid the use of ties and button-up shirts. Some of the finer restaurants in Waikiki ask that men wear sports jackets and women wear dresses or pantsuits. The weather stays warm year-round, so a lot of warm clothing is not necessary for tourists. Some nights on the beach feel a bit cool because of the wind. A light jacket or a sweater will cure that. Trips into the high mountains require warmer clothing. "Liquid sunshine" feels suspiciously like a warm rain. Guard against that. Most of all, bring comfortable walking shoes, beach wear, binoculars, and a camera. If you come from a cold climate, don't forget to dress in layers that you can quickly strip when you land in Hawaii, or bring a change of clothes in your carry-on bag.

All airlines servicing Honolulu allow two checked bags and one carry-on. Checked luggage may generally not exceed 70 pounds. The "puddle-jumpers" that hop between islands are sometimes strict in the number of bags and weight that they'll allow.

RELIGIOUS SERVICES: Unless you plan to make human sacrifices to the volcano goddess Pele, you will probably find a church of your denomination. Hotel rooms often have both a Bible and the teachings of Buddha in English and Japanese.

RENTAL CARS: Stiff competition usually keeps prices low and availability high, although cars are sometimes scarce and expensive if you want to rent one at the last minute. Try to plan at least a few days in advance. Check the local free magazines for ads.

TELEPHONES: Hawaii uses area code 808. Standard U.S. telephone companies service the state. You may occasionally have trouble hooking in with some long-distance services once you leave Oahu.

TIME: Hawaiian time is two hours earlier than West Coast Time, three hours earlier than Mountain, four hours earlier than Central, and five hours earlier than Eastern Standard Time.

TRAVEL TIME BY AIR

To Honolulu:
Chicago: **9 hours 30 minutes**
Los Angeles: **6 hours**
New York: **12 hours**
Toronto: **11 hours**

VACCINATION REQUIREMENTS: None.

VISA/PASSPORT REQUIREMENTS: Standard for the United States. None for U.S. or Canadian citizens.

WATER: Tap water is generally safe to drink. For conservation reasons, restaurants do not always serve it unless asked.

COCO PALMS RESORT

VITAL FEATURES

Type of vacation: **Resort**
Target market: **Couples, families, Elvis Presley fans of all ages**
Location: **Lihue, Kauai**
All-inclusive cost per week: **Not applicable (this is *not* an all-inclusive)**

RATINGS

Value: 💲💲💲

Fun quotient: ☂☂☂☂

Honeymoon suitability: ❤❤❤

Singles meeting ground: 👤

Management professionalism: ☎☎☎☎

Service: 💡💡💡

Food: 🦞🦞

THE REAL STORY

You've seen Kauai, even if you've never traveled to Hawaii. Film-makers come here regularly to shoot scenes. Gilligan chose this as his home before "Fantasy Island" recognized the same beauty a few decades later. Appropriately named the "garden isle," Kauai served as the ape's kingdom in the 1976 production of *King Kong*, as the Huleia River for *Raiders of the Lost Ark*, and as Vietnam for *Uncommon Valor*. Anyone who has visited the island understands why it makes such a great setting. It offers spectacular waterfalls, lush foliage, and rocky mountain peaks.

You can share in cinematic history by staying at Coco Palms, a setting that filmmakers favor for its charm and authentic representation of Polynesia. In many ways, this resort created the world's vision

237

of Hawaii. Michener's *Hawaii*, Elvis's *Blue Hawaii*, and other films have used the island and the Coco Palms Resort to represent the South Pacific. The chapel from Rita Hayworth's wedding in *Sadie Thompson* still stands. Ricardo Montalban welcomed visitors to "Fantasy Island" on the bridge spanning the royal lagoon.

Technically not an all-inclusive resort, Coco Palms deserves to be your haunt on Kauai. It was built on sacred ground that Hawaiian royalty chose as the best in the islands. According to legend, the first *alii* (royalty) from Tahiti landed in the area. They kept Wailua Beach as their personal playground, forbidding commoners its use. The island's last queen, Deborah Kapule, made it her home and built canals to fatten fresh mullet and turtle for her royal feasts; the resort was laid out around these holding ponds. About 100 years ago, a German immigrant planted the coconut trees that give the resort its name.

Visitors stay in Polynesian-style huts and in a modern mid-rise hotel with Polynesian decor. The Lagoon features a long-running Polynesian show that can be viewed by the grandchildren of people who first saw it 34 years ago.

The resort provides something for almost any guest. On the grounds are a museum, tennis courts, mullet-stocked canals, a zoo, a shopping center, and an activities desk. The front desk lends snorkeling equipment and beach mats for the fine beach just across the road.

Elvis Presley loved Coco Palms. It served as the site for his wedding in *Blue Hawaii*. Elvis Presley aficionados come from all over the world, including Japan, which brings Japanese Elvis impersonators and, believe it or not, look-alikes. If your wedding fantasy involves the King (not Kamehameha), the management will re-create Elvis's wedding scene, including the canoes on the lagoon.

The management of the resort also has a flair for less romantic productions. Each night, local men clad in traditional red *malos* (loincloths) run through the coconut fields lighting torches in an elaborate ceremony. The pageantry should not be missed. These forerunners of your lawn tikki torches set the 100-year-old palm plantation aglow. The effect is truly stunning. It is worth making a special trip to visit the resort to see the ceremony, even if you don't stay there. Be sure to bathe your ankles in mosquito repellent if you go to watch the performance.

INCLUDED: Accommodations, beach paraphernalia, some activities.

VALUE

Coco Palms doesn't have the feel of a superluxurious chichi resort. In fact, the decor and ambience are a little dated compared to the megaresorts and new establishments like Kona Village. However, the prices make it affordable for the average couple or family, people who might enjoy paying less for their stay so they can do other things with their money. Besides, Kauai is an island worth exploring. You probably would not want to spend much time in any resort when you are surrounded by so much beauty.

ACTIVITIES, SPORTS, & EXCURSIONS

Every day the Palace Museum and Library exhibits its collection of Hawaiian artifacts and historical information. The zoo houses royal peacocks, gibbons, a donkey, and other pets.

Additional activities include fishing in the canals (the resort furnishes bamboo poles and bait), lei making, haku headband weaving, shellcraft classes and demonstrations, lessons in contemporary and traditional hula dances, ukulele lessons, and a walking tour of the historic grounds.

ACTIVITIES

Arts & crafts	Movies (in room)
Culture/music/language classes	Sunbathing
	Television/movies
Dancing	
Entertainment/shows	

SPORTS: The activities director passes out paraphernalia for Wailua Beach, including snorkeling equipment, boogie boards, and beach mats. Anglers can book trips for deep-sea fishing. The three clay and six hard-surface tennis courts earned Coco Palms a five-star rating by *World Tennis* magazine. Pros teach students and rent rackets.

Aerobics/exercise class (& aquacise)	Ping-Pong
	Shuffleboard
Billiards	Snorkeling (off resort)
Croquet	Swimming (pool big enough for laps)
Crushed coral jogging course	
Golf (extra)	Tennis (clay & hard courts)

NIGHTLIFE & ENTERTAINMENT

Wednesday through Saturday, Larry Rivera brings out the old Hawaiian show in the dining room. Mr. Rivera has hosted the show for the last 30 years, and probably has not changed a joke or a song in that time. He brings people onstage, gets them to dance the hula, and then embarrasses them. All this delights the audience. The resort has dubbed him an "institution" and a "legend in his own time." The audience forgives the dated act in the same way that we all laugh with veteran comedians. If you want to see the show, which is included in the price of dinner, you'd probably do better to eat at Coco Palms's other restaurant, the Sea Shell, across the street. Then have a drink at the Lagoon dining room.

AESTHETICS & ENVIRONMENT

Guests are housed in three-story buildings and thatched-roof cottages.

FACILITIES

Bars (3)
Beaches (public, across the street)
Beauty salon
Concierge

Gift shop (several in a ministrip offering sundries & souvenirs)
Jacuzzi (8-person)
Swimming pools (3)

ROOMS

The good-size rooms have all the conveniences that you would expect of a modern hotel, except that they have a few tropical touches, like a shell sink and aqua fish tiles in the bathroom.

LUXURY LEVEL

Air-conditioning
Clock
Laundry service (extra)
Maid service
Phone in room

Porter service
Radio
Refrigerator in room
Room service
Television in room

FOOD & DRINK

What a pity that a dining room as scenic as the Lagoon does not offer better cuisine. The fried and breaded recipes served when we visited seemed to be left over from the days when Mr. Rivera started playing there 30 years ago. The service left the guests waiting, and people at many tables complained about being served cold food. The breakfast buffet was similarly inadequate. Management renovated the resort a few years ago, and one can only hope that the main restaurant's menu will be updated also. Dinner for two costs approximately $35. The breakfast buffet charges $10 per person.

We did not try the Sea Shell restaurant or the Lotus Court Chinese restaurant, but guests reported that the food at those places was better. Both offer a chance to eat on a terrace overlooking Wailua's sandy beach.

Do not avoid staying at Coco Palms because of the food. It's not included in the package, so you can eat anywhere. Perhaps by the time this book hits the stores, the new management will have upgraded it also. Ask guests you think may be reliable sources for restaurant suggestions.

STAFFING & SERVICE

The front desk and maintenance staff do an outstanding job. The dining room crew gives you plenty of time to enjoy the view.

PRIVACY & RELAXATION

Most people seemed to use Coco Palms as a base to do their island tours. However, it offers much more than a standard hotel. A relaxing environment for tourists, the Jacuzzis feel good after a day on the beach or exploring Kauai. Also, parents can send their kids off to activities or the beach while they find some private time.

The tennis courts, beach, jogging trail, zoo, and activities provide things to do on the property. You might not find enough on-premises to keep you occupied for a week's stay, but it's a great place to hang out for a few days.

SHOPPING

A strip of stores offers souvenirs, sundries, Hawaiian fashions, jewelry, flowers, and local ice cream. The Palms Beauty Shop coifs guests. The prices in these shops tend to be a little high. The macadamia nut ice cream is worth any price.

HONEYMOONERS

Many honeymooners choose to make Coco Palms their base while in Hawaii. They often return to revisit the scene of the crime. A three-night package in a superior room costs $440. A junior suite with a lagoon view costs $595.

SINGLES

North Americans won't find many singles here. We did observe a few groups of single Japanese women, but they didn't speak English.

CHILD APPEAL

Your kids could have a great time here. The beach lies just across the street. There are many places where they can tromp through the woods and fields. Coco Palms offers lots of activities for kids as well as a pool for splashing. The tour desk features many fun family outings. The prices and modest $15 charge for kids make this an affordable place for a family to stay.

NUTS & BOLTS

BOOKING & CONTACT INFORMATION

Coco Palms Resort
P.O. Box 631
Lihue, HI 96766
800-542-COCO
808-822-4921

DEPOSITS/REFUNDS: If you book from December 20 until March 31, you must pay a 2-night deposit, with tax, within 10 days of making reservations. Cancellations must be made 7 days prior to the date of arrival. From April 1 through December 19 guests need a 1-day deposit with 48 hours cancellation. All packages must be prepaid in full. No refunds are given for last-minute cancellations.

HANDICAP ACCESSIBILITY: Two rooms are fitted for handicapped guests, one superior and one deluxe. Both rooms are available at the same rate as the other rooms of their class. Disabled guests will find easy access to most parts of the resort. Just make a request.

PACKING: Casual dress applies for dinner. Breakfast and lunch require nothing more than shorts, shirts, and bathing suit cover-ups. Bring good hiking shoes to tromp around the island, along with mosquito repellent and tennis rackets.

RELIGIOUS SERVICES: Nondenominational services on Sundays at 8:45 A.M. in the chapel that Columbia Pictures built for Rita Hayworth in *Sadie Thompson*.

RESERVATION SCHEDULE: Peak months tend to be February, August, and October. For a visit during those months, reservations should be made three months in advance. For the rest of the year, you should be able to get a room with seven to ten days' notice.

SIZE: 45 acres.

NUMBER OF ROOMS: 416.

NUMBER OF EMPLOYEES: 300.

TRAVEL TIME BY AIR

Chicago: **9 hours 43 minutes**
Honolulu: **25 minutes**

Los Angeles: **5 hours 12 minutes (United & Hawaiian airlines fly direct)**
New York: **12 hours 18 minutes**
Toronto: **12 hours 10 minutes**

ARRIVAL AIRPORT: Lihue, Kauai.

TRAVEL TIME FROM AIRPORT: 20 minutes (7 miles).

Cost Worksheet

	High Season[1]	Off-Season[2]
Accommodations (per night)[3]		
Standard	$110	$105
Superior	$135	$130
Deluxe	$150	$145
Cottages	$180–$240	$175–$235
Suites (main building)	$155–$250	$150–$230
2-bedroom suite	$370	$365

[1] High season dates: December 20 to March 31
[2] Off-season dates: March 31 to December 20
[3] Premium for single person: Double room rates apply. Room prices are based on single or double occupancy. A third person in a double room costs $15 per night.

KONA VILLAGE RESORT

VITAL FEATURES

Type of vacation: **Resort**
Target market: **Couples, families**
Location: **Kaupulehu-Kona, The Big Island, Hawaii**
All-inclusive cost per week: **$1,400–$1,900 plus airfare**

RATINGS

Value: 💲💲💲💲💲

Fun quotient: 🏝️🏝️🏝️🏝️

Honeymoon suitability: ❤️❤️❤️❤️❤️

Singles meeting ground:

Child appeal: 🍦🍦🍦🍦

Management professionalism: ☎️☎️☎️☎️☎️

Service: 💡💡💡💡💡

Food: 🦞🦞🦞🦞🦞

THE REAL STORY

If you've just read a novel about ancient Hawaii, you probably have visions of a volcanic place of pristine beauty, native traditions, and breeze-cooled beaches. This Eden-like setting exists at only one all-inclusive resort in the islands, Kona Village.

In 1801, Mt. Hulalai spewed out rivers of lava, covering much of the western part of the Big Island with a blanket of molten rock. This natural disaster covered villages, beaches, and fish canals, driving away the native Hawaiians. Fortunately, the molten rock stopped just short of a small stretch of beach and fertile land, which would forever be isolated from other settlements. On this beautiful oasis, Kona Village created a gentle resort that complements the natural beauty of the land and adheres to the spirit of many old Polynesian traditions.

At Kona, guests stay in *hales*, thatched-roofed native huts perched up on stilts. Clustered in villages, each representing a different type of South Pacific architecture, including those of Tahiti, Samoa, Fiji, New Caledonia, Palau, Marquesia, and of course, Hawaii. Guests stay cool because the high ceilings and open architecture allow unconditioned island scented breezes to flow through the *hales*.

Modern comforts inside the bungalows show themselves in subtle ways. Visitors awake to the modern technology of another island, Japan, whose electronic, programmable coffee machines grind and brew, filling the morning air with the scent of fresh Kona coffee. Original oil paintings by famed Hawaiian artists decorate the walls. The *hales* come equipped with wet bars, refrigerators, modern baths, and, in some cases, sitting rooms and lanais (patios). From the lanais, you can see the lush foliage-lined ponds, the palm-fringed beaches, and the distant mountains.

The resort itself is separated from the outside world by thousands of uninhabited and uninhabitable acres. The compound itself contains no cars or concrete. The parking lot is likewise camouflaged. You'd have to fly another five hours to Tahiti to get this close to an authentic Polynesian village. However, that village probably wouldn't have Kona's modern conveniences and services.

The resort offers a variety of sports, activities, and arts and crafts. Management philosophy is geared to letting visitors vacation away from the hassles of structured activities, televisions, telephones, and radios. Guests come to totally relax and unwind. They rely on someone else to make the decisions and worry about the details. The only swinging you'll do is from a hammock.

For all its relaxed island charm, Kona attracts a cosmopolitan crowd—celebrities, people with an appreciation for natural beauty, and those with the wherewithal to pay the prices. Consequently, you see a lot of honeymooners and couples who are "established." Kona makes an ideal family vacation because it keeps kids busy with numerous activities. The resort is laid out in such a way that even if it is full of young villagers, you won't necessarily hear their noise.

INCLUDED

Accommodations	Sports
Activities	Sports instruction
Food	

VALUE

If you value your sanity, Kona Village offers a place to buy it back. You don't have to worry about much of anything, because the top-notch staff take care of everything. The guests tend to be seasoned travelers who expect and appreciate top quality and value.

ACTIVITIES, SPORTS, & EXCURSIONS

ACTIVITIES

Arts & crafts
Board games
Culture/music/language
  classes
Dancing

Entertainment (soft music at
  night)
Glass-bottomed boat
Masseuse on-property (extra)
Sunbathing

SPORTS

Basketball
Bicycles (rent them in Kona and have the freight man pick them
  up)
Golf (5 courses; greens fees and other charges extra)
Horseback riding (through lush ranch lands; extra)
Jogging trails (from village to gatehouse)
Outrigger canoes
Ping-Pong
Sailing (Laser & Sunfish)
Scuba (concessionaire on-property, about 50 reefs, trips depend on
  weather & tides)
Scuba resort course & certification (extra)
Shuffleboard
Snorkeling (gear provided)
Swimming (ocean and free-form pool)
Tennis courts (3, all lighted, daily round-robin, pro gives lessons at
  extra cost)
Volleyball

EXCURSIONS: Nothing completes the Hawaiian experience like waking up to Kona coffee in your *hale* and returning later to the sumptuous food of the village after a day's adventure. All of the following excursions, offered by independent tour companies, cost extra. Each presents an experience unique to Hawaii, and all can be arranged with the concierge. Be sure to ask the kitchen for a picnic lunch if you plan to take off for the day. If money is a factor, and you plan to spend several days touring, combine your Kona Village vacation with a few nights at a European-plan hotel, where the rates are cheaper.

There are three ways to see The Big Island: by air, land, and water. Each offers perspectives that cannot be seen by either of the other two. The most spectacular way—some would say the only way—to see Hawaii is by air. Helicopters give you access to the otherwise inaccessible Kohala Coast with its spectacular cliffs, and to Kilauea, the world's most active volcano. Airplanes offer a less expensive, and slightly less satisfying, way to see the island.

The island practically demands that guests visit Volcano National Park, the gulches and rain forests of the Hamakua Coast, the old town of Hilo, Parker Ranch, and the ancient temples of Kohala. If you find beauty in lava fields, meadows, frontier towns, and rain forests, you will love the varied topography and culture of the Big Island. Cars can be rented at Kona Village. You may find it more economical and convenient to have one reserved at the airport for your arrival. This way you can easily travel to the resort and back.

The shoreline can be seen best on a sailing and snorkeling cruise aboard the *Guinevere*. This 38-foot catamaran sails to virgin beaches and colorful reefs. From December through April, passengers can watch whales frolic. Excursions for kids and teens offer snack refreshments and amplified music. Full-day and half-day fishing charters are also offered off the fertile Kona Coast. Reservations for fishing trips must be made two weeks in advance to assure a place. Cancellations must be made 48 hours prior to sailing to ensure a refund. In-house guests can often get space a day in advance.

ITINERARY & DAILY SCHEDULE

First-time guests stay an average of five days, while repeat customers often stay at least a week and sometimes more than two months. Most guests come to Kona Village and don't want to move. First-time visitors often rent a car for one day.

NIGHTLIFE & ENTERTAINMENT

The resort offers music nightly. A trio plays contemporary but mellow Hawaiian music. A classical guitarist entertains in the dining room.

AESTHETICS & ENVIRONMENT

A few miles down the road, the Hyatt took similar terrain and spent $360 million to create a megaresort, complete with canals, waterfalls, and multilevel pools. For all their effort, the Hyatt's beauty pales in comparison with the simple natural setting of Kona Village, which highlights the natural beaches, lush terrain, and distant mountains. Throughout the resort, one sees excavated archaeological sites, including petroglyphs, an old Hawaiian coral water slide, and canals lined with lava rocks. The canals are like those once used to fatten fish for the royal family.

FACILITIES: Local lore says that the Shipwreck Bar is made from the original catamaran that crashed onto the property when the owner discovered Kona Village. It now serves poolside guests. The

Talk Story beach bar keeps sandy guests full of fluids. (*Talk story* means shooting the breeze with blarney in Hawaiian.) In the evenings, the Hale Samoa Longhouse bar serves drinks in the main dining room. Drinks range from $2.50 for a domestic beer to $3.75 and up for a mixed drink. Prices are comparable to a swanky New York City bar.

Bars (3)
Beaches
Concierge
Entertainment coordinator

Gift shop
Safety-deposit box
Swimming pool
Water-sports center

ROOMS

Don't let the primitive-looking architecture fool you, the natives never had coffee makers and mini-bars, much less indoor plumbing. Room service delivers drinks and hors d'oeuvres to guests who wish to sit on their lanais and watch the sun go down. (Order "Kona service" with the concierge. It will be delivered the next day.)

Room rates vary depending on a dizzying combination of size, location, and view. Guests approach each of the *hale*s from trails, and each bungalow is surrounded by natural foliage. Some overlook the ocean or the pond. Standard bungalows contain two twin beds, or one king-size bed, and a bathroom, while Royal *hale*s provide families with a four-room suite, dressing rooms, and a large lanai. Square your needs and costs with the reservation department. Honeymooners get superior rooms with their package.

LUXURY LEVEL

Coffee maker
Laundry service (extra)
Maid service

Porter service
Refrigerator in room
Safety-deposit boxes

FOOD & DRINK

Kona Village guests tend to be very sophisticated. They expect absolutely top-notch food. Few are disappointed. The food is made from fresh ingredients and is exceptionally well prepared with a light touch. Breakfast is served from one of three rotating menus. Fresh juices, island fruits, and eggs are offered every day. Featured items include omelets, banana macadamia pancakes, fresh fish, and waffles. The luncheon buffet offers fresh seafood, salads, and meats.

Two nights a week, Kona guests eat outdoors at a luau and a steak fry. On the other nights they choose between two dining rooms, the Hale Moana and the Hale Ho'okipa. The Hale Moana is the main dining room. It offers a different menu for each day of the week. Every dinner has five entrées, including a lighter fare and a fresh fish plate. The Hale Moana dining room seats 52 people. Its menu concentrates on locally grown, fresh ingredients, with a light Continental accent.

You won't find cruise-style, constant dining at Kona. Guests eat enough at the meals and don't besiege management with requests for a snack bar. A special children's dinner seating starts at 5:30 P.M.

STAFFING & SERVICE

Kona Village provided a case study as one of the best-run companies in America for Robert Wattern's book, *The Renewal Factor: How the Best Get and Keep the Competitive Edge.* The front desk efficiently arranges stays, weddings, and honeymoons. The concierge handles all details for recreational facilities, excursions, travel, baby-sitting, and any special requests that a guest may have.

PRIVACY & RELAXATION

Don't go to Kona looking for wild entertainment. Kona offers an exit ramp from the fast lane where you can park your body, soul, and mind for a while. You can let your engine cool down for a day, a week, a month, knowing that you'll eat nothing but premium fuel.

While Kona offers more activities than you could do, the staff have a philosophical aversion to pushing guests to do anything. The atmosphere is very relaxing. You have to pick yourself up to go to an activity. As one guest said, "There's nothing to do, and by the end of the day, I've done only half of it."

The grounds accommodate the guests with room to spare. You never feel crowded.

SHOPPING

Two shops on the resort property offer souvenirs. The Island Copra and Trading Company General Store sells Hawaiian and resort wear, sandals, and assorted gifts. The Village Goldsmith specializes in more expensive body ornaments.

HONEYMOONERS

If a writer of dime-store romances had to dream up the perfect honeymoon setting, Kona Village would probably be the fruit of her imagination. Special packages cater to those who want a Hawaiian wedding or honeymoon. The honeymoon package includes the following features:

Five days and four nights in a private, thatched *hale.* The price is
based on a superior-class bungalow, which occupies the middle
of the price range. Deluxe class, which is slightly better
located, larger, or newer, costs an extra $50 per day. The
superior class is truly romantic and private, but if money is no
object, you may want to spring for the deluxe. This is one place

and one occasion where you may want to spend a fair amount of time in your room.

Round-trip transportation from Keahole-Kona airport
Fresh flower lei greeting (this is Hawaii, after all)
Reception rum punch, champagne in your room
Three-hour snorkeling sail or two one-hour therapeutic body
    massages
An 11 × 14 art reproduction of your honeymoon *hale*

The wedding/honeymoon plan includes:

The honeymoon package
Marriage license
Minister
Flower bridal leis
Floral decor
Album of 24 photos
Wedding cake and champagne
Music
Personalized wedding announcements to please or shock the folks
    back home.

SINGLES

Forget it. Unless you seek to encounter the spirit of the volcano goddess Pele, you probably won't meet any new flames. Kona Village caters to couples and families.

CHILD APPEAL

The sports and activities keep kids (*keikis*) busy and happy. Children's programs are geared for ages 6 and older, and sample activities include beach games, hula lessons, hula skirt making, fish contests, sand castle building, and seashell and scavenger hunts. Kids eat early, at 5:30, and are entertained with games and movies after dinner.

NUTS & BOLTS

BOOKING & CONTACT INFORMATION: Book with your travel agent or contact:

Kona Village Resort
P.O. Box 1299
Kaupulehu-Kona, HI 96745
808-325-5555
800-367-5290 in continental United States
800-432-5450 in Hawaii

DEPOSITS/REFUNDS: Deposits for the first and last nights of your stay must be paid 14 days after you confirm your reservation. Refunds for cancellations must be requested at least 14 days before arrival. In order to get a refund during the two weeks around Easter you must give sixty days' notice. Ninety days' notice is required for refunds during the Christmas season.

HANDICAP ACCESSIBILITY: Wheelchair ramps and pathways access the main dining rooms and the swimming pool. Two duplexes are equipped for the disabled.

PACKING: The dress here is casual. The dress code strictly forbids coats and ties. Male guests wear slacks and collared shirts. Women wear sundresses or muumuus (Hawaiian casual dresses). Bring comfortable shoes for hiking, swimsuits, and suntanning paraphernalia.

RELIGIOUS SERVICES: Catholic and Protestant churches can be found in town 14 miles away.

RESERVATION SCHEDULE: Make reservations one year in advance for visits during Christmas or the winter high season from early February to late March. During the soft months of May and June, one-week notice is generally sufficient. During the rest of the year, it's best to make reservations a few months in advance.

Usually, there is no minimum stay. During Christmas, and upon request of a specific *hale*, a seven-day minimum is required.

SIZE: 30 acres maintained, 82 acres overall.

MAXIMUM NUMBER OF GUESTS: Approximately 350 in 125 *hale*s.

NUMBER OF EMPLOYEES: 220.

TRAVEL TIME BY AIR VIA HONOLULU

Chicago: **9 hours 57 minutes**
Los Angeles: **6 hours 36 minutes**
New York: **12 hours 21 minutes (via Los Angeles)**
Toronto: **11 hours 27 minutes**

ARRIVAL AIRPORT: Keahole-Kona, Hawaii.

TRAVEL TIME FROM AIRPORT: 20 minutes. Interisland flights connect all the Hawaiian islands. The flight from Honolulu takes just under an hour and costs approximately $50 to $70 one way. United

Airlines flies directly to Kona from San Francisco. That nonstop trip takes 5 hours and 23 minutes.

SPENDING MONEY: You'll need money for taxes, beverages, and gratuities, as well as any extracurricular activities.

Cost Worksheet	YEAR-ROUND RATES[1]	
	Week	Day[2]
Accommodations (7 days)[3] (standard)[4]	$1,155	$165
Food	incl.	incl.
Drinks (average cost)	90	13
Room tax (5.26% of room rate	33	4.50
Sales tax (4.17% state tax)	55	8
Sports	incl.	incl.
Airfare	_____	_____
Sight-seeing		
Tips (automatically add 15%)	$92	$13
Additional sports		
Souvenirs		
Extra[5]	_____	_____

[1] For approximately one week in early December, Kona Village is closed for annual renovations.

[2] The following per-night rates apply to children staying with parents: 13 and older, $117; 6–12 yrs. old, $90; 2–5 yrs. old, $43; under age 2, $20. Make arrangements through concierge or dining room if you need baby food.

[3] Premium for single person: $255 minimum charge. To figure the premium subtract $75 (for food) from double rate.

[4] The standard room is the least expensive.

[5] Offered for extra charge: Nighttime baby-sitting, $27.50 per 5 hours; massage, $27.50 per half hour.

CLUB PERILLO

VITAL FEATURES

Type of vacation: **Resort**
Target market: **Couples, families, singles of all ages**
Location: **Waikiki, Hawaii**
All-inclusive cost per week: **$2,200 (includes airfare)**

RATINGS

Value: $ $ $ $ $

Fun quotient: ☂ ☂ ☂ ☂ ☂

Honeymoon suitability: ♥ ♥ ♥ ♥ ♥

Singles meeting ground: 👤

Child appeal: 🍦

Management professionalism: ☎ ☎ ☎ ☎ ☎

Service: 💡 💡 💡 💡

Food: 🦞 🦞 🦞 🦞

THE REAL STORY

Perillo Tours provides the perfect vacation for people who want to combine sight-seeing, relaxation, and sports. Or maybe you have a family with diverse interests? Everyone from the surfer to the shopper to the beach potato can find what he or she likes.

Club Perillo offers the best in an urban-beach resort. Rather than being focused inward, like resorts with closed campuses, Club Perillo in Waikiki focuses outward, encouraging guests to see the islands, try different restaurants, and experience what modern Hawaii has to offer.

In this type of all-inclusive, you benefit from knowing the cost before you leave, with the warm touch and convenience of a concierge who takes care of most of the details, making the vacation relatively hassle free.

Club Perillo reserves a wing of the Moana Surfrider, a superb renovation of Waikiki's historic hotel set on the beach. The accommodations have character, something found in abundance in nature's Hawaii, but generally lacking in Waikiki. The Moana Surfrider, though fully renovated and newly modernized, retains the charm of the original landmark hotel built in the early part of this century.

Perillo's price includes meals, activities, and air travel aboard regularly scheduled American Airlines flights. The last feature is more important than it may seem at first blush, because the service on American tends to be much better than aboard charters (this is a long flight) and you have flexibility not found on the fixed schedules of charters. For Hawaii, this means that you can tack on tours of other islands to your vacation. If time permits, try to spend at least two weeks on the island visiting Maui, the Big Island, and Kauai.

The club's recreation register gives you a way to communicate with other members of the "inner circle." This way you can easily find a tennis partner, a fourth for bridge, or just a pal. The private club suite gives you a place to meet, by design or serendipity. Most important, the club hostess (or host) gets to know the guests in a short period of time. She (or he) floats as a combination troubleshooter, socialite, matchmaker, camp counselor, and friend.

Your vacation with Club Perillo stays exactly that. A vacation. Everything is effortless, from the baggage handling and prearrival check-in through the week to the return flight.

INCLUDED

Accommodations	Taxes
Activities	Tips
Airfare	Tours
Entertainment & dancing	Transfer to and from airport
Food	Wine with dinner

VALUE

Club Perillo costs about the same as other quality all-inclusive resort packages. It caters to a special market. It takes care of its guests very well. Most guests feel that the Perillo experience exceeds their expectations and that the money is very well spent.

While most water sports are available, they cost extra. If you plan on occasional use, this should not throw your budget off. If you are a sports fanatic, you would probably choose a different trip anyway.

ACTIVITIES, SPORTS, & EXCURSIONS

ACTIVITIES

Arts & crafts
Board games
Culture/music/language
    classes
Dancing
Entertainment/shows

Movies
Nude sunbathing
Sunbathing
Underwater vision boat

SPORTS: A resort staff member will arrange for the sports listed, although they will all cost extra.

Golf
Jogging trail
Pedal boats
Sailing (Sunfish)
Scuba
Scuba resort course

Snorkeling
Surfing
Swimming
Tennis
Weightlifting
Windsurfing

NIGHTLIFE & ENTERTAINMENT

The Perillo package includes a luau, a native show, a dinner cruise, the famous Don Ho show, and other similar diversions. All the attractions of Waikiki—shows, bars, nightclubs—lie within steps of your hotel entrance.

AESTHETICS & ENVIRONMENT

The Moana Surfrider Hotel defines class, charm, and hidden electronic luxury. Its face-lift made the old lady into a beautiful bionic woman that could win any beauty contest.

FACILITIES

Bars
Beaches
Beauty salon
Concierge
Gift shop

Medical station
Piano bar
Safety-deposit box
Swimming pool

ROOMS

The rooms are furnished with hardwood furniture and all the electronic wizardry that Japan has to offer.

LUXURY LEVEL

Air-conditioning
Clock

Laundry service (extra)
Maid service

Phone in room
Porter service
Radio

Refrigerator in room
Room service (extra)
Television/VCR in room

FOOD & DRINK

If you like to try different restaurants and types of food, you'll love the dine-around plan. All of the restaurants are located in the hotels listed below. In general, the restaurants fit in the "fine dining" category. If you have visited these hotels in the past or have read old reviews, you'll be pleasantly surprised. Some of these restaurants are very good, even by the standards of people used to dining in top restaurants. Ask the hotel concierge for precise and up-to-date information.

Sheraton Waikiki: The Hano Hano Room; Contiki; Ocean Terrace, casual American food.
Royal Hawaiian: Surf Room, Continental seafood and steaks.
Moana Surfrider: Ships Tavern, fresh seafood and beef; Captain's Galley, seafood, chicken, and steaks; Beachside Café, breakfast; Ciao, pasta and Italian.
Princess Kaulaini Hotel: Lotus Moon, Mandarin; Momoyama, Japanese; Sheraton Polynesian.

STAFFING & SERVICE

A concierge attends to the needs of the guests, including making dinner reservations.

PRIVACY & RELAXATION

Waikiki has electricity in the air. Even if you lie on the beach all day, it's hard not to be affected by the activity found everywhere.

SHOPPING

Waikiki may have the world's highest concentration of stores. You have to sift through a lot of junk, but truly nice things can be found. Some crafts offer local color at reasonable prices. Typical souvenirs include pineapples and every food item imaginable made out of macadamia nuts.

HONEYMOONERS

For Hawaii-bound honeymooners, Club Perillo provides an excellent way to combine a honeymoon with a relaxing, entertaining, and active vacation, especially if this is your first trip. All arrangements are taken care of, so you have one less thing on your mind when making wedding plans. Also, the charming hotel makes a very romantic setting. You will also find this one of the most economical ways to take a luxury vacation in Hawaii.

SINGLES

Not a lot.

CHILD APPEAL

Children are welcome, although the resort is not geared for them. There is no special day-care or activities program, but the concierge will find a baby-sitter if you desire.

NUTS & BOLTS

BOOKING & CONTACT INFORMATION

Perillo Tours
800-431-1515
201-307-1234

DEPOSITS/REFUNDS: Various cancellation penalties apply. Perillo strongly recommends cancellation insurance. You can purchase this when you buy your package from your travel agent.

HANDICAP ACCESSIBILITY: Ramps and special equipment aid the handicapped traveler.

PACKING: Hawaii is a pretty laid-back place, but you may want to bring a sports coat or nice dress for your meals in Waikiki's finer restaurants; a tie is not necessary. You'll spend most of your time in shorts or bathing wear.

RELIGIOUS SERVICES: If you can't find the church of your choice in Waikiki, Honolulu lies close by.

RESERVATION SCHEDULE: For holidays you probably will need to book at least three months in advance. Other times, you should be able to get a room within several weeks.

NUMBER OF ROOMS: 800 (hotel), 50 (club).

MAXIMUM NUMBER OF GUESTS: 1,600 (hotel), 100 (club).

SPENDING MONEY: You don't need to spend much extra, but budget several hundred dollars for additional excursions, including helicopter and boat tours, plus drinks, sports, and souvenirs.

Cost Worksheet		
	High Season[1]	*Off-Season*[2]
Accommodations		
(8 days, 7 nights)[3]	$1,999	$1,899
Food		
Drinks		
Departure tax	5	5
Sports		
Airfare (from NYC)	incl.	incl.
Sight-seeing	incl.	incl.
Tips	incl.	incl.
Additional sports		
Souvenirs		

[1] High season dates: June through August
[2] Off-season dates: January through May. Shoulder season dates: September through December
[3] Premium for single person: $600.

CLUB MED

INTRODUCTION

THE REAL STORY

If you try to explain the concept of an all-inclusive resort, it's easiest just to say "like Club Med." With over 100 resorts in 33 countries, and more planned, Club Med may offer as many all-inclusive villages as the entire competition combined. It pioneered a concept that others have copied and, in many cases, improved.

Club Mediterranée has attracted a group of devotees who would like nothing better than to spend their lives going from one club to the next. Some come close to doing that. Club Med has a high percentage of repeat guests, and it's not unusual to find people who have been on five or more trips.

Why do they keep going? Most people like the spirit. The carefree "antidote to civilization" appeals to snowbound desk jockeys. Many people originally came for the wild singles activities, met their spouses at Club Med, returned for their honeymoons, and now bring their kids to the mini-clubs.

Club Med achieved its initial reputation as a wild den of sexual activity. Myths die hard, but Club Med has tried to bury this one. The resorts now cater to couples and families as well as singles. Your chance of action depends on which club you choose and when you go. Some people who have avoided Club Meds because of their reputation may be missing great spots for a family vacation. Singles who aren't necessarily looking for romance but don't want to spend their vacations alone will also find a social experience.

Still, Club Med does not offer all things to all people. It caters to people who are interested in sports. The accommodations aren't generally much to speak of, and the entertainment is amateurish. You can find a much cheaper way to lie on a beautiful beach. It is the sports and the spirit that make the vacation a good deal. Some other all-inclusives have fewer extras—Club Med charges for drinks, excursions, golf, deep-sea fishing, and some scuba trips. More luxurious resorts offer a higher level of service.

Some basic Club Med features remain constant throughout the resorts. This is especially true in the more remote locations, where you feel as if you could be on any warm-weather island in the world. All Club Meds include three meals. All offer a spirited atmosphere with a concentration on sports, games, and other activities. The entertainment does not change markedly from resort to resort, nor from year to year. Most sites also keep the same popular touches, such as playing classical music on the beach at sunset.

Club Meds do vary in their target market, sports offered, and excursions. While some are truly islands unto themselves, others offer tours of the Holy Land, Indian ruins, or straw market shopping. You'll also find a big difference between the lush Caribbean islands, with their azure waters, and the drier Mexican climate. Some welcome children; others do not.

CHANGING TIMES: Club Med is changing with the times, becoming more diverse, and in some ways catching up to the competition. An intensive renovation and building program is bringing its facilities up to the standards of competing clubs. This means that it is adding or enlarging swimming pools, renovating rooms, and improving common areas.

The biggest drawback at some Club Meds has been the quality of the guest rooms and other physical facilities. The excuse for the guest rooms, which are often dingy, has always been: "Well, you don't spend much time in your room anyway." This is true, but the excuse does not apply to the pools and common areas, which are often second rate. The new Club Meds are often built to be Club Meds, instead of being converted resorts. The rooms are closer to the standards that people want. This *does* make a difference to a lot of people, especially honeymooners.

SHOULD YOU GO TO CLUB MED: Club Med asked not to be included in this book because it felt that its product was different from everyone else's. Although we find that reasoning difficult to follow, Club Med does offer a consistently good vacation package that varies somewhat from resort to resort. Other all-inclusives orbit around the market they exploited first. Some offer superior products, some inferior.

There are reasons to go elsewhere. Perhaps you've already been to Club Med, seen the shows, and eaten the food. Some other resorts charge less for a similar experience. Others accept couples only, making them more suitable for a first or second honeymoon. Many all-inclusives reflect the local culture more than Club Med, or are more oriented toward tourism or learning. Yacht charters, land tours, and spas, to name only three options, give their participants the benefits of all-inclusives but show them a very different experience.

HOW TO CHOOSE A CLUB MED: Choose a Club Med using the same criteria that you would use in selecting any resort. Your chief decisions will be whether you want to be around kids, are looking for hot singles action, or want to stay at the resort or choose a place that offers more possibilities for tours and nightlife. Decide what kind of experience you want, how much you can spend, and where you want to go. (See the "How to Choose an All-Inclusive Resort" section in the Introduction.) Finally, you should reevaluate whether it's really a Club Med that you're looking for, or if you'd rather try one of the many other options.

The specific features of all the clubs can be found in the voluminous Club Med brochure. Features date quickly because of the extensive ongoing renovation.

TARGET MARKET

The Club Med brochures show only people who are extremely good-looking and incredibly fit. Even models only look that sharp in carefully selected pictures! Club Med sells an image as much as a product. Clearly you don't have to be a triathlete or movie star. Not all the other guests will be either. There is no reason to be intimidated.

While you pay dearly for the many included water sports, a few people go just to relax and romance. Most people seem to be pretty aware of what to expect before they go.

ENTERTAINMENT

Many people say that the shows are their favorite part of the trip. They enjoy watching the performances of the GOs (staff) with whom they partied all day. Although the shows are scripted and predictable, they keep most people laughing.

The shows at each club borrow heavily, very heavily, from each other. Some people report being a little bored after seeing the same show repeatedly. Others still laugh at the same joke told a bit differently. The "stars" display more enthusiasm than talent, and the attitude is infectious. One night each week, guests supply the talent, singing, dancing, and playing the air guitar. GMs (guests) join in the fun and end up chanting the Club Med song. The indoctrination process may be more effective than the Hare Krishna ritual, and you don't have to shave your head.

The discos open in the late evening, playing recorded dancing music until the wee hours. Some weeks they stay packed with revelers, other weeks they pine for attention.

INCLUDED

Accommodations	Sports instruction
Activities	Taxes
Entertainment & dancing	Tips
Food (3 meals only; snacks extra)	Transfer to and from airport
Sports	Wine and beer with dinner and lunch

VALUE

Sports-oriented people generally feel that Club Med gives them an excellent value for the money. The lodging may not be spectacular, but it is consistently clean and adequate. The food is always fresh, plentiful, and satisfyingly good.

For all its innovations and size, Club Med has been surpassed by some of its imitators, and now must play catch-up. Specialty niches have been carved out of the market that Club Med created; drinks and tours are often included. Some cater to couples or families or are specialty sports centers. While Club Med does not include drinks or tours, it does have clubs with children's facilities, and others that offer sports tournaments.

ACTIVITIES, SPORTS, & EXCURSIONS

ACTIVITIES: People do more than sports. Some play chess or bridge. Other times, you can just read a book. All Clubs Meds have libraries consisting of paperbacks that people leave.

On rainy days, GOs lead all sorts of contests and games, such as team Trivial Pursuit. Instructors also teach arts and crafts. Fortunately, they do not hang your works next to the masterpieces that your kids produce in the mini-clubs.

Club Med makes no contingencies for snow, except in their Colorado, Austrian, and Japanese resorts, where they pray for it.

Arts & crafts
Board games
Culture/music/language
    classes
Dancing
Entertainment/shows
Glass-bottomed boat
Nude sunbathing (some
    resorts nude, some
    topless, some "family,"
    some for nude families)
Sunbathing

SPORTS: Club Med revolves around sports. Each resort offers a wide variety of water sports, with first-rate facilities and equipment. The most precious sports skill at Club Med is willingness to learn. Qualified and patient instructors will teach you any skill that you do not possess, from waterskiing to windsurfing.

Many Club Meds offer scuba diving, sometimes at extra cost. If you're not certified, they'll teach you. Some clubs also offer a bona fide scuba certification, requiring a five-day commitment.

Golf festival weeks allow guests to compete in tournaments and driving and putting contests. The program includes two days of practice on the course before the event, video analysis of participants, pro clinics, cocktail parties, and an awards banquet. These are held during the winter and spring at the Sandpiper and Paradise Island. Some resorts offer intensive horseback riding or tennis tournaments. Horseback riding, deep-sea fishing, and golf all cost extra.

ROOMS

Club Meds typically have people stay in very stark accommodations without locks on the doors. This forces people to pack light and survive without the things they thought they needed. The luxury levels vary by resort, but tend to be much higher in the newer and renovated clubs.

FOOD & DRINK

Most people really enjoy the food. They tend to serve a lot of indigenous ingredients, which in the Caribbean means tropical fruits, vegetables, seafoods, meats, and poultry. In Mexico, you might find more species of avocado than Darwin cataloged. The food is also geared to the taste buds of the guests. For example, at Martinique the cooking tends to be more French, and the English-speaking resorts serve more Continental food. And you'll love the baked goods. Breads, croissants, French baguettes, peasant loaves, and outrageous desserts pop out of the ovens on a daily basis.

Days start with a full breakfast, dwindling to light fare by midmorning. Lunch and dinner feature more food than you could shake a sailboat mast at. Between lunch and dinner, and in the evening, snacks can be purchased with drink beads. Few people want more food than they see on the buffet meals.

All Club Meds require that you buy beads to pay for hard and soft drinks. This is a major disadvantage that goes far beyond money. Even though they have substituted one monetary unit for another, the guest still has to think about whether the string of beads is affordable. Many other all-inclusive resorts include drinks in the basic price. However, since wine and beer are served free at breakfast and lunch, and there are a lot of free happy hours, it is possible to stay reasonably tanked at relatively little expense.

STAFFING & SERVICE

The GOs form the heart of any Club Med. Gentil Organizateurs, or congenial hosts, instruct, entertain, help, and often romance guests. They live the life of a camp counselor, forsaking much pay for the glamor, fun, and hard work associated with running the resorts. They interact with the guests on every level, including dancing, eating, and . . . whatever. Their job description demands language skills, entertainment ability, and the willingness to be relocated and devote themselves completely. In fact, they do change resorts every six months. Guests often remark that they are "gorgeous."

PRIVACY & RELAXATION

Club Med does not push people to become involved in activities. No one gets roused from their lounge chair if they don't want to be disturbed. If you perch yourself near the volleyball net or the water sports area, however ... Most guests get involved because they choose their Club Med vacation for that reason.

HONEYMOONERS

Although no special packages celebrate the honeymoon experience, many newlyweds choose Club Med. If you want to share your time with other people and don't mind the spartan accommodations, it could be a great experience. It offers an active, fun week, but not necessarily the romantic trappings of a couples-only resort or the adventure of a land tour.

SINGLES

Club Med started out as a singles resort and many guests still come for that reason. Choose carefully, however, because some resorts attract more families and couples. The age group also varies from club to club.

Traditionally, Club Med will pair you with another guest of the same sex to share a room. At some villages it will now let you stay by yourself for a 20 percent surcharge on the land rate. A few of the villages even let you go solo at no extra charge during certain (off-season) weeks.

CHILD APPEAL

The camp for adults knows how to be a camp for children. At certain sites mini-clubs supervise and entertain children ages 2 through 11. Specially designed sports equipment fits their little fingers and little toes. They also occupy kids with games, workshops, and crafts.

Baby clubs take infants from 4 to 23 months. The age ranges vary with the different clubs. Creature comforts for the kids and mental comfort for the parents include toys, bottle warmers, cribs, playpens, and more. They'll watch your child for as long as you'd like between the hours of 8:00 A.M. and 6:00 P.M. The club will coordinate baby-sitting services after hours.

A Kids-Free program at some resorts allows tykes ages 2 to 5 to stay free with their parents during some off-season weeks. The Sandpiper resort has teamed up with Walt Disney World to offer a combination package of three nights at Disney World in the Disney Village Resort Club with four nights at Club Med. See the reviews of individual Club Meds to learn which ones have mini-clubs and baby clubs.

NUTS & BOLTS

BOOKING & CONTACT INFORMATION: Newspaper travel sections and the Yellow Pages frequently advertise Club Med specials. Call 800-CLUB-MED.

CURRENCY: Drinks and excursions require only your signature and your "plastique." Club Med holds your return airline ticket until you pay your bill at the end. Not that they don't trust you . . .

DEPOSITS/REFUNDS: A deposit of $300 per person, plus the $30 membership and $20 initiation fees, are due within 8 days of booking. The total balance is due 30 days prior to arrival. The insurance included in the membership fee allows for cancellation due to medical problems with no penalty. Other cancellation fees are as follows: 10 percent, 30 to 60 days prior; 25 percent, 21 to 30 days prior; 40 percent, 14 to 21 days prior; 60 percent, last week.

FUTURE PLANS: Club Med is now elbowing in on the turf of its competitors. It is building a "floating village," with a five-masted sailing ship à la Windjammer, but more luxurious and more expensive.

More than anything, Club Med has capitalized on being the first in its marketplace, and advertises heavily. It has developed such a large market share that people think of it first, and in many cases don't know about any alternatives.

After sleeping a bit too long, Club Med has awakened and noticed the competition. The present renovation campaign should revamp Club Med's image from a chain of spartan single resorts to a group of fun spots offering varied activities and the luxury of choice.

LANGUAGES: French and English.

PACKING: From the time you wake until the time you go to dinner, you need wear nothing other than a swimsuit. At some clubs, you won't always need that much.

Ther room doors do not lock. This forces people to pack light and leave valuables at home. Although management dismisses them, we have heard many stories of cameras, tennis rackets, and even clothing thefts at Club Meds. It would be hard to place these items in a safe. Management apparently feels that the advantages of a keyless society outweigh the occasional loss. Guest should bring only inexpensive cameras as a precaution.

RESERVATION SCHEDULE: Winter months fill early in many resorts, but even on short notice you should have a choice of a couple of clubs.

INTERNATIONAL

CORAL WORLD, EILAT, ISRAEL

Israel hosts two Club Meds, one in Coral Beach (Eilat) and the other near the resort town of Nahariya. These give visitors the chance to combine an exhilarating tour of the Holy Land with a warm, relaxing vacation.

The Eilat beaches of fine white sand overlook the mouth of the Red Sea and the mountains of Jordan. Many people swear that the Red Sea has the best scuba diving in the world, bar none. Club Med scuba trips will take you to some of these famous reefs.

MOOREA, SOUTH PACIFIC

Perhaps you've just come from a Gauguin exhibit, and images of Tahiti are bouncing around your head. But your spouse doesn't like the idea of your going to rediscover your artistic proclivities in peace for a couple of years with the well-built natives. Or perhaps your boss won't give you that many personal days. Try Club Med at Moorea for the next closest thing.

Guests stay in rustic two-room huts called *fares*. They are spread out, but all are well located near the beach. There are no screens on the windows, but each *fare* has running water and a little deck. Mosquitoes would be a problem if they didn't give you coils to burn.

Moorea attracts lots of Australians and people from all over. It accepts kids ages 6 and over. Most of the children are locals. They come on the weekends when huge crowds of Tahitians flock to the beaches. The Tahitians tend to be very friendly, but often stick to themselves and don't use the Club Med facilities. The club itself tends to be very mellow. The disco gets crowded at night, and people do party . . . in a civil way. You'll find lots of bare chests on the beach, but no naked bodies. The shows feature some attractive Tahitians dancing in the native style, but they mostly resemble the GO shows of other clubs. A lot of the guests are older than the Club Med average of 35, and a fair number of singles come here as well.

The island itself tends to follow in the pristine *South Pacific* image. There is no town to speak of. You can rent a moped to see the island, or take a Club Med excursion. It becomes very expensive if you want to leave the club to eat or do anything. All the other hotels charge big bucks. You also won't find many souvenirs for sale. In sum, you'll spend the vast majority of your time on the resort grounds.

The ocean water is protected by a reef. It is so calm you won't miss having a pool. It is also perfect for snorkeling and waterskiing. The scuba diving rates with the world's finest.

The food is classic Club Med: fresh seafood, steaks, burgers, pasta, cheese salads, and great breads. You get lots of everything.

TURQUOISE, TURKS AND CAICOS

The island of Providenciales in the Turks and Caicos harbors Club Med Turquoise. Don't feel badly if you don't know where that is. Most people know the island because of the resort, which is fairly new.

Life at Turquoise centers on the pool. An open-air disco, right off the beach, opens after the night's entertainment. Two bars serve drinks. The club attracts lots of singles, but it is a little more mature and less wild than Martinique. People may still have it, but they don't flaunt it. To join the fun, you must be 12 years of age or older.

You'll probably end up staying at the club because there isn't a whole lot else happening on the island. Luckily, the club lies just a short jaunt from the airport. Because the resort has recently been laid out, the plantings haven't had a chance to reach sufficient size to provide shade. People fry. Bring heavy sunscreen and hats and a cover-up.

A new, expanded scuba diving program offers in-depth diving.

MEXICO

CANCÚN: Guests remember Cancún for its great beach, warm water, near-perfect winds, and the number of off-site diversions. The Cancún Club is different from most in that guests go off the grounds quite frequently. The Club Med here shares a long strip of sand with many other resorts. Some people like this because they feel less isolated from the outside world. At night, many guests go to the discos in other hotels. While the on-site diving is just fair, the club offers a great trip to Cozumel. It costs extra, but certified divers find it well worth the price.

The surrounding area also offers many must-see tourist attractions, including the trip to the ruins at Chichén Itzá. You fly on a small chartered flight, land in a dirt field, and take a bus to see the ruins. Club Med orchestrates it very well.

Shoppers will love the silver, ceramics, clothes, papier-mâché piñatas and the rest of the crafts at the markets. Be prepared to bargain.

As at most Club Meds, the rooms don't hold any special attraction. The one-story and two-story motel-style buildings are spread out. The circular pool is not conducive for swimming laps, but most people prefer to spend their days at the beach anyway. There are separate areas for waterskiing, snorkeling, and scuba diving. The sports adhere to the Club Med tradition of excellence. Sailors enjoy the steady winds. Private instructors help you with your tennis game. Other sports include aerobics, volleyball, water volleyball, and a mini (practice) golf course. The lagoon is perfect for waterskiing, but you could wait as long as a half hour to get your turn on the boat.

Club Med veterans will find the kind of food they expect. Huge buffets offer lots of fresh fruits, salads, fresh fish, hamburgers, and more. Mexican food is available even for breakfast, along with chocolate croissants and other fresh-baked goods. All meals are served on the second-floor dining room. The club is not wheelchair accessible.

Ixtapa: Ixtapa offers the usual plethora of Club Med activities and sports. To all the beauty that the West Coast of Mexico has to offer, it adds a beautifully manicured lawn, a bar, a theater, a large swimming pool, an open-air beach restaurant that doubles as a disco, and a safe water supply. Club Med is located 20 minutes away from the old fishing village of Zihuatanejo and the airport. Ixtapa caters to families. The mini-club supervises kids from 2 to 11 years old, giving parents the chance to pay a little extra for deep-sea fishing or playing the 18-hole Robert Trent Jones golf course.

The rooms provide air-conditioned relief from the often sweltering sun. They have twin beds, a sofa, a private bath, and use standard U.S. voltage electricity.

Playa Blanca: Playa Blanca's Club Med blends with its Mexican heritage. The adobe brick haciendas are topped with red clay tile. Located on the Pacific coast, 60 miles north of Manzanillo, it occupies a strategic spot on a calm inlet overlooking rock mini-islands that protrude from the water.

The atmosphere depends on you and the rest of the crowd that week. In general, the atmosphere tends to be almost as calm as the inlet's water. Lots of couples choose this club; 18 is the minimum age. Almost all patrons come from North America.

Entirely remodeled in 1988, it offers a large pool for swimming laps, and games. The common areas boast a new disco and refurbished restaurants. It uses standard U.S. voltage electricity.

The cuisine tastes of French, Mexican, and Continental traditions. Breakfast and lunch are served in the usual huge buffets. Each dinner has a different theme, and is served semibuffet, with an entrée served and the side dishes taken off the buffet table.

Sonora Bay: Sonora Bay is dedicated to the serious athlete. Located in Guaymas, it sits at the foot of plum-colored mountains on a sandy reef that juts into the Gulf of California. It stands out for its intensive sports instruction. Tennis pros will videotape your game and critique you. Dedicated scuba facilities take you to colorful, albeit cool-water, reefs. The horseback riding program offers lessons in English riding including trail rides, jumping, dressage, and horse care. Fishing, golf, and excursions are offered for extra charge.

THE BAHAMAS

PARADISE ISLAND: The Paradise Island Club Med just underwent a $14 million face-lift, and is now being touted as a luxury resort. It has a completely rebuilt and air-conditioned main dining room, two restaurants featuring Italian and Continental cuisine, and larger rooms. Tennis festivals are played on 20 Har-Tru courts; golf packages are available but cost extra.

CARIBBEAN

MARTINIQUE: Martinique's reputation precedes it. Officially called Buccaneer's Creek, it guards the reputation that all Club Meds used to have: wild, young, sex occupied. Although the crowd tends to be young, the resort admits only adults, and adults-only games proliferate. The GOs at Martinique have a reputation for satisfying the guests in every way. This will either entice you or turn you off, depending on your proclivities. Some people want to play and some are not sure.

The biggest rap against Buccaneer's Creek is its remote location. After often torturous plane transfers, you must take what seems like a long bus ride (actually only an hour) from the airport.

More than other Club Meds in the Americas, Buccaneer's Creek draws a lot of Europeans, primarily the French. They do not mix well with the Americans. They mostly stay on the nude beach, while Americans often prefer the topless section. The GOs tend to go topless also.

The crowd is more mixed than you might guess, drawing singles, married couples, and some family groups with adult children. The club also draws lots of rowdy New Yorkers.

The famous Club Med picnic, where everyone drinks a lot of a spiked punch and does things that are subsequently bragged about or hidden, takes on classic form here. Among the favorite games: pairs of men and women run into the water, switch swimsuits, then run back out. Other similarly suggestive games put the crowd in a playful mood, and . . . things happen. By the end of the day, most people get totally naked. Quite a few also get involved.

If you've come to Martinique looking for something (else) on the side, one of the many excursions may interest you. They all cost extra, and take you around the island, which is fairly barren.

A fairly constant wind keeps the temperature cool and the Windsurfers moving. Lots of pool games involve the guests when they are not out snorkeling, playing tennis, or involved in other sports.

The beauty of the physical setting attracts people. The grounds are well landscaped and the accommodations are very clean. In many ways, it looks more like a hotel than a Club Med. The rooms are light and airy. Good breezes come from the wind, ceiling fans, and the air-conditioning. There are accommodations for pairs and triples.

ST. LUCIA: Located close to the airport. St. Lucia's Club Med offers Caribbean island charm to "members" 12 years of age and older. It features intensive windsurfing instruction and horseback riding for an additional fee, along with the usual fun, games, and entertainment. Leave your electronics at home or bring an adapter, because the voltage is European-style 220.

The atmosphere at St. Lucia tends to be relatively calm and conservative, considering that it draws a lot of singles between the ages of 23 and 35. The social life centers on the swimming pool and the bar, while the tropical beaches offer a quiet place to relax. The volcano excursion remains a crowd favorite.

UNITED STATES

FLORIDA INTRODUCTION: Florida's climate is the most tropical in the continental United States. When you cross the border into Florida, you are already farther south than southern California. Key West occupies a latitude almost as low as that of Hawaii. Florida remains very popular with foreigners, especially Europeans and French Canadians. In many ways, they understand the lure more than Americans, who can't see past Miami Beach.

Florida vacations can be more economical and hassle free than traveling abroad. Cut-rate accommodations and supersaver airfares abound as companies compete for a place in the Florida sun. Many Eastern Seaboard and Middle West travelers find that they can pack the family in the car and drive down for even less than the cost of discount flights. This also eliminates many of the hassles involved with transferring luggage and dealing with rental cars and taxis.

Florida's weather, more than other attribute, attracts resorts and tourists. Temperatures generally stay pleasant from early spring to late fall. In the winter, the climate can rarely be called balmy. Yet it usually remains comfortable, certainly warm enough for most outdoor sports, including golf, tennis, walking, sailing, fishing, scuba diving, and windsurfing with a wet suit. Even in the middle of winter, the most dedicated sun worshipers should be able to come back with a "drop dead" tan.

Most all-inclusives in Florida fall into the spa category. Very often they are associated with larger resorts, so a family can travel together but members can take the type of holiday that each chooses.

Walt Disney World belongs in a class by itself. When you are three feet tall, a six-foot-tall Mickey Mouse gives an impression that you will remember your whole life. For adults, the Magic Kingdom also offers EPCOT, the Experimental Community of Tomorrow. It resembles a permanent world's fair. If possible, avoid visiting during school breaks.

Premier Cruises touts itself as the Official Cruise Line of Walt Disney World. It offers combination cruise/resort packages. So do many other cruises that leave from Florida. Club Med also combines Disney vacations with stays at its Sandpiper club.

Also very popular as a vacation destination is Florida's west coast, particularly Sanibel and Captiva islands near Fort Myers. Development here came later, and the slower, more controlled pace produced a far more attractive environment. Unfortunately, the all-inclusive concept has yet to take root here.

SANDPIPER: If you've suspected that Club Med is a Mickey Mouse operation, the Sandpiper will confirm it. Located on Florida's St. Lucie River, this resort combines visits with jaunts to Walt Disney World. Its baby club and miniclub will entertain your little ones while you enjoy the Club Med pleasures you knew as a DINK (double income, no kids). Family jaunts include river cruises, picnics, and guided excursions.

The Sandpiper is also known for its intensive sports program. Imagine that the little white, dimpled ball is your business competitor. Whack—on 45 championship holes. Or you can have your tennis videotaped and critiqued.

The accommodations exceed the primitive facilities that you found on your Club Med trip years ago. They now meet what you'd expect from a modern resort.

CRUISES

INTRODUCTION

Cruises have forged a romantic imprint on the dreams of almost all of us. They are floating resorts, restaurants, nightclubs, and gyms surrounded by water and sun, and highlighted by scantily clad bodies. They appeal to travelers looking for a range of activities in a number of locations. You can find as much variety as you would in land-based resorts, from luxury Princess Love Boats to Windjammer "barefoot" cruises, to dedicated scuba boats such as *Blackbeard*.

Some cruise lines orient their passengers to activities off the ship. American Hawaiian Cruises, for example, really serves as a very enjoyable way to jaunt between islands. Other cruises focus more on life on board, with enough activities there to keep you busy. Some, like Bermuda Star Line, have so much going on that many passengers don't leave the ship during port stops. On most cruises you have a chance to shop, dine, and play ashore.

When picking a cruise, consider the following factors: how much you wish to spend, how much time you want to be aboard ship, and which ports you want to visit. These factors go a long way toward determining the right cruise line and itinerary.

Although cruises probably originated the all-inclusive concept, few would probably meet a narrow definition of the term today. They generally include accommodations and meals; many also include airfare. Most charge extra for drinks, sports, and shore excursions. Perillo Caribbean Cruises on Costa Cruises ships is an exception in the luxury market, because almost everything is included in the base price, but many yacht charters and specialty cruises do as well. Cruises will generally let you charge all your extras and pay the tab (the cruise missile) at the end of the week.

Ship sizes range considerably, from a few hundred feet in length to over a thousand. In addition to smoother sailing, larger ships offer greater resources, more nightlife, and usually better shows. Some ships are so big you may not be able to see all of them in a week. Many people like this. Others prefer the intimacy of small ships, like those of Dolphin Cruise Lines, where you can really get to know other passengers and crew. Your choice may be influenced by your marital status. One decided advantage to large ships is that if you make a faux pas you can easily find new people with whom you can embarrass yourself.

The length of stay in port shapes your impression of the island stops. Most port calls are short, giving you only the slightest taste of the destination. American Canadian Caribbean Line makes excellent use of brief stops by making bow landings on small cays for sunbathing and snorkeling. Even though cruises don't allow you to seriously explore any of the destinations, they make great reconnaissance trips for future visits.

All passengers on a cruise enjoy the same food and activities. Your fare often depends on the type of cabin you want. Philosophy and budget dictate which cabin category you should choose. In this book, we usually quote the lowest priced cabin available for double occupancy.

In general, cruise length and price dictate the market. Young passengers can rarely take off more than a week from work. They also tend to max out at $1,500 per person for a vacation, including airfare. Most cruise ships attract a large number of "mature" passengers, although Commodore, Carnival, and Chandris have structured their cruise lengths and prices to attract younger people as well. Premier Cruise Lines caters to families with young children by combining their voyages with stays at Walt Disney World.

Most cruise ships break meals into two seatings and assign passengers to a specific table for the duration of the cruise. Only the time of the meals differs; the food is the same for both seatings. When you book your cruise, decide if you prefer to dine early or late. Second seating gives you more time to socialize after the meal and more time to work up an appetite after all the food that you've been eating at previous meals. Also, the second seating tends to draw a younger crowd. Large tables give you an opportunity to meet more people. Most large cruises assign you to a table where you must sit for all meals in the dining room. If you don't like your dining companions, the maître d' can often move you to another table. Smoking and nonsmoking sections are almost always available.

The dress on cruises ranges considerably, from simple and casual to formal. The ambience usually follows formality. Formal cruises generally cater to an older market, but the reverse does not hold. Pack for a cruise like you would for a resort. Even on the most formal cruises, daytime dress tends to be casual and functional, allowing shorts and swimming suits. Evening dress depends upon the ship and the events planned. You'll want to wear formal clothing to special dinners and events, but there is no reason to buy a tuxedo. A dark suit and tie work fine for men. Women can wear cocktail dresses or gowns.

Most cruises ask that you leave your bags outside your cabin the last night of the voyage. Pack a small bag in which to store essential overnight items.

Shipboard passengers can be reached by calling the high seas operator at 800-SEA-CALL. Give the name of the vessel. For smaller ships, you may need the "call sign" of the ship. All calls are placed person-to-person through AT&T. It costs $14.93 for the first three minutes, and $4.98 for each additional minute no matter where the ship is. These calls reach virtually any passenger ship. Small boats use marine radios and are usually not accessible by this service. Outgoing calls can usually be arranged through the purser or directly with the ship's radio officer.

Most cruise tickets can be bought at a substantial discount from the "rack" rate. This especially holds true in the off-season or when you book at the last minute. Travel agents often know about these deals. Ask several before you book.

For all their advantages, cruise vacations are not for everyone, particularly people who can't stand motion beneath their feet. Obviously, larger ships tend to be more stable in rough water. Many new ships use stabilizers to minimize the rocking motion of the waves. Still, there is no guarantee that all passengers will feel comfortable in all types of weather. Cruising can be quite uncomfortable when the ship travels through a storm.

Cruise companies pride themselves on the service they provide to their passengers. Indeed, many people take a cruise to be pampered. But "to ensure promptness," managements ask that passengers tip the ships' service staff, who are usually paid very low salaries.

In most cases, it is not necessary constantly to fish out dollars for tips. When charging drinks to your room, a service charge is customarily added. Toward the end of a cruise, management usually recommends an amount to tip the cabin steward, the waiters, and the busboys. Very often the maitre d' has his hand out also. All these amounts should be budgeted. The recommended tip should also be considered a minimum amount. If you do not feel the service warrants at least the suggested gratuity, then you should make your feelings known to the staff or on the evaluation sheet.

SEASICKNESS

If the gentle swaying of the seas makes your stomach do backflips, the following advice of Jeffrey Schaider, M.D., might help:

I often attempt to dissuade patients from taking motion-sickness medications. Preventive measures can often prevent nausea, vertigo, and vomiting, symptoms that can put any vacation on the rocks.

Two preventive measures can help avoid seasickness. Avoid lying in the sun, because an hour under the hot solar rays can contribute to dehydration and fatigue, making you more susceptible to motion sickness. Alcohol is the second thing that must be avoided—motion is not required to feel nauseous when intoxicated.

If these measures are inadequate, then it might be time to turn to medications to calm a butterfly stomach. Anti–motion sickness medications come in three forms for home use: pills, suppositories, and patches. Most people prefer pills—unless they have active vomiting, in which case suppositories might be the preferred route of administration. The French generally prefer suppositories over pills in all situations. Patches have the advantage of easy administration and long duration of action. The only problem is their visibility, which might embarrass some vacationers if they get caught with a patch behind their ear.

Some common oral agents used to control motion sickness and nausea include Dramamine, Atarax, Antivert, Compazine, and Phenergan. Dramamine, Antivert, and Atarax are types of antihistamines that have anti–motion sickness effects. Dramamine should be taken orally 30 minutes before exposure to motion and may be repeated every 4 to 6 hours. Antivert has a slower onset but a longer duration of action. It should be taken 1 hour before motion and may be repeated every 24 hours as necessary. Atarax may be taken every 6 to 8 hours for control of nausea and vomiting. Atarax also provides excellent control of itching due to allergic reactions or insect bites. Compazine and Phenergan are phenothiazine derivatives that have anti-emetic properties. Compazine may be given every 6 to 8 hours for nausea. Phenergan should be taken 30 to 60 minutes prior to motion and may be repeated in 8 to 12 hours. Compazine and Phenergan are also available in rectal suppositories. These should be given 1 hour prior to motion and may be repeated in 12 hours.

Transderm Scop patches are an excellent alternative to the medications above. Each patch is designed to deliver scopolamine evenly over a 3-day period. The patches should be applied behind the ear 4 hours before motion. The patches last for 72 hours and should be left on continuously and changed every 3 days.

All of these medications have side effects and contraindications. Please consult with your doctor previous to their use and for dosing information.

AMERICAN CANADIAN CARIBBEAN LINE

VITAL FEATURES

Type of vacation: **Cruise**
Target market: **Mature couples, younger groups**
Locations: **Bahamas, Belize, Florida, Mexico, New England**
All-inclusive cost per week: **$675–$1,875 plus airfare**

RATINGS

Value: 💲💲💲💲💲

Fun quotient: 🏖️🏖️🏖️🏖️

Honeymoon suitability: Not applicable

Singles meeting ground: 🧍

Child appeal: Not applicable

Management professionalism: ☎️☎️☎️☎️☎️

Service: 💡💡💡💡💡

Food: 🦞🦞🦞🦞

THE REAL STORY

The *Caribbean Prince* made its way toward a semidesolate beach of Anegada. There were no other boats around, and only a few sunbathers lined the beach. From the bow deck we could begin to make out the features of their sunburned faces. One sunbather stared in mild curiosity as we came closer and closer to the shore. His gaze changed to shock when he realized we weren't stopping; his jaw dropped into his Budweiser when we pulled right onto the beach next to him.

It's not surprising that he was startled: the ships of American

Canadian Caribbean Line (ACCL) act like World War II land-shore landing craft. As they approach the beach, an unusual ramp comes apart from the bow, extends slowly, and gently lands on the white sand. Within minutes a crew member exits, scampers down the ramp, and is followed by a line of passengers wearing snorkels, masks, and flippers. It's not the way most people imagine cruise ships.

ACCL's unique features are what make it different from any other cruise line. The president of ACCL, Luther H. Blount, designed his ships with a unique bow ramp and a shallow six-foot draft that allows them to go to beaches and ports inaccessible to other cruise ships. These features eliminate all disembarkment hassles. No lines form to get on and off the ship. No waiting. No crowds. Just more time to enjoy yourself snorkeling or wandering around the town. It's the perfect balance. You have the comforts of a cruise ship and the flexibility to jump ship and wander around the wild side of the islands.

ACCL currently attracts retired people aged 65 and older, but there is no reason why younger passengers wouldn't enjoy these trips. Industry wags say that ACCL is for the geriatric crowd, and the company's brochure gives this impression too. The combination of an adventurous itinerary, exotic ports, invigorating beaches, snorkeling caves, BYO liquor and, of course, the low price makes this package an inviting vacation for passengers of all ages. This would be the perfect cruise for a group of college spring breakers, or a group of young couples. The potential to have fun is unlimited, although it is the "make-it-yourself" rather than the packaged kind.

INCLUDED

Accommodations	Taxes
Activities	Transfer to and from airport
Food	Wine with dinner
Sports	(occasionally)

VALUE

These trips are very good deals although they are as basic as they come. You won't be wined, dined, or pampered as you would be on a larger cruise ship, but you won't have to deal with the crowds, hassles, or stuffiness either.

The BYO policy actually saves you money. You can buy a bottle of rum in the Virgin Islands for less than the price of two drinks on some other ships.

ACTIVITIES, SPORTS, & EXCURSIONS

The active and the nonactive alike will enjoy a cruise on either the *Caribbean Prince* or the *New Shoreham II*. If all you want to do on your vacation is lie in the sun, exert yourself only to eat a meal or refill your drink, then a trip on ACCL is for you. There aren't a thousand planned activities demanding your attention. You won't feel guilty about skipping aerobics classes, for example, because there are none. There is no disco, piano bar, or casino forcing you to decide how to spend your evening. There is a well-stocked, cozy library in the bow, with a VCR and a piano. The one planned nightly activity runs along the lines of a limerick contest or bingo. Yet the same cruise can satiate even a hyperactive appetite. The ships stop at a different island every day, each offering a unique culture of its own. There are hundreds of things to do, see, eat, drink, and absorb on each of the islands.

ACTIVITIES: Board games, sunbathing.

SPORTS: No rigorous sports are offered on the ship because participation would be low. This might change if ACCL experiences a change in its passenger makeup.

Sailing (there is a Sunfish   Stretch class
    aboard for passengers'   Swimming
    use)
Snorkeling

EXCURSIONS: Taxi drivers give half-day tours of the larger islands; they usually cost $10 to $18. The *Caribbean Prince* also offers a perfectly timed excursion on the tenth day of the trip. Passengers feeling antsy find relief at the beach picnic. Blue skies, conch fritters, volleyball games, music, and an open tab at the beach bar exorcise any seasickness or boredom from being at sea.

ITINERARY & DAILY SCHEDULE

Home port for ACCL's two ships is Warren, Rhode Island. The *Caribbean Prince* and the *New Shoreham II* travel through New England and up to Saguenay, Canada, during the summer. The first cool breeze sends them to the Caribbean. An intercoastal cruise is offered on the way down, ending in Florida. The ships split up there; the *Caribbean Prince* goes to St. Thomas in the U.S. Virgin Islands, and the *New Shoreham II* goes to Belize and Mexico.

The first part of the winter, the *Caribbean Prince* offers 7- and 12-day trips through the Virgin Islands. It stops at St. John, St. Croix, Tortola, Virgin Gorda, Peter Island, and then returns to St. Thomas. The ship visits the islands of Anegada and Jost Van Dyke on the 12-day tours. In mid-February, the *Prince* heads to St. Martin and travels in a circle, stopping at St. Barts, Saba, Anguilla, Tintamarre, and several other small islands.

The rest of the winter the *Prince* travels through the Lesser Antilles. Twelve-day cruises depart from Antigua and travel down to Grenada. The ship lands at the following ports of call: Guadeloupe, Dominica, Martinique, St. Lucia, Bequia, Canouan, Mayreau, and Carriacou. The *Prince*'s last Caribbean cruise of the winter departs from Antigua and ends at St. Martin. Along the way, it visits Nevis, St. Kitts, Barbuda, Saba, St. Barts, Grand Case, Flat Island, Oriente Bay, and Anguilla.

NIGHTLIFE & ENTERTAINMENT

If you define nightlife by contemporary standards, then there is no nightlife aboard ACCL's ships. No discos. No parties. Not a bit of fooling around. The passengers on our cruise did not seem to notice that there was no entertainment. People played card games and conversed. Many friendships formed on the cruise and sad farewells ensued when it ended.

There is plenty of nightlife on the islands. The ship usually docks at a town during the night. The sea anchorages come as a welcome relief to the drinking passengers, who need time to recover from the "pain-killers" (a favorite island drink).

AESTHETICS & ENVIRONMENT

ACCL's ships are not glittery, glitzy, floating Love Boats. They are small, comfortable craft that serve the passengers' needs. When you walk on board you get the buckled-in, secure feeling that everything is in place. This is comforting, especially during rough seas.

FACILITIES: beaches, entertainment coordinators, medical station, refreshment counter with free soft drinks.

ROOMS

The cabins on the *Caribbean Prince* don't change drastically from one classification to another. The staterooms on the main level (called the 50s deck) are the most expensive. These cabins can be made up with a double berth, in which case you can have a table and chair, or two single berths. Add a bunk, and they can accommodate three people. The cabins on the main deck aren't that different from those on the 50s deck except they have a hanging bar instead of a closet and can only accommodate two people. The least expensive cabins are on the lower deck. Rather small and without a window, they tend to feel a bit cramped. These cabins are for budget travelers who don't plan to spend much time in their room.

Don't expect anything lavish. The cabins are kept clean and a central air conditioner keeps them very cool. They give you a good place to sleep and that's about all. But you won't want to stay in your cabin for long periods of time anyway.

LUXURY LEVEL: Air-conditioning, maid service.

FOOD & DRINK

A bell announces meals three times a day, but this draws only a few people from their cabins because most people are already gathered around the dining room tables. Meals are a time to socialize, eat good food, and watch the Caribbean sky turn from aqua blue to azure through the huge windows lining both sides of the dining room.

ACCL doesn't provide the gastronomical orgy found on the larger cruise ships. The food is plentiful, usually American, and served family style. The chef on the *Caribbean Prince* is imaginative, but his creativity is restricted by the desires of guests. Most passengers on our cruise wanted their food on the mild side. Sometimes the chef slips a few spices or an ethnic meal in between the meat and potatoes. Desserts are much more creative. He causes quite a bit of excitement with his flaming jubilees.

Breakfast is served at 8:00 A.M. The buffet table is laden with hot and cold cereal, fresh fruit, and nuts. Bacon and eggs or something along the same lines is served as the main course. Lunches are hearty. A fresh salad or interesting soup precedes sandwiches or a hot dish. As you probably suspect, people dress casually for meals. A cocktail hour before dinner lends a formal air to the meal. Homemade bread is baked daily and served with dinner. Main fare alternates between seafood and meat. The chef occasionally serves fresh fish from the local seafood markets.

STAFFING & SERVICE

How can you go wrong with a captain named Roy and a first mate named Dixie? They're also husband and wife, and he has a soft southern drawl—the Love Boats would love to get them on board. The captain and first mate are very professional: not only do they know the waters well, they also understand what the passengers want and tailor the itinerary accordingly. The rest of the crew are young and enthusiastic. They actually appear to enjoy what they're doing. Both ACCL's office staff and ship crews work hard to please, and they succeed. They're as quick with their work as they are with a smile. Passengers appreciate the quality of service throughout the cruise.

PRIVACY & RELAXATION

If you got any more relaxed than this, you'd be dead. It's a perfect place to be a couch potato in the sun.

SHOPPING

An entire day is reserved for shopping at Charlotte Amalie on the St. Thomas cruise, but this time would be spent more wisely at the beach or sight-seeing. You might find a bargain if you don't mind crowded, noisy streets and hordes of people all looking for that same bargain. The town is famous for linens, gold, and perfumes, but they can be bought at home for just about the same price.

HONEYMOONERS

This trip is not suitable for a honeymoon. It might be OK for a second honeymoon, if you are not attached to young romantic ideals.

SINGLES

ACCL definitely does not compete with Hedonism II in attracting young singles. In fact, the aboard-ship possibilities are slim to none. Older singles may have better luck in finding companionship.

NUTS & BOLTS

BOOKING & CONTACT INFORMATION

American Canadian Caribbean Line
P.O. Box 368
Warren, RI 03885
800-556-7450
401-247-0955

CURRENCY: All you need is U.S. currency. Traveler's checks are best.

CUSTOMS/DUTY: Once aboard, there are only two things you will have to do for customs: give your passport to the cruise director, and fill out a customs declaration form. Everything else is taken care of.
You will also have to clear customs at the airport. In the Virgin Islands, the process consists of a quick glance toward your luggage by a customs officer and filling out a form that declares how much money you spent in the Islands.

DEPOSITS/REFUNDS: Deposit for all cruises is $100 per person. The balance is due 60 days prior to date of sailing.
For a full refund, a written request must be sent 60 days before date of sailing (and it will be given only if the space is resold). The cancellation charges after 60 days, but prior to departure, are as follows: 25 percent for cancelling 59 to 45 days prior to departure date; 50 percent charge for cancelling 44 to 30 days prior; 75 percent for cancelling 29 to 11 days prior; and 100 percent charge for cancelling 10 or fewer days prior to departure date.

ELECTRICITY: 110 volts 60 cycles.

HANDICAP ACCESSIBILITY: There have been handicapped passengers before, although accessibility is limited.

LANGUAGE: English.

PACKING: The only thing that is absolutely necessary is a bathing suit. Dining is very informal, but you may want to bring one nice outfit for special occasions. You may want to bring your own snorkel and mask if you don't like the idea of community equipment.

RELIGIOUS SERVICES: There are no services offered on board, although the cruise director will arrange for you to attend local services when the ship is in port.

RESERVATION SCHEDULE: Book six months ahead for winter cruises, three months for the summer.

SIZE: Length, 160 feet; width, 35 feet.

Cost Worksheet

	Year-Round Prices[1]
Accommodations (7 days)[2]	$675–$1,875
Food	incl.
Drinks[3]	
Departure tax	varies with itinerary
Sports	incl.
Airfare	
	_____
Sight-seeing	
Tips[4]	
Additional sports	
Souvenirs	
	_____

[1] Rates do not change because the ship travels to New England in summer and the Caribbean in winter, avoiding off-seasons altogether.

[2] Premium for a single person: If you agree to share a cabin you pay no extra. Otherwise you may pay up to 175 percent of the double rate.

[3] Drinks: ACCL has a bring-your-own policy on alcohol. Coolers are provided for beer and wine; mixers are free as well. There are no problems with disappearing bottles; liquor bottles are left everywhere and everyone is pretty honest.

[4] Tips: There is a formula to figure out exactly how much to leave the crew. Ignoring the complications, it should be between $100 and $150 per person per week. The crew is really excellent and you will probably want to tip the higher amount.

NUMBER OF CABINS: 38.

MAXIMUM NUMBER OF GUESTS: 76.

NUMBER OF EMPLOYEES: 14.

VACCINATION REQUIREMENTS: None.

VISA/PASSPORT REQUIREMENTS: Passport needed.

SPENDING MONEY: You don't have to spend a cent once on board, but you will want to bring money to tip the crew and of course for shopping in port.

AMERICAN HAWAIIAN CRUISES

VITAL FEATURES

Type of vacation: **Cruise**
Target market: **Mature couples, singles, and families**
Location: **Hawaiian Islands**
Home port: **Honolulu**
All-inclusive cost per week: **$2,000–$5,000 including airfare**

RATINGS

Value: 💲💲💲

Fun quotient: 🏝🏝🏝

Honeymoon suitability: ❤❤❤

Singles meeting ground: ▮

Child appeal: 🍦🍦

Management professionalism: ☎☎☎

Service: 💡💡💡

Food: 🦞🦞🦞

THE REAL STORY

American Hawaiian Cruises (AHC) sails a dramatic route that answers almost any passenger's prayers. The Hawaiian Islands exude beauty when viewed from near or far. AHC executes the voyage spectacularly, circling the islands during the day and passing molten lava at night. The results are truly memorable. In addition, the close proximity of the ports allows long stays ashore.

AHC revived U.S.-flagged passenger ships and, until recently, remained the sole major U.SA. carrier. The all-American crew seems like an anomaly for seasoned passengers. However, the largely Hawaiian staff know the islands well. The name American Hawaiian suits the cruise line because the ships have the same mosaic of mainland and Hawaiian culture found on the islands themselves: the continental *haole* way of doing business is laced with native language, dress, attitudes, and aloha spirit.

During your time at sea, the staff keep you quite busy with Olympic games, ukulele lessons, and hula time. One evening is topped with the crowning of Ms. and Mr. S.S. *Constitution*.

Although the ship offers most of the activities that you would expect during a cruise, the schedule orients passengers toward touring the different islands. Most people leave the ship as soon as it docks and come back right before the crew pulls away the gangplank. By late evening, most passengers seem fatigued from their day of sight-seeing. Many make it to the shows, but the crowd thins out for the disco and nightclub acts.

Most of the passengers are active seniors, who often come in groups. Much of the cruise is oriented toward them, from the music, to the shows, to the food. The chefs cook special low-cholesterol meals (classic Continental, lightly seasoned), and the crew makes special provisions for people who have physical disabilities. Also, a majority of the excursions do not demand strenuous physical activity.

A minority of younger passengers keep the noise level up slightly. Many of them hop aboard for three or four days as a way to travel interisland. For a few days, they don't seem to mind the demographics. Most of the young folks are coupled up; many are honeymooners. You may find this trip a delightful way to do a grand tour of the islands.

INCLUDED

Accommodations	Food
Activities	Transfer to and from airport
Entertainment & dancing	

VALUE

AHC cruises cost considerably more than cruises of the same quality in the Caribbean. However, they do offer a very easy and pleasant way to see the Hawaiian Islands. The total sight-seeing experience would be hard to beat.

ACTIVITIES, SPORTS, & EXCURSIONS

ACTIVITIES

Arts & crafts	Culture/music/language
Board games	classes

Dancing

Entertainment/shows

Horseback riding

Sunbathing

Sports: Don't take this trip to get that old form back. It is far more oriented to touring than to sports and onboard activities. The barely adequate gym and the slow exercise classes will keep you limber. Long walks around the islands offer the best opportunity to get in shape. To do this, rent a car to get to your destination, then get out and explore Hawaii's beautiful geography. Glorious promenades take you around the caldera at Volcano National Park and through the Maui Tropical Plantation.

Aerobics (low-impact)

Golf (driving off the stern)

Shuffleboard

Snorkeling (extra)

Swimming

Weightlifting

Excursions: The cruise offers almost 40 distinct shore excursions during the five days on land, plus an additional dozen on the base island of Oahu. The cornucopia of choices ranges from sight-seeing and sports to leisure activities. All cost extra, ranging from $10 for a glass-bottomed boat tour to $155 for a helicopter tour of Haleakala Crater. Visitors should plan on spending about $50 per person per day for the shore excursions. Tours on Oahu must be booked on land, and can probably be booked cheaper through discount coupons found in some of the free advertising magazines at most hotels. All the ship-sponsored excursions are exceptionally well organized. Guides meet passengers on the dock and take care of all arrangements. The prices tend to be higher (sometimes significantly) than those offered from more competitive companies that advertise locally, but the convenience and time saving more than compensate for the extra cost. Most people find the trips interesting and well planned out. The bus tours suffer from fixed schedules and cramped seating, but the interesting guides spin yarns about old Hawaii, keeping the crowd amused.

Far more economical than the organized tours is renting your own car, and Dollar Rent-A-Car brings its autos to the dock and its keys on board. U.S. roads and customs make driving easy. The island roads are laid out simply, for the most part, so navigation rarely becomes a problem. The tourism booths at many docks often offer maps and self-guided automobile tour booklets. An investment in a guidebook to the islands would be money well spent. Split several ways, a car can be cheap, flexible, and more comfortable than the buses.

Early bookings for rental cars often deplete the supply. Advance reservations for all the islands are strongly recommended. If you decide not to take the car at the last minute, there is often a line of people who will gladly relieve you of the responsibility. If you should get stuck without a car, a company at the local airport will often pick you up at the dock. Expect to pay more. Here again, the supplies are limited, and there is often trouble supplying the walk-in traffic.

 Jason's Tips:

Gold credit card holders can often avoid the expensive "Collision Damage Waiver" insurance option. Find out your privileges before you leave home, then stand your ground with the rental car clerk, no matter what scare tactics he or she might employ. A lost-leader rental rate of under $30 per day offers a car with manual transmission and no air-conditioning; unlimited mileage is included. If you are prepared to accept this, you will often find that you get a car with automatic transmission and air-conditioning for the same rate.

Before you rent a car with other people, do a nose count of smokers and nonsmokers. Setting the rules before the journey can make the trip more enjoyable for everybody.

ITINERARY & DAILY SCHEDULE

Even though each of the Hawaiian Islands offers enough activities for a long stay, many visitors prefer to see several of the islands. AHC knows Hawaii well and provides a sensible itinerary. The ships circle around and between the islands, keeping close to spectacular views of volcanos, mountains, villages, and the inlets. Our cruise was trailed by a constant rainbow.

Both of AHC's ships cruise the same route, only they do it in reverse directions. Each ship departs from Honolulu Saturday evening and spends the first day at sea, allowing passengers to relax and get acquainted with the ship. The S.S. *Constitution* visits the islands of Oahu, Maui, Hawaii, and Kauai. The S.S. *Independence* stops at the same islands, but in the reverse order.

AHC also accepts people for three-day or four-day cruises. Many couples will find this preferable to a week-long cruise because it gives them a chance to sample the cruise and the different islands, while still allowing vacation time for relaxing on a single island.

Passengers originating outside California may stop off (before or after the cruise) in Los Angeles, San Francisco, or Las Vegas for an additional airline charge of $60.

NIGHTLIFE & ENTERTAINMENT

"Early to bed, early to rise" dictates the pattern of a large percentage of the passengers. The after-dinner show marks the end of an active day for most of the ship's sight-seers. This includes young people as well as senior citizens. A few nocturnal diehards keep things rocking in the disco, attend the nightclub acts, or drop by the Starlight Lounge for its late-night piano shows.

The shows deserve a mention for their level of energy and choreography. Many of the performers have exceptional talent. The orchestra is well rehearsed. The show suffers only because the short contracts of the performers don't allow them a lot of time to get comfortable in their routines or with each other.

AESTHETICS & ENVIRONMENT

The ships are plush, modern, attractively decorated, and immaculately maintained. The recently renovated ships feel like new vessels.

The outside common areas are cramped for the number of passengers. For example, it can be hard to find a couple of lounge chairs together. This is rarely a problem, because the ship is more oriented to shore excursions than sunbathing on deck. Passengers spend time on the ship during the evening, when space in the lounges, bars, and disco is adequate.

FACILITIES

Bars	Gift shop
Beaches (on shore)	Medical station
Beauty salon	Piano bar/lounge
Concierge	Safety-deposit box
Disco	Swimming pool
Entertainment coordinators	

ROOMS

The recently refurbished rooms please the visual and tactile senses. They contain modern baths and allow plenty of room to move around. Unfortunately, few contain double beds, so romantic types must sleep real close. Just think back to your days at the college dormitory, if you attended school after the days of parietals.

LUXURY LEVEL

Air-conditioning	Porter service
Laundry service (extra)	Radio/music in room
Maid service	Refrigerator in room
Phone in room	Room service

FOOD & DRINK

The food features mostly American-style cuisine, and is geared to the tastes of an older crowd, although the menus also include foods lower in cholesterol and salt. These dishes, which are found in each menu category, are clearly marked. Fresh quality ingredients go into the dishes.

The food tends to be lightly seasoned and is often smothered with sauces. If you request sauce on the side or additional seasonings, the waiters will accommodate you with short delays. Passengers who have palates sharpened by nouvelle or ethnic cuisine sometimes find the food disappointing. However, the wide selection ensured that nobody ever seemed at a loss to find enough of something to eat.

The morning starts with pastries and coffee on deck. Soon after, breakfast is served in the main dining room and on a deck buffet. Both menus feature a full cadre of juices, cereals, eggs, meats, and fresh-brewed coffee. The dining room also offers smoked salmon and capers. An omelet chef makes eggs to order on the outdoor buffet.

After the first day, few people come back from touring for lunch, even though the half-day tours allow you to do that. An outdoor buffet offers lunch meats and salads. A dining room lunch offers a full-course meal. At dinner, a wide selection of juices, soups, hors d'oeuvres, main courses, vegetables, and desserts offer choices for even the most picky eaters. You won't find anything exotic, but you won't have to guess what's on your plate either.

A midnight buffet offers munchies for the few diehards. On the night that you pass by the active volcano on the Big Island, a magnificent midnight buffet artistically presents seafood galore. It opens up a half hour in advance for picture taking. Pretty as it is, you will probably find better uses for your film.

STAFFING & SERVICE

The brochure gives excellent information on company policies, cabin placement, and available packages. Similarly, the shore excursion brochure is descriptive and complete. You may need a cryptographer to discern which combination of discount packages is available for your sailing dates, class of cabin, and advance booking.

The entertainment staff and cabin stewards do their job with charm and efficiency. The dining room staff get only an average grade.

PRIVACY & RELAXATION

Our cabin steward told tales of the imaginative places that people have found to be alone on board. That really is not necessary, because the ship was originally designed to carry 1,003 passengers (it now sails with a maximum of 798). In your cabin you have complete sound privacy from the other passengers.

After the first day, most people stay extremely active touring the islands. Many people are up early, sipping coffee and eating Danish before the breakfast buffet opens at 6:30 A.M. Most morning tours depart shortly after 9:00 A.M.

The ship offers activities all day long. The morning exercise classes draw a good-size crowd. The rest of the day's activities are as hokey as "Napkin folding with Tom." Few except the infirm remain on the ship during the day, so this is of little consequence.

Game activities occupy the day at sea. These consist of the standard silly, but fun, team pursuits of chugging contests, walking with a ball between your legs, and the like. The participation level is high.

SHOPPING

Except for pineapples and macadamia nuts, most items are imported from the mainland or from Japan. Waikiki is full of trendy shops and much *schlock*. A few interesting items can be found at the International Market located on Kalakaua Avenue, Waikiki's main drag.

HONEYMOONERS

A honeymoon cocktail party will start off your cruise. Most of the honeymooners book a three- or four-night package, then stay at other islands for the rest of their trip.

SINGLES

Young singles may have a tough time finding interesting company. If you are preretirement, this is definitely not the place to meet your mate.

CHILD APPEAL

AHC welcomes children of all ages, but the excursion orientation of the cruise may not work well for families.

NUTS & BOLTS

Booking & contact information

American Hawaiian Cruises, Inc.
550 Kearny Street
San Francisco, CA 94108
800-227-3666
415-392-9400

Deposits/refunds: A minimum of 25 percent of your total fare is due one week after booking. You must pay the balance 60 days before departure.

If you cancel, you lose $25 no matter what. Let them know 61 days before the cruise and you'll get the rest back. From 31 to 60 days, you lose 25 percent; from 16 to 30 days you sacrifice 50 percent; up to 3 days before, you get 25 percent back. After that, you lose it all. This policy applies even for medical reasons.

HANDICAP ACCESSIBILITY: The staff go out of their way to accommodate people with physical disabilities. On some of the port stops, the angle of the gangplank makes it difficult for people in wheelchairs to get onshore.

PACKING: The ship generally reflects the informal nature of the islands. One semiformal outfit should suffice for the formal dinner and a possible invitation to the captain's cocktail party. This is the place to bring those Hawaiian shirts and shorts; people really wear them here.

Bring your own snorkeling gear for familiarity and to save money on rentals. Binoculars will give you a better view of the erupting volcano and the islands.

RELIGIOUS SERVICES: On Sunday, the cruise director conducts an interdenominational service accompanied by the music of Haunani's Hawaiians. You might want to go just for the experience.

RESERVATION SCHEDULE: Good things come to those who plan in advance. Those who deposit 30 percent within 7 days of booking and pay in full 90 days prior to sailing receive all sorts of bonuses.

SIZE: Length, 682 feet; width, 89 feet.

MAXIMUM NUMBER OF GUESTS: 798.

NUMBER OF CREW: 330.

TRAVEL TIME BY AIR

Chicago: **9 hours 30 minutes**
Los Angeles: **6 hours**
New York: **12 hours**
Toronto: **11 hours**

TRAVEL TIME FROM AIRPORT: 30 minutes.

SPENDING MONEY: Plan to spend lots of cash on the shore excursions. These run approximately $50 per person per day for six days, plus approximately $130 for a helicopter tour, which should be considered a mandatory part of the trip. The islands can be toured for far less money by renting cars and splitting the cost two to four ways.

Cost Worksheet

	High Season	Off-Season[1]
Accommodations		
(7 days)	$1,125–$3,695	$1,025–$3,595
Food	incl.	incl.
Drinks	U.S. bar prices	
Port charge	$33	$33
Sports	incl.	incl.
Airfare[2]	————	————
Sight-seeing	$450	$450
Tips		
Additional sports		
Souvenirs	————	————

[1] During the off-season, special rates are offered, as well as children's packages.

[2] Discounted airfare via American Airlines runs from $495 round-trip from New York to $269 round-trip from Los Angeles.

BERMUDA STAR LINE

Type of vacation: **Cruise**
Target market: **Couples, singles, families**
Location: **Mexican Riviera**
Home port: **San Diego, California**
All-inclusive cost per week: **$1,200 including airfare**

RATINGS

Value: 💲💲💲💲

Fun quotient: 🌴🌴🌴🌴

Honeymoon suitability: ❤️❤️❤️

Singles meeting ground: 🚹🚺🚹

Child appeal: 🍦

Management professionalism: ☎️☎️☎️☎️☎️

Service: 💡💡💡💡

Food: 🦞🦞🦞

THE REAL STORY

Are you ready for a week-long fest of eating and activities? The *Bermuda Star* offers just that. Leaving from San Diego, she cruises down the coast of Baja California to the Mexican Riviera. Seven nights and six full days allow the passengers three days in port and a disproportionately long three days at sea. Because you spend that much time cruising, *Bermuda Star* offers lots of ship attractions: food, entertainment, munchies, music, snacks, sports, activities, and a bit to eat. It provides it all in large quantities. With that much fun and food, you're virtually guaranteed to have a good time and gain weight.

Not surprisingly, this cruise is oriented toward the time at sea. In fact, many people elect not to take advantage of shore excursions, remaining on board the entire time. Land is visible during most of the cruise, and dolphins often show off to the delight of the passengers.

The *Bermuda Star* makes a comfortable home for your voyage. Christened in 1958 and built to cross the Atlantic, the ship retains the feel of her era, when ships were built with relatively large staterooms and a lot of rich woods and brass. She navigates the seas in a stable and confident manner. Her low center of gravity and solid construction provide an extremely stable footing. While passengers may detect some pitching and rocking, the ship experiences substantially less motion than the newer, taller vessels. In addition, the use of steam turbines, instead of diesels, all but eliminates vibration and noise.

The passengers come from all age groups, the majority being retired. Still, passengers in their thirties or even their twenties comprise a significant percentage of the guests. Very few children come aboard.

INCLUDED

Accommodations	Food
Activities	Sports
Airfare	Sports instruction
Child care	Taxes
Entertainment & dancing	Transfer to and from airport

VALUE

Bermuda Star Line's rates place it in the ranks of budget cruises. The fine vessels, competent crews, good food, and spacious accommodations guarantee a fun and relaxing holiday. All passengers we interviewed agreed that they enjoyed the experience and felt that they had received their money's worth.

ACTIVITIES, SPORTS, & EXCURSIONS

ACTIVITIES: Each day offers new activities. Programs, slid under your door every evening, allow the next day to be planned. An AP news wire keeps you abreast of world events.

At sea, daily activities revolve around eating. Leave your diet on shore, because everything is squeezed between major sit-down meals and almost constant buffets. An average morning offers golf (a humorous demonstration of driving on the ship's fantail), Ping-Pong, dance classes, shuffleboard, bingo, a mileage pool, and wooden horse racing. After lunch you might listen to one of several bands on deck, or watch a couple of recently released movies. Aerobics classes offer

exercise each afternoon for both neophytes and those experienced in
self-punishment.

The ship's nightlife includes a Las Vegas–style casino that includes
four blackjack tables, a roulette wheel, and slot machines rigged for
quarters and dollars. Several clubs, discos, and a seemingly unlimited number of bars assure that evenings never become dull.

Arts & crafts	Movies
Board games	Sunbathing
Dancing	Underwater vision boat (in
Entertainment/shows	ports)

SPORTS: Aerobics classes aside, swimming and weightlifting provide the only exercise on board. The small saltwater pool becomes
too rough for swimming in heavy seas. Much of the water in the pool
ends up on deck and so would a swimmer's lunch if he stayed in the
water. The pool is drained each evening and filled with fresh, lightly
chlorinated seawater each morning. The pool water tends to be a bit
cool.

The small exercise room contains a Universal machine and free
weights. Unfortunately, the low ceiling only allows presses for people under the height of four feet 3 inches. A masseuse for men and
women loosens muscles for a market fee.

Aerobics/exercise classes	Scuba (extra)
Bicycles (extra; in port)	Shuffleboard
Gold driving	Snorkeling (extra)
Horseback riding (extra; in	Swimming
port)	Weightlifting
Jet skiing (extra)	
Parasailing (extra)	

EXCURSIONS: At each port of call, the excursion office offers tours
at extremely reasonable rates. The ship also gives information about
local facilities, customs, and what to avoid.

ITINERARY & DAILY SCHEDULE

As with all cruises, your time is your own. Many night owls sleep
late. Don't worry about missing breakfast, because food is always
close at hand. Other passengers begin the day early and pack in as
many activities as possible. Port visits usually last for several hours,
giving you a chance to shop, tour, or wander around. You'll probably
have just enough time to get really interested in something before
having to return to ship.

The Bermuda Star Line operates three ships: the *Bermuda Star*,
the *Queen of Bermuda* (the *Bermuda Star*'s sister ship), and the *Veracruz*, a smaller but equally fun and friendly ship. The *Queen of
Bermuda* sails from New Orleans to Cancún, Cozumel, and Key West

during the fall and winter months. During the summer she sails from Bermuda to New York. The *Veracruz* makes two-to-five-day trips from Tampa to Cancún and Cozumel on Mexico's Yucatán Peninsula. The *Bermuda Star* cruises the Mexican Riviera during the winter, when western Mexico has its dry season. In the summer, she sails through the Panama Canal and on to New York. From there she plies the North Atlantic until it's time to return to the Pacific.

NIGHTLIFE & ENTERTAINMENT

There is at least as much to do in the evenings as there is during the day. Floor shows attract a considerable crowd, as do the casinos. Those who like to dance can choose between big band music, jazz, or rock and roll. The bars serve drinks throughout the night. Of course, you can always leave the crowds and lights behind and take a quiet walk on the deck beneath the stars.

AESTHETICS & ENVIRONMENT

The *Bermuda Star* does not claim to be the most elegant ship afloat. The ship underwent a major refurbishment in 1973, when many of her cabins were redone. She is starting to feel her 30 years and shows the innumerable coats of paint that soften the outlines of her steel fittings. All during the cruise, crew members can be seen chipping, painting, varnishing, and polishing. Some of the cabins suffer from lack of maintenance. The ship's interior is disappointingly Spartan, but the crew keeps the ship clean and functional. Keep in mind that most time is spent on deck or in the dining room. The rooms creak a bit while under way. In a way, this gives a nautical feel to the voyage. A few passengers complained of loud, distracting noises in their cabins.

The ship has a well-staffed radio room that provides ship-to-shore radio-telephone services and a daily newspaper. The ship also holds an unusually large and well equipped hospital. It has a two-position coronary care unit, an examination room, a dentist's chair, and an isolation ward. The doctor and nurse show pride in their facilities and claim to be able to handle any kind of emergency. The purser's office dispenses aspirin, Band-Aids, and Dramamine free of charge.

FACILITIES

Bank	Gift shop
Bars	Laundry (coin-operated)
Beaches	Massage
Beauty salon (extra)	Medical station
Casino	Piano bar
Disco	Safety-deposit box
Film lab	Swimming pool

ROOMS

The cabins vary widely. Some rooms in the same class have tubs while others do not. Sometimes the beds are at right angles to each other; in other rooms they are parallel. Some cabins have paintings on painted walls while others have wallpaper. Most rooms have windows that can be opened, a few are painted shut, and others have fixed windows.

LUXURY LEVEL

Air-conditioning	Phone in room
Clock	Porter service
Desk	Room service
Maid service	

FOOD & DRINK

The food makes the cruise. A Bermuda Star cruise ship is a floating hotel and restaurant. The flow of great food never ends.

Dinner sittings are at 6:00 P.M. and 8:15 P.M. This leaves plenty of time for leisurely dining at both seatings. The maître d' assigns guests based on their preference for a large or small table, age group, and smoking habit. A waiter, busboy, and wine steward serve you through the entire cruise. Each handles his job professionally. They can accommodate almost every possible food request.

The menu offers a wide selection and changes each day. The waiters describe the entrées and express their opinion about what should be ordered. The quality of the food is good, but not great. The desserts are very good, and the selection seems unlimited. At first blush, the portions may seem a little small. But since you rarely go into the dining room ravenously hungry, this waste reduction technique goes unnoticed by all but the most gluttonous of passengers. Of course, you can order additional servings if desired.

The wine steward totes a limited selection. The wine list also lacks descriptive information.

If you miss a sit-down meal, or don't want to get out of bed for a scheduled feast, fear not! Plentiful buffets assuage the munchies between meals. The selections at these times are substantially more limited and the quality is somewhat lacking, but it does give you the opportunity to eat in casual dress on deck.

STAFFING & SERVICE

The crew comes from more than 20 countries. The officers tend to be European, and the staff originates from the Caribbean, Mexico, and the South Pacific. The entire crew works hard to make the cruise pleasant for the passengers. The almost invisible room stewards clean the staterooms on a continuous basis. You can almost come back from the beach to use the bathroom and find the sand vacuumed from your room before you emerge.

PRIVACY & RELAXATION

With the exception of your stateroom, little privacy can be found on board the ship. You can often escape the crowds on deserted beaches during the shore stops. Poke about the ship, and you should find a nice place to curl up with a book or a friendly body. Some passengers claim that the gentle rocking of the ship assists them in sleeping. Others can't get used to it. Most people get a good night's sleep and wake early.

SHOPPING

Each port offers its own special items. Mexico has especially good prices on leather goods and woven items. With the strength of the dollar in comparison to the peso you should find some good deals. The shops aboard ship can provide for most of your shopping needs.

HONEYMOONERS

Evening strolls around the decks and daytime sun lounging make for romantic moments. Few rooms have double beds, and the twin beds are poorly suited to honeymoon calisthenics. Some passengers remove the mattresses and place them side by side on the floor. This may upset the cabin steward, but it does say much for the size of the staterooms.

SINGLES

The atmosphere is conducive to romance, but pickings tend to be slim. The male officers attend all the singles functions. While not outwardly aggressive, they tend to lie like jungle cats waiting to pounce on passing prey that is often enthusiastic about being caught.

CHILD APPEAL

There's not much for kids to do but hang around the Ping-Pong table or go to the movies.

NUTS & BOLTS

BOOKING & CONTACT INFORMATION: Tickets must be purchased through travel agents. Special rates are sometimes available close to departure dates.

Bermuda Star Cruises
1086 Teaneck Road
Teaneck, New Jersey 07666
800-548-8208 (brochures)
800-237-5361 (information)
201-837-0400

CURRENCY: A special ship's credit card allows you to charge drinks and shipboard purchases. This "tab" is then resolved with the purser prior to departure.

Pesos are the official Mexican currency, but vendors would rather take your dollars. Stores quote prices in both pesos and dollars. We recommend that you not convert currency.

CUSTOMS/DUTY: Passengers place their luggage outside their rooms the day before returning. Customs agents come on board to clear the vessel. After the officials clear the ship, the passengers may disembark and claim their bags. They then proceed through the inspection phase, where the bags are rarely opened. Passengers may bring back one liter of liquor and $400 in merchandise without having to pay the 10 percent duty tax.

DEPOSITS/REFUNDS: Confirmed reservations require a $200 deposit per passenger. The balance must be paid no later than 45 days prior to departure. Written cancellations received 30 days before sailing will get a full refund. Cancellations received 30 to 14 days prior to departure will be charged a $100-per-person cancellation fee. Under 14 days' notice will cost half of the cruise fare. No-shows receive no refund.

ELECTRICITY: 110 volts 60 cycles.

HANDICAP ACCESSIBILITY: The *Bermuda Star* is well equipped for the handicapped. There are two elevators on board and the doors open wide enough for wheelchairs. The ship's crew will always assist handicapped passengers.

PACKING: Passengers dress casually aboard ship except during dinner, when jackets often appear. Two times during the cruise dinners become formal. The first, the "Captain's Welcome-Aboard Gala," is a black-tie formal affair, although suits are acceptable. The "Captain's Farewell Dinner" requires semiformal dress.

RELIGIOUS SERVICES: Except when docked, nondenominational services are held each day in the movie theater. An interfaith renewal of marriage vows is conducted in a mass ceremony on the last full day of the cruise. If you've looked longingly at Reverend Moon's weddings, you'll love the *Bermuda Star*'s ceremony.

RESERVATION SCHEDULE: Reservations for shore excursions require that you sign up at least 24 hours in advance.

SIZE: 617 feet long.

NUMBER OF CABINS: 358.

MAXIMUM NUMBER OF GUESTS: 713.

NUMBER OF CREW: 300.

TRAVEL TIME BY AIR

Chicago: **4 hours 17 minutes**
Los Angeles: **55 minutes**
New York: **6 hours 15 minutes**
Toronto: **6 hours**

ARRIVAL AIRPORT: San Diego International Airport.

TRAVEL TIME FROM AIRPORT: 5 minutes. The *Bermuda Star* departs from the B Street pier, which is across the street from the airport. You could walk to the ship, but a taxi ride may make more sense considering the amount of luggage that most people carry on a cruise. Prior to departure you can make arrangements with the cruise operator to be shuttled to the ship and back after your return. Parking is available at the cruise terminal for $3 per day.

Embarkation begins at 12:30 P.M., with the ship sailing at 3:00 P.M. Passengers should board the ship at least 30 minutes prior to departure. Do not arrive earlier than the designated time, because you will not be permitted to board early.

VACCINATION REQUIREMENTS: None.

VISA/PASSPORT REQUIREMENTS: Passengers must prove citizenship or U.S. residence to clear customs in San Diego. A birth certificate, driver's license, or a passport will all suffice.

SPENDING MONEY: The amount of money spent on board depends on your drinking habits. Mixed drinks go for $2.50 and soft drinks cost $1.25. Shore excursions cost anywhere between $10 and $60 per person. All are well worth the price. You may want to bring money for purchases from the duty-free gift shop on board and from the Mexican shops while on shore. A couple can expect to leave $100 or more in tips for a one-week cruise, not including the 15 percent added to the bar tab.

Cost Worksheet

	Winter Season[1]
Accommodations (7 days)[2]	$895–$1,795
Food	incl.
Drinks	
Port tax	varies with itinerary
State tax	none
Hotel tax	none
Sports	incl.
Airfare	incl.
Sight-seeing	
Tips	$50 per passenger
Additional sports	
Souvenirs	

[1] Only sails to Mexican riviera in winter.
[2] Premium for single person: Single rates are available at 150 percent of ppdo rate.

BLACKBEARD'S CRUISES

VITAL FEATURES

Type of vacation: **Cruise for scuba divers**
Target market: **Certified divers of all ages and marital status**
Location: **The Bahamas**
Home port: **Miami, Florida**
All-inclusive cost per week: **$575 per person plus airfare.**

RATINGS

Value: 💲💲💲💲💲

Fun quotient: ⛱⛱⛱⛱

Honeymoon suitability: ♥

Singles meeting ground: Varies

Child appeal: Not applicable

Management professionalism: ☎☎☎☎☎

Service: 💡💡💡💡

Food: 🦞🦞🦞

THE REAL STORY

Blackbeard's Cruises takes scuba divers on a warm-water, warm-air adventure. Each of its 65-foot sloops provides a floating scuba fest in the reefs and wrecks of the Bahamas Out Islands.

While the subtropical climate and friendly crew provide a pleasant atmosphere aboard an intimate ship, Blackbeard's is, above all, a diving cruise. The Bahamas offers diving tour sites as diverse as the different cities of Europe. The captain and the dive master work together to find the best combination of underwater adventures that give each day variety and keep the sport diver well within decompression limits. Along with trips to coral forests, we were taken to several underwater locations where a James Bond movie and *Jaws 3* were filmed. We also dove spectacular underwater cliffs that dazzled even the most experienced diver.

You will feel comfortable no matter what your age or marital status. The ages on our tour ranged from 19 to a just-certified 61-year-old. Some divers brought their spouses, some didn't, and some were single. There was a bit of frolicking among the singles, although this is far from your classic singles vacation. It's OK to come alone, without a diving or partying buddy. Many do, and they immediately become a part of the boat scene.

If you're not a diver, the trip's not for you. Consider getting certified, though; it's well worth the effort. The skill level of the divers on this trip ranged from several just certified to some with over 100 dives. The dives are not difficult, none require decompression, and the reefs and wrecks are so colorful and varied that any sport diver will find them enjoyable. If you dive, bring along an underwater camera—better yet, plan ahead and take an underwater photography course. You'll fill a lot of pages in your dive log, and if you are experienced, you'll want a new challenge. In most spots, you are prohibited from spearfishing or taking lobsters under scuba. Hawaiian slings (a combination spear and slingshot) are available on board if you want to snag a grouper while snorkeling. Fishing gear is also available.

INCLUDED

Accommodations	Food
Activities	Sports
Drinks	Taxes
Entertainment & dancing	Wine with dinner

VALUE

Blackbeard's offers very solid value for the money. The trips are fun, well run, and reasonably hassle free. The destination—the Bahamas—offers some of the finest weather and diving in the world. Diving trips tend to be expensive, but Blackbeard's Cruises' cost per dive has to be among the lowest anywhere.

ACTIVITIES, SPORTS, & EXCURSIONS

Almost the sole activity is scuba diving. Depending on the weather-driven itinerary, you might get to visit Bimini, Nassau, or both. The captain will often lay out the options and let the passengers vote on how they want to spend their time.

Sailing	Spearfishing
Scuba	Sunbathing
Snorkeling	Swimming (ocean)

ITINERARY & DAILY SCHEDULE

The itinerary varies with the weather, the underwater visibility, and your whim. The captains take great pride in steering a course that will maximize diving, partying, and sunny weather.

NIGHTLIFE & ENTERTAINMENT

The onboard nightlife revolves around topside topple-over parties. Depending on the guests, these can turn into cocktail parties or frat parties, or a little of both! At night, the crew concocts a huge cooler of rum punches, including their infamous "frog." That stuff is too good, and it's a secret only *you* can discover. Have you ever mourned the decline of conversation? This is the place to rediscover it. Divers tell stories that could make fishermen incredulous.

Sometimes you'll travel down into the sea for a night dive. You'll see different fish that feed at night, and you can usually spot a lobster or two roaming the white sandy bottom in search of a meal.

At least one night during the week-long trip, the boat goes into town for some native nightlife, usually to Nassau or Bimini. In Bimini, go to Hemingway's old digs, the Compleat Angler (that guy drank in more places than Washington slept in).

AESTHETICS & ENVIRONMENT

The boats are efficient, functional vessels from which you can see tangerine sunsets, aqua-clear waters, and countless stars. The 65-foot sloops are designed to navigate the shallow waters of the Bahamas and to weather any nasty storms that could come along.

FACILITIES: Beaches (on the islands), gift shop (sells T-shirts), medical station (CPR-trained personnel).

ROOMS

Imagine cabin-camping with your food and dishes taken care of; a basic, shared bathroom; 30-second showers; and an experienced guide. Float that cabin, and you get an idea of a Blackbeard's cruise. It's not exactly roughing it, but there's no formal captain's table either. It's strictly casual: seven days of alternating between a bathing suit and a pair of shorts and a T-shirt.

The cabins and galley are air-conditioned, which keeps the air fresh and dry. This is especially nice in the summertime.

FOOD & DRINK

There is plenty of food—fresh, frozen, and canned—very ably prepared by the chefs. The fare is wholesome American—roasted meats, chicken, turkey, and lasagna. Salads, vegetables, and desserts are served with every dinner. Breakfasts revolve around eggs, cereals, grits, and bacon, and lunches are often sandwiches with potato salad. Meals are served buffet style down in the galley and are usually eaten up on deck, with plenty to go around. There is a big hammock full of fresh fruit in the galley for between-meal snacks. Those who don't like a meal or who miss one can always find something to eat. Late risers can usually round up a peanut butter and jelly sandwich if the 8:30 A.M. breakfast is a little early. Beer, soda, juices, and alcoholic drinks are always available.

If you want seafood, including the terrific Bahamian conch specialties, you can buy them in a restaurant on shore. The extremely budget conscious can eat on board, even during the port stay.

STAFFING & SERVICE

The crews are extremely competent. Our captain and first mate knew the waters, islands, swimming coves, and local watering holes like most people know their neighborhoods. They strike a good balance of being highly professional and good party masters. They will get as involved as you want them to. The dive master and engineers are real pros.

Front office support is one of Blackbeard's strengths. It has a full-time reservation staff and a warehouse that contains just about any spare part that a boat may need, including whole engines and generators. This is important, because it increases the chance that your trip will go without a hitch.

PRIVACY & RELAXATION

There are no portholes in the cabins. You have no idea what time it is until you hear a "last call for breakfast" or "get ready if you're diving" call. For a solid week, you'll hear no ringing telephones or alarm clocks.

The boat easily accommodates couples, although seven days of close quarters can test any relationship. There are at least two berths to a cabin, some single, some double. The fact that there is someone sleeping above you acts as a sort of "berth control." Visual privacy comes from a pulled black curtain, and audio separation from other cabins is left solely to the louvered wood door. For intimacy, you might have to make the kind of arrangements that you did in your college dorm room.

Topside, there is virtually no privacy. People socialize on the adequate, but not excessive deck. Passengers tend to be very friendly: scuba people come from all walks of life and share their passion for the ocean and the other things that they are doing in their lives. As a whole they tend to be interesting people and good conversationalists.

SHOPPING

Among piles of junk in the Nassau straw market is some very beautiful local handiwork. You can watch local craftspeople create their art. The prices are good compared to what you'd have to pay in the States, and you can get some real bargains if all of the other cruise ships aren't in town on the same day.

Blackbeard's sells fun T-shirts that you'll probably want as a souvenir of the trip. They cost about $10 each.

HONEYMOONERS

Unless your new spouse is a scuba fanatic, your marriage will last until the first Bahamian divorce court. This trip is perfect for taking a spouse or friend, even one who does not dive. But privacy is hard to come by.

SINGLES

The atmosphere is conducive to getting close, but the pool is limited. It varies from week to week.

CHILD APPEAL

This is not a trip for young children, although older teenagers would enjoy it.

NUTS & BOLTS

BOOKING & CONTACT INFORMATION

Blackbeard's Cruises
P.O. Box 66-1091
Miami Springs, FL 33266
305-888-1226
800-327-9600

You can also book with a travel agent. Some dive shops run trips.

DEPOSITS/REFUNDS: A $75 deposit is required to confirm a reservation. The balance is due 45 days before departure. No refunds are given for cancelled trips.

HANDICAP ACCESSIBILITY: None.

PACKING: You'll need to bring scuba or snorkeling gear, except tanks and weight belt, plus your dive log and certification card. Nothing more formal than a polo shirt is needed. During the summer, you need only bring a few bathing suits, shirts, and T-shirts. Foul weather gear and motion sickness pills are a must, just in case. . . .

RELIGIOUS SERVICES: None, unless you choose to pray to Neptune.

RESERVATION SCHEDULE: Many cruises fill up far in advance, especially during the winter months.

Cost Worksheet

	Year Round
Accommodations (7 days)	$575
Food	incl.
Drinks	incl.
Departure tax	$5
Sports	incl. (with own scuba gear)
Airfare	_____
Sight-seeing	
Tips	$20–$50
Additional sports	
Souvenirs	_____

SIZE: 65 feet long.

NUMBER OF SHIPS IN FLEET: 5.

SPENDING MONEY: You'll need very little. Bring a few dollars to buy souvenirs in the Nassau straw market and to order a few "back-packers" at the Compleat Angler in Bimini. Tip the crew $20 to $50 in toto, although we suspect that you'll want to give them the higher amount. Plan on $10 for cyalume sticks for night diving.

VACCINATION REQUIREMENTS: None.

VISA/PASSPORT REQUIREMENTS: You need only proof of citizenship, a passport, or a voter's registration card.

 Jason's Tips:

As with most cruises, you really get two fewer days than is advertised. The first day you embark in the late afternoon, the last day you debark early in the morning. As on all scuba trips, make your decision based on the number of diving days.

The crossing from Miami to Bimini, the "Gateway to the Bahamas," can be rough. If you have enough time and money, the seven-day cruise is recommended.

CHANDRIS FANTASY CRUISES

VITAL FEATURES

Type of vacation: **Cruise**
Target market: **Singles and couples in their late twenties to sixties**
Location: **Caribbean**
Home ports: **San Juan, Montego Bay, Barbados, Miami, New York, Venice**
All-inclusive cost per week: **$649–$1,649 plus airfare**

RATINGS

Value: $$$$$

Fun quotient: (3 umbrellas)

Honeymoon suitability: (4 hearts)

Singles meeting ground: (couple)

Child appeal: (ice cream cone)

Management professionalism: (4 telephones)

Service: (5 light bulbs)

Food: (4 lobsters)

THE REAL STORY

Any psychiatrist would prescribe Chandris Fantasy Cruises as therapy for Eskimos and other snowbound inhabitants of the Northern Hemisphere. Chandris ships ply the Caribbean and Mediterranean seas, dispensing healthy doses of sunshine to passengers who dream of tropical isles and relaxing vacations.

Chandris offers conservative, middle-of-the-road-type cruises. They are not luxury ships, nor are they economy trips. You'll experience a quiet vacation, without a party atmosphere or a big-spending,

313

high-rolling crowd. Yet you'll enjoy the benefits cruising has to offer: port calls in tropical places, good food and entertainment, nightlife, and social activities. Chandris is a Greek-owned cruise line, and its ships sail in traditional Greek style with festive music and entertainment, tasty food, and hospitable service. The staff generally go out of their way to accommodate people, and to see that passengers are having a good time.

The ships in the Chandris fleet may be older and less luxurious than most, but passengers seem pleased with their vacations. The majority of passengers come from the East and Midwest, and range from the late twenties to late fifties, with a few kids and senior citizens mixed in. Many guests come from middle and lower-level executive positions. Some are schoolteachers and others are blue-collar workers. Everyone mixes well.

INCLUDED

Accommodations	Food
Activities	Sports (some extra)
Airfare	Transfer to and from airport
Entertainment & dancing	

VALUE

You definitely get your money's worth on this cruise. You'll spend less per day for food and lodging during the cruise than you would on only a hotel in San Juan. Its an especially good value when you throw in the entertainment, travel, and cruise experience.

ACTIVITIES, SPORTS, & EXCURSIONS

For a complete description of activities, see the section "Food & Drink." Seriously, Chandris provides a number of shipboard activities, but sunbathing by the saltwater swimming pool seems to be the most popular. Organized activities are run-of-the-mill—aerobics, dance instruction, movies, card games, and cooking demonstrations. Trap shooting costs extra and is only available while the ship is at sea. Games such as Ping-Pong, shuffleboard, and darts will be arranged "on demand." None of the activities draw much of a crowd. The crew does not invest much time or energy into making the included activities inviting. Instead, they direct their efforts toward those that cost extra: the waiters push drinks during the entertainment shows; the casino, bingo, and wooden horse racing provide gambling opportunities; and ship photographers snoop about the ship (photos cost $5 each). The weight room on the M.V. *Victoria* is small and poorly equipped, with a few free weights, an exercise bike, and a rowing machine.

ACTIVITIES

Arts & crafts
Board games
Dancing
Entertainment/shows

Movies
Sunbathing
Topless sunbathing

SPORTS

Aerobics/exercise classes
Jogging on deck
Shuffleboard
Snorkeling (in port)

Swimming
Volleyball
Water polo
Weightlifting

EXCURSIONS: Chandris arranges several shore excursions at every port. Each night a short slide show helps you decide which ones you want to take the next day. Generally, excursions involve sight-seeing tours, beach trips, or shopping sprees. They range in price from $14 to $48 per person per excursion.

ITINERARY & DAILY SCHEDULE

Chandris ships generally sail at night and arrive in port in the morning, so the passengers can make a day out of shore excursions. The ship's newspaper, *Seascape*, informs the guests of daily activities. Port activities usually involve sight-seeing excursions or shopping. During days at sea, activities focus on the deck. You can always be as active or sedate as you like.

Chandris offers numerous itineraries, lasting from 6 to 14 days. Its ships sail the upper and lower Caribbean, New York to Bermuda, and the Mediterranean.

NIGHTLIFE & ENTERTAINMENT

The ship really rocks at night. Pardon the pun. Every evening brings a different revue, followed by dance music and a late-night disco. The shows usually involve showgirls, magic, and music. The productions are always enjoyable, though they are not up to Las Vegas standards. The cast consists of four entertainers, the showgirls and a band. They have a large repertoire, but attendance tapers off during the week. The casino never flags in popularity.

AESTHETICS & ENVIRONMENT

Chandris ships are small and old by cruise line standards. The ship we reviewed, the M.V. *Victoria*, is the oldest and smallest in the Chandris fleet. Though built in the 1930s, the ship was recently refurbished; she wears her age like Lauren Bacall—some wrinkles here and there, but still very attractive. The carpets and furnishings look excellent in the common areas, but are a little worn in the cabins. The rooms don't match "Love Boat" standards, but they are large, clean, and functional. Chandris's ships offer less facilities than the larger vessels of other cruise lines. Our ship featured one formal dining hall, one casino, and two bars. The intimate size of the ships makes it easy to learn your way around.

FACILITIES

Bank
Bars
Beaches
Beauty salon
Casino
Concierge

Disco
Entertainment coordinators
Gift shop (2)
Medical station
Safety-deposit box
Swimming pool

ROOMS

The room sizes and furnishing remain similar throughout the ship. Most cabins contain two twin beds and a fold-down bunk bed. Few double beds are available. All rooms come with private showers. The staterooms have bathtubs, but no other extra features. Outside cabins sport portholes, which make it possible to tell the time of day or type of weather from inside your cabin.

LUXURY LEVEL

Air-conditioning
Laundry service (extra)
Maid service

Phone in room
Porter service
Room service

FOOD & DRINK

The food never stops. Breakfast can be eaten in your room, on deck, or in the restaurant. Lunch comes buffet style on deck or as sit-down service in the dining room. A box lunch can be ordered for shore excursions. The dining room serves lunch and dinner at two sittings. Unfortunately, Chandris does not offer an open seating at lunch. The food from the deck side buffets tastes ordinary. In contrast, excellent dishes are served in the dining room. The menus change with every meal, and generally relate to some theme, such as Caribbean Night. Appropriate decorations and costumes accompany meals. The cooking staff presents a spectacular midnight buffet, though it only attracts a small group of hard-core eaters. The ship features an extensive wine selection and several bars. Drinks cost extra. Special diets such as vegetarian, low-sodium, or kosher can be arranged in advance.

STAFFING & SERVICE

The service is fantastic. At meals, your waiter and busboy cater to all your needs. The cabin steward keeps your room clean and constantly stocked with fresh supplies. The crew works very long hours seven days a week for only $10 per week wages. The ship suggests $7.20 per passenger per day for tips. Tip generously, and factor this into your budget in advance.

PRIVACY & RELAXATION

Although the *Victoria* was small, we did not feel crowded. We walked the promenades at night with plenty of privacy.

Noises pervade the ship day and night; the constant sounds of the engines vibrate through the walls and floors. The ship rolls constantly while at sea. Many passengers feel the need for Dramamine.

SHOPPING

Grenada is called "the spice island" for good reason. There you'll find native spices and plants such as cocoa and nutmeg, costing next to nothing. The spice that islanders call saffron is called turmeric in the States. Most people buy it, mistaking it for expensive Indian yellow saffron. Also, the ships have duty-free shops and souvenir shops with clothing and sundries.

HONEYMOONERS

The ships allow for intimate moments in quiet places. You can image the sunset scenes on deck. While the deck may create romantic moments, the rooms may not. Few double beds are available, so unless you plan ahead, sleeping arrangements will be distant or extra cozy.

If honeymooners book 90 days early for a six-day or seven-day cruise they get $100 off the cabin fare. All honeymooners receive a bottle of champagne, a cake, a photo album with free photos, a fruit basket, and a cocktail party with other honeymooners. Newlyweds must bring a marriage certificate to verify the proximity of their marriage.

SINGLES

Chandris tries to accommodate singles by holding cocktail parties and get-togethers. However, the cruise line caters more to couples. Many singles are women in their mid-thirties, typically two friends traveling together.

CHILD APPEAL

Children receive discount fares, though few families bring children, because baby-sitting and children's activities are not available.

NUTS & BOLTS

BOOKING & CONTACT INFORMATION: Most passengers book through a travel agent.

Chandris Fantasy Cruises
4770 Biscayne Boulevard
Miami, FL 33137
305-576-9900
800-423-2100

or

900 Third Avenue
New York, NY 10022
212-223-3003
800-621-3446

CURRENCY: Chandris uses American dollars. Traveler's checks and credit cards are accepted on board. Most places in the Caribbean accept U.S. currency but give you change in local currency. Be sure to bring small-denomination bills and traveler's checks to avoid accumulating foreign money.

CUSTOMS/DUTY: Standard U.S. customs.

DEPOSITS/REFUNDS: Confirmed reservations require a $200 deposit per person. Final payments come due 30 days before sailing. For a full refund, written cancellations must be received no later than 30 days before departure. Refunds for cancellations made later depend upon the resale of the accommodations and the discretion of the management. Chandris requires that all documents issued by the company be returned before refunds will be processed. Cancellations under 48 hours will receive no refund.

ELECTRICITY: Electricity varies from ship to ship. Check with the cruise line to see if you'll need an adapter.

HANDICAP/ACCESSIBILITY: Chandris ships have no special facilities, but the cruise line does welcome disabled passengers. It requests that they make themselves known at the time of reservation.

LANGUAGES: The crew speaks English, among other languages. The officers are Greek, and the crews are international.

PACKING: Dress tends to be casual. Most passengers wear shorts and light shirts during the day. Sweaters keep you warm on deck in the evenings. Dinner is usually informal. Men wear long pants, but no tie or jacket. For formal nights men should pack a suit or dress slacks and a dinner jacket. Women can get by with party dresses. Chandris asks female passengers not to wear halter tops or short shorts when going ashore.

RELIGIOUS SERVICES: Chandris provides religious services on board only during holidays. At other times, you'll have to find services while in port.

RESERVATION SCHEDULE: Chandris recommends that passengers book four or five months in advance for holidays. In other months, if you want special accommodations, such as a certain room or particular itinerary, you should book at least three months prior. Passengers not looking for anything special can usually book within a week or two. Sometimes Chandris offers last-minute specials.

SIZE OF SHIPS: 466 to 700 feet.

NUMBER OF CABINS: 162 to 550.

MAXIMUM NUMBER OF GUESTS: 671 to 1,413.

Cost Worksheet

	Year-Round Prices
Accommodations (7 days)[1]	$649–$1,649
Food	incl.
Drinks	
Departure tax	$55 (approximate, varies for each itinerary)
State tax	incl.
Hotel tax	incl.
Sports	incl.
Airfare[2]	incl.
Sight-seeing	
Tips	
Additional sports	
Souvenirs	

[1] Premium for single person: 150 percent of normal fare.
[2] Airfare prices are based on zones of travel, roughly divided into the Northeast, South, Midwest, and West.

NUMBER OF CREW: 320 to 546.

FUTURE PLANS: New ship in 1990.

VACCINATION REQUIREMENTS: None.

VISA/PASSPORT REQUIREMENTS: U.S. and Canadian citizens need only proof of citizenship (passport, birth certificate, or voter's registration card) when traveling in the Caribbean. Passports are required for Mediterranean cruises; some ports of call require visas. Check with Chandris for up-to-date information.

SPENDING MONEY: You'll need money for shore excursions, drinks, gambling, tips, and activities that cost extra on the ship. Several hundred dollars should cover things, unless you are a big gambler.

All rates per person, based on double occupancy for a seven-night stay.

Always ask if any special packages, promotions, or airfare discounts are in effect before booking.

All vacations described in this guide can be booked through any competent travel agent; we advise you to do so.

See the general introduction and area introductions for more details.

COMMODORE CRUISES

VITAL FEATURES

Type of vacation: **Cruise**
Target market: **Singles and couples, generally aged 22 and up;
    children during the holiday season**
Location: **Caribbean—Miami to San Juan, Puerta Plata, St.
    Thomas, St. John**
All-inclusive cost per week: **$595–$1,295 plus airfare**

RATINGS

Value: 💲💲💲💲

Fun quotient: 🏖🏖🏖🏖

Honeymoon suitability: ❤❤❤

Singles meeting ground: 👫👫

Child appeal: 🍦🍦🍦

Management professionalism: ☎☎☎☎

Service: 💡💡💡💡

Food: 🦞🦞🦞

THE REAL STORY

Commodore offers one of the least expensive big-ship tours of the Caribbean. It has some of everything that you'd expect to find on the truly luxurious ships—gambling, food, entertainment, island tours, and pampering service. Although Commodore doesn't serve the gourmet cuisine of your fantasies, the value is excellent. Commodore bills itself as the "Caribbean's best cruise value" and can make a good case for that statement.

Most cruises cater to a mature crowd. Commodore adds a wrinkle to its sailings that attracts younger passengers as well. Theme weeks include Rock 'n' Roll, Country Western, Big Band, Oktoberfest, Valentine's Day, Mayfest, and Jazz.

Cruises are arranged so that you'll be able to meet passengers with similar interests. There are two meal shifts, an earlier one that caters to those who retire early, and a later one that most of the younger people go to. A special honeymooners' party brings the blissful couples together. Other parties and activities draw singles. Many types of entertainment run concurrently: a "period" stage show, preceded by bingo, delights the older crowd; at the same time, the bar and disco begin to warm up.

The staff keep guests well apprised of the program with a daily activity sheet; a separate sheet reports world events.

Commodore offers quality at a reasonable price, made more so by its Miami departure (meaning cheap port access) and its many promotions. In many ways, this is a beginner's cruise because it is short, consistent, affordable, and offers a good variety of ports of call.

INCLUDED

Accommodations
Activities
Airfare
Child care (during school
   holidays)

Entertainment & dancing
Food
Transfer to and from airport

ACTIVITIES, SPORTS, & EXCURSIONS

ACTIVITIES: You can always find something to do on the ship, from gambling to dancing, till the wee hours. The casino keeps long hours. The dealers are equally friendly to experienced gamblers and neophytes; during the slow times, they will teach the different games.

The calypso band rocks the boat while at sea. Staff entertainers organize picnic games such as beer chugging, which entertain both the participants and onlookers.

Arts & crafts
Board games
Dancing
Entertainment/shows

Movies
Sunbathing
Video games

SPORTS: Commodore's "Aquanauts" offer a resort diving course. They teach scuba in the ship's pool, then take students on a guided underwater tour of some remarkable diving sites. The brochure is somewhat misleading by saying that you will return an "experienced diver" or a "Resort Diver." You will have tried diving, but in no way will you possess the certification that is recognized by any of the professional diving boards. On our cruise, people who took the diving and snorkeling programs said that they were highly satisfied.

Aerobics/exercise classes	Scuba (extra)
Golf driving	Shuffleboard
Horseback riding (extra, in port)	Skeet
	Snorkeling (extra)
Jogging on deck	Swimming
Mallet pool	Weightlifting
Ping-Pong	

EXCURSIONS: Tours are offered at an extra cost at each of the ports.

ITINERARY & DAILY SCHEDULE

Commodore's one ship, the *Caribe I*, sticks to a fixed itinerary, Saturday to Saturday. The ship sails on the high seas for the first full day (Sunday) and the last two full days (Thursday and Friday). Monday, from 11:00 A.M. to 5:00 P.M., is spent in Puerta Plata, Dominican Republic. All Tuesday you can tour Puerto Rico or roam the streets of Old San Juan. On Wednesday, the ship touches down near both St. John and St. Thomas in the Virgin Islands. A ferry taxis people between the two close islands, so visitors can spend time on each.

NIGHTLIFE & ENTERTAINMENT

If you like to party, Commodore should suit you well. After dinner, a stroll to the foredeck offers refreshing Caribbean air, moon, and stars. Variety shows follow Las Vegas formats. Comedians, magicians, singers, and dancers perform with the ship orchestra. Nightly events encourage guests to dress up for the masquerade ball or perform for the talent show.

The disco rocks the boat until the wee hours of the morning. If you thought that ships were just for the retiring crowd, you'll be amazed at how hard and long the evening pulses. A core group of late-night partiers keeps things going almost until breakfast. A respectable percentage of all the guests filled the disco until an unrespectable hour.

We sailed on the Rock 'n' Roll cruise, which featured mostly music of the fifties and sixties, including Motown, Elvis, and contemporary "light rock." While the overall quality of the entertainment was inconsistent, the featured act displayed talent, good choreography, and excellent song selection. A comedian, a magician, and the entertainment director/singer rounded out the entertainment.

AESTHETICS & ENVIRONMENT

The *Caribe I* was originally built as an ocean liner. Although the ship is smaller than many of the newer ones, some of the staterooms are quite large. It reflects an elegant era, shown in the wood paneling and trim throughout. Maintenance is good, and the crew keeps everything spotless, including the rooms and baths.

The mazelike floor plan is baffling at first; it was designed to separate the first-class passengers from the lower classes in the ship's transatlantic days. While of Panamanian registry, the ship sails with a European crew and Caribbean staff.

The differences among the cabins are quite pronounced, and people sensitive to space may find the extra few hundred dollars well spent. However, little time is spent indoors, and all guests are treated the same and eat the same food. If you sailed with Commodore because of the price, you may find your dollars better spent on shore excursions, drinks, and souvenirs.

FACILITIES

Bank
Bars
Beaches
Beauty salon
Casino
Disco
Gift shop
Jacuzzis (2)

Medical station
Movie theater
Parking in port (extra)
Pool (small)
Purser
Safety-deposit box
Water-sports center

ROOMS

The *Caribe I* does not rank with the superluxurious ships. Its age, physical layout, and price range do not allow this. Except at breakfast time, room service, for example, suffers from being sparsely staffed. But, the ship is extremely well run, the food is tasty, and the service is generally excellent. The luxury level, in many ways, surpasses that of a medium-price resort. The cabins are very comfortable and many have double beds. Size and amenities vary with the price level, but all are tastefully decorated and airy.

LUXURY LEVEL

Air-conditioning
Bar in room
Laundry service (extra)
Maid service

Phone in room
Porter service
Refrigerator in room
Room service

FOOD & DRINK

The price includes all food. The kitchen supplies lots of it. Three full-course meals are served in the dining room on tables covered with cloths and decorated with fresh flowers.

Seating is reserved, except for the midnight buffet. You dine with the same people all week. If you come with friends and wish to sit with them, this can be arranged with advance notice.

Slow risers or morning romantics have the option of starting the day with a Continental breakfast in bed. Motivated morning people can eat their first meal on deck while watching the sun rise. The chefs prepare a full selection of rolls, eggs, breakfast meats, and fish. Midday diners can choose to take lunch in the dining room or dig into the informal grill on deck.

Dinner offers a choice of relishes; hors d'oeuvres; chilled juices; soups; entrées of seafood, meat, and fowl; vegetables; salads; cheeses; and desserts. The quality and quantity of dinners is very good. The kitchen does an admirable job of putting out meals that are well prepared, hot, and attractive. If asked, the waiters will serve seconds on anything, including lobster.

The port tours are timed with meals in mind, so you'll be able to eat on board even when the ship is docked.

Midnight buffets consist of fruit and cleverly rehashed leftovers, along with added treats such as shrimp and cheese. The disco serves pizza at midnight.

Guests restricted to a special diet will be accommodated; tell the head waiter about your needs.

The drinks are priced at what you'd expect to pay in a medium-priced U.S. bar. Most cabins have mini-bars (that is, a refrigerator with mini-bottles of booze and mixers); drinks here cost slightly more than ones from the bar.

STAFFING & SERVICE

The crew work hard to please. Service is efficient and friendly. From the captain to the cabin stewards, they all do their best to make your cruise as pleasant as possible.

PRIVACY & RELAXATION

Although the ship's not one of the largest ocean liners, married couples and honeymooners will find it spacious enough to be able to get away from the crowds. The size of the larger cabins allows for comfortable times to be intimate.

The schedule of the trip leads to relaxing during the first day at sea, hustling during the next three days in port, then winding down during the last two days at sea. The pace of the ship feels far slower than that of others, which may dock in ports five or six days out of seven, instead of Commodore's three.

SHOPPING

Commodore docks at many of the world's famed shopping ports. Puerta Plata offers deals in native handiwork. St. Thomas sells duty-free liquor; cruisers from high-tax states should find this especially attractive. Local and internationally known artists exhibit their work in the galleries of Old San Juan. The stores also sell the high-fashion clothes that many Puerto Ricans like to wear.

The ship store sells liquor, perfume, and other times at duty-free prices, along with sundries, souvenirs, clothes, cameras, film, and reading material.

"Duty-free" means only that the stores do not pay import taxes. Sometimes (but not always) they pass the savings on to the customer. St. Thomas used to be known as a place to get perfume, cameras, watches, and electronic items at bargain prices. To a large extent, the reputation no longer fits reality. Perfume manufacturers have fixed the sales prices at all the stores. The lowering of U.S. import duties has also closed the price gap. Very often you will find that you can get better prices at home. If you plan to shop for major items, bring along catalogs or know the prices before you leave. Also, be ready to carry the items home and pay the applicable duties.

HONEYMOONERS

This is a good cruise choice, especially for the budget minded. If your spouse is a serious gambler, don't bring the nest egg along.

SINGLES

Commodore offers a lot of activities to help singles break the ice. (This is not to be confused with what the *Titanic* did.) Singles events let guests know which attractive passengers did not come with jealous, and potentially violent, mates. It also gives the crew a chance to check out the guests. A singles party starts things off the first night. Games on deck have the same effect, resulting in a lot of guests finding each other on this ship. You'd have a tough time convincing the crew that Commodore isn't the official "Love Boat." They never bother you, but they often make themselves available to entertain the guests.

CHILD APPEAL

Commodore has programs planned for kids during the Christmas, New Year's, and Easter holidays, as well as during the summer. Other times, kids may feel a bit lonely.

Prices for children sharing a cabin with their parents make this trip economical for families, especially if they can drive to Florida.

NUTS & BOLTS

BOOKING & CONTACT INFORMATION

Commodore Cruises, Ltd.
1007 North America Way
Miami, FL 33132
800-327-5617
305-358-2622

CURRENCY: U.S. dollars are good on the ship and at all ports of call.

CUSTOMS/DUTY: U.S. customs agents greet you and your baggage upon return. Drug dogs often nuzzle your luggage.

DEPOSITS/REFUNDS: Commodore requires a deposit of approximately $225. Cancellations made less than 35 days prior to sailing are assessed a 25 percent penalty. No refunds are given for reservations unclaimed or cancelled the day of sailing.

ELECTRICITY: 110 volts 60 cycles.

HANDICAP ACCESSIBILITY: Only one cabin is designed to accommodate handicapped persons.

PACKING: Bring bathing suits for the pool area, otherwise comfortable clothes such as sundresses, shorts, slacks, and knit shirts are OK. The same dress applies on the island tours. Dinner attire is dressy. Women will want to bring a cocktail dress, pant suit, or even a semiformal gown. Formal Night encourages cruisers to wear long dresses, tuxedos, or dark suits. The casino/nightclub tour of San Juan requires this as well.

RELIGIOUS SERVICES: Interdenominational services are conducted every Sunday.

RESERVATION SCHEDULE: You should book up to six months in advance for a vacation during the high season.

TRAVEL TIME BY AIR

Chicago: **Three hours**
Los Angeles: **Five hours**
New York: **Three hours**
Toronto: **Four hours**

ARRIVAL AIRPORT: Miami International Airport.

TRAVEL TIME FROM AIRPORT: 25 minutes.

SPENDING MONEY: You'll want to bring a few hundred dollars to cover drinks, gambling, shopping, tours, and tips.

Cost Worksheet		
	High Season[1]	*Off-Season*[2]
Accommodations		
(7 days)[3]	$595–$1,1295	$595–$1,095
Food	incl.	incl.
Port tax	35	35
Departure tax	none	none
State tax	none	none
Hotel tax	none	none
Sports	incl.	incl.
Airfare	_____	_____
Sight-seeing		
Tips	50	50
Additional, sports[4]		
Souvenirs	_____	_____

[1] High season dates: December 22 to March 31, June 15 to August 23
[2] Off-season dates: April 1 to June 14, August 24 to December 21
[3] Premium for single person: There are single cabins available, and rates start at $795. When the single cabins are filled you have the option of sharing a double occupancy cabin.
[4] Offered for extra charge: Special arrangements are made for those people who arrive in Miami a day early. Drive-&-cruise, Amtrak/cruise, and Walt Disney World/cruise packages are also available.

COSTA CRUISES

VITAL FEATURES

Type of vacation: **Cruise**
Target market: **Married couples, groups, families of all ages**
Location: **Florida, Bahamas, Virgin Islands**
All-inclusive cost per week: **$975–$1,670 including airfare**

RATINGS

Value: 💲💲💲💲

Fun quotient: ☂☂☂☂

Honeymoon suitability: ♥♥♥♥

Singles meeting ground: 👫👤👤👤

Child appeal: 🍦🍦🍦🍦

Management professionalism: ☎☎☎☎

Service: 💡💡💡💡💡

Food: 🦞🦞🦞🦞

THE REAL STORY

Italians are romantic. They created Rome, Venice, and Florence. They are the only people in the world who can sing corny lyrics with a deep mesmerizing accent and send your imagination swooning. This is why Costa can state simply "We are Italian" to explain the style of its cruises.

The Costa *Riviera* is similar to other large cruise ships, with a full complement of activities, sports, bars, discos, and dinning. But the fact that Costa is Italian makes everything seem livelier. There is plenty of opportunity aboard to absorb Italian style. Meals have pasta galore. The deckhands yell in Italian. You can even practice your Italian at the Galleria Via Veneto by pronouncing the words *Gucci*, *Fila*, and *Ferre*.

INCLUDED

Accommodations
Activities
Airfare
Child care

Entertainment & dancing
Food
Sports
Transfer to and from airport

VALUE

A tremendous value. Considering what there is to see, do, eat, drink, and enjoy, it is worth every penny.

ACTIVITIES, SPORTS, & EXCURSIONS

You name it, they've got it. You almost feel guilty because you can't possibly keep up with the daily list of "fun." There are contests and dances. They'll also teach you a little blackjack, photography, and Italian. First-run movies are shown in a plush cinema. The Galleria Via Veneto has a number of boutiques that make for good browsing.

The music never stops, and enticing smells keep you dancing from dining room to patio to pizza parlor. The cruise director will supply you with tips on things to do on the island stops.

ACTIVITIES

Arts & crafts
Board games
Culture/music/language
    classes
Dancing (a steel band plays on
    the deck daily)

Entertainment/shows
Movies
Sunbathing

SPORTS

Aerobics/exercise classes for
    all levels of fitness)
Basketball
Bicycles
Golf
Jet skiing
Jogging track

Shuffleboard
Skeet shooting
Snorkeling
Swimming pool (a little
    cramped for doing laps)
Weight room

EXCURSIONS: Offered in the price of the cruise is a day picnic on St. Croix. *Molto bene.*

ITINERARY & DAILY SCHEDULE

The Costa *Riviera* departs from Fort Lauderdale Saturday, spends three days at sea, and arrives at St. Thomas Tuesday morning. It leaves late that night and arrives at St. Croix Wednesday morning, spends the day there, and departs in the afternoon. All day Thursday is spent at sea. Friday the ship arrives at Nassau, Bahamas, at 1:00 P.M., leaves that night, and is back in Fort Lauderdale Saturday morning.

NIGHTLIFE & ENTERTAINMENT

If empty places at breakfast indicate how much fun went on the night before, then there are plenty of people who like to party.

The Monte Carlo Casino stays open all night. It apes Las Vegas. Instead of waking to a neon Vegas sky you can lumber up to the Sports Deck, crawl into the hot tub, and drown your hangover under a Caribbean blue sky.

The La Scala Showroom has all the glitter and the glitz that you would expect on a cruise ship. There are showgirls, Liberace-style singers, and musicians.

You won't have to walk far to find a lounge or bar. There are plenty of them scattered throughout the ship, and one of the lounges turns into a disco late in the evening. You could spend the entire trip exploring the different bars.

AESTHETICS & ENVIRONMENT

The decor is a bit dated on the Costa *Riviera* and could use some sprucing up. When decorating the cruise ship, someone went a bit overboard with the velour couches. They are everywhere. The only thing that redeems them is the fact that they are incredibly comfortable. The staterooms are attractive, fresh, and very clean. The crew polishes brass day and night on the decks and sweeps and scrubs into the wee hours.

FACILITIES

Bars	Gift shop
Beauty salon	Hot tub
Casino	Medical station
Disco	Safety-deposit box
Entertainment coordinator	Snack bar, grill

ROOMS

The cabins are light and airy, although the decor is basic Holiday Inn; pastels predominate. A few nautical paintings can be found here and there. If you spend the extra money it's possible to have a very luxurious cabin. Some of the deluxe cabins even have queen-size beds.

LUXURY LEVEL

Air-conditioning	Bar in room

Clock   Phone in room
Maid service   Room service

FOOD & DRINK

Just say "Mamma mia," and into your head pops the image of a fat Italian woman serving big bowls of steaming pasta and thick, crusty bread. Costa sticks to this imagery. It follows Italian tradition and makes the cruise one big gastronomical delight.

The food is plentiful and always top-notch. There are informal breakfasts and lunches outside, or you can opt for the formal dining room. While you sunbathe you can enjoy salads, pastas, hamburgers, fruits, desserts. If you doze through the first lunch shift there is always a second. There are afternoon teas, hors d'oeuvres, pizza, ice cream vendors, midnight buffets—something to please even the most finicky of eaters.

Dinners include lobster, lamb, incredible pasta dishes, steak, broiled seafood galore, and tons of exquisitely prepared vegetables. Each night features a different theme. There is a wine list rich with Italian *vino*.

STAFFING & SERVICE

The brochure gives you all the information you need, and if you have any questions the office staff are very knowledgeable and helpful.

It's hard to believe the crew and staff do not become jaded, taking these trips every week, but the staff, from the captain to the cabin boys, are charming, helpful, and downright fun.

PRIVACY & RELAXATION

It's hard to believe how many people the ship holds. You never feel hurried, hassled, or lost in the crowd; it's not difficult to find private places to relax. Deck chairs are incredibly comfortable. Hibernate in them and stay away from the thick of things. Don't be surprised if you spend the majority of the cruise lying in them. On some cruise lines you feel obligated to participate in the activities and at the end of the cruise you end up feeling frantic, having run from one activity to another. Costa never treats passengers like a herd of cattle being rounded up for activities or meals.

SHOPPING

The Galleria Via Veneto aboard the ship consists of very chichi boutiques offering Ferre fashions, Fila sportswear, Gucci leather, and products of other Italian designers. All the boutiques are duty free, although with the number of digits on the price tags, you'd think prices were quoted in lira. Guess again. The merchandise is expensive, but it would be anywhere.

St. Thomas also offers duty-free shopping. There are some bargains to be found in the jewelry and watch section if you don't mind pushing your way through gobs of tourists in congested Charlotte Amalie. Try to stay calm. The shopping frenzy is contagious and you may find all your purchases for the same price at home. The straw market at Nassau is worth bringing a couple of extra dollars ashore with you.

HONEYMOONERS

If you're sure rolling seas won't affect either of you and you don't mind cramped bathrooms, then this could be ideal. Watching the sun set and sharing a hot tub under the moon are certainly romantic enough for a honeymoon. On the *Riviera*, the first three days are spent at sea, giving honeymooners an opportunity to get to know each other better. There are no specific honeymoon packages, but it's more than likely that Costa will upgrade your cabin if you let it know in advance it's your honeymoon. Once aboard, honeymooners will be spoiled by the staff.

SINGLES

There are plenty of singles roaming around and lots of meeting grounds. The Riviera Lounge, which turns into a disco late in the evening, seemed to be the place where most people entered alone and exited in pairs.

CHILD APPEAL

Two clubs offer activities for children, the Teen Club and the Pinocchio Room. Both have video games, dancing, drawing competitions, scavenger hunts, educational programs, and a variety of classes. Most children have a ball just romping around with their newly made friends.

NUTS & BOLTS

BOOKING & CONTACT INFORMATION

Costa Cruise Lines
One Biscayne Tower
Miami, Fl 33131
800-462-6782
305-358-7325

CURRENCY: There are no problems with currency exchange. American currency and traveler's checks can be used for everything. Most major credit cards are accepted.

CUSTOMS/DUTY: You clear customs only one time, upon returning to Port Everglades. It is just a minor nuisance; it takes about an hour or so of waiting around the lounge of the ship. There is no heavy-duty searching or questioning. It is all very civil. Customs officers ask what you bought and want to see receipts.

DEPOSITS/REFUNDS: A deposit of $200 is required for a 7-day cruise. Final payment is due no later than 6 weeks prior to sailing. Cancellations and requests for refunds must be submitted, in writing, to Costa Cruises. Cancellation charges, per person, will be assessed as follows: 42 to 31 days prior to sailing—$75; 30 to 15 days prior to sailing—$150. Cancellations less than 14 days prior to sailing and no-shows lose their full fare 14 to 2 days prior to sailing—refunds are subject to resale of the cabin. If accommodations are resold, a cancellation charge of $200 per person will apply.

ELECTRICITY: 110 volts 60 cycles, same as in the United States. You cannot use your hair dryer, curlers, curling iron, or electric shaver in your cabin. Separate rooms at the end of each hall are provided for this.

HANDICAP ACCESSIBILITY: If you have a physical disability that may require special attention, you must report it in writing at the time you make reservations. Costa can accommodate most wheelchair passengers.

LANGUAGES: English is spoken everywhere. The crew speaks English well enough to understand it most of the time. Surprisingly, Spanish was more common than Italian among the cabin staff and waiters.

PACKING: Unless you are a party animal, leave your formal gowns and jewels at home. One interchangeable jazzy outfit will suffice. There are shops aboard if you forget toothpaste or your bathing suit. Bring along a lightweight jacket and some scarves; it gets very windy on deck at night.

RELIGIOUS SERVICES: The crew conducts services in the chapel during holidays, although there are no services during regularly scheduled cruises.

RESERVATION SCHEDULE: We recommend booking one year in advance for a winter cruise and six months to a year for summer.

SIZE: Length, 700 feet; width, 93 feet.

NUMBER OF CABINS: 487.

MAXIMUM NUMBER OF GUESTS: 1,260.

NUMBER OF EMPLOYEES: 500.

TRAVEL TIME BY AIR

Chicago: **3 hours 30 minutes**
Los Angeles: **5 hours 30 minutes**
New York: **3 hours**
Toronto: **6 hours 50 minutes**

ARRIVAL AIRPORT: Fort Lauderdale or Miami.

TRAVEL TIME FROM AIRPORT: 15 minutes.

VACCINATION REQUIREMENTS: None.

VISA/PASSPORT REQUIREMENTS: U.S. and Canadian citizens need proof of citizenship. A birth certificate or passport will suffice.

SPENDING MONEY: You'll need money for drinks, tips for the staff, shore excursions and shopping, and shipboard activities—massages, casino, day trips.

Cost Worksheet

	High Season[1]	Off-Season[2]
Accommodations (7 days)[3]	$1,049–$1,830	$999–$1,760
Food	incl.	incl.
Drinks		
Port tax	$35–$58	$35–$58
Sports	incl.	incl.
Airfare	incl.	incl.
Sight-seeing		
Tips	$45	$45
Additional sports		
Souvenirs		

[1] High season dates: December 17 to March 31; June 17 to August 25 (higher prices apply Christmas to New Year's)
[2] Off-season dates: April 1 to June 16; August 26 to December 16
[3] Premium for single person: $1,400 to $2,200

PERILLO CARIBBEAN CRUISES ABOARD COSTA

VITAL FEATURES

Type of vacation: **Cruise**
Target market: **Couples, singles, families**
Location: **Caribbean**
All-inclusive cost per week: **$1,400 including airfare from JFK**

RATINGS

Value: 💲💲💲💲💲

Fun quotient: 🏖️🏖️🏖️🏖️

Honeymoon suitability: ❤️❤️❤️❤️

Singles meeting ground: 👫👫👫

Child appeal: 🍦🍦🍦🍦

Management professionalism: ☎️☎️☎️☎️☎️

Service: 💡💡💡💡💡

Food: 🦞🦞🦞🦞🦞

THE REAL STORY

Most cruises cost more than they would appear to because of extra charges for tips, taxes, drinks, and excursions. Perillo created perhaps the only truly all-inclusive luxury cruise by bundling Costa cruises with all the trimmings into one prepaid price. Even better, that one price is less than Costa's "rack" rates.

In addition to all the normal Costa features, Perillo adds some of the same homey touches found on its resorts. These include private cocktail parties (including one with the captain), unlimited wine with dinner, and shore excursions or a beach party in all ports. A host/concierge/ombudsman ensures that all your sea needs are handled well.

Passengers traveling solo have the option of requesting a roommate, which, if one is available, will allow them to pay the double-occupancy rate. Prices include regularly scheduled flights from New York City. Passengers from other cities should contact Perillo to arrange air transportation. Add to this all the other features found on Costa's Italian-style cruises and you have a terrific cruise vacation. See the Costa review (pp. 329–35) for more details.

INCLUDED

Accommodations	Sports
Activities	Taxes
Airfare	Tips
Child care	Tours
Entertainment & dancing	Transfer to and from airport
Food	Wine with dinner

VALUE

The all-inclusive nature of Perillo's Costa package, along with the quality and discount price of the cruise, make this an excellent vacation value.

Cost Worksheet	High Season[1]	Off-Season[2]
Accommodations		
(7 days)[3]	$1,400	$1,300
Food	incl.	incl.
Drinks		
Departure tax	incl.	incl.
Sports	incl.	incl.
Airfare (from N.Y.)	incl.	incl.
Sight-seeing	incl.	incl.
Tips	incl.	incl.
Additional sports		
Souvenirs		

[1] High season dates: Mid December to Mid April, summer
[2] Off-season dates: Mid April to Mid December, excluding summer
[3] Premium for single person: $750 off-season, $850 high season

ROOMS

All Club Perillo guests stay in outside cabins on the top foredeck. These large rooms all have windows.

NUTS & BOLTS

BOOKING & CONTACT INFORMATION

577 Chestnut Ridge Road
Woodcliff Lake, NJ 07675
800-431-1515
201-307-1234

DEPOSITS/REFUNDS: Perillo requires a $300 deposit and payment in full seven weeks before departure. Cancellation penalties apply. Perillo sells cancellation insurance, which it strongly recommends.

DOLPHIN CRUISE LINE

VITAL FEATURES

Type of vacation: **Cruise**
Target market: **All ages, shorter trips attract a younger crowd**
Location: **Bahamas, Caribbean**
All-inclusive cost per week: **$845–$1,795 including airfare**

RATINGS

Value: 💲💲💲💲💲

Fun quotient: ⛱⛱⛱⛱

Honeymoon suitability: ❤❤❤❤

Singles meeting ground: 👤👤👤👤

Child appeal: 🍦🍦🍦

Management professionalism: ☎☎☎☎☎

Service: 💡💡💡💡💡

Food: 🦞🦞🦞🦞🦞

THE REAL STORY

Veteran cruisers consistently rank Dolphin as one of their most pleasurable cruising experiences. Dolphin does week-long cruises of the upper Caribbean, and three-day and four-day cruises from Miami to the Bahamas. The shorter trips are especially attractive to people who want a sun fix but can't take the whole week off. The combination of length, quality of food, and entertainment makes this the perfect brief getaway. If you've made a big sale this week and you want to celebrate with your extra cash, this cruise is a good way to catch a little R&R and go double or nothing on your riches in the ship's casino.

The food, staff, and service are top-notch. Both of Dolphin's ships

339

boast international crews that work extremely well together. Personal service comes with a smile. The entire staff is conscientious and genuinely concerned about the passengers. In fact, one passenger commented that the management remembered her special dietary needs without her ever reminding them.

INCLUDED

Accommodations
Activities
Airfare
Entertainment & dancing

Food
Sports
Transfer to and from airport

VALUE

Dolphin cruises offer a solid value. You'll come home very pleased with the time you had for the money you spent.

ACTIVITIES, SPORTS, & EXCURSIONS

ACTIVITIES

Board games
Culture/music/language
    classes
Dancing

Entertainment/shows
Movies
Sunbathing

SPORTS

Aerobics/exercise classes
Basketball
Horseshoe pitching (in port)
Jogging
Kayaks/canoes (extra)
Pedal boats (extra)

Ping-Pong
Shuffleboard
Snorkeling (extra)
Swimming
Volleyball (in port)

EXCURSIONS: Dolphin offers a free daytrip to Blue Lagoon Island in the Bahamas. Passengers leave the cruise ship to travel aboard a ferry boat, complete with wet bar and reggae band. On the island, you can enjoy the water, party at the bar, or just relax until it's time for the beach barbecue.

Dolphin's entertainment coordinators also organize shore excursions for extra cost. Most trips cost $20 to $30 per person and last for several hours. Usually you have time for one trip during the day and another in the evening if the ship is staying late in port. Excursions take passengers on traditional sight-seeing tours and shopping sprees. In the Bahamas, passengers can also visit casino shows.

ITINERARY & DAILY SCHEDULE

The *Dolphin* sails from Miami on three- and four-day cruises to the Bahamas. The *Sea Breeze* alternates between two seven-day itineraries. One week she plies the eastern Caribbean with stops in St. Martin, St. John, St. Thomas, and Puerta Plata. The other week she sails the western Caribbean, making port calls in Montego Bay, Grand Cayman, Playa del Carmen, and Cozumel.

NIGHTLIFE & ENTERTAINMENT

Night owls enjoy dancing, drinking, and gambling. Movies and a midnight buffet entertain the more sedate crowd. The romance of the open sea enchants most couples. Whether aboard ship or visiting a port of call, you will almost certainly find yourself entertained.

AESTHETICS & ENVIRONMENT

Dolphin ships are well maintained, clean, comfortable, and warm. Passengers do their own thing, without infringing on the privacy of others.

FACILITIES

Bars	Gift shop
Beaches	Medical station
Beauty salon	Piano bar
Casino	Safety-deposit box
Disco	Snack bar, grill
Entertainment coordinators	Swimming pool

ROOMS

Cabins are small, yet comfortable. Some couples may find themselves in a room with two single beds. Pack light—drawer space is limited.

LUXURY LEVEL

Air-conditioning	Porter service
Clock	Radio in room
Maid service	Room service
Phone in room	

FOOD & DRINK

Dolphin raises eating from a fun activity to an art form. Literally. Its chefs sculpt watermelons into artistic figures, such as a woman holding a child or an Indian head. The cuisine tastes as good as it looks. One veteran cruiser told us, "I've never eaten as well as I have on Dolphin."

Dolphin serves three formal meals a day in the tastefully appointed dining room, and buffet-style breakfasts and lunches can be enjoyed poolside. A midnight brunch stuffs those who still have room for more food. Breakfasts range from cold cereal to eggs Benedict. Formal lunches consist of meals such as fresh fish or chicken, and the buffets dish up burgers, burritos, and similar fare. At dinner, passengers enjoy lobster, veal, and steak, with cherries jubilee or baked Alaska for dessert. The midnight buffet assuages the munchies with pasta dishes, Mexican food, cold cuts, fruits, and desserts. All the meals are lavishly prepared and elegantly served. Kosher, diabetic, and salt-free diets can be accommodated on request. Passengers say these meals taste great. Special dietary requests should be submitted in writing when booking the cruise.

Before the cruise, Dolphin distributes VIP cards, so there is no need to carry money for drinks. All you do is sign the bill and settle up at the end of the trip.

STAFFING & SERVICE

If you want to be pampered and made to feel like royalty, look no further than Dolphin cruises. One of the waiters even calls the female passengers "my lady." All staff members do their best to accommodate your needs. If for some odd reason they can't help, they will point you in the direction of someone who can.

PRIVACY & RELAXATION

Most activities occur on the poolside deck, leaving the upper deck relatively quiet. In the evening, the bow attracts couples who want a bit of privacy. To really get away, you can always retreat to your room, or wander off while the ship is in port.

SHOPPING

Islanders enjoy bargaining with tourists. Brush up on your haggling skills and you'll come home with some good buys. Remember, many items are not unique, even if the vendor says they are. If you're patient, you can usually get the price you want.

HONEYMOONERS

Dolphin cruises are ideal for honeymooners. The crew takes care of you, so you can spend time with each other. If you're looking to spend quality time in your cabin, a Junior Suite is a must.

Dolphin offers a unique seven-night honeymoon package that includes a four-day cruise with champagne and flowers in your cabin on arrival, a honeymoon party, a commemorative gift, and a portrait. The night before the cruise you stay at the Marriott Hotel, and after the trip you are taken to the Mayfair House in Coconut Grove,

Florida, for a two-night stay. At this all-suite hotel, you receive champagne and Continental breakfast in bed.

SINGLES

The shorter cruises attract a fair amount of singles, but don't expect the odds to be as good as they are at some of the resorts.

CHILD APPEAL

Counselors plan children's activities during summer vacations and school holidays. Depending on their age, kids can romp in a toy cabin, play video games, watch movies, go on scavenger hunts, and play poolside games. Older kids hang out in the disco during the early hours. Occasionally counselors arrange a kids' picnic with limbo contests, crab races, and other activities. Few organized activities are available when kids are normally in school.

NUTS & BOLTS

BOOKING & CONTACT INFORMATION

Dolphin Cruise Line
1007 North American Way
Miami, FL 33132
800-222-1003
305-358-5122

CURRENCY: The purser's office cashes traveler's checks but not personal checks. Credit cards are accepted in the gift shop.

CUSTOMS/DUTY: Standard U.S. customs.

DEPOSITS/REFUNDS: Confirmed reservations require a $100 deposit to be paid at the time of booking. Final payment is due no less than 60 days before departure. If written cancellations are received 50 to 30 days prior to departure, you will get a full refund, less a $100 cancellation fee. Cancellations received 29 to 4 days before departure cost you 50 percent of the gross fare. No refunds will be returned for cancellations with less than 3 days' notice.

ELECTRICITY: Both ships have 110 volts and 220 volts. Your hair dryers and electric razors will run without an adapter.

HANDICAP ACCESSIBILITY: Dolphin ships are not readily accessible to wheelchair-bound passengers. The elevators do not go to all decks. Steps in the cabin doorways make entry and exit awkward for wheelchairs. Dolphin passengers should be self-sufficient, and should have a companion to help them in case of an emergency.

LANGUAGES: The crew speaks English, Spanish, and Greek. Dolphin's officers are Greek: the crew is international.

PACKING: Passengers wear informal clothing for daytime activities and shore excursions. After sundown etiquette requires more formal attire. On the shorter cruises, women are asked to wear nice dinner dresses, and men are asked to wear jackets and ties. On seven-night cruises, Dolphin holds two formal nights. People tend to get a little more dressed up. Some passengers wear gowns and tuxedos, but cocktail dresses and suits are acceptable. Limited storage space demands that you leave nonessentials at home.

RELIGIOUS SERVICES: Dolphin does not hold religious services on a regular basis, but it does conduct services at Christmas and Easter.

RESERVATION SCHEDULE: Dolphin offers discounts for reservations made 90 days in advance. Book early and save money, in addition to getting the cabin and itinerary you want. Dolphin recommends six months notice for many cruises. Holiday cruises begin filling up a year in advance.

SIZE: 501 or 605 feet.

NUMBER OF CABINS: 294 or 400.

MAXIMUM NUMBER OF GUESTS: 588 or 800.

NUMBER OF EMPLOYEES: 280 or 400.

TRAVEL TIME BY AIR

CHICAGO: **3 HOURS 30 MINUTES**
LOS ANGELES: **5 HOURS 30 MINUTES**
NEW YORK: **3 HOURS**
TORONTO: **4 HOURS**

ARRIVAL AIRPORT: Miami International Airport.

TRAVEL TIME FROM AIRPORT: 20 minutes.

VACCINATION REQUIREMENTS: None.

VISA/PASSPORT REQUIREMENTS: U.S. and Canadian citizens need proof of citizenship in the form of a passport or birth certificate with a photo ID.

SPENDING MONEY: Bring enough for tips, drinks, gambling, shore excursions, and souvenirs. Unless you are a serious gambler, a few hundred dollars should be plenty.

Cost Worksheet	High Season[1]	Off-Season[2]
Accommodations		
(7 days)[3]	$995–$1,795	$845–$1,645
Food	incl.	incl.
Drinks		
Port tax	$29–$37	$29–$37
State tax	incl.	incl.
Hotel tax	incl.	incl.
Sports	incl.	incl.
Airfare	incl.	incl.
Sight-seeing		
Tips	$25	$25
Additional sports		
Souvenirs		

[1] High season dates: February, March 3 to 31, May 26 to September 1, December 22 to January 2
[2] Off-season dates: September 8 to December 18, January, Regular season dates: April 3 to June 9, September 4, November 20
[3] Premium for single person: *Dolphin*, 150 percent double occupancy rate; *Sea Breeze*, 125 percent double occupancy rate

PREMIER CRUISE LINES

VITAL FEATURES

Type of vacation; **Cruise**
Market: **Families (also couples and singles)**
Location: **Bahamas, Florida's east coast**
All-inclusive cost per week: **$600–$1,015 per person double
 occupancy; $1,700–$2,930 for a family of four**

RATINGS

Value: 💲💲💲💲💲

Fun quotient: 🏖️🏖️🏖️🏖️🏖️

Honeymoon suitability: 🖤

Singles meeting ground: 🧍🧍🧍

Child appeal: 🍦🍦🍦🍦🍦

Management professionalism: ☎️☎️☎️☎️

Services: 💡💡💡

Food: 🦞🦞🦞🦞

THE REAL STORY

A trip on Premier Cruise Lines is like a well-balanced meal. There
is something from all four food groups. The concept is prepared
perfectly and is filling. The cruise, with stops in Nassau and Salt Cay,
combined with three days at Walt Disney World to make the trip
balanced, offers something new and exciting every day. It's highly
unlikely you will hear anything similar to the backseat moan, "When
are we going to get there?"

Premier has two luxurious cruise liners, the *Star/Ship Royale* and
the *Star/Ship Oceanic*. Both offer a day and a half at sea, with a range
of sports, social activities, good eating, gambling, and entertainment

on board; a day in Nassau featuring sight-seeing, beaches, shopping, and nightlife; a day on Salt Cay, a small island in the Bahamas where "Gilligan's Island," *Splash*, and other features have been filmed, with snorkeling and other water sports, beautiful beaches, hammocks under swaying palm trees, and a variety of activities. The cruise features a truly excellent program for kids, with activities ranging from cartoons, to treasure hunts, to costume parties, and best of all, to live Disney characters who help entertain and play with the kids on every trip.

Along with the four-day cruise, the package includes a three-day pass to Walt Disney World, a rental car and hotel accommodations in Orlando, and free admission to Spaceport U.S.A. at the Kennedy Space Center. Food costs in Walt Disney World are not included. It's a terrific vacation value, sure to enchant everyone in the family. Watch out, though. You might get this question from your five-year-old: "Can we live at Disney World?"

INCLUDED

Accommodations	Entertainment & dancing
Activities	Food
Child care	Sports

VALUE

Premier is the "Official Cruise Line" of Walt Disney World. There is no competition, making this the only package you will find. The brochure says you are only paying for the cruise and the three days at Walt Disney World are free. If this were entirely true it would be a very expensive cruise. Slick advertising aside, it's still a very good deal. More than likely, you would spend the same amount or more on a trip only to Walt Disney World. And it wouldn't be as much fun.

ACTIVITIES, SPORTS, & EXCURSIONS

On board ship, activities go nonstop. There is something for just about everyone. In addition to sports and entertainment, there's casino gambling, bingo, video games, bridge, trivia quizzes, mock horse racing, talent shows, tours of the bridge, get-togethers for grandparents, wine-tasting seminars, perfume seminars, and much more. Your head will spin from all there is to do.

There is a terrific program for children aged two through the teens, featuring visits with live Disney characters, cartoons, movies, treasure hunts, costume making, and a talent show. Your kids will actually want to go to the kids' programs, leaving their parents some (gasp) time alone. The program goes until 10:00 P.M., after which group baby-sitting is available for a fee. Baby-sitting is limited to children under two.

ACTIVITIES

Arts & crafts
Board games
Culture/music/language
    classes

Dancing
Entertainment/shows
Movies
Sunbathing

SPORTS: There is a fitness program aboard called "Sea-Sport," which offers continual planned fitness events. The incentive to participate lies in prizes offered to those who've accumulated the most gold stars. Gold stars are placed on your Star Card when you attend such activities as jumpercise, stretchercise, juggling, tap dancing, and many others. They make it look like so much fun you'll soon join in.

Aerobics/exercise classes
Basketball
Golf (driving into the ocean)
Jogging (running track at Salt
    Cay)
Parasailing
Pedal boats
Sailing

Shuffleboard
Snorkeling (extra)
Swimming pools
Volleyball
Water polo
Weightlifting
Windsurfing (extra)

ITINERARY & DAILY SCHEDULE

The cruise leaves from Port Canaveral in the afternoon and arrives in Nassau the next day. After an afternoon and evening in Nassau, the ship spends a day at Salt Cay, one of the Out Islands in the Bahamas, and then returns to Port Canaveral. The three days at Walt Disney World can be added either to the beginning or at the end of the cruise.

NIGHTLIFE & ENTERTAINMENT

Who could be more fun than Mickey Mouse? The Disney characters create the best entertainment on board the ship. At least four of them show up on each cruise. They appear at various events and make fun for all ages. Don't bother trying to tell your four-year-old that there is really a man or woman inside the costume. The characters create a magic aura that would make Walt Disney himself proud.

On board there are cabaret singers and Broadway-style revues. These were enjoyable, but not the highlight of the trip; most of the Disney shows are better. There are movies, several bars, a casino, a disco, and a masquerade party on the last night.

In Nassau it's easy to get sucked into the excitement of the fire dancers, island shows, and of course the casinos. Tickets for a native island calypso show are about $28, and $21 for a Las Vegas–style show. The cost includes transportation and one drink. You can free yourself of any loose change in the thousands of slot machines.

Walt Disney World offers numerous shows of various types at Epcot Center and the Magic Kingdom. There are also evening night-club-type shows at several Disney resorts.

AESTHETICS & ENVIRONMENT

Premier's two ships do have mice in the hull, but they answer to the names of Mickey and Minnie. The *Royale* and the *Oceanic* stand out in a crowd. Not only can goofy characters be found walking around the decks, but the ships are painted a distinctive vibrant red and white. The color is an example of the lively environment that is created aboard the ships.

FACILITIES

Bank
Bars
Beaches
Beauty salon
Casino
Disco (matinee disco for kids
    and teens)
Entertainment coordinators

Gift shop
Hot tub
Medical station
Piano bar
Safety-deposit box
Snack bar, grill
Water-sports center

ROOMS

Both on board ship and at Walt Disney World, the degree of luxury depends on what you pay for. The typical cabin resembles a slightly cramped, vintage 1965 Howard Johnson's room with bunk beds, which are turned down by a steward every night. The steward service is courteous and prompt. Each cabin has plenty of closet space, towels, pillows, and blankets, plus a radio and on-ship telephone. Bathrooms are clean and include showers with plenty of water pressure. If you're willing to pay an extra couple of hundred dollars, you can get a genuinely luxurious and spacious cabin, some with a private veranda.

The quality of accommodations in Orlando also depends on price and location.

LUXURY LEVEL: Air-conditioning, phone in room, radio.

FOOD & DRINK

The food is very good and plentiful. In addition to the three standard meals, there is a buffet breakfast and lunch, do-it-yourself sundaes all afternoon, a hearty "tea time" snack, pizza at 11:30 P.M., and a splendid midnight buffet. If one of the kids still has the munchies, have no fear. Candy, chips, and similar snacks can be purchased at the duty-free shop. Lunch and dinner offer at least five entrée choices, and there's a different international theme every night. Special diet requests can be met if requested at least a month in advance of departure.

Food at Walt Disney World (which you pay for separately) offers tremendous variety and ranges from adequate at the snack bars in the Magic Kingdom to excellent in Epcot's international restaurants.

STAFFING & SERVICE

The office staff are efficient, competent, and handle things well. The professionalism of the ship's officers and crew add to the fun and your peace of mind.

PRIVACY & RELAXATION

If you're looking for a calm, relaxing trip, this cruise is not for you, although the ship is big enough so that you can find some privacy. Even in your cabin you may be disturbed by the 8:30 A.M. shipwide announcements.

SHOPPING

On board ship, there are duty-free shops, which offer prices competitive with those in Nassau. Items include souvenirs, liquor, china, cigarettes, and sundries, as well as Disney and cruise memorabilia. The shops and markets of Nassasu offer everything from straw hats to sophisticated calculators, all within walking distance of the harbor. Bargains can be found, but comparison shop carefully.

HONEYMOONERS

For some reason the thought of spending a honeymoon with hundreds of children and the Disney characters does not seem blissful. But the cruise does attract some honeymoon couples. Maybe they want a sneak preview of family life.

The size of the ship and the itinerary allow for solitary romantic strolls—as well as a lot of fun. Premier is trying to attract honeymooners with a package including complimentary champagne and a honeymooners' cocktail party hosted by the ship's captain. Attention Donald and Daisy, Mickey and Minnie.

SINGLES

It would be a good story to tell your kids that you met at Walt Disney World. Several organized activities and parties are arranged for single parents, with the same lighthearted touch that guides the children's programs.

NUTS & BOLTS

BOOKING & CONTACT INFORMATION

Premier Cruise Lines
P.O. Box 573
Cape Canaveral, FL 32920
407-783-5061
800-327-7113

CURRENCY: American currency and traveler's checks are fine. MasterCard and Visa are accepted on the ship.

CUSTOMS/DUTY: U.S. Presidents can bring back up to $400 worth of duty-free merchandise per person. Customs is handled fairly quickly and without hassles at Port Canaveral; just fill out your return card and follow the rules.

DEPOSITS/REFUNDS: A $150-per-cabin deposit is required within 7 days of booking. Final payment is due 60 days before departure. There is a minimum cancellation charge of $150 per cabin if you cancel before departure. The charge climbs to 50 percent if you cancel less than 30 days in advance, and there are no refunds for no-shows or cancellations on the sailing date.

ELECTRICITY: 110 volts 60 cycles, same as in the United States.

HANDICAP ACCESSIBILITY: There is limited mobility for wheelchairs aboard the *Oceanic*.

LANGUAGE: The crew is multinational, but all speak English, as does everyone in Nassau.

PACKING: Bring a sweater or jacket for cool evenings. The Captain's Dinner requires a coat and tie for men and a nice dress for women. Bring your own diapers, bottles, and other paraphernalia for young kids. They do sell disposable diapers aboard.

RELIGIOUS SERVICES: None is offered on board. A sign listing services at Nassau is posted in the lobby of both ships.

RESERVATION SCHEDULE: Six months advance reservations are needed if you want to stay at a Disney on-site resort for no extra charge. Otherwise two months to six weeks will be fine, except during school vacations, when you should plan a year ahead.

SIZE: *Atlantic*, 671 feet; *Majestic*, 545 feet; *Oceanic*, 782 feet.

MAXIMUM NUMBER OF GUESTS: 1,500.

TRAVEL TIME BY AIR

Chicago: **3 hours 30 minutes**
Los Angeles: **4 hours 30 minutes**
New York: **3 hours 30 minutes**
Toronto: **3 hours 50 minutes**

ARRIVAL AIRPORT: Orlando International Airport.

TRAVEL TIME FROM AIRPORT: 45 minutes.

VACCINATION REQUIREMENTS: None.

VISA/PASSPORT REQUIREMENTS: U.S. and Canadian citizens must carry documentary proof of citizenship, such as a passport, birth certificate, or voter's registration card. A driver's license is not valid.

SPENDING MONEY: You will need money for tips, port charges, tours in Nassau, souvenirs, drinks, and gambling.

Cost Worksheet		
	High Season	*Off-Season*
Accommodations		
(7 days)[1]	$710–$1,095	$675–$1,070
Food	incl.	incl.
Drinks		
Departure tax	$30	$30
Hotel tax	6%	6%
Sports	incl.	incl.
Airfare	_____	_____
Sight-seeing		
Tips	$22–$30 per passenger	$22–$30
Additional sports		
Souvenirs	_____	_____

[1] Premium for single person: $350 to $550 over per person double rate. Accomodations are for 7 days: 3 or 4 on ship, or 3 or 4 at Walt Disney World.

PRINCESS CRUISE LINES

VITAL FEATURES

Type of vacation: **Cruise**
Target market: **Couples, families, singles of all ages**
Location: **Caribbean, Trans-Canal, Mexico, South Pacific, Alaska, Canada and New England, Europe, the Orient, South America**
All-inclusive cost per week: **$1,199–$3,359, airfare sometimes included**

RATINGS

Value: 💲💲💲💲💲

Fun quotient: ⛱⛱⛱⛱

Honeymoon suitability: ❤❤❤❤❤

Singles meeting ground: 🧍🧍🧍

Child appeal: 🍦🍦🍦

Management professionalism: ☎☎☎☎☎

Service: 💡💡💡💡💡

Food: 🦞🦞🦞🦞

THE REAL STORY

When you think of a cruise ship, you probably envision a Princess ship. ABC-TV made the ships famous when it used them for its popular program, "The Love Boat." Now, thanks to hours of television time, Princess Cruise Lines sets a cruise standard in the public's mind.

The Princess cruise staff rate a solid five on smiles and service. If you've never been on a cruise before, you're in for great surprises. If you're a veteran cruiser, you're sure to find Princess right up there with the best. From beginning to end, you'll get much more than you were promised. About the only thing you won't get from a Princess

353

cruise is an autograph from Gavin MacLeod, a.k.a. Captain Stuebing.

On a Princess cruise, you can be a sight-seer, couch potato, or superathlete. Even shore excursions come in three categories: one for beach loungers, another for sight-seers, and a third choice for those who want to engage in water sports. The ships act as floating resorts with health clubs, casinos, kids' centers, swimming pools, bars, and lecture rooms. Not only do the ships offer the benefits of a resort, but they also eliminate the hassles of getting from one place to another. You see numerous ports of call without dealing with transportation and transfers, or check-ins and checkouts. A Princess cruise may be the ideal solution for couples who normally can't agree on what to do on their vacation. They can be together, yet each can enjoy his or her own activities.

Young couples are finally catching on to what older folks have known all along: cruising is fun. Princess attracts passengers of all ages and backgrounds. We spent time with a 22-year-old model from Los Angeles and a 45-year-old émigré Russian musician. At least half the passengers had cruised with Princess before, and one couple had been on 27 previous cruises.

Princess recently acquired Sitmar Cruise Line. Both lines have excellent reputations for fine luxury cruises. The size and amenities differ somewhat among the ships, but all offer high-quality vacations.

INCLUDED

Accommodations	Sports
Activities	Sports instruction (some
Airfare (sometimes)	sports)
Child care	Taxes
Entertainment & dancing	Transfer to and from airport
Food	

VALUE

Compared to other types of vacations, a Princess cruise is a tremendous value. You know before you leave how much the trip will cost. You get six meals a day and a luxurious room; drinks are inexpensive. You are waited on hand and foot. You'll be so pleased with the value you'll probably book another cruise.

ACTIVITIES, SPORTS & EXCURSIONS

If you have always thought of a cruise as a continual eating orgy with nothing to do but play shuffleboard, you're only half right on this one. Whether at sea or in port, you can choose from many organized activities, games, or classes. Or you can lounge on the deck by the pool. Some people limit their physical activity to lifting cocktail glasses and walking to the dining room.

Each day you receive a schedule of the planned activities for the next 24 hours. For example, you may choose a mix-and-mingle game, volleyball tournament, dance lessons, or take classes in choosing your best colors and applying makeup. Health and fitness programs keep you in shape with stretch, exercise, and aerobics classes. At night passengers listen to music and dance in one of the many lounges. Gamblers play slot machines, blackjack, roulette, craps, and more. Bingo games entertain those who like to limit their losses.

ACTIVITIES

Arts & crafts
Board games
Culture/music/language
   classes
Dancing

Entertainment/shows
Gambling
Movies
Sunbathing
Video games

SPORTS

Aerobics/exercise classes
Bicycles (extra)
Golf (extra)
Hiking
Horseback riding (extra)
Jogging
Paddle tennis
Ping-Pong
Scuba (extra)
Scuba course (extra)

Shuffleboard
Skeet and trap shooting
Snorkeling (extra)
Swimming
Volleyball
Walking classes
Waterskiing (extra)
Weightlifting (Nautilus)
Windsurfing (extra)

EXCURSIONS: Port days feature three categories of organized activities: sight-seeing tours, beginner water sports, and advanced water sports. The ship offers free snorkeling and scuba diving lessons, but a sport diving certification costs $300. The price includes all equipment, instruction, and the required number of dives. Guided shore activities cost from $20 to $65. You're on your own for individual shopping, sight-seeing, and suntanning.

ITINERARY & DAILY SCHEDULE

Each cruise operates on a scheduled itinerary. However, the captain may, at his discretion, change the order in which you visit the various ports. If, for example, the captain learns that six other large cruise ships are scheduled to arrive in St. Croix on the same day, he can take the ship to St. Thomas instead, returning to St. Croix later.

NIGHTLIFE & ENTERTAINMENT

Nighttime activities separate the younger and older passengers. Early in the evening, passengers watch live entertainment in the main auditorium and feature films in the ship's movie theater. The nightlife continues after the older passengers and children have retired to bed. Those in their twenties, thirties, and forties dance the night away to live bands in the bars, lounges, and discos. The casino crowd swells at night, as more gamblers try their luck. Theme parties such as Fifties Night, a pajama party, and a costume party add variety to the normal entertainment. Couples always manage to find semisecluded spots on the decks and among the nooks inside.

AESTHETICS & ENVIRONMENT

Boarding the ship feels like entering a beautiful, tastefully decorated hotel. The cabins and public areas would not only pass a white glove inspection, they would pass a white sock inspection as well. Cleaning crews scrub and polish both day and night. A button next to each bed summons the cabin steward, who shows up quickly with a smile and a desire to help solve almost any problem or respond to almost any request. This attitude pervades the ship's entire crew.

The ship combines the best of a luxury resort with the convenience of a shopping mall. Boutiques carry countless items a passenger may want or need. A beauty and barber salon offers facials, manicures, and hairdressing. Massages await those in need of relaxation. Costs for these additional services are similar to prices in the United States.

FACILITIES

Bank	Hot tub (some ships)
Bars	Medical station
Beauty salon	Piano bar
Casino	Safety-deposit box
Disco	Snack bar, grill
Entertainment coordinators	Swimming pool
Gift shop	

ROOMS

All the amenities of a first-rate luxury resort are found on Princess ships. The cabins are large, clean, well appointed, with excellent closet and drawer space.

LUXURY LEVEL

Air-conditioning	Laundry self-service (extra)
Bar in room (some rooms)	Maid service
Desk	Phone in room

Porter service
Radio
Refrigerator (some rooms)

Room service
Television (some cabins)

FOOD & DRINK

Passengers can eat from 6:00 in the morning until 1:30 the next morning. And if for some reason you can't make it through the night, the cabin steward will stock your room with snacks and fruit. Elaborate menus suggest house standards, as well as specials that change each day. You can eat as often as you like and order as much as you want. Buffets and room service provide an alternative for those who don't feel like eating during their assigned seating.

Lunch and dinner menus change each day. Breakfast specials are offered each morning. Meals always involve multiple courses with several selections of appetizers, soups, salads, main courses, and desserts. The food is well prepared, beautifully served, and usually at the proper temperature. Everything tastes superb. On French Night you may select escargots sauced with Bordeaux, mushrooms, and garlic in a puffed pastry; a lobster bisque; crisp roasted duckling in orange sauce with fresh yellow squash; and for dessert, a Napoleon. If nothing on the menu looks appetizing (not likely), you may ask for something different or go to the pizzeria for a few slices of pizza or a calzone. Come back to the dining room for dessert, though. The ultimate dessert experience is the march of the baked Alaska. The lights go down and the music comes up. Orchestra music plays as the waiters parade through the dining room with flaming baked Alaskas.

Princess always serves several dishes approved by the American Heart Association for their low fat, cholesterol, and salt contents. Special dietary arrangements are made for people who have diabetes, allergies, or other dietary restrictions. Be sure to let the company know your requirements when you make your reservations.

The entire dining room staff works efficiently and quickly to provide for all your needs. The personable service adds immeasurably to the enjoyment of the meals. The staff dresses in costume for theme dinners such as the Welcome Gala Dinner and Italian Night, and the dining room is decorated to fit the theme.

Although drinks are on the house at occasional cocktail parties, passengers must usually pay for cocktails and soft drinks in the bars. Wine with dinner also comes at extra cost. Drink prices are very reasonable. Each day at least one special cocktail sells for $1.50, and several others go for $2.25. Wine costs less than you would normally expect to pay for it in a restaurant at home. Our cruise featured a special wine-tasting class, but neither the wine nor the lessons were worthwhile.

STAFFING & SERVICE

The crew is extremely well trained and professional. The captain is very experienced, and all of the senior people have been with the Princess or Sitmar line for many years. The instructors are excellent and are able to work equally well with beginners and advanced people in whatever they are teaching. The social staff is very creative and, for the most part, quite friendly and helpful. Not all of the staff were equally familiar with all the ports, but the staff member who does know a port quite well holds briefings for all the passengers. We were told all we needed to know about the island we were visiting, shopping, customs regulations for our purchases, and interesting things to do on shore.

PRIVACY & RELAXATION

We always found quiet, relatively isolated spots to sit and talk, in spite of the fact that there were 1,200 people on board our ship. A library on board offers passengers a quiet refuge from 8:00 A.M. until midnight. Its arrangement gives the illusion of several small and comfortable rooms. You can also find relatively private lounges scattered throughout the ship.

The cabins are reasonably quiet, much like rooms in better hotels. Occasionally, we could hear showers running in an adjacent cabin. Sleep is easy to come by, but you probably won't have much time for it. A lot of people sleep on the decks in the sun after a late night and an early morning of activities.

SHOPPING

Each port features its own special items at bargain prices. We discovered that the best prices are often found in the shops on board. Our ship had a shopping arcade with boutiques, a jewelry store, and gift shops. Shipboard merchandise includes sundries, clothing, crystal, and jewelry. Prices range from very expensive to moderate; most items are marked at prices commensurate with their quality.

HONEYMOONERS

Princess cruises create a romantic atmosphere ideal for honeymooners. Newlyweds enjoy king-size beds, dinners for two, and champagne celebrations. Some passengers decide to take the honeymoon first and get married later.

SINGLES

Passengers are extraordinarily friendly, and single passengers are included in all the activities. In fact, the cruise director takes special care to provide daily opportunities for singles to meet and mingle. Summer and holiday cruises see more singles than other months. Singles also seem more plentiful on shorter trips.

CHILD APPEAL

A children's social director keeps an eye on the kids while parents are away doing their own thing. Children play video games, board games, and playground games. They hang out at the ice cream bar, attend beach parties, and go on escorted shore excursions. For younger kids the ship provides a nursery and a playroom. Parents must get their children for meals and bed. Baby-sitting can be arranged so parents can have a night out on their own.

The extent of children's activities depends on how many children are on board. More children travel during school vacations.

NUTS & BOLTS

BOOKING & CONTACT INFORMATION

Princess Cruise Line
10100 Santa Monica Boulevard
Los Angeles, CA 90067
213-553-1666
800-421-0880

CURRENCY: Princess ships use only United States currency. You may settle your bills with cash or credit cards. Some ships accept personal checks to pay the final bill. Some ships will change U.S. dollars to foreign currency. Sometimes bank representatives come aboard in port to change money.

CUSTOMS/DUTY: U.S. residents may return to the United States with $400 worth of duty-free merchandise and one quart of liquor. On cruises stopping in the U.S. Virgin Islands, passengers may return with $800 worth of duty-free goods and one gallon of liquor, provided at least $400 worth of merchandise and the extra liquor were purchased in the U.S. Virgin Islands. Canadian citizens may, after eight days, return to their country with $300 (Canadian) worth of duty-free items. It usually takes at least two hours to clear customs upon reaching the point of debarkation. The cruise director gives a talk explaining customs procedures and allowances.

DEPOSITS/REFUNDS: Seven-day cruises require a $250 deposit per person. Longer cruises need a deposit of $450 per person. Initial payments come due 7 days after booking, with the balance due 60 days before sailing. Optional cancellation waiver insurance costs an additional $50 per person and is due upon deposit. For cancellations made 60 to 30 days before sailing, you only lose your deposit. If you cancel 29 to 15 days before departure only 50 percent of your fare will be refunded. If you cancel with 14 days or less remaining before your cruise the entire amount is forfeit.

ELECTRICITY: 110 volts 60 cycles; same as in the United States.

HANDICAP ACCESSIBILITY: On most ships, several staterooms are especially adapted for wheelchair access. All elevators accommodate wheelchairs. On our cruise, several wheelchair-bound passengers participated in many of the activities. They appeared to be having a very good time.

LANGUAGES: All crew members speak English. On Sitmar ships all officers are Italian; the crews are predominantly Portuguese and Italian. On Princess ships, the officers are British and the crews are Portuguese and Italian.

PACKING: During the day passengers wear sports clothes in keeping with the ports visited and the temperature. On a ten-day cruise, you will need three formals. Actually, a suit and tie will do for men who don't have a dinner jacket, and women can get by in a nice dress or dressy pants outfit. On other evenings you'll need three semiformal outfits plus casual clothes. Shorts and jeans are never appropriate in the dining room in the evening, or in any of the lounges, bars, or discos at night. Don't forget to bring a bathing suit for the pool and Jacuzzi and a light sweater or shawl for cool evenings at sea.

RELIGIOUS SERVICES: Religious services are held on board for those who wish to attend. Some cruises have a priest, a minister, and a rabbi. Most religious holidays are observed. A Catholic mass is celebrated every morning.

RESERVATION SCHEDULE: Most passengers make reservations a year in advance. Book at least seven months in advance to get the cabin type and sailing date you want. Nine months in advance is not too early for holiday periods. Seasonal cruises, like Alaska and New England, also fill up a year in advance.

SIZE: 535 to 761 feet.

VACCINATION REQUIREMENTS: Vaccinations are not required, but they are recommended for some South American destinations. Check with your travel agent or cruise line.

VISA/PASSPORT REQUIREMENTS: U.S. and Canadian citizens need only proof of citizenship (passport or birth certificate) for cruises in the United States, Canada, the Caribbean, Panama Canal, and Mexico. In Mexico, travelers also need a Mexican Tourist Card, obtained before beginning the cruise. Passports are required for cruises to South America, the South Pacific, the Orient, and Europe. Visa requirements vary, so be sure to check with your travel agent or the cruise line. Also be sure to fill out and bring the immigration form that comes with your ticket.

SPENDING MONEY: Most money you spend will be on shopping, so set your own budget. The social staff can tell you where to buy the items you want at the best prices. Organized tours cost extra. Before you sail, the ship provides a list of shore tours and the cost of each. Be sure to bring enough money to tip the staff. We were so impressed with the excellent service that we felt the recommended tips were too low and chose to give more.

Cost Worksheet

	Year-Round Prices
Accommoodations (7 days)[1]	$1,199–$3,359
Food	incl.
Drinks	
Departure tax	$30–$200
State tax	incl.
Hotel tax	incl.
Sports	incl.
Airfare	incl. on some sailings
Sight-seeing	
Tips	15% ($4 to $5 per person per day)
Additional sports	
Souvenirs	
Extra[2]	

[1] Premium for single person: 150 percent of regular fare
[2] Offered for extra charge: massage, $30 per session

WINDJAMMER BAREFOOT CRUISES

VITAL FEATURES

Type of vacation: **Cruise**
Target market: **Singles and couples, aged 20 years and up**
Location: **Caribbean**
All-inclusive cost per week: **$675–$850 per person plus airfare**

RATINGS

Value: 💲💲💲💲💲

Fun quotient: 🌴🌴🌴🌴🌴

Honeymoon suitability: ❤️❤️❤️

Singles meeting ground: 👫👫

Management professionalism: ☎️☎️☎️

Service: 💡💡💡💡

Food: 🦞🦞🦞

THE REAL STORY

Barefoot describes the soul, as well as the sole, of Windjammer cruises. Simple, earthy, relaxing, rowdy, fun. It depends on the week and on you. These cruises resemble a floating Club Med. The highlight of the day comes when the sails go up while the speakers play "Amazing Grace." The drama is not lost on the passengers.

Windjammer has a reputation for having a young crowd. It's true that there are a lot of people in their twenties, but many guests in their thirties, forties, fifties, and over sail on the Barefoot Cruises and they like it equally as much.

Different itineraries offer assorted blends of tourist sights, shopping, and isolated beaches. Travelers with an independent streak

362

will probably like these cruises. Nobody meets you at the airport or holds your hand on the shore excursions. The captain holds a humorous "storytime" and accurately tells you what to see and where to go. After that, you're on your own.

Windjammer offers 6-day and 13-day cruises throughout the Caribbean. Each of the ships has its own itinerary. See the "Itinerary & Daily Schedule" section for a description of the different ships and their routes. "Old Salt" tours give a $50 discount on a second week with free "stowaway" nights in between. Because some of the ships do different routes on alternating weeks, this is an attractive option to a 13-day cruise.

INCLUDED: Accommodations, activities, food.

VALUE

Windjammer cruises give excellent value in terms of the total experience and as a way to see the different islands.

ACTIVITIES, SPORTS, & EXCURSIONS

ACTIVITIES: Windjammer has no activities coordinators. The ship does not arrange tours or activities ashore, but the crew will point you in the right direction.

SPORTS: The *Flying Cloud* in the British Virgin Islands emphasizes diving and snorkeling activities. It is the one cruise where Windjammer makes outside arrangements with a dive company. There's also sailing (you can help sail the ship), snorkeling (bring your own equipment), and swimming.

EXCURSIONS: You make your own adventure.

ITINERARY & DAILY SCHEDULE

Most times the Windjammer ships sail at night, giving the passengers a full day on the islands. Breakfast is served around 8:00 A.M. Between 9:00 and 10:00 the captain holds "storytime," telling the passengers about the island, what to see, and when to be back. Skiffs then ferry passengers to shore for a free day of play. Lunch runs from late morning to late afternoon. Most passengers come back for dinner or just before the ship leaves port.

Itineraries depend on the cruise offered. All of Windjammer's trips combine fun on the boat with time on shore for sight-seeing, shopping, or just playing around. The following paragraphs briefly describe the ships and their itineraries. For descriptions of the island stops see the appropriate chapter introductions.

FANTOME: The Windjammer flagship, *Fantome*, combines a mixture of isolated beachcombing with tourism and duty-free shopping in the West Indies and British Virgin Islands. This one-week cruise accommodates 126 passengers and a crew of 45. The itinerary alternates weekly. On odd weeks the *Fantome* sails from Roadtown, Tortola, in the British Virgin Islands, and it visits Salt Island, Peter Island, Cooper Island, Norman Island, Virgin Gorda, Marigot (St. Martin), and Anguilla before ending in St. Matin, West Indies. On even weeks the cruise is reversed, with Phillipsburg, St. Martin, marking the beginning of the voyage. Those stops include: Prickly Pear, Antigua, St. Barts, Saba, Statia, Virgin Gorda, Jost Van Dyke, Peter Island, Norman Island, Cooper Island, and Tortola.

Although small for a cruise ship, the *Fantome* is the largest four-masted ship in the world. It measures 282 feet from bow to stern. Originally built in 1927 for the Duke of Westminster, the *Fantome* was later owned by the Guinness brewery family. Next she was purchased by Aristotle Onassis as a wedding present for Prince Rainier and the late Princess Grace. Never delivered, the ship joined the Windjammer fleet in 1969 after a complete reconstruction.

FLYING CLOUD: The *Flying Cloud* patrols the Caribbean like a privateer from the Revolutionary War. Instead of hunting ships to plunder, it tours Drake's Passage and the Treasure Isles of the British Virgin Islands. All 78 passengers are guaranteed to have a jolly good time on either of the *Flying Cloud*'s alternating itineraries. Both offer white sand beaches with superb snorkeling, historic tours, and markets with local handcrafts. On odd weeks the *Flying Cloud* cruises Drake's Passage, stopping at Salt Island, Virgin Gorda, Beef Island, Green Cay, Sandy Cay, Norman Island, Cane Garden Bay, and Deadman's Bay. The intinerary for even weeks covers Cooper Island, Virgin Gorda, Beef Island, Green Cay, Sandy Cay, Norman Island, Jost Van Dyke, Cane Garden Bay, and Peter Island. All trips depart Roadtown, Tortola, midday Monday and return early Saturday.

The *Flying Cloud* was built in France in 1935 as a cadet training ship for the French navy. Tahiti was her home port during World War II and she received the honorary Croix de Lorraine for sinking two Japanese submarines. Windjammer purchased the ship in 1968, and she was christened the *Flying Cloud* after being converted to her present form.

YANKEE CLIPPER: The blend of tropical paradise and West Indian charm on a *Yankee Clipper* cruise is almost as intoxicating as the ship's cold rum swizzles served at sunset. This 197-foot clipper ship carries 66 passengers and 24 crew members on its weekly tours of the West Indies. Visiting the North Leeward Islands during odd weeks, the *Yankee Clipper* stops in St. Barts, St. Martin, St. Kitts,

Anguilla, Nevis, and Statia. On the even weeks she heads for the South Leeward Islands, exploring Montserrat, Barbuda, Banana Bay (St. Kitts), Dominica, Guadeloupe, Isles des Saintes, English Harbour, and Falmouth. Both cruises leave St. John's, Antigua, on Monday and arrive back early Saturday in time to catch morning flights.

Probably the only armor-plated private yacht in the world, the *Yankee Clipper* was built in 1927 by German industrialist and manufacturer Alfred Krupp. She was taken as a war prize during World War II and used by the U.S. Coast Guard for the duration of the war. Later purchased by the Vanderbilts, the clipper's home port was Newport Beach, California, until she was rechristened the *Yankee Clipper* by the Windjammer fleet.

POLYNESIA: Every Monday the *Polynesia* leaves Phillipsburg, St. Martin, for a week of exploration and relaxation. Volcanoes, uninhabited cays, and topless beaches add spice to this cruise through the West Indies. Windjammer standards such as shipping, sightseeing, and late-afternoon swizzles are also included. The *Polynesia* sails the Leeward Islands on the first two weeks a month, with ports of call in Columbia Beach (St. Barts), St. Barts, St. Kitts, Saba, Statia, Prickly Pear, and Anguilla. The ship varies her routine in the latter half of the month by sailing to Columbia Beach, St. Barts, Nevis, Montserrat, Banana Bay (St. Kitts), St. Kitts, St. Barts, and Anguilla. All cruises return to St. Martin on Saturday in time to make travel connections.

The *Argus*, as the ship was originally called, was constructed by the Dutch in 1939. She first served as a cod boat in the Portuguese Grand Banks fishing fleet. The ship became a celebrity when the fleet was featured by maritime writer Allen Villiers in his book *The Quest of Schooner Argus*. In spite of her fame, she was dropped from the fishing fleet when motorboats became more economical. Windjammer acquired her in 1975 and turned the 248-foot work boat into a cruise ship capable of carrying 126 passengers and 45 crew members.

MANDALAY: The *Mandalay* is "the queen of the Windjammer fleet." With three masts and more than 22,000 square feet of sail, this 236-foot yacht carries her 72 passengers and 28 crew members in style and luxury. The cabins are paneled in rosewood and the baths are finished in marble. As on all Windjammer cruises, the crew is friendly and helpful, and the equipment is state-of-the-art. You won't want to spend all your time aboard ship, though. The scenery in the Grenadines and West Indies is difficult to top.

The *Mandalay* offers two 13-day cruises each month. Both combine swimming and snorkeling opportunities with tourist activities. At the beginning of the month, the *Mandalay* sets sail from Grenada to

Antigua with stops in Palm Island, Mayreau, Tobago Cays, Mustique, Bequia, St. Vincent, St. Lucia, Martinique, Dominica, Isles des Saintes, and English Harbour. After a two-day layover the ship begins another cruise, sailing back to Grenada. On the return trip she calls on St. Barts, Nevis, Montserrat, Isles des Saintes, Martinique, St. Lucia, St. Vincent, Bequia, Mustique, Tobago Cays, Mayreau, Palm Island, and Carriacou. From June through October it's possible to take a six-day mini-cruise, catching or leaving the ship in St. Lucia.

The *Mandalay* was built in 1923 by famous shipwrights Cox and Stephens for financier E. F. Hutton. Originally christened the *Hussar*, she was known to be the most luxurious personal yacht in the world. Later she served as a training ship for the U.S. Merchant Marine and as a charting vessel for the Lamont-Doherty Geological Observatory. Columbia University used her as an oceanic research vessel to gather evidence confirming the theory of continental drift. Instead of scientific studies, she now sails the West Indies and Grenadines in pursuit of pleasure.

AMAZING GRACE: From the Bahamas to the Grenadines, passengers on the *Amazing Grace* see the Caribbean and more. Every 19 days she sails south from Freeport, Bahamas, to resupply the other ships of the Windjammer fleet. It may be a working trip for the ship, but for the passengers it's all vacation. The ship visits Nassau, San Salvador, Puerta Plata, Santo Domingo, Tortola, Virgin Gorda, St. Martin, and Antigua. Between rendezvous there are plenty of stops for swimming, sight-seeing, and shopping. There is also ample opportunity for the 44 passengers and 30 crew members to form friendships. The *Amazing Grace* sails from Freeport on the second Sunday of each month and returns 19 days later. If you don't have time for a full trip, you can arrange one-week or two-week stays.

The *Amazing Grace* is the youngest ship in the Windjammer fleet. She was built in 1955 in Scotland for the British navy for service in the North Sea. When she was not aiding lighthouse keepers along the rugged north coast, *Amazing Grace* served British royalty. The queen, the queen mother, and other members of the royal family have all been passengers on her guest list. Windjammer acquired her in 1987.

NIGHTLIFE & ENTERTAINMENT

Most nights are spent on the ship. Windjammer does not have a cruise director, but the crew plans activities such as toga parties, costume contests, boat races, and a talent night. There is no regular band, although the ship does have live music on stowaway nights. Occasionally there is a double party with another Windjammer ship. Passengers can be skiffed ashore for nightlife if the schedule allows. Usually people make their own entertainment.

AESTHETICS & ENVIRONMENT

Windjammer possesses the largest fleet of "tall ships" in the world. Heir to a legacy of fast metal clippers, Windjammer has refitted the former cargo vessels and yachts to accommodate passengers comfortably. They now house guests in relative comfort, which includes air-conditioning and a bar.

FACILITIES: Bar, gift shop, medical station, safety-deposit box.

ROOMS

Windjammer ships have three types of cabins. All rooms are air-conditioned and ship-size (small). They sleep you comfortably enough and allow you to change, but they aren't meant as sitting rooms. The cabin you choose depends on your budget and desire for a porthole.

The least expensive cabins are the bachelor/bachelorette dormitories for single passengers. These rooms are reminiscent of your college days, when you shared a small room and bathroom with six other people. A berth goes for $675 per person for a five-to-six-day cruise. Close families can rent the whole room.

The most common type of accommodations are the regular cabins, which are double occupancy with an upper and lower berth and a private bath. These rooms cost $725 per person for six-day cruises. Deck cabins are similar to the regular cabins, but you pay an extra $125 for a porthole. An Admiral's Suite provides particular passengers with a double bed, private bath, and porthole.

LUXURY LEVEL: In spite of the mystique of Windjammer's being a floating cooperative where passengers help trim the sails, guests are relatively pampered. The crew clean the cabins and make the beds every day. They also cook, maintain the ship, and swab the decks. If you wish, you can help them hoist the sails and keep the ship on course.

FOOD & DRINK

Guests are given two choices for meals: eat them or not. Exaggerations aside, think of it as going to a restaurant for the atmosphere and view instead of the food. Selection is limited, but food is hearty and acceptable. Don't come here expecting cruise line food and you won't be disappointed. Breakfast selections include eggs, French toast, fruit, cereal, and juices. You will rarely see lunches except for the island picnics or buffets on the top of a mountain. Dinner usually consists of soup, a main course, vegetables, and dessert.

All guests receive two complimentary drinks a day, plus wine at dinner. Swizzles, made with rum, fruit juice, and grenadine, are served at sundown and at midnight. Throughout the day, a bartender sells mixed drinks and sodas. Beverages are paid for with a "drinker's doubloon," a voucher available from the purser. Hard-core drinkers can get up early and help themselves to free Bloody Marys and pastries.

STAFFING & SERVICE

The company organizes the trips very well. The brochures accurately describe the nature of the voyage, what you need to pack, and what to expect. The deckhands keep everything shipshape, provide friendly service, and occasionally let the guests beat them in volleyball.

PRIVACY & RELAXATION

You set your own pace. Although most people leave the ship during the day, you don't have to. In fact, the ship is at its quietest at midday, making it perfect for lazy tanning. The rooms below deck are quieter than those above. All of the rooms lock from the inside, but for fire protection none lock from the outside. There is usually no problem with theft, but the captain has a small safe for valuables.

The ship is not large for the number of people that it carries. If privacy is your goal, choose an itinerary that goes to the smaller islands.

SHOPPING

The Caribbean has some excellent shopping opportunities. You can usually find good buys on gold jewlery, watches, camera equipment, stereo equipment, perfumes, and china. Be sure to check the prices at home before you leave to ensure really getting a bargain. Partygoers might want to try the fabled Saba Spice rum.

HONEYMOONERS

If you have the personality to like Windjammer, and you don't have visions of heart-shaped tubs or a stable of servants, you might find Windjammer to be perfect. Passengers experience the cruise as a group. The close quarters and unguided island drop-offs lead to fast friendships. Extroverts seem to have the best time.

Windjammer won't give you a bottle of champagne, a slice of cake, or a honeymooners' party, although you probably will find a fair number of other couples on their honeymoons. A comment by a young bride summed up the feelings of many honeymooning couples: "We've been living together for a couple of years. We don't need to be alone 24 hours a day. After the hassle of the wedding, we wanted a vacation where we could cut loose and have some fun."

The *Flying Cloud* offers the "ultimate" honeymoon cabin. The roomy stateroom combines two converted dorm rooms. It sports a four-poster canopy double bed, private bath with gold fixtures, a small refrigerator, wallpaper, carpeting, and a real window instead of a porthole. But wait, there's more. . . . It also has a dumbwaiter going from the room to the bar. Now how much would you pay? All of this can be yours for only $950 per person for a six-day trip.

SINGLES

The atmosphere lends itself to all guests (married, single, and various combinations of the two) meeting in a festive party environment. Windjammer cruises spark quite a few shipboard romances. Management says, "You'd be surprised how many passengers meet on board and then call back for a honeymoon trip."

CHILD APPEAL

Kids must be at least seven years old. There are no special children's activities or baby-sitting services. Frequently kids get special attention from the crew members, who teach them knots and other sailing lore. Families might enjoy taking this cruise together. Independent teens may feel somewhat left out.

NUTS & BOLTS

BOOKING & CONTACT INFORMATION

Windjammer Barefoot Cruises
P.O. Box 120
Miami, Beach, FL 33119-0120
301-327-2602 (reservations)
305-672-6453 (management)
800-327-2601 (U.S.)
800-432-3364 (FL)
800-233-2603 (Canada)

CURRENCY: Every island accepts U.S. dollars. Many of the countries will also take Eastern Caribbean units, Bee Wees (British West Indian dollars), and French francs. Bring lots of small bills so you won't have to take change in the local currency. Otherwise, bring traveler's checks, also in small denominations.

CUSTOMS/DUTY: You face local customs upon returning.

DEPOSITS/REFUNDS: Deposits for a cruise are $250 per person to hold a space on the ship and $100 for airplane space. This amount must be paid within 10 days of making your reservation. The final payment is due 45 days before sailing. If you make a reservation for a trip less than 30 days ahead, full payment is due immediately; there is an additional $25 charge for quick handling.

Written cancellations must be received 45 days or more before your sailing date. Windjammer holds $35 per person per cruise in penalty. The rest of the cruise money comes back in credit for a future cruise. If you also wish to cancel airfare purchased through Windjammer you will pay an additional penalty of $35 per person. The rest of the airfare money is returned to you. If you cancel less than 45 days from sailing date, you forfeit the entire cruise. The airfare still comes back less the $35 fee.

Windjammer offers cancellation insurance through Cigna Insurance. It costs $38 per person for a six-day cruise and $58 per person for a thirteen-day trip. The insurance is only for fully paid passengers. It covers cancellations for illness and interrupted travel plans due to airline problems. You are not covered if you simply change your mind.

ELECTRICITY: 110 volts 60 cycles; same as in the United States.

HANDICAP ACCESSIBILITY: Handicapped passengers have been ingenious in the past, and it has paid off. You must be at least semi-mobile in order to negotiate the inside stairs and climb the stationary ladder for the skiff. There is no wheelchair access.

LANGUAGES: English will do. On St. Barts a French translator is sometimes needed.

PACKING: Leave your fancy duds at home. You'll spend most of your time wearing nothing more than your bathing suit. The only concession to civility you must make is to wear a clean shirt at dinner.

RELIGIOUS SERVICES: You won't be aboard on a Sunday, unless you are taking a 13-day cruise or are doing back-to-back trips. There is no chaplain aboard.

RESERVATION SCHEDULE: It's best to book at least six months in advance, particularly for the Admiral's Suites. Christmas and New Year's trips begin to fill up a year in advance. As with most all-inclusives, the more particular you are about your accommodations, the sooner you should make your reservations.

SIZE: 197 to 282 feet.

NUMBER OF CABINS: Varies.

MAXIMUM NUMBER OF GUESTS: 66 to 126 passengers.

NUMBER OF EMPLOYEES: 26 to 44.

Cost Worksheet

	Year-Round Prices
Accommodations 6 days[1] (Cabins prices are the same all year.)	$675–$850 per person
Food	incl.
Drinks (some included)	
Departure tax	
Sailing tax	
Sports	N/A
Airfare	Windjammer offers package deals at a discount from most major U.S. and Canadian cities
Sightseeing	
Tips	Recommended tip is $35 per passenger. Tips are split among the crew.
Additional sports	
Souvenirs[2]	
Essential Extras[3]	

[1] Premium for Single Person: Whatever the per person cabin rate is plus 75 percent.

[2] Offered for extra charge: The gift shop has souvenirs and sundries.

[3] Essential extras: Sailing and departure taxes vary according to the country your cruise ends in. If you are in Antigua for more than 24 hours you must pay a $6 (U.S. currency, as are all taxes given here) departure tax. Grenada has similar rules but the tax is $10. In the British Virgin Islands the tax is $5 by plane and $4 by boat. The British Virgin Islands also charges a sailing tax on all yachts. This varies with the season but is approximately $10. It must be paid to the purser before departure.

VACCINATION REQUIREMENTS: None.

VISA/PASSPORT REQUIREMENTS: For all cruises a passport is the best proof of citizenship. A birth certificate or voter's registration card *and* a photo ID such as a driver's license will also be accepted in most cases. When boarding the ship all passengers must give the ship's purser their passports and immigration cards for daily immigration and customs clearances. The documents will be returned at the end of the cruise. The *Amazing Grace* and *Mandalay* absolutely require passports.

SPENDING MONEY: $200–$250 will leave you money for shopping. The ship does not take credit cards, except in the Sea Chest gift shop.

YACHT
CHARTERING
SERVICES

INTRODUCTION

Unlike the resort feel of a cruise ship, yacht charters give an up-close, personal sailing experience. When you charter a craft, you move under your own power and at your own pace. Instead of visiting deep-water harbors—often tourist traps—you can anchor in dozens of secluded bays. You can also explore the land at your leisure.

Go with friends you can live with. Most of the boats have compact living quarters. These trips present the perfect way to get to know your buddies well through long discussions and shared experiences. If someone absolutely drives you nuts or talks your ear off, however, your ship may experience a mysterious "man overboard." Rumor has it that sword fights on the gangplanks originated because of matters more trivial than an annoying twitch . . . after seven days at sea.

The price per person depends on how many mates you pack into your boat. The maximum number of guests given here usually includes use of full bunks in the galley and other small spaces. In practice, people often abandon those spaces for the fun of sleeping on deck. Couples looking for a romantic vacation will probably want to limit the number of pairs to the number of cabins.

Charter yachts range in size from relatively small, 30-foot sloops to larger, 60-foot vessels. Prices vary according to the size of the boat, its condition, the time of year, food stocks, and additional sports equipment.

Charters come in two types: crewed and bareboat. If you choose a crewed boat, the price frequently includes meals and drinks, but bareboats can also be stocked with full provisions.

The experience on a crewed charter differs somewhat from that on a bareboat one. Choose a crewed charter package for an all-play sailing vacation. The boats tend to be a bit larger and more luxurious. The crew attends to all your needs from sailing the vessel to preparing your meals and mixing your drinks. Most important, they also do the dishes (keeping your boat from becoming "crude"). They know the waters and the islands so you get tour guides in the package as well. Crews are trained to be around when you need them and to be tactfully "absent" during private moments. Charter companies require their crews to have bona fide sailing credentials and a long résumé of experience. The crew will assist you as much as you want. If you are a novice, your captain takes care of all the sailing so you can relax. If you wish, many captains will teach you to sail while underway. For intermediate sailors, not quite comfortable on their own, the crew can serve as consultants.

Many experienced sailors choose bareboat charters. This lets you explore the seas. The term *bareboat* does not mean an empty boat; shipboard facilities often compare favorably to crewed boats. The difference is that you and your friends serve as the only crew. Sailing alone creates more responsibility, but also has advantages: a lower price, more room for passengers, and complete privacy. Groceries, liquor, and sports equipment can usually be included for an additional charge.

Before you can sail away on your own, you must prove that you have the experience to handle the boat of your choice. This precaution protects you from your ego and also assures the boat owner that the craft sails in competent hands. To charter a boat, you must know more than the difference between a jib and a spinnaker—you need to know how to use them and how they affect the boat. In addition to basic skippering, you should know how to read charts and translate the information into navigation, be able to anchor or moor the boat, and feel comfortable handling inclement weather. Previous charter trips or skippering time on slightly smaller boats should be enough to qualify you. Charter trips in the Virgin Islands require less experience than do charters in the Bahamas and Grenadines, where the seas are rougher and the passages longer between islands.

When you book a charter you will be asked to specify the following: type of boat, dates of arrival and departure, number of people, preference for crewed or bareboat (if the company offers both), and necessary provision requirements.

Companies usually offer three types of provision packages. In the first type, you supply everything yourself and get specifically what you want and need for the trip. This option is probably the best course if you have special dietary needs or plan to eat on shore frequently. Keep in mind, however, that grocery stores on the islands have limited selections and are more expensive than mainland markets. On the smaller islands, the grocery stores resemble Moscow markets after the first 5,000 people in line have raided the shelves.

The second option, a fully provisioned boat, comes with a complete food-and-staples package. This plan saves you the hassle of shopping. Unless you bring things from home, you probably won't beat the volume discount purchases of the charter company. Most charter companies will stock the boat with fresh meats and vegetables. Be sure to check the menu before placing an order. Custom menus are sometimes available.

The third option is a hybrid of the first two. The charter company provides a starter kit. You fill the gaps with your own menus. Some companies offer half-day provisions so you can eat out at night.

Base your meal plan decision on how much effort you are willing to put into shopping, your time limitations, and the pickiness of your eating habits. If you depend on the small island grocery stores, your crew may discover how cannibalism started.

RATINGS: Wide variations among boats, food plans, itineraries, and options make rating yacht charting services practically impossible. The narrative introduction at the beginning of each chapter should give you the objective and subjective information necessary to decide whether to choose this type of vacation. It should also give you a head start toward choosing a yacht chartering company.

PACKING: Regardless of the itinerary you choose, island supplies are scarce. Pack as if you were going camping. You will want comfortable, casual clothes for sailing and swimming. A windbreaker protects you against wind and rain; deck shoes keep you from slipping after you've swabbed the deck. Many boats include snorkeling gear, but bring some if yours doesn't. Scuba divers have the option of bringing scuba gear; most dive boats will gladly rent equipment, but at a dear price. Binoculars make touristing more enjoyable and navigation easier. Your personal kit should include all medications and bug repellent. Be sure to pack everything in collapsible bags. Hard suitcases are difficult to store in the small storage spaces provided.

DRUGS: Drug smuggling has become a fact of life throughout the Caribbean. Many people use pleasure craft to smuggle drugs surreptitiously. Don't be surprised if customs officials search your boat. Also avoid lifting any unmarked buoys. A favorite method of smuggling drugs, they are watched constantly. The owners get very annoyed when people interfere with their trade. Also, they often contain explosive devices.

SAILING AREAS

THE BAHAMAS: The Bahamas have been a popular sailing destination since Columbus made his first landfall in the New World, reportedly at San Salvador. Now you too can launch an exploration party without having to pawn your jewels to fund it.

Several factors make sailing the Bahamas more difficult than cruising United States coastal waters. Markers and beacons are often scattered. You may require multiple bearings to get an accurate location fix. (This also makes it difficult to locate wrecks for diving.)

Sailing the Bahamas requires two types of piloting. First is straightforward open-water navigation across the channels and sounds separating the islands. The second type involves reading the shallow waters close to shore. Most cruising guides have helpful tips on deciphering the varying shades of blue and green water to locate coral heads and dangerous shoals. Average cays can be seen four to five miles in the distance. Higher islands can be located farther off. Winter winds are inconsistent. Summer winds blow predominantly from the east. Strong currents run in the narrow passages between cays.

All vessels entering Bahamian waters must clear customs at one of the dozen ports of entry. United States and Canadian citizens need only proof of citizenship, meaning a passport, birth certificate, or voter's registration card. Cruising permits, picked up on arrival, must stay with the boat and be returned upon departing from the Bahamas.

THE U.S. AND BRITISH VIRGIN ISLANDS: Protected waters, innumerable anchorages, and consistent easterly trade winds make Virgin Islands sailing among the best in the world. Located 60 miles east of Puerto Rico, the Virgin Islands have lured sailors for centuries. Hundreds of years ago pirates used the protected coves as strongholds for their forays in the Caribbean. Today you can safely sail Drake's Passage, the inside route between the islands, enjoying the sea and sand by day and safe anchorages by night.

Most sailing takes place in the 45-miles-long-by-15-miles-wide area that stretches from St. Thomas in the east to Anegada in the west. You can navigate predominantly by sight, since land is always close by and there are few natural hazards. Reefs and shoals are easily seen when the sun is overhead. The islands are close enough to allow use of visual reference points for finding locations. You should not need to use navigation instruments. Ideal sailing conditions do not, however, substitute for proper equipment and caution.

Distances between the islands are so short that it's possible to visit several spots in a single day, but you'll probably want to slow the pace and savor each one. Virgin Islands highlights include the baths on Virgin Gorda, where giant granite boulders meet the sea, forming caves and secluded swimming holes. Norman Island's sea caves and the "bight" inspired Robert Louis Stevenson's famous novel *Treasure Island*. Nature and history buffs will love the Virgin Islands' National Park on St. John, where old sugar plantations lie half hidden in the jungle growth. Buck Island off St. Croix has such spectacular reef life that it has been declared an underwater national monument.

Since the Virgin Islands are both American and British, you will be crossing international boundaries in your sails. It is mandatory that you clear customs in both territories upon entering *and* leaving. Failure to do so may result in serious fines or the loss of your boat. At the time of clearance, the skipper should bring the boat's papers and previous customs clearances. All passengers must be present with proper identification. To clear customs, U.S. and Canadian citizens may use a passport, birth certificate, or voter's registration card. All other nationalities need a passport.

THE LEEWARD ISLANDS: Located approximately 70 miles east of the Virgin Islands, the Leeward Islands is another popular sailing ground. With seven principal islands and six separate nationalities, the Leeward Islands deliver an assortment of sailing conditions and convivial accommodations ashore. The warm weather, consistent winds, and minimum rainfall make for pleasant vacations.

Unlike the protected waters of the Virgin Islands, the seas between these islands are wide open-water passages. While rich in tropical beauty, the Leeward Islands demand significant sailing experience and an ability to deal with a variety of sea and weather conditions. Navigation between the more distant islands requires the use of charts and equipment. You can "eyeball" it on short hops and around the coasts. However, visual navigation should be used only as a backup for chart reading, because underwater hazards are better marked on charts than on the hull of your boat.

The boundaries of the Leeward Islands are marked by Anguilla on the north, Saba to the west, and Nevis on the southeast. Between them are Statia, St. Barts, St. Martin, and several smaller islands. Each island offers distinctive flavors and cultural experiences. St. Martin, where you'll probably pick up your charter yacht, is worth visiting before rushing off to the outlying islands. The half-French, half-Dutch island (the Dutch half is spelled Sint Maarten) blends tourist-oriented activities with remote spots. The Dutch port of Phillipsburg launches most of the cruise ships and has most of the shopping, while the French side contains most of the pristine beaches. Scuba divers and snorkelers will want to explore Oranje Bay on Statia, where cannons, coins, and coral lie submerged amidst sunken ships and abandoned fortifications. British Anguilla remains undeveloped, with miles of uninhabited beaches and unspoiled reefs.

Because several nationalities occupy the Leeward Islands, different rules and regulations apply. For short visits to all of the islands except St. Barts, Americans and Canadians need only proof of citizenship and onward transportation. St. Barts, a French island, requires a passport for all visitors. Cruising charges and departure taxes vary with each island. Check with your charter company for more information.

THE WINDWARD ISLANDS: The Windward Islands form a 200-mile arc of low-lying cays and steep, mountainous islands in the southern Caribbean. Beginning with French Martinique in the north, and ending with Grenada in the south, the island chain offers an assortment of culture, topography, and adventure. All the islands are independent, unspoiled by large development, and relatively untouched by tourism. Local residents are friendly, and the sailing is superb.

Blue water passages and day sails in open water separate the

Grenadines. The north-south oreintation of the islands and the eastern trade winds make sailing easy. Since land is never far off, you can navigate predominantly by sight. Mild tides and near-perfect weather add even more pleasure to a sailing vacation.

The big islands of Martinique, St. Lucia, St. Vincent, and Grenada attract many sailors. These wet islands feature lush interior rain forests and secure harbors beneath steep dramatic headlands, such as St. Lucia's volcanic pitons. Smaller islands such as the Tobago Cays are uninhabited atolls with empty beaches, clear clean waters, and ideal snorkeling.

The islands are independent and they take their sovereignty seriously. Standard customs regulations apply. Passports are best, but U.S. and Canadian citizens may get by with birth certificates, or voter's registration cards and a driver's license. You must also have proof of outgoing transportation such as the yacht charter or a plane ticket.

Yacht charters are also available in the Mediterranean, South Pacific, and off the coast of western Mexico. For more information on yacht charters in these areas contact the area tourism boards.

THE MOORINGS, LTD.

VITAL FEATURES

Type of vacation: **Yacht charter**
Target market: **Vacation sailors**
Location: **Virgin Islands, St. Martin, St. Lucia, Mexico, Tahiti, Tonga, Mediterranean**
All-inclusive cost per week: **Crewed charters begin at $1,099 per person for a party of 4 (summer) and $1,302 (winter). Weekly bareboat prices begin at $420 per person in 4-person group (summer), $707 (winter), including provisions, plus airfare.**

THE REAL STORY

Whether you want to sail the Grenadines or the Gulf of Mexico, the Turkish coast or the Tahitian islands, the Moorings provides sailing yachts and support services. One of the oldest charter companies in business, the Moorings began operations in the British Virgin Islands and now operates bases halfway around the world. The Moorings's reputation hinges on quality and dependability; its services provide an industry benchmark. The company offers both crewed and bareboat charters. Discounted airfares are available through the Moorings' accredited travel agency, Mariner International Travel.

BASES OF OPERATION

The Moorings maintains more bases than any other charter company we have reviewed. Its cruising areas are listed below (home ports are in parentheses).

Caribbean:
The Virgin Islands (Roadtown, Tortola)
The Leeward Islands (Anse Marcel, St. Martin)
The Grenadines (Marigot Bay, St. Lucia)

Mexico:
Sea of Cortez (Puerto Escondido, Baja California)

Polynesia:
Tonga (Neiafu, Vava'u)
Tahiti (Uturoa, Raiatea)

The Mediterranean:
The Saronic Islands and Peloponnesian Coast (Athens, Greece)
The Dodecanese Islands (Rhodes, Greece)

The Ionian Islands (Corfu, Greece)
Adriatic Sea (Trogir, Yugoslavia)

THE BOATS

The Moorings keeps all its yachts clean and well maintained. It replaces the boats every two to three years to keep the fleet up-to-date and in good condition.

CREWED YACHTS

Moorings 51—up to 3 couples and crew.
Moorings 60—up to 9 guests plus crew.
Gulfstar 60—up to 3 couples and crew of 3.

BAREBOATS

Moorings 51—up to 4 couples.
Moorings 500—up to 10 passengers.
The Moorings 37—up to 2 couples.
Endeavour 37—up to 2 couples.
Moorings 43—up to 6 people.
Moorings 432—up to 7 passengers.
Oceanis 390—up to 6 passengers.
Oceanis 430—up to 8 passengers.
Moorings 370—the only motor yacht in the fleet. Up to 8 passengers.

The Mediterranean is handled by the Moorings's sister company, Kavos. All models are available in the following locations: **Athens, Corfu, Rhodes, Gocek,** and **Trogir.** Kavos does not offer full crews, but it does hire out skippers.

Kavos 32—carries 2 to 3 couples.
Kavos 35—holds 3 to 4 couples.
Kavos 40—accommodates up to 4 couples.
Kavos 43—takes 8 to 10 passengers.
Kavos 50—carries up to 5 couples.

INCLUDED

Accommodations
Activities
Captain and crew (depending on package)
Charter essentials (for example, cruising guides, navigation equipment, radio)

Galley & cooking equipment
Provisions (depending on package)
Sports
Taxes (extra, but paid in advance)
Transfer to and from airport

ACTIVITIES, SPORTS, & EXCURSIONS

Sailing
Scuba (extra)
Snorkeling (equipment not
    included in
    Mediterranean)

Sunbathing
Swimming (ocean)
Windsurfing (included with
    crewed yachts, extra for
    bareboats)

ITINERARY & DAILY SCHEDULE

When you charter a yacht, it is yours to sail where you wish. The Moorings suggests an itinerary that allows you to hit the highlights of your chosen sailing area; you can follow it or not at your discretion. The average Caribbean charter lasts seven days, and Pacific charters tend to be slightly longer. Bareboat charters must last a minimum of five days; crewed trips have a three-day minimum. All charters begin and end at noon.

FOOD & DRINK

We did not sample the Moorings' food, but it claims to supply fresh fruit, vegetables, and meats. When you confirm your reservations, you will receive an order form specifying what is available and at what cost. All Moorings meal plans allow you to swap items in your packages. For instance, if you want to eat out more often, you can swap dinner foods for more hors d'oeuvres and snacks. Vegetarians can trade the meats for more fruits and vegetables. Beverages cost extra. The price of a crewed yacht includes the cost of full provisioning. If you fill out the food-and-liquor preference sheet in advance, the items will be waiting when you arrive. For your money you get all breakfasts, lunches, hors d'oeuvres, and all evening meals except two, which you eat ashore. Don't worry about deciding which meals to eat out, you can decide while under way.

Bareboat charters have two provisioning options. First, you can supply everything yourself by shopping in town or at the Moorings' commissary. Another twist on this option is to save time and hassles by purchasing a charter starter kit that includes basic items necessary for any cruise, such as condiments, toilet paper, and soap. This way you shop only for the meals you want to prepare. The second option, a split-provisioning package, gives you a chance to eat ashore. In addition to the charter starter kit, the Moorings provides all breakfasts, lunches, and hors d'oeuvres for the week, plus four dinners. For the remaining three evening meals, you can dine ashore and sample local specialties.

In Tahiti, Tonga, and Mexico, bareboat charters should get full provisions to make up for the lack of restaurants. In the Mediterranean no cooks or provision plans are available, but open-air markets and restaurants are plentiful.

STAFFING & SERVICE

The charter information packages and cruising guides provide a wealth of information about your vacation. The front office staff and base operations managers provide five-star service. They are friendly, courteous, kind, and help old ladies across the street. We did not deal with the charter crews, but if they are up to the Moorings' standards, you should be in for a great trip.

SPECIAL PROGRAMS & PACKAGES

The Moorings Offshore Sailing School teaches landlubbers and small-boat sailors how to handle 37-to-51-foot yachts. The weeklong course brings students of all ages up to bareboat skipper competency. The course balances instruction with free time, and ends with an overnight solo trip. Upon successful completion, you are ready to charter a yacht on your own.

Sail-and-drive packages combine adventures above and below the waterline. For a week you live on a Moorings yacht and rendezvous with an Underwater Safaris drive boat for daily lessons, guided dives, and more. At the end of the day you meet the rest of your party at a prearranged destination. (Underwater Safaris can be contacted at 809-494-3235 or 494-3965.)

Shore-and-sail packages provide four nights ashore at either of the Moorings's resorts (Tortola or St. Lucia) and three nights on a crewed yacht with full provisions. Shore-and-dive packages are available for groups of six or larger.

The Moorings Commodores' Club rewards repeat customers. Beginning with your fifth charter, bareboat or crewed, your cruises cost 15 percent less. Automatic membership also includes a free "welcome to the club" dinner for the entire party.

NUTS & BOLTS

BOOKING & CONTACT INFORMATION

The Moorings, Ltd.
Suite 402
1305 U.S. Route 19 South
Clearwater, FL 34624
800-535-7289
813-535-1446

DEPOSITS/REFUNDS: Reservations are confirmed upon receipt of a 25 percent deposit. Another 25 percent deposit is due 90 days before departure, with the remaining 50 percent due 30 days prior to the charter date. After receiving the first 25 percent deposit, the Moorings sends out a charter information pack including verification of date, equipment, and payment schedule.

Cancellation refunds require a written request. For a full refund, less a $100 cancellation fee, the request must be received 90 days prior to departure. No refund will be returned for cancellations under 90 days. The Moorings offers cancellation insurance to cover this contingency.

Security deposits on the yachts are also required. Two plans are available. A nonrefundable insurance premium of $10 a day covers the charter for all liability or damage over $50. A $500 refundable insurance premium covers the charter for all liabilities. Security deposits in the Mediterranean differ, so check with the company.

ELECTRICITY: 110 volts 60 cycles.

HANDICAP ACCESSIBILITY: Yachts are not equipped for wheelchair access. For people who get about with some difficulty, the Moorings recommends the 432 model, which features molded steps in the transom for easier access.

LANGUAGE: All employees speak English.

RESERVATION SCHEDULE: Reservations are best made a year in advance, particularly during holidays and spring break. The larger

---

Cost Worksheet

	Cost per person per week	
Crewed Charters	Winter	Summer
Moorings 60	$1,337–$3,164	$1,015–$2,779
Gulfstar 60	same	same
Moorings 51	$980–$2,541	$840–$2,191

Extra[2]

	Cost per boat per week	
Bare Boats	Winter	Summer
Moorings 51	$3,997	$2,513
Moorings 432	$3,241	$1,785
Moorings 37	$2,380	$1,232

[1] Prices given are for the Caribbean. They are similar to those for Mexico, Polynesia, and the Mediterranean.
[2] Extra: Skipper, $71 or $76 per day including food; cook, $56 or $66 per day including food; split provisioning, $16 per person per day; cruising tax; gratuity for crew; insurance.

boats sell out almost a year in advance all year round. June and September are the slowest months, but they too fill up quickly.

VACCINATION REQUIREMENTS: None.

VISA/PASSPORT REQUIREMENTS

The Virgin Islands: Passports recommended. Proof of citizenship acceptable for U.S. and Canadian citizens.

St. Martin, St. Lucia, and Tahiti: Passport and French visa. Visas are obtainable upon arrival.

Mexico: Proof of citizenship and a tourist card. Passports are recommended.

Greece, Turkey, and Tonga: Passports only.

Yugoslavia: Passports and visas. Visas are available at point of entry.

STEVENS YACHTS

VITAL FEATURES

Type of vacation: **Yacht charters**
Target market: **Great weather sailors**
Location: **Tortola, British Virgin Islands, St. Lucia, Antigua**
All-inclusive cost per week: **$150 plus airfare**

THE REAL STORY

To find Stevens Yachts on Tortola you must go several miles down the road, heading away from the island's main marina. Stevens Yachts is quietly tucked away from the hustle and bustle at the west end. The bay is quiet, the atmosphere peaceful. The anchorage is one of the best protected on the island. Of course, you won't spend your sailing vacation on a mooring, but the initial serenity soothes your travel-weary nerves and allows you to relax, anticipating a "hassle-free" vacation.

The remote location of Stevens Yachts is just one indication that it's not your average "Joe" charter company. The fact that all the boat slips are empty during the winter months is proof that they are doing something right at Stevens.

Stevens Yachts offers complete all-inclusive vacations on water. This trip is for you if you have always wanted to charter a yacht but thought it would require too much energy. The crew will sail your vessel, serve you drinks, and present you with three meals a day.

BASES OF OPERATION

Stevens Yachts operates out of Tortola, St. Lucia, and Antigua.

THE BOATS

The staff at Stevens Yachts shower the vessels with tender loving care. The staff are meticulous about maintaining and caring for the fleet. All crewed yachts have separate crew quarters. They are equipped with snorkeling equipment, Windsurfers, and dinghy with outboard. Below is a list of the many boats available.

CREWED YACHTS

Spirit of Carib: 80-foot Camper and Nicholson cutter. Maximum number of guests: 2. The *Spirit of Carib* was built in 1912 and shipwrights have restored her, adding technology to her Edwardian splendor. They installed a water maker, an ice maker, a refrigerator, video equipment, snorkeling gear, Windsurfers, and scuba equipment. Available only in the Grenadines.

Imagine: 66-foot custom ketch. Maximum number of guests: 6. Just "imagine" sitting at a huge dinner table laden with delectable food. The walls of the main galley are rich mahogany and music is softly piped through a high-tech stereo system. Comfortable lounge chairs are scattered around the deck, and the three snug staterooms invite you to effortless sleep. Available in the Grenadines only.

Eclipse: 53 foot ketch. Maximum number of guests: 4. This is the perfect boat for two couples. There are two double staterooms, each with its own head and shower. The *Eclipse* is fully equipped with snorkeling equipment, scuba equipment, and a Windsurfer.

Indio Rosa: 52-foot sloop. Maximum number of guests: 4. This yacht is luxurious and fast, traveling at up to 12 knots. There are two separate double staterooms, each with its own head.

Anne-Marie II: 47-foot cutter; *La Gitane:* 47-foot cutter. Maximum number of guests: 4. These yachts are perfect all-around cruisers. They are available fully crewed, as well as bareboat, out of either Tortola or St. Lucia.

Locura: Derrfoot 72. Maximum number of guests: 6. Locura is one of the fastest offshore cruising ketches. It has the freedom to sail anywhere between St. Thomas and Grenada, offering the ultimate yachting vacation. The spacious quarters and main salon make the trip luxurious. It is equipped with full scuba equipment, including an air compressor to refill the tanks.

BAREBOATS

St. Lucia, Windward Islands, Leeward Islands: Stevens Custom 47, Peterson 44, Moody 422.

Tortola, British Virgin Islands: Stevens Custom 47, Stevens Custom 40, Moody 422.

INCLUDED IN CREWED CHARTERS

Accommodations
Activities
Captain and crew
Charter essentials (cruising guides, navigation equipment, radio, etc.)
Cruising permits

Custom clearance fees
Dinghy
Fuel
Galley & cooking equipment
Provisions (food and reasonable amounts of beer, wine, and liquor)
Sports

INCLUDED IN BAREBOAT CHARTERS

Accommodations
Barbecue

Charter essentials (cruising guides, etc.)

Dinghy   Linens
Galley ware   Sports

ACTIVITIES, SPORTS, & EXCURSIONS

Sailing   Swimming (ocean)
Scuba   Windsurfing (included with
Snorkeling   crewed yachts, extra for
Sunbathing   bareboats)

ITINERARY & DAILY SCHEDULE

You plan your own itinerary with the help of the skipper. You may choose a route anywhere between St. Thomas and Grenada. The itineraries are flexible, allowing for a whimsical trip to ... "that beautiful island over there."

You can do as little or as much as you like on the trip. Learn windsurfing. Snorkel in crystal-clear waters. Troll for deep fare. Or explore the islands.

NUTS & BOLTS

BOOKING & CONTACT INFORMATION: Travel arrangements can be made directly or through a travel agent. Contact the company at:

Stevens Yachts
50 Water Street
South Norwalk, CT 06854
800-638-7044
203-866-8989

DEPOSITS/REFUNDS: A deposit of 50 percent of the total cost is required to confirm a reservation. If you cancel 60 days before departure you will be charged a $200 service charge. After 60 days Stevens Yachts will retain your deposit, and if the yacht is rebooked your deposit will be returned and you will be charged only the $200 service charge.

ELECTRICITY: 110 volt 60 cycles; same as in the United States.

HANDICAP ACCESSIBILITY: None.

LANGUAGE: All employees speak English.

RESERVATION SCHEDULE: You should reserve a yacht four to six months in advance during the winter months and three to four months ahead during the summer.

VACCINATION REQUIREMENTS: None.

VISA/PASSPORT REQUIREMENTS: In the Virgin Islands passports are recommended. Proof of citizenship is acceptable for U.S. and Canadian citizens.

Cost Worksheet

Crewed Charters	Cost per person per week[1]	
	Winter	Summer
Eclipse	$1,313–$2,415	$1,040–$1,869
Anne Marie II	$1,155–$2,100	$910–$1,593
La Gitane	$1,155–$2,100	$910–$1,593

[1] Extra: 10% gratuity for crew

Bare Boats	Cost per boat per week[1]	
	Winter	Summer
Stevens 47	$3,500	$2,394
Stevens 44	$2,450	$1,792
Stevens 42	$2,875	$1,890
Stevens 40	$2,765	$1,715

[1] Extra: Skipper/cook, $70 (Tortola), $60 (St. Lucia), daily rate including food; split provisioning, $15 per person per day; full provisioning, $22 per person per day; cruising tax, $50–$100, per person per day in British Virgin Islands; fuel; insurance, $1,000 (refundable deposit); gratuity for crew.

LAND TOUR

BRAZILIAN SCUBA AND LAND TOURS

VITAL FEATURES

Type of vacation: **Land-based scuba and sight-seeing tours**
Target market: **Scuba divers and their nondiving travel partners**
Location: **Brazil, including Rio de Janeiro, Fortaleza, Cabo Frio, and Bay of Dolphins**
All-inclusive cost per week incl. airfare: **Fortaleza, $1,649 from Miami, $1,849 from L.A.; Cabo Frio, $1,397 from N.Y., $1,597 from L.A.; Bay of Dolphins, $1,400 from N.Y., $1,600 from L.A.**

RATINGS

Value: 💲💲💲💲💲

Fun quotient: ☂ ☂ ☂ ☂

Honeymoon suitability: ♥♥♥

Singles meeting ground: 👤👤

Child appeal: Not applicable

Management professionalism: ☎ ☎ ☎ ☎

Service: 💡💡💡💡

Food: 🦞🦞🦞🦞

THE REAL STORY

Dive Brazil? You haven't seen T-shirts because Brazilian dive sites rest unspoiled and virtually unexplored. Tour Brazil? Ah, Rio! Just the name conjures up romantic images of exotic people and mysterious Amazonian lands. Divers can now be among the first to probe the long, serpentine coast of a land whose waters are just beginning to welcome divers. After an ocean splash, the charms of Rio and the playgrounds of wealthy Latins welcome voyagers to a world that few Americans know.

Scuba diving remains in its embryonic stages in Brazil. People who come here to dive must be adventurous and eager to explore wrecks that may not be well charted. Local dive masters—American trained with Yankee gear—regularly open new dive stations. Rewards for the adventurous diver can be unique experiences and treasures that might include an occasional gold coin. Your underwater slides and videos will draw attention because they will be unique; how many of your friends have been to Brazil?

The diver who picks Brazil is the same skier who eschews the well-groomed trails of Aspen for the thrill of helicopter skiing, risking uncertain conditions for the possibility of a run on virgin snow. Dive masters too have a fresh attitude, unjaded by lots of tourists.

Brazil, comprising half the landmass of South America, with 11,919 miles of coastline, provides a full spectrum of diving and snorkeling. Some sites differ from anything that you are likely to see elsewhere. Others offer the chance of a spectacular find on a wreck that may have been found only days before.

Most of Brazil lies just south of the equator, so the warm climate varies very little. Temperatures in Rio, for example, average a high of 84 degrees F. in January and dip to a low of 75 degrees in September. Brazil's Southern Hemispheric seasons are the reverse of North America's. November, its spring, brings the short rainy season. Avoid that month. In tropical Fortaleza, which lies close to the equator, the temperature remains constant year-round. Unfortunately, the seas become too choppy for diving from August through December. BSLT does not book tours during those months.

Our winter, starting in January, is the best time to go. Conditions should be good everywhere through July. The Brazilians celebrate *Carneval*, their contribution to partying, in March. More than the Amazon or the sea, Brazil's greatest natural resource lies in its warm people, a multiracial society of European, Asian, and African origin. The national language is Portuguese, and the favorite saying is *tudo ben*, meaning "everything is OK." Brazilians are extremely friendly and can't wait to tell you about their country. They like Americans without being overly jealous. Many have lived or traveled in the United States. They came back because they love Brazil, forsaking the wealth of the United States for a rich cultural life in their homeland. They ask nothing of you other than that you have a good time. In general, the people are not money motivated. The prevalent attitude at most resorts is "come party with us." Management projects a friendly, family atmosphere that does not demand that employees be servants. Their laid-back attitude is contagious when you talk to them, frustrating when you have to depend on them.

Visitors would be well advised to learn a little of their culture, their language, and the people. People will smile, and take you that extra mile—literally. For example, our bus driver took us on a detour so that we could see some of the scenery. The countryside is often so beautiful as to be shocking. The pastoral and rough landscape paints a table of green pastures dotted with white stucco and red Spanish-tiled houses. Rio excites visitors with its pulsating beat and its wide white beaches leading up to pastel buildings that seem etched on a backdrop of emerald and jade mountains.

At present, only one company, Brazilian Scuba and Land Tours, offers English-speaking guided scuba tours to Brazil. Reviewed are some of the destinations that its 6-to-16-day tours offer.

 Jason's Tips:

Any healthy adult diver or spouse should like this trip. On land, the drivers are maniacal, and trips on the country roads can rattle the bones. To enjoy this trip, you must be able to roll with the punches and laugh about it.

RIO: No trip to Brazil could be complete without a stay in Rio, a city that has often been described as the world's most beautiful. The city protrudes into the Atlantic, which surrounds it on three sides. Copacabana Beach is the most famous beach, but it is only one of the golden sand strips that define the center city's social life. Elegant shops, an outdoor "hippie market," gourmet restaurants, and spark-ling discos line the wide mosaic sidewalks along Atlantica Avenue. Shuttered buildings in pink, lime green, and aqua-blue play host to the world's jet-setters. When you encounter the "girl from Ipanema" on the beach, you can bet that she'll be dressed in one of Brazil's famous thong bikinis, alternately described as two dots and a dash or two Band-Aids and a cork. Men dress skimpily also. Rio ranks as one of the world's fashion capitals, but visitors don't need warm clothes, and even the best restaurants don't require a tie and jacket.

You may be tempted to party all night, but don't miss the morning dive boat because it offers one of the best views of the city. Sailing out of Rio, city buildings cut a ragged edge against the dark green mountains that jut up sharply from the shore. Rio does not offer world-class diving, but the scenic boat ride, coupled with the chance to get wet, makes it worth the trip. Eight new wrecks have been recently discovered off the coast of Rio, and new ones are found on a regular basis. The water becomes cold when you hit the thermocline. You'll need a full wet suit, including a hood.

FORTALEZA: Fortaleza offers tropical and drift diving at its best. Close to the equator, it is located well over 1,000 miles north of Rio and just south of Macau, where a major African oceanic current hits South America. The warm, crystalline waters cover the 30-to-40-mile-long continental shelf, which varies in depth from 60 to 160 feet.

One of the richest fishing grounds in the world, the waters teem with lobster, red snapper, octopus, angelfish, jewfish, squid, pompano, 40-foot grouper, parrot fish, and more. If you long to see sharks, Fortaleza has reefs where you are almost guaranteed to see five or six species of sharks. The dive sites here have just recently been discovered; most of the fish have not seen divers before. That makes for interesting encounters.

Fortaleza's tropical location sits almost directly under the sun year-round. This sunshine, combined with the clear waters, produces incredible luminosity, even at 100 feet. Bring your cameras because you can get pictures full of colors and curious fish.

A dive in Fortaleza can cover 3 to 5 miles, as divers follow a 2-to-4-knot current around coral heads and through schools of tropical fish. Swimming is hardly required, so exertion and air consumption are low. The water temperature remains in the low 80s, but the dives are long, so a thin wet suit is recommended.

Diving facilities are adequate but not fully commercialized. A 55-foot schooner equipped with a compressor and tanks takes 15 divers and 6 crew members, including 3 dive masters. Igor Materovsky, the local contact for BSLT, is building new facilities.

The diving boat returns adventurers to a town that resembles the Rio of 30 years ago. World-class restaurants, virgin beaches, nightlife, and hospitable people should make Fortaleza a major tourist destination. Fortunately, it has not found its way onto the tourist loop yet, making it a real undiscovered gem. Hurry!

CABO FRIO: Over 80 wrecks lie off the coast of Cabo Frio. Most of them have not been fully explored, so the pickings are pretty good. The water may not be the warmest or the clearest, but you will see more unusual things per dive than you will at most other places. Turtles, octopi, lavender eels, and giant starfish can often be seen in one dive. The village is located due east of Rio, just a few hours' ride by car.

ANGRAS DOS REIS: Angras dos Reis (Harbor of Kings) is a beautiful resort located just two hours south of Rio. The bus ride down gives visitors a good chance to see rural Brazil. The road, carved through red clay mountains and lush terrain, is lined with peasant houses and farms of palm trees and banana plants.

Angras is noted for its 365 islands in the bay, ranging from those too small to be inhabited to the Ilha Grande, with its many beach resorts on the lee side. The bayside water is protected and usually calm and clear, making it perfect for a scenic boat ride out to the dive sites.

The "Wall" provides the best diving here—as its rocky surface slopes down to the 40-foot bottom of the cove. The shallow and protected coves also make it ideal for snorkelers. These waters are inhabited by unusual marine life, including lavender sea urchins, large starfish, groupers, octopi, angelfish, crabs, and giant turtles.

The Hotel Fraje accommodates divers in complete comfort, with air-conditioned rooms, sparkling modern toilet facilities, and televisions. The natural-brick-and-beamed Spanish architecture provides the charm. A full-scale resort, the hotel offers horseback riding to a spectacular waterfall, windsurfing, chariot riding, golf, swimming, parasailing, and, of course, diving. The rooms are large, romantic, and overlook the sea, sandy beach, and palm trees. From your room you get the feeling that you are the only guest. Nightlife is mellow and tends to revolve around the bar. Most divers welcome the quiet after the daytime activities and the excitement of Rio.

FERNANDO DE NORONHA & THE BAY OF DOLPHINS: Fans of "Flipper" have a fantasy home in Brazil. Situated 200 miles off the coast of Brazil and 400 miles from Fortaleza (far north of Rio), the Fernando de Noronha Islands surround the Bay of Dolphins, a natural breeding ground for spinner dolphins, green sea turtles, booby birds, and other rare wildlife. Underwater schools of groupers, snappers, squirrel fish, and eagle rays occupy a sandy bottom with patches of coral, caves, and walls.

Scuba divers scare the wildlife, but the playful dolphins will allow snorkelers to come close and play. The clear, calm water and the plentiful, friendly sea life make this a natural place to take videos that probably could not be shot anywhere else in the world.

The Brazilian government has strictly limited the development of this small, rocky island, so naturalists must compete for the rare opportunity to visit this sanctuary. Brazilian Scuba and Land Tours can secure a few slots with advance notice. While nightlife does not exist on the island, this unique natural habitat offers a rare chance to photograph marine life in pristine surroundings. Serious naturalists will find it well worth the trip.

INCLUDED

Accommodations	Sports
Activities	Taxes
Airfare	Tips
Entertainment & dancing	Tours
Food	Transfer to and from airport

VALUE

Do not compare this to a charter trip in a cramped plane that drops you off in Rio. BSLT offers a true adventure package with fairly luxurious accommodations. It also uses Varig Airlines, whose fare takes the major chunk of your travel dollars. All told, these trips offer extraordinary value.

ACTIVITIES, SPORTS, & EXCURSIONS

ACTIVITIES: Vary with location.

SPORTS: On this trip, scuba rules the day. The diving at Fortaleza ranks with the best in the world. Apart from that, the water is not as warm or as clear as that at Bonaire or most of the Caribbean locations. You go on this trip for the total experience, underwater and on land. You will be one of the first to explore Brazilian diving. This is a tour for the tourist who likes to dive, or the diver who likes to tour. The person who insists on the guaranteed number of world-class dives may be disappointed. But there are enough other things to do that, no matter what the diving conditions are, you can have fun.

You probably will not have time for any other sports. The Hotel Fraje offers horseback riding, tennis, hiking, golf, and the like. Water sports abound in Rio, including jet skiing, parasailing, windsurfing, and sailing.

EXCURSIONS: BSLT includes a tour of Rio de Janeiro, including Sugarloaf Mountain, Corcovado (Christ on the Mount), and other sights in each of the tours.

ITINERARY & DAILY SCHEDULE

The trip to Fortaleza stays five nights in Fortaleza, then stops in Rio for two nights. This is the trip for those who come primarily to dive. The six-night Cabo Frio trip spends half of its nights in Rio de Janeiro. The Bay of Dolphins trip usually spends the whole week there.

We recommend taking the Fortaleza trip, then extending your trip a few days to really enjoy Rio de Janeiro.

NIGHTLIFE & ENTERTAINMENT

Brazilians love to party. *Carneval* dominates their life, and to a large extent, defines their culture. Rio comes alive at night. People pack the restaurants, sidewalk cafés, and discos. We suggest that you mix freely with the locals, who tend to be extremely friendly.

AESTHETICS & ENVIRONMENT

The natural environment of Brazil can best be described as alternatively spectacular, third-world, and cosmopolitan. BSLT chooses

Jason's Tips: ────────────────────●

The trip offerings change according to conditions and demand. Seven days and six nights makes for a short trip, and you will feel as if you have just scratched the surface of a giant country. A country as big as Brazil demands a larger stay. But don't expect to be able to see the whole country. It is as big as the continental United States. Manaus, a city in the heart of the Amazon, for example, takes five hours to reach by jet. If you want to visit that area, see if you can fly that direction on the way back, or save it for another trip. All you can realistically expect to see is the southeast of Brazil.

Unlike most charters, Varig Airlines, the national airline of Brazil, will usually allow you to extend your trip at no extra charge if you make arrangements in advance. A longer stay in Rio, trips to other dive sites, or a stop in Manaus makes the travel time worthwhile. Brazilian Scuba and Land Tours will help you make the air arrangements. Ask them or your travel agent to book the additional land portion.

hotels that are well-maintained and, for the most part, luxurious. Sometimes, as in the Bay of Dolphins, where there is only one hotel, you take what you can get. Luckily, that one has just been renovated.

FACILITIES

Bank	Safety-deposit box
Bars	Snack bar, grill
Beaches	Swimming pool
Disco	Tour guide
Gift shop	Water-sports center

ROOMS

The luxury level of the different hotels varies. Most are extremely charming and have all the modern conveniences, including maid service, porters, telephones, refrigerators in the room (you need this for the bottled water), and televisions (for whatever good shows in Portuguese will do you).

Varig Airlines deserves note for the extraordinary quality of its coach service. Except for the size of the seat, you would swear that you were in first-class. It offers an open bar, free headsets, great food, friendly efficient service, and hot cloth towels after the meals. Typically, a traveler dines on a shrimp cocktail, filet mignon, white wine, and a demitasse of Brazilian *café*. Needless to say, this far exceeds the quality of charter flights. It also adds about $200 to the price of the trip. But for an overnight trip (the best way to go to Brazil is to take the red-eye) it's probably worth it.

In sum, BSLT offers a luxurious adventure tour at a very reasonable price.

FOOD & DRINK

Different. High quality. Tasty. Worth trying. Brazilian food and drinks taste different than any other. Try a grilled meat restaurant where they slice high-quality skewered beef, veal, and pork on your plate until you beg them to stop. In general, they prepare food with sweet, aromatic spices. Much of it is baked and topped with sauces. Meals include plenty of tropical fruits, preserves, and unusual cheeses and dairy products. The coffee is delicious. Brazilians take it very strong and sweet.

Of the new words that you'll learn, probably half will be the names of drinks. Try the Caiparinhas, a blend of sugarcane alcohol, *cachaca* sugar, lime, and ice. The Caiparoska tastes more conventional because it contains vodka.

Drink only bottled water, liquor, and sodas as a precaution. If you avoid tap water, you probably will not get sick. On our trip, people used ice cubes, ate unpeeled fruits and vegetables, and some drank the water. No one, including those with weak stomachs, got sick.

STAFFING & SERVICE

Brazilian Scuba and Land Tours takes care of all arrangements, including getting your visa, arranging for all transfers from your outbound flight, picking you up in the Brazilian airport, and whisking you away to your dive destination. It provides guides who take care of your every need. Its buses effectively navigate the treacherous roads of Brazil—made so by the drivers, not the conditions. The staff in the New York office are exceptionally competent and accommodating.

BSLT is a relatively new company. It is supported in its marketing and promotional efforts by Varig, the national airline of Brazil. Bill Smith, BSLT's owner, has invested his personal fortune and reputation into making this work.

PRIVACY & RELAXATION

You won't get much privacy on this trip. The whole group travels around together on chartered minibuses. Most of the places you stay in are small and devoid of other anglophones, so the group tends to eat together.

However, all rooms offer couples complete privacy in romantic settings. Also, it's always possible to sneak away for an evening stroll.

This is a very busy tour. You are constantly doing something. The travel time is long, both getting to Brazil and to your destinations. Don't count on getting much sleep. There are too many places to go and things to do.

SHOPPING

H. Stern and his competitors sell jewelry on every tourist street of Rio. Bargain for high-quality high-karat gold, topaz, aquamarine, emeralds, and diamonds. Jewelry made from semiprecious stones makes a less expensive souvenir. If you want to buy jewelry, we suggest that you get an idea of prices in the States and that you set a budget. Keep in mind that Brazilians use only 18-karat gold. The widest selection is at the H. Stern factory, which offers an interesting tour in Rio, even if you have no intention of buying anything. Strangely, the lowest prices on jewelry can often be found at the duty-free store in the airport, which often offers prices 15 percent below those at the factory.

Most bargains are in consumable goods: food, hotel rooms, transportation. Most clothing and other durables seem to cost at least as much as in the United States. Brazilians are very fashion conscious. You can get styles in Rio two seasons ahead of those in the States—if they ever make it into American fashion at all. Don't expect buys on leather until the end of their summer (the end of our winter). Fashion shoes are a real bargain, but the quality tends to be less than that of American-made footwear.

HONEYMOONERS

If you both enjoy adventure, you won't find a more romantic city than Rio. And this trip is bound to be memorable. Keep in mind that you will get little rest during this trip. Will you need that after your wedding? Also, the first night is spent on the airplane.

SINGLES

The tour groups tend to be small, so the pool of talent would appear to be limited. Despite that, divers frequently couple up on these trips. Blame it on Rio.

If you are looking for romance with the locals, note that the Brazilians tend to be extremely good-looking. This warrants a note of caution, however. The discos fill with more beautiful women than you could dream of. Unfortunately, a large number of them are prostitutes. In Discoteca Help, for example, women outnumber men two to one. A guide told us that 99 percent of the beautiful women in the bars are prostitutes. A friend corrected that figure by saying that the true figure was closer to 99.9 percent.

Ask at your hotel for discos that are OK. You might meet the "girl [or boy] from Ipanema." Very often the hotel has disco passes that will save you the cover charge.

CHILD APPEAL

The extensive traveling and scuba orientation of the trip make it unsuitable for young children. Any certified diver from the early teens (traveling with guardians) and older should enjoy the trip.

NUTS & BOLTS

BOOKING & CONTACT INFORMATION: Dive shops and some travel agents know about this program. You'd do best to contact BSLT directly.

Brazilian Scuba and Land Tours
64 Division Avenue, Suite B3
Levittown, NY 11756
800-722-0205
516-797-2133

CURRENCY: Stores accept only Brazilian cruzados. The value of the U.S. dollar remains strong in Brazil because of astronomical inflation. There is an open black market where a dollar buys more cruzados than it does at the bank. Often shops and restaurants will give you a rate as good as that of the black market. Credit card purchasers receive only the official rate. While you may feel like a poor boy in Europe, in Brazil you can still live like a rich American.

CUSTOMS/DUTY: Usual U.S. customs. A Brazil stamp on your passport does not draw undue attention.

DEPOSITS/REFUNDS: A $100-per-person deposit is required at the time of booking, and full payment is due 30 days prior to departure. If you cancel 30 days before date of departure you will receive a full refund.

ELECTRICITY: 110 volts 60 cycles.

HANDICAP ACCESSIBILITY: None.

PACKING: Before our trip, we asked people in my local dive shops about Brazil. No one could give us much advice, except one man who thought that I should wear shorties. Don't listen to this. You need a full 1/4" wet suit with a hood and gloves. Bring mosquito repellent, a phrasebook, and all your own scuba gear except tanks and weights.

You'll have no need for warm clothes. A waterproof windbreaker will suffice. Here, the rain is as warm as the people. Leave your sports jacket and fancy dresses at home. You can go to the nicest places without them. Just bring sports clothes and comfortable walking shoes.

RELIGIOUS SERVICES: The itinerary does not lend itself to finding religious services. Over 90 percent of Brazilians are Catholics, so you might be able to find a mass if you are so inclined.

RESERVATION SCHEDULE: BSLT schedules trips according to demand. You might be able to hitch on to one with short notice. More advanced planning will, of course, allow you to select the tour that you want. Also, you should allow time for the embassy to process your visa application.

Groups should book about a year in advance for the best choice of times, although BSLT can sometimes put together a trip with as little as three months' notice.

TRAVEL TIME BY AIR

Los Angeles: **13 hours**
Miami: **8 hours 30 minutes**
New York: **9 hours 30 minutes**

ARRIVAL AIRPORT: Rio de Janeiro.
Note: People in other cities will most likely transfer planes in New York or Miami.

TRAVEL TIME FROM AIRPORT: Cabo Frio is a two-hour ride from Rio's airport.

VISA/PASSPORT REQUIREMENTS: You must get a visa to travel to Brazil. BSLT will handle this for you, but you must send them your passport and give them a few weeks to take care of the details.

SPENDING MONEY: You'll need money for restaurants in Rio, which cost little compared to those in the United States. The nightclubs charge a cover that seems steep to all except New Yorkers. Approximately $300 in traveler's checks should suffice. You can charge major purchases if you decide to bring home some jewels. Imported electronics goods are very expensive in Brazil, as is scuba equipment. You can often get good prices for your camera, radio, or regulator. Bring the equipment that you'd like to replace anyway, and you might find a buyer.

PORTUGUESE—A FEW WORDS

A few words of the native tongue will go a long way. The pronunciation varies in different regions. Rio has its own. Give it your best shot. We've left out questions that can't be answered with a gesture or number, because you won't understand the answers anyway.

Good morning	*Bom dia*
Good afternoon	*Boa tarde*
Good evening	*Boa noite*
Please	*Por favor*
Thank you	*Obrigado*
How much does it cost?	*Quanto custo/Quanto è?*
I don't speak Portuguese	*Não falo português.*
Yes/no	*Sim/não*
Help	*Soccoro*
Good/bad	*Bom/máu*
Wine (red/white/rosé)	*Vinho (tinto/bronco/rosé)*
Beer	*Uma cerveja/um chopp*
Mineral water (carbonated)	*Água mineral (com gas)*
Milk	*Leite*
Menu	*Menu*
The bill	*A conta*
Rare	*Mal passado*
Medium	*Ao ponto*
Well done	*Bom passado*
Where is . . . ?	*Onde é . . . ?*

Cost Worksheet

	High Season	Off-Season
Accommodations (7 days)[1]	$1,650	$1,650
Food	150	150
Drinks	30	30
Departure tax		
Sports	incl.	incl.
Airfare	incl.	incl.
Sight-seeing	incl.	incl.
Tips	incl.	incl.
Additional sports		
Souvenirs		

[1] Premium for single person: $300